RELATIVITY

ANTONIA HAYES
RELATIVITY

corsair

CORSAIR

First published in Australia in 2015 by Penguin Group Australia

First published in Great Britain in 2016 by Corsair

13 5 7 9 10 8 6 4 2

A CIP catalogue record for this book
is available from the British Library.

ISBN: 978-1-4721-5168-1 (hardback)
ISBN: 978-1-4721-5171-1 (eBook)

Printed and bound in Great Britain by Clays Ltd, St Ives plc

Papers used by Corsair are from well-managed forests
and other responsible sources.

MIX
Paper from
responsible sources
FSC
www.fsc.org   FSC® C104740

Corsair
An imprint of
Little, Brown Book Group
Carmelite House
50 Victoria Embankment
London EC4Y 0DZ

An Hachette UK Company
www.hachette.co.uk

www.littlebrown.co.uk

For Julian

Do I dare
Disturb the universe?
In a minute there is time
For decisions and revisions which a minute will reverse.

– TS Eliot

We are lived by powers we pretend to understand.

– WH Auden

I

MOTION

Before you hear any words, you can hear the panic.

It surfaces as an irregularity of breath, a strain of vocal cords, a cry, a gasp. Panic exists on a frequency entirely its own. Air into air, particle by particle, panic vibrates through the elastic atmosphere faster than the speed of sound. It's the most sudden and terrible thing, piercing the calm and propelling us towards the worst places. Before the words come out the anxiety is there, roaring on the other side of silence. Before your brain can register what you're being told, you know that something is wrong. And before you can respond it's already too late. Because once you've heard those words, an event is set in motion and everything will change.

'Help,' he said. 'He's not breathing.'

2

TIME

Ethan took his mum by the hand and led her into the tunnel. Graffiti covered the walls – veins of green and silver – with patterns and symbols sprayed into stories like sacred paintings in a cave. Cryptic characters spelled strange words; the mismatched letters reminded Ethan of formulas and equations. Aerosol fumes lingered, but nobody else was there.

'Come on, Mum!' The tunnel threw Ethan's voice further ahead. 'Hurry up! We'll miss it.'

They emerged in the darkness, rushing under the brick archway of the golden viaducts and into Jubilee Park. Along the footpath by the mangrove habitat, past the oval and cricket pavilion, over the mossy bridge, they ran towards Blackwattle Bay. It was low tide: empty stormwater drains, shallow creek, a bank of exposed mud where water lapped at the shoreline walls. Across the bay was the Anzac Bridge, its cables stretching from the pylons like strings of a harp. Street lamps dotted along the bridge reflected in the dark water, staining it with orange stripes.

Ethan frowned. 'There's too much light. We should've gone to the country.'

His mum gave him a weary smile. 'You're lucky we're even here; it's two o'clock in the morning. You have school tomorrow, I have work. We live in the middle of the city. This'll do.'

She spread out a blanket and they sat by the promenade. Both of them were wearing their pyjamas. The park was silent and empty; the air smelled like wet grass and salt. Ethan concentrated, letting his eyes adjust to the dark. It was a cloudless night and the moon hadn't risen yet. Optimal conditions for seeing the meteor shower, and tonight was its peak. Behind them, the glare of Sydney's skyline turned the horizon amber. He worried about light pollution, that the glowing metallic city would stifle the secrets in the sky.

'There!' Ethan pointed. 'See the row of three stars? That's Orion's belt. And there's Rigel, the constellation's brightest star. That means the Orionid meteor shower is happening over here. Look!'

Mum kept her eyes on him. 'How long until we go back to bed?'

'Tonight there'll be somewhere between twenty-five and fifty meteoroids per hour. They're actually dust from Halley's comet entering our atmosphere. Air friction makes them glow with heat and then *swoosh*! They vaporise.'

His mum lay down on her back. 'So I guess we wait then?'

'Yeah, we wait.' Ethan nestled in beside her, resting his head on her arm. He looked up at the northwest corner of the sky and connected the dots of the constellation Orion. One of its bright stars – Betelgeuse, a red supergiant – floated near the belt. Red supergiants were the largest stars in the universe and Betelgeuse was so big that if it replaced the sun, it would spread all the way out to Jupiter.

Ethan squinted, focusing on the vague pink spot. Betelgeuse was a dying star. Eventually, it would run out of fuel and collapse under its own weight. He imagined the red star exploding, the cosmic boom as it went supernova, shockwaves sweeping across the galaxy. Violent plasma bursting into the brightest ball of light. He could almost see it burning. But Betelgeuse wasn't going to explode for hundreds of thousands of years, maybe not even a million.

In a million years, Ethan thought, these constellations will break apart. People would need to make new maps and tell new myths for the changing patterns in the sky. Orion would be a different shape; the Southern Cross might become a square. Ethan watched the stars move, like a movie on a massive screen. He saw the cinematic trajectories of darkening dwarfs and brightening giants. Everything was slipping and unthreading, disappearing and beginning. Up in the celestial jungle, there were no static stars.

In two billion years, the galaxy Andromeda would be so close to the Milky Way that every night sky would light up like fireworks. And in four billion years, the two galaxies would spin closer and closer together and finally collide, swirling and twisting, giving birth to new stars. Becoming one galactic knot. But all that was so far away. There were so many things in the distant future that Ethan would never see.

He dragged his knees up to his chest. 'Mum, do you ever think about the future?'

'Right now I'm thinking about what we're going to eat for dinner tomorrow night.'

'No, not like that. I mean The Future. Like in a million years. Or a billion.'

Mum smiled. 'Not very often, sweetheart. I won't be alive in a billion years.'

Ethan turned to face his mum, propping himself up on his elbows. 'But I don't want you to die. What if I sent you away on a spaceship travelling at nearly the speed of light? Because of time dilation, it'd only feel like one year for you. But for me it would be twenty. So when you got back to Earth, we'd almost be the same age.'

'I wouldn't want to spend twenty years away from you, though.'

'Neither.' Ethan scratched his nose. 'Okay, what if we were both on the spaceship together? We could travel close to the speed of light or through the deepest parts of the fabric of space-time where gravity makes it warp. By the time we got back home, millions of years would've passed. But we'd still be alive. We could see Betelgeuse go supernova, and the Milky Way collide with Andromeda. Maybe if we just fly around the universe for the rest of eternity, then we never have to die. Or maybe we could go faster than the speed of light. There must be some loophole in theoretical physics that makes living forever possible.'

His mum studied his face, the hypnotised way people stared at paintings or sunsets. 'Ethan, sometimes I have no idea where you came from.'

'Yeah, you do. I came from inside you.'

'As usual, you're right,' she said, rolling onto her stomach.

'Mum, want to know something crazy? Statistically, the probability that I exist is basically zero. Did you know you were born with two million eggs? But when you were thirty you'd lost 90 per cent of them, and by the time you turn forty you'll only have about fifty thousand left. So the chance that I was born was 0.008 per cent. I'm one in two million eggs, plus I'm one in two hundred and fifty million sperm. That's approximately how many sperm are in each male ejaculation.'

Mum looked confused. 'How do you know all this?'

'We're doing sex ed at school. Mr Thompson even made us watch a video of a real birth. I saw an actual vagina and everything.' Ethan paused. 'Mum, do you think they ever miss me?'

'Who?'

'The other eggs. My brothers and sisters inside your ovaries. So far, I'm the only one who's successfully made it out.'

'Oh,' she said. 'Well, the other eggs would all be your sisters. Only men have the Y chromosome that makes baby boys. At the moment, all the eggs are girls.'

'So I used to be a girl?'

'You also used to be an egg.'

'It must be scary for them,' Ethan said. 'Sending one egg down the fallopian tube every month, like a sacrifice. It's like *The Hunger Games* in there. And you only have a few more years left before the whole system shuts down. What if the other eggs run out of time? Mum, what happens if all my sisters die before they get to exist?'

Her hand found his. 'Ethan, do you have survivor's guilt?'

'No,' he said, in a clipped voice. She was making fun of him. But he'd been one of those eggs once, made of the same proteins, and they were still stuck. Trapped in an eternal moment before life could begin. Ethan couldn't save his sisters, couldn't let them know he didn't mean to abandon them. He hunched his shoulders and sighed.

'What's wrong?'

He wasn't sure. He didn't want her to have another baby. And besides, to make another baby she'd need a man to contribute another set of chromosomes. Mum wasn't a Komodo dragon; she couldn't reproduce by herself. But as Ethan thought of his thousands of sisters – squashed together in his mum's ovaries, waiting – he suddenly felt very alone.

He rubbed his eye. 'Nothing. I'm fine.'

'You're tired.' Mum kissed him on the forehead. 'And I'm freezing.'

'But the meteor shower!'

'Ten more minutes. That's it.'

Ethan leaned forward and focused on Orion; it was high above the horizon now. The night sky was a gauze of symmetries and spirals, an ocean of darkness and light. Ultraviolet and infrared, filled with invisible radiation and empty vacuums. Ethan felt like he could split the yawning universe open with his eyes and see its boundless dimensions, look beyond the blueprint of space and time. He'd always had an aptitude for spotting patterns, finding the geometry in chaos.

His mum looked out at the water; maybe she didn't care about the meteor shower. She pulled the sleeves of her jumper over her hands and shivered. Ethan gave her a hug to help her molecules expand. In the dark, her pale skin and fair hair seemed blue. When Ethan looked at his mum, he saw another universe – a world intact, of soothing shapes and soft textures, of beautiful angles and the warmest light. His universe.

Above them, three hundred sextillion stars rearranged themselves. Expanding, tightening, collapsing – new stars were born and old stars died. Quasars and pulsars, novae and nebulas, clusters of galaxies woven together like a spider web. Ethan watched the marbled universe dance over his head, ever-shifting and spinning towards its ultimate fate.

A tiny flicker of light shot across the sky.

Swoosh!

The meteoroid vaporised. Flashing and fading in the same instant, like a phosphorescent memory.

Ethan blinked. It was already gone. 'I think I saw one.'

'A shooting star?'

'Meteoroid,' he said, correcting her. 'It was really fast.'

'Did you make a wish?'

'Yeah. But if I tell you, it won't come true.'

Mum ruffled his hair. 'Come on, pumpkin. Let's go home.'

∞

Claire watched Ethan gaze at the stars. Wriggling with excitement, mouth slightly open, head tilted back as he scanned the sky. His spellbound expression made it impossible not to smile. She loved her son in unexpected ways, with the same sort of visceral obsession that one might have for the idiosyncrasies of a lover. Claire loved his physicality – the way Ethan laughed so hard he farted, how he picked at the dry scabs on his knees, the weight of his musty head resting on her shoulder as they sat together on buses or trains. She enjoyed that silent intimacy most of all.

Ethan shuffled closer and pressed his face against her arm. He wasn't self-conscious about adoring his mother yet, still needed her affection. Claire knew these easy days were numbered. Adolescence was sneaking into her son – faint whiffs of body odour, scatterings of hair growing on the back of his neck and down his legs, a tiny line of blackheads forming on his nose.

'Mum,' he said, 'look!'

But on nights like this, when the dark sky was crisp and cloudless, Claire hated looking at the stars. After sunset, she'd taught herself to keep her eyes fixed on the ground. Star visibility wasn't great in Sydney but sometimes they came out to shine, reminding the city they were still there. That night they were sharp, flaring, and Claire looked up. She still knew where to find her star – it was always there. It never seemed to wander the night sky.

Their wedding was fourteen years ago now, just family and a few close friends at the registry. Claire wore a vintage lace dress that had belonged to her mother. Instead of a reception, they invited friends to dinner at their favourite Indian restaurant and everyone drank champagne and chatted over butter chicken and rogan josh. Toasts were made to the happy couple and Claire and Mark held hands under the table, looking over at each other occasionally to exchange a smile. She got a bit drunk, spilled curry on her dress. It stained the lace and she remembered running her finger over the orange mark when – years later – she threw the dress in the bin.

After dinner, Mark took Claire to Centennial Park. They lay together on the grass, looking up at the sky. It was a warm Sydney evening, the middle of January, and the balmy breeze cloaked Claire's skin. She closed her eyes and sniffed the summer air, so thick with humidity that she could reach out and touch the night. The grass was freshly mowed and a chorus of cicadas chirped behind the trees.

'Are you happy?' Mark's fingers moved down her arm, his breath on her face.

Claire kept her eyes closed but smiled. It was unusual for Mark to ask for reassurance and it made her feel drunk with confidence. 'Why wouldn't I be?'

'This probably wasn't the wedding you wanted. You deserved a big ceremony, hundreds of guests, a church, a gift registry. You must be disappointed.'

She sat up and looked at him. Blades of grass were stuck in his black hair, and she picked them out with her fingers, noticing how thick and full his eyelashes were. It was peculiar to feel as though she owned him now, that she could say he was hers, that they were married. But he should've known that she didn't care about the wedding. They were young and in love. The thing that mattered most of all was Mark.

'I'm not disappointed,' Claire said. 'Today was perfect.'

Mark nodded but seemed unconvinced. Bats flapped overhead, flying into the park to feed on the nectar of the paperbark and gum trees. She knew him well enough to suspect that maybe it was Mark who was disappointed, who wanted things to be grander.

'I have something for you,' he said.

She hadn't bought him anything. Sometimes Mark made her feel naive, like she'd lived her life in a bubble, oblivious to the rest of the world. 'You didn't have to,' Claire insisted. 'I have enough things.'

Mark stood up and offered his hand. She pulled herself upright and brushed the grass off her dress.

He kissed the back of her neck and pointed at the sky. 'There. It's for you.'

Claire looked up. 'I don't understand.'

Mark linked his fingers around hers. 'Can you see that star, right here?'

She stared out to beyond where her fingertip grazed the sky. 'Maybe,' she said, closing one eye so the stars came into focus.

'It's yours. I bought it for you.'

'You bought me a star?' She gave him a sceptical look.

'Because you're my light,' he said. 'My constant.'

Even though it was a hot night, Mark's lips against her earlobe made her shiver.

Much later, Claire removed all traces of Mark: letters, clothes, books, the wedding dress. She erased him completely. But Claire couldn't throw away a star. She prayed that somehow, up in space, her star would extinguish and disappear. This star didn't, though. It remained steadfast in the sky, and the further away Mark felt, the brighter the star seemed to shine.

After the meteor shower, Claire peeked through Ethan's bedroom door. When he was a baby, she'd stand over his cot and listen to him breathe, soothed by the perfect function of his lungs and steady heartbeat. Now Ethan was twelve years old and Claire still watched him sleep, still sending herself into a panic if she couldn't see his ribs move. She'd survey the landscape of his face – the smiles and frowns of his dreams, the shadow his long eyelashes cast on his cheeks, the crease that ran through the middle of his nose. His long limbs were often a shock, caught in his rumpled bedding. Her son was always taller and older than she thought he was in her head. Claire could never picture him properly.

But Ethan gave the vagueness of her life definition. And although Claire complained about his clothes and Lego scattered about the house, she needed them there to punctuate her existence. He made their house a home. They were similar in many ways, softly spoken and prone to dreaming, half-listening to conversations and lost inside their heads. Echoes of her bone structure bloomed in the lines and angles of her son's face. But something about Ethan was from another planet.

Even when he was a baby, Claire knew he was unique. He saw the world with different eyes. Sensitive to light, he'd become entranced by prisms and patterns. Ethan lost hours watching shadows bend and flex, shrinking and elongating against the carpets and walls. Amazing – that didn't seem like normal behaviour for a baby – but alarming too.

Everyone was worried. Ethan didn't meet his developmental milestones; it was frightening how late he was to walk and talk. He didn't coo and babble, or respond to his name. Claire took him to specialists, tested his hearing, read him stories, sang him songs. She did everything in her power to draw her son out from his interior world and into hers. But Ethan was stuck, caught in the net of delay.

Doctors warned her that he might never speak, but Claire refused to believe them. It took almost a year of speech therapy but Ethan's first word was 'Mama'. Behind those quiet eyes, she saw flashes of something brilliant hiding there. His second word was 'moon'.

This uneven brilliance was coupled with a dark intensity. Quickly agitated, Ethan often threw toys across the room; his wild temper was easily broken. Claire saw her son get frustrated with his homework, angry with himself, to a point where he'd detonate and explode. When

Ethan was like this, she couldn't be near him. It was too familiar. During those crackling moments when her son lost his cool, Claire locked herself in the bathroom and burst into tears.

That wasn't who she wanted to be. She often felt like an amateur at motherhood, even though it was a job she'd had for twelve years. Unconditional love and quiet affection both came easily to her. Leadership and being stern did not. She wanted to be Ethan's ally, preferred to make him happy than focus on the prosaic drills of discipline. At times, Claire did let things slip. The duties of parenting – jumping from tutor to coach, manager, cook, seamstress – needed an ensemble cast and she was just a one-woman show.

Ethan spotted her standing in the doorway. 'Mum, can you stay here until I fall asleep?'

'Sure.' Claire lay down beside him. She shouldn't have let him go out past midnight; he'd be tired for school tomorrow. She succumbed to his strange requests too much.

Outside, the moon finally rose: a slim crescent like cupped hands waiting to catch a star. As her son settled into sleep, he automatically shifted his solid body closer to hers – that undeniable umbilical pull. He offered his cheek for a kiss. Claire pressed her lips to the back of his head, taking in his doughy smell.

'Goodnight,' Ethan whispered.

'Sleep tight.'

'Don't let the bed bugs bite.' He paused for a moment. 'Mum, did you know that bed bugs have the geometry of an ovoid? Their bodies are dorsoventrally flattened. That means their vertical plane is flat like a leaf, so it's easier for them to hide in carpets and beds.'

Claire laughed. 'Ethan, go to sleep.'

∞

Time had stopped.

It was an ordinary pocket watch: pale gold with a white face, a halo of black Roman numerals around its edge. But the enamel of the dial had browned, the golden casing was coated in orange rust. Gears and shifts had frozen; there was no tick to follow the tock. No hand heaving forward, shaving another second off the future. Ethan pushed his nose against the glass. Time had stopped at seventeen minutes past eight.

Underneath the pocket watch was a white plaque. Its lettering was black and small. The watch belonged to a Japanese man named Kengo Nikawa, who was riding his bicycle along Kan'on Bridge in Hiroshima on his way to work on 6 August 1945. He was only sixteen hundred metres from the point of impact. The blast left him with serious burns all over his body and sixteen days later he died. He was fifty-nine years old.

Ethan stepped back from the display and the tip of his nose left a smudge on the glass. The Hiroshima exhibit upset him – a chill skimmed down his spine. He'd seen a corroding metal lunch box with an uneaten meal and burnt rice from 1945. A small tricycle that belonged to a child, who would have been playing in his yard when that bright August morning turned dark. The ribbons attached to the handles were black. Ethan glanced back at the pocket watch.

He heard the rest of his class moving to the next part of the exhibition, his teacher Mr Thompson telling them to hurry up. But Ethan stayed behind. He couldn't stop thinking about that Japanese man and his pocket watch. In a single moment, Kengo Nikawa's whole world changed. After that atomic bomb had fallen, and his watch stopped.

'Ethan!' Will's voice echoed through the museum hall. 'Where are you?'

Will had been Ethan's best friend since they'd started school. On their first day of kindergarten, five-year-old Will made a paper plane and threw it across the classroom. It landed on Ethan's desk.

Will's plane was flawed, clumsily folded, badly designed. Ethan uncreased the paper. It needed bigger wings to give it more lift, a more aerodynamic structure. He refolded the paper and threw it back. It floated above the small tables, hovered instead of flew, and Will stood up to catch it. He had a look on his face as though nothing impressed him more than that paper plane. After that, they were always together, talking about rockets over lunch, how to build a time machine, how the universe began.

But now that primary school was ending and Year 6 was almost over, Ethan noticed something was different. They never spoke about rockets, time machines or the universe any more. Recently, Will had started spending all his time with another group of boys; all they talked about was footy and farts. Once, Will rolled his eyes after Ethan spoke in class. His best friend stopped coming over on the weekends and after school. He didn't understand why Will was suddenly embarrassed to be seen with him. Nothing had changed. Ethan hadn't changed.

Will's new mates called Ethan 'Stephen Hawking', repeating things he said in a slow, electronic-sounding voice. Maybe it was meant to be mean, but to Ethan this was the greatest compliment. Stephen Hawking was extraordinary. Ethan would smile as they imitated the famous cosmologist.

The rest of their class gathered under the shadow of the dinosaur in the foyer of the Australian Museum. The bones of the Tyrannosaurus Rex swayed in the yellow light. Ethan imagined what the creature had looked like millions of years ago, wishing he could travel back into the past along the curvature of space-time. Ethan often thought about space-time intervals and the space-time continuum. How it was made up of lots and lots of intervals like beads on a huge cosmic necklace. Like fireworks that branched off into an explosion of four different directions, we continuously filled up the universe with our pyrotechnic lives. Ethan looked up at the skeleton again but Will was dragging him back to the group.

Daniel Anderson was one of those boys who puberty found early, already a foot taller than most of the kids in the class, tufts of impatient facial hair bursting from his skin. At eleven, he was almost the size of a fourteen-year-old but still had the voice of a small boy. He tried to make it sound deeper by grunting at the end of sentences.

'Where'd you go, Will?' Daniel asked. 'You and your boyfriend get lost?'

'Ethan's not my boyfriend.'

'Yeah, he is. You love Stephen Hawking. You're gonna marry him.' Daniel looked pleased with himself.

Will glanced back at Ethan. 'He's not even my friend.'

Ethan pointed at the dinosaur. 'Fossils show that the Tyrannosaurus Rex was alive during the Cretaceous Period, which was the last segment of the Mesozoic Era. Did you know the Mesozoic Era is an interval of geological time that started about 250 million years ago?' He swallowed his breath. 'That sounds like ages, but dinosaurs were only alive for a little bit of our planet's history. Radiometric dating shows that Earth is approximately 4.54 billion years old.'

Daniel put on the electronic Stephen Hawking voice, moving his hands like a robot. 'Radio dating. Shows that the Earth. Is 4.54 billion years old.'

The boys laughed.

'You're such a freak, Ethan,' Will said. He and the other boys walked away.

Ethan climbed back up the stone stairs of the museum. They were wrong. It wasn't called radio dating. And he wasn't a freak. The foyer was full of people, moving in and out of exhibitions, collecting their tickets, buying toy snakes and bendy souvenir pencils. Nobody stopped to look at the dinosaur and Ethan felt sorry for it. Lonely, stuck up there, suspended by wires. Only one here of its kind. He wanted to tell the Tyrannosaurus Rex that he understood how it felt to be alone. He wanted to ask it what the stars looked like when it was still alive.

The dinosaur nodded. Ethan blinked – it looked like it really moved. Its skeleton arm reached across the foyer and the wires started to swing. Maybe the Tyrannosaurus Rex wanted to shake his hand. The dinosaur tilted its head and opened its jaw like it was about to say something, but no sound came from its sharp-toothed mouth. Ethan looked down at the crowd. Nobody else at the museum entrance noticed that the dinosaur's bones had come back to life.

'Ethan,' Mr Thompson called out. 'Stop wandering off. The bus is here.'

The Tyrannosaurus Rex stopped moving. Ethan swung his backpack over his shoulder and joined the class. As they walked out onto College Street, he squinted into the afternoon light. It was one of those clear Sydney days, sun bouncing off buildings, windows glinting bright and blue. The children pushed and shoved, trying to get the best seats on the bus. Daniel, Will and his new friends sat at the back and threw soggy paper at the girls in front. Ethan took a seat near the middle of the bus and waited for somebody to sit beside him. Face after face passed, but the seat next to Ethan remained empty.

When they arrived back at school, he saw his mum waiting for him near the front gate. She was by herself again. Sometimes Ethan wished she'd talk more to the other parents, try to make a friend. He watched her stretch her leg like she was warming up. In old photographs – back when she'd been a professional ballerina – his mum looked like someone else. She held her head higher, bones in her face were more prominent, and something was different behind her eyes. Mum waved at the bus window. With one shrinking hand, Ethan waved back. It was a secret wave – opening and closing his hand quickly – as he didn't want anybody else to think it was for them.

Ethan was last off the school bus, hoping that Will, Daniel and the rest of them would finally leave him alone. He negotiated his way through the afternoon swarm of parents. How much kids in his class resembled their mums and dads was something Ethan often thought about – he wanted to figure out where each gene came from and where it'd landed. Ethan didn't look exactly like his mum, although they had similar eyes. But he was dark and his mum was fair; she was slight and he was sinewy.

'Mum, do you remember when the atomic bomb fell on Hiroshima?' Ethan stood beside her. He was as tall as her chin now, but being adult-sized like his mum still seemed impossible.

She laughed. 'How old do you think I am? That happened a very long time before I was born.'

'Oh, yeah.' Ethan looked at her face. He couldn't imagine her being born; Mum had always been a grown-up. It was strange to think that she'd been twelve like him – that his mum had grown and developed, changed and aged. Luckily, no bombs had fallen on her. Ethan thought again about Kengo Nikawa and his pocket watch.

'Mum, do you think we care about time when we die?'

His mum made a face, the one she made when she was having a serious thought. 'No, I don't think so. You'd stop noticing it. You'd be dead. When you die, time doesn't matter any more.' They stood at the traffic lights, waiting to cross the street. 'You okay?'

Ethan nodded.

He looked over the horizon at the grenadine sky. They lived under the flight path and he could hear another jet engine bellow overhead. Above Sydney, plane after plane flew past, leaving streaks of white vapour in the dry evening air.

3

SPACE

The shock of the turbulence woke Mark. The 'Fasten Seatbelt' sign above his head flashed and beeped. Grit collected in the corners of his eyes and he rubbed his face. The angular shape of the plastic window had left a deep imprint in his cheek. He ran a finger over it – the pink groove felt hot and tender – knowing at least this wasn't permanent like the ugly scars that lived elsewhere on his skin.

He stretched his arms; his shoulders felt stiff. It was only a five-hour flight, but there'd been the drive from Kalgoorlie to Perth too. And in the claustrophobic hull of an aeroplane, time behaved differently. It stretched and distended, every minute counted impatiently by every passenger.

Before last week, Mark hadn't spoken to Tom for nine years. Hearing his brother on the phone jolted him back into their childhood: the two boys laughing as they hid from their mother under the orange formica kitchen table; talking until they fell asleep as they lay beside each other under the stars on family camping trips; yelling at each other as teenagers, fighting over the stereo. The sound of Tom's voice shot through Mark's nervous system, rushing along every fibre and cell.

'Mark,' he said. 'It's me. Tom.'

'Hey.' Mark paused. 'Yeah, I know.'

'Listen, Dad's dying. Cancer.' Tom's breathing was heavy on the other side of the line. 'You should probably come home.'

Mark had chosen a seat at the back of the plane. Luckily, the flight was reasonably empty and nobody sat beside him. He didn't want to talk, answer questions about his life in Western Australia or explain why he was coming back to Sydney. A boy across the aisle, perhaps around fourteen or fifteen years old, looked up from the game on his tablet for a moment and smiled at Mark. Mark smiled back, but the corners of his mouth laboured over the movement. He didn't know how to interact with children. And this boy wasn't a child any more. It didn't feel like long ago that Mark was that age, his whole life ahead of him, his future bright. The boy returned to his game.

Mark looked out the window at the darkening blue air. The altitude made him feel queasy. They were flying over the South Eastern Highlands of New South Wales now, across the Great Dividing Range, as the plane approached the sandstone cliffs on the edge of the Sydney Basin.

Western Australia had been a salve for Mark: its different air, its alien light, a sun that set behind the water instead of rising from it. Over there he lived under another sky. In Sydney, it felt like the city and sky both grew from the ground. Space wasn't infinite there – it had a limit, a lid – but it was the opposite out west. Everything was open and endless; the wide land seemed to hang from the wider stars. There was nothing familiar in Kalgoorlie to anchor him. He lived a new life on a new planet.

Mark adjusted his seatbelt. The plane rocked over pockets of air. He was calm through the turbulence, understood the science of it: the way jet streams were caused by differences in atmospheric heating and planetary rotation, the mixing of warm and cold gas in the troposphere, creating large gradients in wind velocity. The wings rattled; the fuselage dropped. They descended further, breaking the clouds. Now he could see the sparkle of the Pacific Ocean as the plane tilted, turning towards the city.

At Kingsford Smith's arrival terminal, nobody was waiting to meet him. No open arms would greet him at the gate. He'd collect his bags from the conveyor belt and wheel them out into the staring faces. Other people would have joyful reunions. Couples would kiss; children would run to their parents and hold them tight. But Mark would make the lonely journey into the city by himself.

As the plane plunged towards the airport, Mark's stomach jumped. He caught his first glimpse of the city that used to be his home. Tarmac swelled below them; the runway glowed neon orange and red. Sydney's lights quivered in the distance as he stared out the tiny window of this soaring machine, piloting him straight into his past.

∞

If Ethan's hands could lie, they wouldn't hurt so much. Knuckles not scraped raw, no tiny scratches nestled between each ridge of his joints. But the ache in his bones told the truth. Last year, he'd memorised the names of all the bones in the body. The eight carpal bones of the hand were collectively known as the carpus: scaphoid, lunate, triquetrum, pisiform, hamate, capitate, trapezoid, trapezium. They sounded like a circus. Ethan studied his fingers and nails, the groove of his palms, the swirls of his fingertips. He knew he had his father's hands.

Ethan had no memories of his father. He'd left when Ethan was a baby. One crushed photograph, found at the back of his mum's wardrobe, was the only picture he'd ever seen. In the photo, Ethan was a newborn. His father was giving him a bath, looking down, his splayed hand holding the back of the baby's head. At that angle, Ethan couldn't see the colour of his father's eyes or the details of his face. His hair was dark, dark hairs ran along his arm. But Ethan could see his hands. Long thin fingers, broad palms, wide fingernails and big thumbs. As Ethan grew, he noticed his own hands become those other hands. He kept the photo of his father hidden in the drawer of his bedside table. This man had made him – pieced him together from his genes and cells – but he was a stranger.

Although Ethan didn't remember his father, there were a handful of things he knew about him. He'd collected them over the years – small details from his birth certificate, fragments of overheard conversations. It was exactly a handful because there were only five things, a tiny snatch of information. Ethan knew these things like the back of his hand; they were all he had to hold on to of the father who'd disappeared from his life.

On his thumb, Ethan knew that his parents were married on 13 January. On his index finger, he knew that his father's birthday was 14 October, and on his middle finger Ethan knew that when he was born, his father was a student. These were all written on his birth certificate. On the next finger, Ethan counted the black hair he'd seen in the photograph, and on his pinkie was his father's name: Mark Hall. But it was only a handful. The questions Ethan still had about his father could have filled up all the fingers on all the hands of everyone in the universe.

The Year 6 boys had been playing tip in the playground at lunch. Their runners squeaked as they dodged the younger kids, knocking over lunch boxes and drink bottles. 'You're it!' they yelled at each other. Ethan watched from the seats underneath the shaded area – he'd forgotten his hat that day and wasn't allowed in the sun. It didn't really bother him, though. He had his copy of *A Brief History of Time* to read and he got sunburnt easily.

A Brief History of Time was his favourite book; he'd already read it five times. Ethan stared at Stephen Hawking's diagram of what would happen if the sun died. The future light cone of the dying sun was a big triangle, pouring out litres of time. Stephen Hawking said that if the sun stopped shining right now, we wouldn't know on Earth until eight minutes after it'd happened. Maybe the sun had already exploded, sucking up all of our solar system, and we only had eight more minutes to live. He glanced back up at the boys across the playground. They'd have no idea they were about to die because of the collapsing sun.

'Hey, freak,' Daniel shouted. 'Stop staring.'

Ethan buried his face back in *A Brief History of Time*.

A shadow fell across the page as Daniel stood over him. He knocked the book out of Ethan's hands. 'Guess you can't pick that up from your wheelchair, can you, Stephen Hawking?'

'Obviously, I don't have motor neurone disease,' Ethan said.

'Obviously. Don't. Have. Motor. Neurone. Disease.' Daniel mimicked Stephen Hawking's digital voice again.

Ethan tilted his head. 'But that's how you'd sound if you did have it. Because you wouldn't —'

Daniel kicked the book further away. Other Year 6 boys gathered around them now: Nathan Nguyen, the twins Harry and Hank, Ramesh from Bangladesh, who everyone called Ram. Ethan saw Will out of the corner of his eye.

'Don't be a dickhead, Stephen Hawking,' Daniel said.

'I'm not.'

'Leave him alone.' Will picked *A Brief History of Time* off the ground and handed it back to Ethan. The real Stephen Hawking smiled his lopsided smile on the cover. 'He's just reading.'

'Sorry, Wilhelmina, I forgot Stephen Hawking was your boyfriend,' Daniel said. 'When are you two homos getting married and having babies? Don't you sleep in the same bed when you have sleepovers?'

Ethan nodded but Will shot him a look. They hadn't had a sleepover since the school holidays now. Earlier that year, the two boys tried to find Ethan's father together, staying up late and using Will's computer. There were thousands of Mark Halls on the internet: one lived in Chicago, one in Beijing, another in Brisbane, one was an actor in a soap opera. As Ethan clicked through picture after picture of unfamiliar faces – hoping to see that nose, that chin, those hands – he felt defeated. None were the man in that creased photograph. None of them were the right Mark Hall.

Will pulled at the sleeves of his uniform. 'Ethan's not allowed to stay at my place any more. Because I might catch some freak disease from him.'

'As if,' Daniel said. 'You probably already have that freak disease from kissing each other goodnight, Wilhelmina. You're a freak too.'

'Ethan's the freak,' Will insisted. 'He used to wet the bed. And he's scared of the dark.'

Daniel shrugged and started to walk away.

'Ethan's such a freak, even his dad left him right after he was born.' Will looked over at Daniel for approval. 'He didn't want a freak for a son.'

That was a secret – a secret Will had sworn never to share. Ethan knew it was his fault his father had left. That he'd been a difficult baby. That he'd cried too much. That his father didn't want him.

Ethan stood up. 'You knew, you knew not to tell.' He dropped his book. All the frustration he'd stored inside his body now barrelled through his veins. He clenched his hand into a fist. 'You knew.'

Will's face was difficult to read. He didn't seem to notice Ethan's elbow move back and his torso twist, or the hand that moved steadily towards his face. When Ethan's fist slammed into his nose, Will was looking the other way.

The first punch stung Ethan's knuckle, the snap of impact burning his joints.

'You knew,' Ethan repeated. He raised his hand and hit Will again. This time Will scrunched his eyes, expecting the blow. He shielded himself, but Ethan struck him one more time. It was a strange feeling: cartilage against cartilage, sinew on sinew, bones colliding with flesh. Ethan punched him again.

'Stop,' Will cried, falling to the floor.

The rest of the children looked on in silence. Even Daniel took a step back as Will recoiled and curled into a ball. Ethan sat over Will's body and struck his jaw.

Will let out a moan. 'Stop,' he said again, choking on the word.

And in that word was a flicker of a memory: Will and Ethan lying head to toe in bed when they were nine years old. Bedtime, lights just switched off, Will pushing his feet into Ethan's face. Even with a smelly foot in his nose, Ethan was smiling. He tickled Will's toes.

'Stop,' said Will, trying not to laugh. He tangled the sheets as he flipped over onto his stomach. 'Stop.'

Ethan pulled the blanket back. 'Do you think we'll always be best friends?'

'Yeah. Always. Even when we're grown-ups. Even when we're really old and living in a retirement home and have no teeth and can only eat pumpkin soup.'

Ethan pulled a face. 'Yuck. I hate pumpkin soup.'

'I know,' Will said. 'I know everything about you. We're best friends.'
They fell asleep with their dirty feet resting on each other's bodies.

That seemed like a very long time ago as Ethan slammed his fist into
Will's face again. But it didn't look like Will's face. To Ethan, it looked
like the cosmos. Filled with ultraviolet flares, yellow gamma-ray bursts
and red interstellar clouds.

Ethan saw the sun explode; each planet in the solar system disappeared one by one. Goodbye, Mercury; au revoir, Venus; adios, Earth;
so long, Mars; farewell, Saturn; see you later, Jupiter; cheerio, Uranus;
sayonara, Neptune.

He saw radar pulses and radio waves, spirals and loops unfurling
into time and space. He saw fistfuls of planets and satellites, monuments
of ice and dust. He saw past light cones and future light cones radiating
out from the present. He saw Galileo and Newton and Einstein.

He saw the hydrogen and helium that make up incandescent stars,
whirling distant pinwheel galaxies. He could see everything, all the
ripples of the universe, spinning in a galactic soup around him.

But when a dribble of blood appeared at the corner of Will's
mouth, and he spat out a tooth, Ethan froze. A crowd of kids stood in
a circle around the two boys, fearful but unable to look away. Will was
crying. Teachers on playground duty ran over. Nathan Nguyen pulled
Ethan off Will's hunched body.

Ethan trembled and stepped back. The backs of his hands tingled; his
knuckles were red and swollen. Will was curled up on the ground. As he
wiped his mouth with the back of his hand, Ethan tasted the stale tang
of blood mixed with sweat. His sweat, but not his blood. What was going
on? Ethan went cold. He remembered every detail of the sun dying – the
solar system swallowed whole, the stellar explosion of a supernova – but
he couldn't remember what he'd just done with his own hands.

∞

Claire waited for her coffee at the cafe below her office. A group of dancers ordered their own drinks at the till. She noticed the way the barista looked at them with wonder, like they were mythical creatures from another planet, some breed of rare bird. It made her smile, before she went unnaturally stiff.

When nobody could see her, Claire liked to dance. She danced along vacant streets, in empty rooms; she danced whenever she was alone. The nightly preparation of dinner was a performance – the kitchen her stage, eighty-watt globes her spotlight, ingredients her audience, the sound of boiling water her applause. But these were dances for no-one. Those strange days of stages and spotlights, audiences and applause, were over. But the desire to move her body was chiselled into her muscle memory.

It felt like a lifetime ago, when she was that nervous sixteen-year-old girl rushing to her ballet classes, her blonde hair slipping out of her bun and pointe shoes dangling from her bag. People used to stare, especially during her peak as a soloist in the Sydney Ballet Company. Now she was twice as old and nobody looked at her any more. Her face was rounder, her legs softer, but the residue of ballet still saturated every fibre of her body. Grace in the fingertips, pointing toes. Bending over became an *arabesque penchée*; instead of turning she'd pirouette; music moved her body until she broke into a *demi-plié*.

More than anything, Claire loved the way dancing made her feel. There was boldness to it; that boldness was a drug. She wasn't as flexible or coordinated these days but to lose herself – in the rhythm, music, moment – was a bliss she couldn't begin to describe.

Claire watched the ballerinas disappear into one of the studios.

She took her coffee back to her desk and sat in front of her computer, tapping her feet.

The phone number flashed across the screen of Claire's mobile. Ethan's school. It triggered her fight-or-flight response, a rush of adrenaline. She let it ring a few times before answering. It probably wasn't an emergency; he was probably fine. Chances were he'd forgotten his lunch again. She held the phone to her ear.

'It's Duncan Thompson. From school. Are you free to talk? It's urgent.'

Claire looked around the office and stood up. 'Mr Thompson. Yes, of course,' she said quietly. She walked over to the elevator. 'What's happened? What's wrong?'

There was a brief silence down the other end of the phone line. Claire heard children yelling in the background.

'Ethan was involved in an incident in the playground. He's not hurt,' Mr Thompson said quickly. 'But I think you'd better come and pick him up. He's in sick bay.'

'Is he not feeling well?'

'He's not sick. He's in shock, I think. Ethan hit one of the other boys.'

'He did what?'

'I'll explain everything when you get here. The principal would like to speak with you too,' Mr Thompson added.

'I'll be there right away.' Claire hung up the phone. 'Shit,' she said to herself. She rested her forehead against the cool hallway wall to steady herself. Calm down. Don't be emotional at work.

Claire worked in philanthropy and corporate relations at the Sydney Ballet Company. Still in the company, just behind the scenes. Although Claire liked staying in the world of ballet, sometimes she felt pangs of regret watching the serene faces of the principals disappear into their choreography. It was hard to look at them. She missed the sprawling mirrored studios, the stampede of rehearsals.

Claire walked straight into her boss's office.

Natalie raised an eyebrow. 'Lice again?'

'Not lice.' Claire looked down at her phone. 'Ethan's in sick bay. I've got to pick him up from school early. Is it okay if I leave now?'

'Of course.'

Claire felt her boss's eyes on her as she returned to her desk. She ignored the new black and bold emails accumulating in her inbox. Even though the official office policy was meant to be flexible for families, sometimes it felt like it meant a certain flavour of family. Claire suspected her boss judged her for struggling with the chaos of single parenting. When she'd interviewed for the job, Claire hadn't mentioned Ethan but cooed over the silver-plated frames with studio portraits of Natalie's little girl. Her daughter never forgot her lunch or went to the sick bay.

Out on the street, Claire hailed a taxi. The driver tapped on the steering wheel as they stopped at a red light. She fished for the lipstick down the bottom of her bag and reapplied it, before quickly wiping it off again. She didn't know why she'd bought this colour; she was too old to wear bright coral. A pink smear stayed on the back of her hand. The taxi changed lanes, found a gap in the George Street traffic and accelerated out of the city. Claire opened the window and closed her eyes.

The school principal offered a chocolate biscuit. Claire's fingers hovered over the jar. It seemed impolite not to take one but it also felt like something the principal offered to children. She felt twelve years old again, called into the office because she'd done something naughty too. She gingerly picked up a Tim Tam and took a tiny bite.

'We're concerned about Ethan,' Mrs Doyle began.

Mr Thompson interrupted. 'Ethan is a bright boy; he's won every maths and science award since kindy. I've been ability-tracking him all year and he's in my high-expectations group. But he's been visibly emotional at school lately. I know that's normal at his age, but I'm worried about him. We need to develop some behavioural strategies to help Ethan control his temper.'

Claire sat up straight in her chair. 'What happened?'

'Some other boys were teasing him. Kids in the gifted stream tend to be easy targets. Usually Ethan's pretty good-humoured about it, but today something struck a nerve. We've spoken to all of the boys involved and nobody is talking. You see, Ethan repeatedly punched one of the boys in the face.'

'We take a tough stance on bullying at this school,' said Mrs Doyle. 'But we take an even tougher stance on violent behaviour. This other boy lost a tooth.'

Claire felt light-headed. She tried to imagine the tiny hands of her little boy inflicting a bruise, let alone knocking out a tooth. He was only twelve. 'Which boy was it?'

The teachers exchanged a look.

'Will Fraser,' Mr Thompson said.

'But they've been best friends since they were five.' Claire felt the chocolate biscuit melt between her fingers. She could just see Helen Fraser now, taking Will to their GP – or casualty. 'Will must've said something to upset Ethan.'

'We're not sure. Ethan won't tell us,' Mrs Doyle said. 'But we need to take disciplinary action. Not only with Ethan, but with the other children involved too.'

'I understand,' Claire said. The sticky Tim Tam slipped from her grip. She wished she could say Ethan losing his temper was out of character. She wished she didn't believe it. 'Can I please see my son now?'

Ethan was asleep in the sick-bay cot. His cheeks were red and Claire brushed the side of his face with her hand. His hair was damp with sweat. As he stirred, he looked fragile, harmless, but Claire could see scratches all over his puffy hands.

'Mum, I didn't mean it. I don't remember what happened.'

'We can talk about it later. Let's get out of here.'

They walked home together in silence. The streets were empty before the end-of-school rush. Ethan reached for her hand. Their arms swinging in unison, Claire felt a knot inside. In the fractured beams of afternoon light, there was something about the way the sun hit Ethan's face that reminded her exactly of Mark.

4

MOMENTUM

At the hospital entrance, there was a stained-glass window – small panels of emerald and ruby glass, fused into a story told with colour and light. It was a memorial for the Australian Hospital Ship *Centaur*. Off North Stradbroke Island, a Japanese torpedo hit *Centaur* before the sun rose on Friday 14 May 1943, sinking the ship and almost three hundred passengers aboard. The window was dedicated 'to the memory of those who perished'.

The old hospital chaplain stood beside Mark and they sipped their takeaway coffees together. He told Mark about how sinking a hospital ship was a war crime under the Hague Convention but they didn't discover the identity of the guilty Japanese submarine until the 1970s.

'Those bloody Japs should've been tried at a war crimes tribunal,' the chaplain said. 'Avenged those poor drowned nurses.'

It had been a hospital for the Australian Army, built in 1942. There was something totalitarian, Soviet even, about the hospital's architecture. Not that Mark had travelled to Russia or East Berlin – he hadn't even been to Europe – but he imagined the bleak eastern bloc to have the same monolithic severity. Grey upon grey, concrete tower after tower – it reminded him of a prison.

Inside, there was a large foyer with a miserable-looking florist.

Mark wondered for a moment if he should buy his father a bunch of flowers but quickly decided against it. John hated flowers. Mark hated hospitals. The corrosive smell of the corridors, the bite of the air-conditioning, the abrasive squeak his shoes made against the polished floor caused the hair on the back of his neck to stand up. He could taste the cloying vapour of disinfectant in the air. He couldn't breathe. Coming back was a terrible idea.

Mark stood at the reception desk. 'I'm looking for a patient. John Hall?'

The nurse glanced at the whiteboard. 'John Hall. Room 8, Bed 24.' Her eyes scanned over his features. 'Are you family? You look exactly like his son.'

'I am his son.' Mark paused. 'You must mean my brother.'

'I didn't realise Mr Hall had another son. Just down the corridor on the left. Third door.' She smiled at him with the sudden warmth of familiarity.

Mark walked down the corridor to his father's room. The door was shut. He glanced across the hall at another elderly patient flicking through channels on the television, toothless mouth agape. Mark would feel more comfortable approaching that other man. When he was a boy, his father's door was always closed so Mark would stand there quietly, examining the fissures running through the wood until he'd forgotten why he needed to speak to his dad. Even now, he still had to gather his nerves, hesitating for a long time before opening the heavy hospital door.

The room was dark, the blinds drawn. A sliver of sun fell across one wall, particles of dust hanging like fog in the single shaft of light. On the bed, the old man was as small as a child, curled beneath a green hospital blanket. His hair was completely white. Mark did a double take. He'd never seen his father robbed of pigment before.

John lay on his side. 'You,' he said quietly. His faint speech was a pale imitation of the booming voice that once struck Mark with fear.

'Dad, it's me. Mark.'

'Thirsty,' John croaked, his eyes searching for a face. His head jerked forward, exposing his wrinkled neck. He reached out and touched his son. The shock of physical contact made Mark flinch; the rawness of skin on skin felt like electricity. Mark held his father's hand. Crooked fingers, blue veins bloated beneath grey skin. 'Thirsty,' John said again.

Mark sat in the chair beside the bed. He offered John a cup of water, placed a bent drinking straw near his mouth. There were no teeth left inside his jaw – just a gummy cavity of fleshy holes and sticky saliva. The old man's lips hunted clumsily for the straw. Pipes and drains came out of his father's body. Amber urine collected in a bag hanging off the bed frame. Mark listened to John's laboured breathing, unsure what to think – should he feel sad? He'd resented his father for longer than he could remember.

When they were kids, John was strict with the boys; they needed to be the best, top of the class in every subject. Occasionally, there were beatings – the leather belt came out whenever they misbehaved or failed to achieve. Tom thrived under the rules, but although Mark did well at school, he wasn't tough enough for his dad. His knee-jerk sensitivity made him an easy target; he couldn't control his feelings. Their mother did her best to protect her children from her husband's violent outbursts. Although he never saw his father hit his mother, Mark knew he did. It was clear from the muffled sounds that reverberated through the house, the occasional darkness in Eleanor's eyes.

'Mark,' the old man said finally. His sour breath quickened, his sweaty chalk-coloured hair stuck to his temples. The whites of his father's eyes were a dirty yellow. Tom said John only had a week left, if they were lucky. Luck had little to do with it – it was cancer. The room stank of shit and piss masked by bleach.

Mark squeezed his father's hand. 'I'm here, Dad.'

John sucked at the plastic straw with his thin lips, drinking with such force that Mark wondered whether he was trying to drown. Choke intentionally on a glass of water. He inhaled the fluid until he gasped for air.

Tom stood at the door. 'Don't let him drink so fast. Use the sponges to give him water. Dad has dysphagia.' He placed firm and possessive hands on their father's frail body, pushing Mark aside. Mark pictured their mother scolding them about it, imploring the boys to share. 'Let Mark have a turn, Thomas,' she would have said. 'You're the older brother.'

Tom quickly grabbed the cup from Mark's hands. Water spilled over their father's front and soaked his blankets. The old man blinked helplessly.

'Now look what you've done,' said Tom. 'Help me clean him up.'

Mark nodded. They lifted their father's limp body and changed his gown, raising his arms like John was a doll. The two brothers hadn't stood so close to one another for such a long time and Mark was surprised by how his brother had aged. Wrinkles and creases covered Tom's face, light brown liver spots on his arms as though he'd spent too much time in the sun.

'Mark,' Tom said loudly. 'Can you please get the nurse?'

John was struggling to breathe, his eyes bulging and wet. His chin quivered; he reminded Mark of a newborn baby.

'Mark,' Tom repeated. 'The nurse. Quickly!'

'Right.' Mark reached for the call button. 'Which one do I press?'

'Just go outside and get someone yourself.'

Mark rushed out into the ward. There was a Filipino nurse named JP by the sink, washing his hands. He followed Mark back to John's bed.

Tom was flustered now, adjusting their father's posture. 'Help,' he said. 'He's not breathing.'

The nurse checked John's nose and mouth. 'Hi, Mr Hall,' JP said sweetly to the old man. He turned to face the two sons. 'He's not in major respiratory distress, but his breathing is shallow. Some oxygen might help.' The nurse stuck the prongs of the cannula up John's nostrils.

John pulled on the chain around JP's neck, making the nurse's glasses swing.

'No, Mr Hall,' JP said, prying the chain from John's hands. 'You're very strong. But those aren't for you.'

John released his grip on the chain. His yellow eyes searched the room, straining to focus, darting from the nurse to Mark, and back to Tom. With an assertive stare, John ripped the nasal cannula and oxygen out, his nose wrinkling as the tube scratched the insides of his nostrils.

'Dad, what are you doing? Doesn't he need that?' Tom asked the nurse.

JP shrugged. 'At this stage, the most important thing is that he's comfortable. We don't need to force him.'

Mark thanked the nurse while Tom sat beside their father's bed, running his hands over his face. His brother's complexion was pink, like the blood in his body wanted to flee.

'Maybe you need a break,' Mark suggested. 'Go home, get some rest, see your family.'

'I haven't eaten all day,' Tom said. 'It's funny, when Dad was first diagnosed they said it'd happen quickly. But these have been the longest months of my life.'

John let out a low groan. He reached for Mark, looked into his eyes with a quiet urgency. The desperation of his father's stare ruffled him.

'I want to see.' John pulled on Mark's hand.

Mark moved in closer. 'I'm here.'

'No, I want to see him.' John coughed. 'I want to see my grandson.'

Mark looked at his brother. Tom and his wife, Jasmine, only had daughters. There was a framed picture of his brother's family on John's bedside table: three beautiful girls. But John wasn't talking about his granddaughters. He wanted to see Ethan.

Mark remembered when his father had visited baby Ethan in hospital, over twelve years ago now. As John held the small bundle, an unrecognisable smile filled his face. But Mark's exit splintered the family, untied any ties that were supposed to bind. Ethan. This was something Mark couldn't negotiate for his dad, an impossibility where hazard outweighed hope.

'Dad, I can't. I haven't seen him since —'

John interrupted. 'Please let me see my grandson.'

They watched their father fall asleep, muttering to himself. John's sunken eyes rolled into the back of his head. Mark didn't owe him anything. He'd come home because he wanted to let his dad leave the world with a feeling of peace, to restore some sense of harmony.

Tom glanced stiffly at his brother. Mark looked away. His mind ran through thousands of unordered ideas but he couldn't focus on a single thought. All he could do was count the beeps of the patient monitors, as the droning machines murmured the flat music of his father's vital signs.

∞

Claire found solace in tedium. Her hands absorbed the choreography of domestic life the way a body swallows a dance, automatically travelling through every movement. The sun was coming up, pink light scattering through the window, making the white kitchen tiles blush. There was something reassuring about having a clean house. It was one thing Claire controlled when life felt uncontrollable.

The letter had arrived at her office yesterday. Crisp white envelope, her name written in handwriting that Claire wished she didn't recognise. The stamp was a portrait of William Lawrence Bragg, an Australian-born scientist who'd discovered x-ray diffraction, who won the Nobel Prize for Physics in 1915. She wondered if he'd done that on purpose. No sender, no return address, but Claire didn't need to see his name to know the letter came from Mark.

She couldn't open it, though. She didn't want to know what was written inside. The previous night she'd stared at the envelope for hours, starting to tear open the flap, stopping herself, hiding the letter in the remotest parts of overlooked drawers, then finally salvaging it again. Haven't you punished us enough? Claire asked the envelope. Mark was abstract now; she couldn't remember the details of his face or the sound of his voice. Time and space had turned him into a ghost. Everything about Mark had long faded into the background.

Love didn't work like that; it didn't fade. You couldn't turn it off like a tap; its plumbing was impossible to plug. To Claire, love was much more like a bad smell. Like spoiled meat – its rotten stench crawled into every corner and was absorbed by every surface, and you'd forget it was there only to have the bad smell resurrected by a warm breeze.

Claire held the letter over the stove. She turned on the gas, the metronome of the electric ignition clicking until the burner was alight. As she watched the envelope disappear into the blue flame, she thought back to her younger self. The paper burned quickly; white turned wafer black.

Once, she'd read anything he wrote over and over again until she knew paragraphs off by heart. Now the letter was ablaze. She blew out the rising fire before it reached her fingers. Smoke filled the kitchen. Claire opened the windows and wiped the greasy ash off the stovetop.

Quark, Ethan's pet rabbit, skidded down the hallway. He was a grey lop rabbit with white streaks, Ethan's seventh birthday present. Particle physics was his obsession then; he'd watched documentary after documentary. Claire often worried her son watched more documentaries than he had friends. Ethan had put Quark in the palm of his hand and the little bunny shot off, thudding along the floorboards, an escape artist from his makeshift home in a drawer. The baby rabbit had made Ethan think of a quark. Ethan often spoke to the bunny like he was a dog, saying, 'Up, Quark!' or 'Down, Quark!' and sometimes he called him Hover Rabbit. Quark liked to eat bok choy, Dutch carrots and – on very special occasions – Anzac biscuits.

Claire scooped up Quark to her chest and took him into Ethan's bedroom.

'Time to get up, sweetheart.'

'Mum,' Ethan groaned. 'I'm really sick.'

Claire put the rabbit down and touched Ethan's forehead. His skin was pink, but he wasn't feverish; his eyes looked clear and bright. Definitely not sick. Claire knew she should send him off to school. But she remembered those rushes of anxiety she'd felt at that age: the stress of whispers, the poisonous stares, the weight-filled gaps in strained conversations.

'You can stay home.' Claire sat on the edge of his bed and ran her fingers through his hair. 'I'll call school.'

Ethan brushed her hand away. 'I want to go back to sleep.'

'Maybe we talk about what happened yesterday at school? With Will.'

'Mum, I told you. I don't remember,' Ethan said, rolling onto his side.

'I'm not mad.' She reached out to pat his back before thinking twice of it and retracting her arm, placing both hands neatly in her lap. 'I just want to understand what happened. Did Will say something to upset you?'

'He didn't do anything.'

'Was it about me?'

Ethan shook his head.

She tried not to sound accusatory. 'You can tell me what he said.'

Ethan's hands were covered in beige bandaids and he picked at the dirty, fraying edges. He mumbled something indecipherable.

Claire stared at her son's downcast face. 'What was that?'

'Freak,' Ethan said clearly this time. 'Will called me a freak.'

'You're not a freak, my darling.'

'Maybe I am. They call me a freak all the time.' Despite Ethan's efforts to appear composed, Claire could hear his voice start to tremble. 'He said it was all my fault. Because I'm a freak.'

'What was?'

'Never mind.' Ethan pulled the bedclothes over his face. His voice was muffled but she just made out what he said. 'That he left.'

It took a moment for Claire to register. Sometimes that pain struck her like a cramp – some spasm of ancient trauma. If anyone were at fault, it was Mark. But Claire understood the irrationality of feeling responsible. She felt it too. 'You were four months old when he left. You were just a baby. It wasn't your fault.'

'How do you know?' Ethan pulled the sheet down his torso. His t-shirt had gathered up around his chest, exposing his bellybutton. 'Did he tell you? You don't talk about him, Mum. You never told me why he left. Or where he is. Or if he's coming back.'

Claire's stomach twisted as she remembered the letter. 'Let's talk about it when I'm home from work,' she said. Ethan had a mathematical clock on his bedroom wall – fractions and equations instead of numbers – and she couldn't figure out the actual time.

'You always do this,' Ethan complained. 'You always change the subject.'

'I know you're curious. But it's complicated. You're not going to understand yet.'

Ethan crossed his arms and looked her steadily in the eye. 'You don't understand. You make everything worse. I hate it. He's my dad.'

Claire felt hollow. His dad. Mark didn't deserve the word; he'd never really been a dad, especially the kind Ethan needed or deserved. It hurt Claire that she wasn't enough, that her son felt something was missing.

'You act like he doesn't exist,' Ethan continued, his voice quieter. 'He's my father. And I've never heard you say his name out loud.'

Claire could see Ethan searching her face for a response. She stared at her son's features so much, she knew the exact location, size and colour of every freckle on his face. Quark chewed a sock on the floor.

'I've got to go to work,' she said quickly, rescuing the sock from the rabbit.

Ethan climbed out of bed, ignoring his mother. He stomped down the hall, his footsteps echoing, and slammed the bathroom door. She heard him piss loudly into the toilet bowl.

Claire lingered behind, fixing the sheets on Ethan's bed.

'Mark,' she said into the empty room. 'Your father's name is Mark.'

The last time Claire had seen Mark, they didn't speak to each other. The room was crowded and she didn't want to approach him. Mostly she knew that she shouldn't, but she also didn't know what to say. There were too many things she wanted to tell him, conflicting things: that she hated him but still loved him, that she hated herself for loving

him, that she was comforted by hatred she couldn't help but feel. She'd
wanted to slap and hold him at the same time.

Mark knew she was there, but went out of his way to avoid eye
contact. He was nervous – understandably – she could tell by the
way he incessantly pulled at his hair. Claire knew him so well, every
idiosyncrasy. How he tugged at a strand of hair when he was worried;
the way he chewed on the ends of pencils when he concentrated; the
way he gestured like a conductor when he was excited. She stared
at Mark while he looked down at his feet. That swollen silence was
excruciating; they were only metres away from each other but already
light years apart.

How could you know somebody so entirely, so intimately, one
minute and then suddenly not at all? The solidity of their love, even
the shape of it, had been deceptive: Claire thought it was circular
when it was actually square. They were married, parents together,
they'd been unbelievably happy. But it was so brief. Did all marriages
end up like this, whether the couple stayed together or broke apart?
Strangers – toxic hostility wedged between them – and the room filled
with thoughts that could never be said.

The night they first met, Mark taught Claire how to play pool.
It was a mutual friend's birthday drinks at a pub on King Street in
Newtown. Mark seemed shy, couldn't maintain eye contact. But after
a few beers he was a pool shark, winning game after game, fuelled by
a quiet confidence. Claire found his scientific approach to the game
charming. Mark nailed every shot. She felt like she couldn't hold the
cue correctly.

'What am I doing wrong?' Claire laughed as she missed another
ball.

Mark shrugged. 'It's just physics. I'll show you.' He took the cue
from her hands and quickly brushed his fingers on hers. Claire wasn't

sure if it had been accidental or deliberate. 'Think about it like this: it's a system. The balls, the cue, and the force you hit the ball with. All of it together makes a system,' Mark told her. 'The momentum in the system before the balls collide has to be the same as after the collision. It's conserved. You can't destroy momentum.'

Claire pulled her hair off her face. 'I'm not sure that explanation helps.'

'Watch this.' Mark bent over the pool table and stretched his long arm along the pool cue. With effortless fluidity, he sent the white ball flying across the table. It struck the red three ball, knocking it straight into the pocket.

'See? The white ball stopped and the red ball gained its momentum. So the momentum of the red ball after the collision is exactly the same as the white ball before the collision. Or the momentum in the system once the white ball has been struck is the same after the white ball has collided. When the white ball struck the red ball, it gained the momentum the white ball lost.'

'I have no idea what you just said,' Claire said, scrunching up her nose.

'Come here.' Mark took her hand and pulled her towards him.

She moved into the gap between his body and the pool table, her back skimming his front.

'Bodies in motion have momentum, but when they collide momentum is exchanged,' Mark whispered in her ear as he leaned over her, cradling Claire, pushing her body against his. She inhaled him. 'They move. They collide. They push each other into different directions.'

Mark hit the white ball again, propelling it down the green felt. It knocked into the yellow ball – sending it on a collision course with the green ball – and they separated, forced onto different paths. The green ball went straight into the pocket. Mark squeezed Claire's torso as he pulled back the cue.

'Now, that happened because of the laws of the conservation of momentum,' he began.

'Stop,' she said. 'Enough physics.'

Mark put his arms on Claire's waist and turned her around to face him. She could feel his breath on her face as their noses touched. His scent reminded Claire of being outdoors, of crisp saltwater breezes, eucalyptus leaves. Her top lip grazed against his bottom lip and their mouths lingered in one spot as they shared the same air: swapping nitrogen, oxygen, carbon dioxide. Mark ran his hand up along Claire's back and into her hair. With his fingertips, he lightly touched the back of her neck, drew her closer, and warm mouth upon mouth, they kissed.

Claire never had a mind for theories and science, but she always remembered that when bodies collided momentum was exchanged. Despite everything that happened and no matter how hard she tried, Claire couldn't forget their beautiful collision. How they'd crashed into each other; how something was exchanged between them. She still carried a piece of Mark inside: his momentum, his energy, his force. She felt it when she saw Mark appear in Ethan – sometimes it was in a gesture, a glance or the way her son spoke. Claire loathed it. She hated that she was never allowed to forget. Perhaps Mark still felt it too. But as much as she willed it to go away, that was the problem. Momentum couldn't be destroyed.

∞

Ethan swallowed the shower water, taking big gulps and spitting them out. Mum left for work; he heard her footsteps against the wooden floor. The front door slammed. He washed his hair and used the remaining shampoo to lather his body. He didn't have a lot of pubes yet – just a light scattering of coarse hairs – but they were definitely there. His body was changing. As he rubbed the area near his groin, his penis stiffened, his legs grew tight. Heat soared to his head.

These urges had only started recently, a photo or glimpse of a breast through a shirt suddenly sending Ethan into a quiet frenzy. He stroked his penis hastily, wanting to do this as fast as possible. Warmth spread to his stomach and he tilted his head backwards, allowing the hot water to fall over his face. He was annoyed with his mum; she treated him like a baby. He wasn't stupid; he wasn't a child. Children might not understand complicated things, but they also didn't do what Ethan was doing right now.

When he came – a thread of fire escaping his body – Ethan let out a low moan. He choked on the sound, hoping it was dampened by water slapping the tiles, but remembered Mum wasn't home. His tiny emission clung to his body before snaking down the drain. Ethan shivered, a ridge of goosebumps appearing on his arms. He rinsed his body one more time and turned off the tap. Then he quickly got dressed and went to eat breakfast.

It was a rare treat to be home alone. Ethan made himself a huge bowl of cereal, staring at milk being absorbed into the grains. Sometimes the finality of things struck him, like the sadness of mixing Weet-Bix and milk. They could never be unmixed – even if Ethan had a centrifuge and separated the milk particles from the cereal particles, he still couldn't undo how they'd changed. Other things like this made him sad too: breaking eggs, mixing a cake, untwisting the cap of a new bottle of Coke. None of those things could be undone. He ate his breakfast in front of the television.

After morning talk shows replaced morning cartoons, Ethan

wandered over to his mum's bedroom. He loved the smell of her bed. White sheets steeped in her scent – flowery perfume, laundry powder, the nutty smell of her shampoo. Her smell attached itself to everything in their home. Being in her bed reminded Ethan of having nightmares, waking up terrified and creeping into her room. She'd hold him, stroke his hair, promise that there were no monsters under his bed; she was the only person who knew how to make his heart beat normally again. Sometimes Ethan sneaked into her bedroom, rested his head on the cool cotton pillow and inhaled her smell. It made him feel safe. He lay under her blankets, watching the day change from the other side of the curtain.

Outside, people walked past, cars started and stopped; the postman who listened to Radio National made his rounds. Next door, the little kids played in their front yard; it sounded like they were having a tea party. The rhythm of daily life lulled Ethan back to sleep.

He was woken abruptly by a loud knock at the front door. Ethan wasn't allowed to answer the door when he was home alone. He sat up in the bed and pretended he was a statue. Mum's bedroom overlooked the street, but with the curtain drawn Ethan couldn't see who was there. Another knock. Someone stood outside at the window. The silhouette of a tall man.

The man paced the front of the house and Ethan tried to quiet his breathing. Maybe the man was planning a robbery. Ethan quickly listed the places he could hide: under the bed, inside the wardrobe, in the triangle of space behind the door. All the good hiding spots were in the back of the house. His palms started sweating. Once a robber broke into Will's house and took their television, computer and all of his mother's jewellery. Mum would be upset if everything was stolen when she came home from work. Or if Ethan was murdered. Maybe it was a murderer.

Something slid under the door. Then footsteps and the creaky front gate banging against the latch.

Ethan didn't move for a while. His body was so still it felt like blood stopped moving through his arteries and veins. Once he was positive the robber wasn't coming back, Ethan went to the door. There was an envelope, addressed to Mum. The handwritten letters were squished together with an agoraphobic compression, scared of the vast whiteness of the envelope. Ethan held it up to the light to read the overlapping words. He saw his own name and brought it closer to his face. This paper had an exotic smell, of dust and damp and petrol.

Ethan knew he shouldn't open it but the letter had a pulse. It felt alive. Sentences beating and pounding, the paper persuaded him to rip it open and read. He peeled the envelope's flap, the sticky seal tearing apart in fine filaments like a spider web. Squiggly lines turned into words that fell out from the page.

Dear Claire,

I'm sorry to get in touch out of the blue like this but I urgently need to speak with you. I sent a letter to your office but I'm not sure you received it. Your old phone number is disconnected. I don't know your email address. Hopefully this is still your address, Anna gave it to me a while ago. She said you two weren't close any more, which was a surprise. It's been a long time.

I want to ask how you are but it feels like a stupid question after all these years. I want to ask how Ethan is too. I hope he is well. He's my son, but I don't know anything about him. Maybe I should've sent him birthday cards, called him at Christmas. I don't know. I wasn't sure if you wanted to hear from me. And I needed to focus on getting my own life back on track. I often wonder what you've told Ethan about me and about what happened. I'm his father. How have you explained the fact that I'm not around?

I'm back in Sydney. Dad is really sick. He's asked to see Ethan.

I'm staying at my parents' house. Maybe you could give me a call?

Mark

Ethan's face burned and his legs shook. He read the letter several times. Pen marks moved around the page, words collided with other words, until Ethan couldn't read any more. It was just a jumble of ballpoint lines, curves and hoops, dancing across the paper.

There was a dirty fingerprint in the right-hand corner. Ethan pressed his finger against it. His father's fingertip. His father's handwriting. This was an object his father had held, folded and touched. Just moments before, his actual father had stood at the front door. He'd knocked, sighed, breathed. That shadow against the curtain had been the shape of his father's body. He was tall. He had loud footsteps. He was real. All that had separated them was a pane of glass, a length of fabric. What might have happened if Ethan had opened the door – would that have broken the universe?

Western Australia was far away but right now his father was here, in Sydney. The letter was written on the personal stationery of a man named John Hall. Was this his grandfather who was sick? Ethan didn't know anything about the other side of his family – what were their names, where did they live, what did they look like, how did they smell? John Hall lived in Woollahra. Ethan looked up the address: 5.6 kilometres away, a fifteen-minute drive, or a one hour and twenty-three minute walk. All this time he'd had family nearby, but they may as well have been on the moon.

The Year 1 class were making cards for Father's Day. Ethan was six years old. He liked using crayons and drew a picture of himself as an astronaut, surrounded by stars and on his way to the moon. But then he got stuck. He didn't know what his father looked like. Beside him, Will had drawn himself and his dad at the beach making a big yellow sandcastle.

'Will,' Ethan whispered.

'Yeah?' Will said, drawing a bright red crab with huge claws.

'Can I copy your dad? Dunno what mine looks like.'

'You don't?' Will gave his crab black beady eyes.

'Never met him.'

'Then how are you going to send him the card?'

This was a good question. If Ethan didn't know where he was, how would he get the card to him? He wondered if Mum knew. They'd lost him like a set of keys. Was there a Father's Day Fairy, just like the Tooth Fairy or Santa, who knew where all the lost dads were and could deliver all the unaddressed cards?

Will stopped colouring and looked at Ethan's card. 'That's a good drawing of the moon.'

'The moon has craters,' Ethan told him. 'But not very much oxygen.'

Oxygen. This gave Ethan an idea. He took a black crayon out of the plastic bucket and outlined a bigger astronaut standing on the moon's surface. Astronaut Dad needed a helmet to breathe, so he didn't need to draw his face. When the kids took the cards home that afternoon, Ethan wasn't sure what to do with his. He slipped it into one of his favourite picture books, just in case.

On Father's Day that year, Ethan stood with his mum outside on the street, on a Telecom junction box that he called their special star-watching stone. He took her there to study the night sky. They held hands and looked up at the indigo horizon, stargazing together at their concrete observatory. Sometimes when they held hands, Ethan pretended her fingers belonged to somebody else.

'I want to see the moon,' Ethan said. It was behind the trees.

Mum lifted him up. 'Can you see it now?'

Ethan nodded. It was a brilliant full circle, shadowy craters dotted over the glowing milky surface. 'Mum, can we go there one day?'

'We can go right now,' his mum said. 'Close your eyes.'

Ethan shut them tight.

'Are you on the moon?' asked Mum.

'No, I'm still on the street.'

'Look harder. Keep your eyes closed.'

Ethan was confused because he couldn't look harder with his eyes closed, all he could see were the backs of his eyelids. There was no moon when he closed his eyes – nothing, no colours, no shapes, just darkness.

Mum kept talking. 'We've just arrived on the moon, and we're standing beside a big rocky hole. Around us is silver terrain as far as the eye can see. All the stars are so clear, tiny twinkles of flickering light. Earth is far away, blue and green and brown, covered in cloudy swirls. It looks like a marble from the moon. It's quiet here, and everything is grey. At our feet there's lunar dust shifting along the ground. Can you see it?'

He opened his eyes. 'I saw it,' he said, wrapping his hands around his mum's neck. 'Thank you.'

She squeezed his dangling leg and kissed him on the cheek.

Ethan studied the dark patches on the moon's surface, counting its basins and seas. 'Mum?' he asked eventually. 'Can my dad see the moon where he is too?'

'I'm sure he can,' she said, suddenly dropping an octave. Ethan knew this was her sad voice.

'Is he looking at it right now?'

'He might be.'

Ethan thought about his father, wherever he was, looking up at the moon. Did he like to study the stars as well? Was he thinking about Ethan too?

Mum put him back onto the ground. 'That's one small step for Ethan,' she said in a silly voice.

They walked towards home. The moon hid behind an apartment block but Ethan needed to see it one last time before he went to bed. He let go of his mum's hand and sprinted back to their star-watching stone.

'Happy Father's Day,' Ethan whispered to the moon.

There were seven cards now: one with the astronauts, another that he'd painted with a picture of the ocean and a boat, one that looked like a comic book. Every year his class made those cards. Sometimes he wanted to throw them in the bin but there was always a flicker of hope – that one day his dad might walk through the front door and say, 'Hello, son, I'm home!'

Now there was an address. Now there was somewhere to send them.

Ethan copied John Hall's address on an envelope. He placed the cards inside in chronological order and stuck on several stamps, just in case. Ethan wrote a note, sealed the envelope, and threw it into the dark slit of the post-box.

The note said:

Sorry these are so late. I didn't know where to find you.

5

ENTROPY

Mark sat alone in the empty house. It was a sandstone estate in Woollahra – heritage listed, north-facing parterre garden – although these days it looked tired, needed to be restored. Rooms held the same smells, their faded walls splashed with familiar lines of light. His childhood home was suspended in a quiet lacuna of time.

Even the boys' bedrooms were stuck in the past: John had never packed away their things. School textbooks still piled high on their desks, forgotten toys assembled on shelves in straight lines. Mark's wooden train set still coiled around one corner of his room, covered in dust. Old leather school shoes lined up underneath his old bed, old school blazers hanging off the back of the old door.

Tom drove him back after another long day at the hospital. They ate baked beans they'd found in the pantry for dinner and watched the 7 p.m. news, falling back into their easy rhythm of easy silence, the way family members do. But the house played tricks on Mark: he swore he saw his father sitting in his armchair and reading the newspaper, his mother knitting on the sofa, basket of lavender balls of wool at her feet. Tom hadn't invited Mark to stay at his own home, hadn't insisted he sleep in their spare room. Mark didn't actually know if his brother had a spare room, but it would've been nicer to stay with people. That option was never put on the table. Maybe there was no space. Or maybe there was.

After Tom went home, Mark rifled through old newspapers and unopened mail, wiped dust off the photo of his mother on his father's bureau. Among the stacks of papers, Mark recognised a worn paperback – his tattered copy of *Jude the Obscure* by Thomas Hardy. He picked it up and leafed through the book, surprised to find there was an ultrasound stuck between its pages. The thin sonogram paper had yellowed, the dark ink faded to grey, but Mark remembered the round belly of the foetus. He hadn't looked at this monochrome image since Claire's ultrasound appointment. It reminded Mark of trawling through his father's slide collection, of the overseas trips John made before his children were born, looking through the light to find toy-sized Athens, Rome and Cairo like vivid jewels trapped in tiny white frames.

It was Claire who recommended *Jude the Obscure*. She'd sat up late one night reading the book, later urging it into Mark's hands. Between the chapters of textbooks and journals, Mark found himself; he didn't like getting lost in novels. Claire was the fiction reader, would happily lie in bed and devour stories, retelling the plot as if it were her own life, chatting about the characters as if they were people she knew.

But Mark wanted to read *Jude the Obscure*. The title drew him in. His mother loved to garden, was never happier than in those moments he'd watched her balanced on her knees, her hands deep in the soil. Mark liked sitting in the dirt with his mother and talking to the plants below the Moreton Bay fig. He'd pass her the fork and trowel, help her press the seeds into the ground, and water the flowers. Even when she was dying, even when she wouldn't eat or drink, she still watered those flowers.

Roses were her favourites. Eleanor grew them in every colour: yellow, red, pink, orange, white, blue. Those roses were Mark's childhood friends and he could call them by name: *Benjamin Britten, Wise Portia, The Nun, The Swan, Scarborough Fair*. Mark still thought of his mother whenever he smelled a rose.

The cancer spread quickly towards the end, metastasising impatiently from cell to cell. In a matter of months, the colour of her skin changed, her eyes grew dull, clothes fell off her shoulders and hips. She was in and out of hospital, and Mark was in and out of waiting rooms, until the treatments stopped working. The doctors let Eleanor come home to die.

In those last few days, she was barely conscious but Mark sat at the foot of her bed and spoke to her like nothing was wrong. Tom stood by the door and couldn't speak, couldn't stay in the room for more than five minutes at once, but Mark wanted to be close. He was nineteen years old then, taller than her, but still needed his mother. Her hair was black and long, and although she was forty-two and had been ill for several years, Eleanor hardly had any grey hairs. Mark brushed it and told her she looked beautiful. She smiled and held his hand.

Two hours later, she passed away. Mark was the only one with her in the room. He felt her leave him. Her hands were still warm but something else changed. His mother wasn't inside her body any more.

After the ambulance took Eleanor away, Mark spent the night in the garden. He moved from one rose to the next. Now that she was dead, these flowers were the only part of her left alive. He put on her gardening gloves, although they were too small for his hands, and started to turn the soil. The earth smelled rich and rotten, of metal and spores. His trowel hit the roots of one rose bush and Mark broke the dirt away. Its roots were white, thick and deep. Anger flew through him; he pulled at the plant. The rose bush fought back, reluctant to withdraw from the soil, but eventually Mark unearthed it. In the horrible quiet of that night, every rose was trampled, every precious bush hauled out of the ground, as Mark slaughtered her garden.

But there was one large rose bush, where the powdery petals turned apricot as they bloomed, that was Eleanor's favourite. It smelled of sweet white wine; the flower formed the perfect shape of a round cup. These roses were the only survivor that night. Despite the following years of neglect, barely watered and undernourished, this bush stayed alive much longer than his mother.

Its name was Jude the Obscure.

Mark started the novel the day he found out Claire was pregnant. He wasn't a fast reader; he found fiction difficult, its twists and turns mostly implausible. But he'd loved *Jude the Obscure*. He didn't exactly identify with Jude Fawley – Mark grew up privileged, walked right into university without any effort, then felt he didn't belong there. It was the book's haunting grief that resonated with Mark. That scene where Little Father Time killed his siblings and hanged himself always stayed with him, he couldn't stop thinking about it: 'Done because we are too menny.'

He'd read that scene as they waited for Claire's ultrasound. She was silent, sipping a bottle of water. Mark felt relieved to have a distraction. Hospital smells made him think of death, even though new life brought them there today. The sonographer called them into her dark room and Claire lay down on the bed. Mark watched as blue gel was squirted onto her stomach.

On the screen, the image started to move. The sonographer shifted her hands over Claire's belly, trying to find the best position for the probe. Flashes of the baby's body appeared on the monitor until the sonographer settled on the perfect angle. The baby moved its hands to its oversized head and the sonographer captured the image, printing it out with thick thermal ink. Claire's eyes welled up as she watched the baby move. Rather than looking at the screen, Mark watched his wife. The glow of the display lit her face; she was visibly besotted with this blob on the screen. Mark looked at the image of his child again, knowing he should feel something – anything – but he was numb. Nothing about these vague pictures moved him.

'Do you want to know if it's a boy or a girl?' the sonographer asked.

Claire shook her head. 'We want it to be a surprise.' She reached for Mark's hand, moving his fingers to her stomach. The gel was slippery and cold. He was indifferent to the foetus, the way he was unmoved by abstract art. It made him feel guilty, especially when Claire's bond with the thing was so tangible. So he faked it. He faked smiles and excitement, was attentive to her needs. If Claire knew how he really felt, she'd worry. Even Mark was worried. Once it was born – once he could see it and hold it, once it was real – this would all be different.

The sonographer handed him the ultrasound. Claire got dressed and went to the bathroom and Mark waited outside, continuing his book. His heart broke for Sue when she found all her children dead – 'the triplet of little corpses' – and how she blamed herself for it on top of her pain. He wanted to be sick as he thought of those dead children hanging from those hooks. Mark closed the pages.

When they returned home, Claire asked for the ultrasound. Mark searched through his jacket and his pockets. He couldn't remember where he'd put it. He looked everywhere. The ultrasound had disappeared.

'I can't believe you lost it,' Claire said, starting to cry. 'It was the first picture of our baby and now it's gone.'

'We could go back and get another one,' Mark offered.

'That's not the point. The baby will never be this small again. I was going to frame it. This is the worst thing that's ever happened.'

Mark couldn't stand it when she was like this. Everything was a catastrophe. He knew the baby made her irrational. It was hormones; she'd be his Claire again soon. They were nearly halfway through the pregnancy. All he had to do was be patient; it would be over in five months.

When Mark moved out of their home, *Jude the Obscure* was one of the few items he took with him. When he left Sydney to work in the mines, the novel was packed away in his parents' garage. He'd forgotten all about it and now it was on his father's desk.

The following day, a bulging brown envelope arrived. Mark hadn't expected to receive any mail; nobody knew he was here. Only Claire. His name was written in the unsteady hand of a child. Inside the envelope, there was a note and seven handmade cards. Happy Father's Day, they said. Each year that Hallmark holiday – gift sets in the supermarket, ads on TV, fathers and sons exchanging smiles on the back of the bus – made Mark feel like he'd been punched in his gut.

A tear fell down his face. These cards were beautiful. Finally – twelve years too late – something in him stirred. Mark suddenly knew exactly how Claire had felt looking at the blob.

He had a son.

∞

The two boys and their parents were called in for an official disciplinary meeting at school. As much as Claire dreaded the idea of a formal meeting, at least it might unearth some answers. Punishing her son felt futile anyway when he was punishing her back. Ethan shut himself away: closed his bedroom door, refused to speak during dinner. This secrecy, this lack of eye contact, was unusual. Claire missed him and the relaxed ease of their bond.

'We just want everyone to touch base, discuss the matter face to face,' Mr Thompson had said over the phone.

Claire shrank. 'I suppose Will's parents will be there too?'

'Yes, I've already spoken to Helen and Simon. I'm sure this will be quality face time.' Mr Thompson paused. 'Claire, I want to reassure you that this won't be a blamestorming session.'

'Thanks,' she'd said, in a measured tone.

Claire ran late to the meeting. The ballet company held a fundraising afternoon tea with the new artistic director and she got stuck speaking to one of the most generous philanthropic supporters. As she sat on the bus, she felt jittery and agitated. The neckline of her dress was too tight. Claire dreaded Ethan's disciplinary meeting but mostly she hadn't prepared herself to see Simon again.

They'd met five years ago at the school Christmas play. Claire knew Helen, but Simon worked long hours and was never home when she dropped Ethan off at their house. That Christmas, Ethan and Will were wise men in the nativity, clutching oversized frankincense and myrrh in their tiny hands. Helen had insisted on sewing Ethan's costume so that all three wise men matched.

After the production, Claire ran into Simon, who was leaning against the school gate.

'These things always go on forever,' he said. 'And your kid is only on stage for five minutes but they still make you watch the whole school perform.' Simon smiled. He reminded Claire of one of her high-school boyfriends, with his warm face and sensible haircut, the sort of practical boy she'd fancied before disappearing from her local school to study ballet full-time.

'I'm embarrassed to admit I don't know your name,' Claire said.

'I only know other parents by the names of their children. You're Will's dad.'

'Simon. I have the same problem. You're Ethan's mum.'

'Claire.' She reached out to shake his hand.

He had a firm handshake. 'Will talks about Ethan all the time. So you're Claire.' Simon said her name slowly. He looked at her for a moment; the intensity of his stare made her feel uneasy. 'The ballerina, right? Helen mentioned something, when we were at the Opera House recently. That you work there.'

'Oh, ex-ballerina. Now I just work behind the scenes.'

'More interesting than my job, anyway. I'm an accountant. Punch-line to lots of jokes. Everyone is more interesting than me.'

They briefly maintained eye contact. Simon fiddled with the sleeve of his shirt. He looked at her in a way that she'd forgotten. Like she was visible, under the spotlight on a stage.

'Funny you mention it, but I need an accountant,' Claire said. This wasn't true. She'd never had any trouble sorting out her tax returns.

Simon took a business card out of his jacket. 'Here,' he said, putting it in her hand. 'Call me if you have any questions. About accounting.'

'Thanks,' Claire said and walked away to collect Ethan from backstage.

She didn't call him. The glossy business card turned grey at the bottom of her handbag, lost beside the old receipts and grimy bus tickets. But their offices were nearby and they kept running into each other around Circular Quay. Suddenly, Simon was everywhere. He'd always be so friendly, invite her to have a coffee or lunch; Claire always refused. Over time, she grew addicted to his persistence and if she didn't see him for a while, she'd miss getting her fix. Finally, after a long day at work, Simon persuaded Claire to have a drink with him.

They sat at a bar overlooking Campbell's Cove. Across the water was a row of identical storehouses, a sandstone procession of triangular rooftops. Claire twisted her napkin with her hands and ordered another drink.

'Tell me about being a ballerina,' Simon said.

Claire tried to laugh off the request. 'It was so long ago. I don't really remember any more.'

She knew all about being cast as that mystical object – the dancing figurine in the music box spinning on its axis. It used to annoy her, the fetish and fixation that went hand in hand with her career. She wanted to be taken seriously, to have her dedication and discipline acknowledged, not be degraded to some spectacle of bodices and tulle.

Mark never saw Claire that way; they shared this unspoken drive. He loved her perfectionism and hunger, how she'd practise and practise until her hips crumbled and feet bled. He was just as obsessive about his work, chasing some elusive original idea so he could challenge existing theories, change the world. Ambition and mastery – that was the foundation of their relationship. Their common ground.

'Do you miss it?' Simon asked.

'Not really,' she lied.

'I'm sure when you were on stage, nobody could take their eyes off you.' He leaned forward and touched her elbow.

Claire felt embarrassed by how much she enjoyed the thrill of being desired. It seemed trivial, superficial, but there was something restorative about Simon's attention. Like coming up for air. Nobody had touched her since Mark. In those solitary years since their divorce, Claire knew she was lonely. But she'd instinctively brush the constant hum of loneliness away, as if it were a whining mosquito buzzing at her ear.

Under the table, Simon pushed his knee against hers. 'Would you like another drink?'

Claire shook her head. She already felt a little drunk. 'Maybe we should go.'

He seemed to take that as a challenge. 'Or maybe we could stay?' His proposition hung in the air for a moment, resting between them, waiting for someone to react.

Something inside Claire just wanted to run with it, to be choreographed, to be pliable, to have someone else tell her the sequence of steps. It was unlike her to be this passive, but perhaps that was the point. She knew she'd play a role for Simon – the star, the ingénue – where embodying his fantasy was like wearing a mask. He didn't know her; she didn't need to be herself. Getting into character meant shedding her genuine skin. It was anaesthetic.

It was only meant to be a one-night stand. Simon was clever, made Claire laugh, but he was such an unexpected choice for a lover. She enjoyed speaking to him about politics, sparring over word games, but any conversation that wasn't flirtatious felt strained. She couldn't let her guard down. And it was such a relief he went home to someone else. Even though sour rushes of guilt often shot up the back of her throat, Claire didn't feel like a threat to their marriage. She kept Simon at arm's length; she couldn't get hurt that way. Even though Simon was married, Claire was more unavailable. Her heart had been trampled enough.

Occasionally they'd meet after work at the Observatory Hotel. The bleached hotel light – snow-coloured and cool Egyptian cotton sheets, pale silver embossed wallpaper – made the trysts feel incandescent. But there was always something wretched about these rendezvous, the wide gloom of the king-sized bed and sterile modern amenities. After the white heat of sex cooled, their mood did too. While it was still exciting – though it had become monotonous, routine – Claire could never push aside the colourless melancholy of those long Thursday evenings.

Simon ran his hand down Claire's back. They were both naked and she hated this part: the exposed vulnerability that came after sex. She sat up in bed.

'You're so beautiful,' he cooed. Claire had noticed something in him change lately; he seemed sloppy, more affectionate. 'Maybe I'm falling in love with you.'

She shook her head. 'Simon, you're not.'

'But isn't that what you want?'

'I like things the way they are.'

Simon frowned. 'What happened to you?'

'What do you mean?'

'It must have been pretty bad if you've closed yourself off to love.' He touched her bare shoulder. 'You can tell me.'

'Nothing,' Claire said. 'It was nothing.'

'Tell me. I promise I won't fall in love with you.'

And that autumn Thursday evening as the overcast sky turned dark, for the first time – not because she wanted him to love her, but because Simon offered to listen – Claire told somebody else her secrets.

The affair lasted barely a couple of months. Maybe there were feelings there, below the surface, although Claire only knew how to suppress them. When they weren't together, she felt relieved, but there was something comforting about being wanted, a validating ferocity that kept her coming back for more. It made her feel like she still existed, like a part of her she'd thought had died still had a beating heart.

Inevitably, the excitement atrophied – like any building without a solid foundation, it was always destined to collapse. Claire called it off. She didn't want anybody to get hurt, though perhaps it was too late for that. Afterwards, she was struck by expected grief. Simon was distant when they ran into each other again at soccer games or school functions; his aloofness stung.

Sometime later, Helen began to ostracise Claire, forgetting to invite her to trivia night, parent meetings, accidentally leaving her name off the Christmas gift to the boys' teacher. Claire was terrified Helen knew everything. But why would she? It made no sense for Simon to admit to his own infidelity.

More than that, Claire feared that by trying to dull her own pain, it had snowballed instead. That by running with Simon's anaesthetic effect, she'd created an avalanche of new pain for somebody else.

Claire stood irresolute at the principal's office door. The meeting had started half an hour ago. She took a deep breath and straightened the creases in her dress. This wasn't the moment to be nervous. What mattered here was Ethan; her personal shit and petty insecurities were irrelevant. She held her head high and let herself into the room.

∞

The chairs in the principal's office were arranged in a circle. No edges, no corners where Ethan could hide. Mum was late but Will's parents were early. Both of them looked very dressed up, like they were going to a concert or church. Ethan swung his feet and stared at the floor; his school shoes were scuffed, one lace undone. He stopped moving and fixed the collar of his uniform. Will looked at him quickly, then turned back to his mother. He was wearing a patch to cover his black eye that made him look like a pirate.

Other adults were gathered in the office too: the principal, Mrs Doyle, Mr Thompson and the school counsellor. Miss Alexander, the counsellor, looked over at Ethan and gave him a closed-lipped smile.

'Should we call your mother?' Mr Thompson asked.

Ethan nodded. Mum wasn't usually this late; he was scared she'd forgotten the meeting. Mrs Doyle offered the phone and he dialled, but it didn't ring. 'No answer,' Ethan said, deflated.

He looked at the empty seat. Everyone's eyes were on him; he could feel the burn of their stares.

Will's mother crossed her legs impatiently one way and then the other. Ethan used to want a mother more like Helen, who volunteered at school, made cakes for the bake sales, worked at the canteen. But Will's mum never looked very happy. She fidgeted all the time like she couldn't stay warm.

'Can't we get started, Mrs Doyle?' Helen asked. 'It's not our fault that Claire is running late.'

Mrs Doyle turned to Ethan. 'Are you okay to begin without your mum here?'

He shook his head, then nodded. He didn't have much choice.

Mr Thompson took out his notepad. 'Thanks everyone for coming to this meeting. Obviously, we're here to discuss the incident in the playground that occurred at around 1 p.m. last Wednesday afternoon. The two parties involved were William Fraser and Ethan Forsythe.'

Helen cut the teacher off. 'That wording sounds wrong, Duncan. Two parties? You really should say William was the victim and Ethan was the perpetrator.'

Mum opened the door. 'I'm so sorry I'm late.'

She stood in the frame for a moment. Her cheeks were pink and she stammered, as if she were about to give a speech but had forgotten where to start. She smiled stiffly at the teachers and took the empty seat. Ethan relaxed back into his chair. Mum put a hand on his knee and gave a gentle squeeze. Her touch heartened him; if Ethan had a tail he would've wagged it.

'Chaos on public transport. Sorry to keep you all waiting.'

Helen tapped her foot. 'Like I was saying before, we need to be clear about culpability. We have to get the wording right and my son was an innocent bystander. He didn't do anything wrong. Just minding his own business when that boy punched him in the face.'

Mr Thompson and the school counsellor shared a funny look. Ethan wasn't sure what it meant; adults often spoke another language with their eyes. He wanted to interject and say, Excuse me, that's not true. But he kept his mouth closed.

'Ethan wouldn't do that for no reason. He was provoked,' Mum said.

Mr Thompson read from his notepad again. 'Neither boy gave us an indication of how one thing led to the next. But other children reported a verbal fight.'

'Verbal!' Helen snorted. 'Will needed stitches. Lost a tooth. You should pay our dental bill.'

'Of course I'm really sorry this happened to Will. I know Ethan is sorry too,' Mum said. 'And I'm not saying Ethan is innocent. But you know him.' She looked at Will's dad, Simon. 'The boys have been best friends for years. He usually wouldn't hurt a fly.'

'We know,' said Simon. 'Ethan's a lovely boy —'

Helen looked at her husband with a pinched expression. 'I read a recent study that said children from single-parent families are responsible for the epidemic of violence in schools. He's wild. He's clearly not getting enough discipline at home.'

Ethan wound a loose thread around his finger. His hands felt heavy and hot. On the opposite side of the circle, Will didn't know where to look. He played with the elastic of his eye patch and pursed his lips. Without his gang of allies, Will seemed more like himself. Just as scared and uncertain as Ethan. He felt sick looking at Will's swollen jaw and wanted to apologise but now it felt too late. Fighting parents, official statements and reports – this had escalated beyond the boys' control.

'Not to mention,' Helen continued, 'that it's a well-known fact kids raised by single mothers are twice as likely to have behavioural issues than those born into traditional two-parent families.'

The school counsellor intervened. 'Hold on, Mrs Fraser. A single mother raised me and I've never heard anything about these studies you're quoting. There's not enough evidence to support any link between violence and single-parent homes.'

Helen scowled. 'Ethan should be expelled.'

'Student welfare is our top priority,' Mrs Doyle said. 'But this doesn't meet our criteria for expulsion. The boy doesn't have a record of persistent or serious misbehaviour. It was a one-off incident.'

'Maybe for now,' Helen said, flapping a hand dismissively in the air. 'But scientists have found genetic links to violence and delinquency too. He's a ticking time bomb. It won't be long before Ethan attacks someone again.'

Will's dad repositioned himself in his chair. 'We're here to resolve the conflict between the boys,' said Simon. He looked uncomfortable, like his clothes were the wrong size. 'Let's not forget that's what this meeting is all about.'

Mum rearranged her face. She had a tigerish look about her, watchful and fierce. She turned to Helen. 'What are you saying?'

'What I'm saying, Claire, is that the apple doesn't fall far from the tree.'

Ethan chewed on a fingernail and looked at his mum. He hated when adults spoke in riddles; he didn't have a feel for them. That didn't make sense – was he an apple, was his mum the tree?

'We were thinking detention,' Mr Thompson cut in. 'For both boys.'

Helen ignored the teacher and kept her eyes on Claire. 'Like father, like son,' she said slowly. 'Shouldn't Ethan know what sort of genes he has before it's too late? Don't you think we should tell him?'

'This is completely inappropriate,' Simon muttered to his wife. 'You promised you wouldn't do this.'

Mum's face went pale; she'd lost her ferocity. 'Helen, please don't. You're angry with me. And you have every reason to be. I take full responsibility. Blame me. Don't take it out on Ethan. He's just a child.'

'I don't understand,' Ethan said, turning to his mum. 'What's going on?'

Mum squeezed his knee again. 'Don't worry. This hasn't got anything to do with you, sweetheart.'

'Yes, it does,' Helen shot back. She swooped and put a protective arm around Will. 'Your son attacked my son. Ethan is a dangerous child. Will doesn't feel safe around him. I don't want my son at a school with wild and unruly kids like him. Kids with fathers who went to jail.'

'Claire, I'm so sorry.' Simon looked at her with a strange expression, like an astronaut who'd just discovered his helmet was leaking in space. Ethan had never seen anyone look at his mum like that before. 'I didn't think. This wasn't what . . .'

Ethan fixed his eyes on the shiny fabric of Will's mother's dress. A geometric pattern of pink and blue diamonds – wavering colours and contours – danced across the material like the pattern was alive. Something inside him twitched.

'Kids with fathers who what?' Ethan asked.

'Jail. Your father went to jail,' Helen said quickly. 'And as I said before, like father, like son. That's why you're violent. Your father is a criminal.'

Heat filled the room suddenly – hot wind buffeted by hot bodies – before Ethan saw air molecules surge across the office in thick convection swirls. Criminal, jail, violent: those words gnawed at him. He wanted to unhear them, to pull them out of his ears. He felt sick. Everybody was watching his face. The clock ticked forward, the walls wobbled, the air expanded. Nothing was reversible. Ethan blinked at the staring faces, stood up and rushed out the office door.

He ran outside to the playground, dodging some aftercare kids playing by the tennis courts. There was a sour taste in his mouth, like acid on his tongue. Maybe he was going to vomit. He pushed the school gate open and dashed onto the street.

'Ethan!' Mum yelled. 'Stop!' She was behind him, pulling off her high heels and chasing him barefoot along the concrete. 'Please stop.'

But he couldn't stop; he had to run. He had to get away. Ethan didn't look back. He ran fast and he ran hard; his mouth was dry, he gasped for breath. He turned around the corner and ran block after block. Cars beeped their horns as he sprinted across the street. He felt hot, feverish. Ethan ripped off his school jumper and threw it to the ground. His feet pounded on the pavement; his hamstrings stretched and tendons extended. His hips flexed, driving his knees forward. Ethan's body moved faster than ever until his legs tingled and his chest heaved.

Tears obscured his vision until his surroundings were opaque. The further he ran, the more fragmented everything looked. Buildings didn't look like buildings; trees stopped being trees. Boundaries blurred. Patterns of patterns inside patterns. The one thing Ethan saw clearly was a spectrum of light: red into orange, yellow into green, blue into violet. Panting, with sweat rolling down his face, the inside of his stomach hardened. He thought he might suffocate in the shallow air. Then his body froze – locked muscles, eyes rolling back into the hollows of his head. Ethan fell, hard, on the pavement.

Above him, an electric arch of refracted colour scattered the wavering light of the afternoon sky. One side of his body jerked – his limbs flailed, his eyelids fluttered. As Ethan lay on his back and stared upwards, his spine bent and he began to shake. He was powerless to resist it; things fell apart. His lungs went rigid and his joints got stuck. Although Ethan saw all the colours of the rainbow, he couldn't feel a thing.

6

LIGHT

Before Ethan opened his eyes, bright light made them sting. He woke up in a haze, blinded by a flood of white. Slowly it morphed into shapes – vague square panels lit by fluorescent bulbs. His body was stiff; his muscles were sore. Ethan shifted his arm and tried to cover his eyes, but his hand trembled and a plastic tube scratched his face.

Things came into focus. Tubes were strapped onto the back of his hand, a sack of liquid dangled over his head, clear fluid pumped straight into his veins. Ethan looked down at his feet and wiggled his toes. His body was covered with a thin white blanket, trapped inside some strange metal barricade. Various pieces of electronic equipment made regular high-pitched sounds. Ethan craned his neck up to look around the room. Where was he? Where was his mum? Nobody else was here.

Beside his bed, a curtain was drawn closed. Ethan noticed the reflection of coloured beams shifting across the ceiling. A muted television. Someone else was in the room, on the other side of the curtain. He tried to talk but his tongue felt furry and his lips were locked; he'd forgotten how to speak. Ethan didn't know the day or date, his memory was stuck behind a layer of fog. He stared at the rippled TV light – flashes of blue, green and yellow.

A burst of laughter filled the room.

Ethan coughed. 'Hello?' he called out. It didn't sound like his voice; the back of his mouth felt full of gravel. He heard a rustling, a creaking bed, dampened footsteps. The curtain rings screeched against the metal rod.

'Hi,' said a girl, taking a step forward into Ethan's cubicle.

She wore a bright yellow jumper that was far too big – it looked like a dress – with long sleeves that hid her hands. Ethan peeked under his sheets, surprised to find he was only wearing a pale mint robe. The girl's head was covered with a brightly coloured swimming cap, an interlocking grid of red and gold, but it wasn't for swimming. It was different. Her long hair plunged out from underneath the cap, a flood of brown waves. She made Ethan think of a lifeguard – standing there, alert with perfect posture, waiting to rescue the drowning.

'Hi.' Ethan tried to sit up. Flashes of sharp pain shot up his neck and he closed his eyes again for a moment.

'I was wondering when you were going to wake up. You've been asleep forever. And you were snoring, you know.'

'Where are we?'

'Ward C1 North.' The girl feigned a zombie voice and raised her arms like the undead. 'Brains!'

He touched his forehead. 'Sorry?'

'Paediatric neurology unit. Where they give children lobotomies.'

Ethan gave the girl a blank look.

'Seems you've already had yours,' she said with a grin. 'I'm Alison.'

'I'm —'

'Ethan Francis Forsythe, born 12 August, lives in Glebe. I've already read the clipboard at the end of your bed.'

'This is maybe a dumb question,' he began. 'But are we in hospital?'

'It's not a five-star hotel,' Alison said, pushing down the side

rail and lifting herself onto Ethan's bed. 'And yes, that was a dumb
question.' She lifted his hand. 'You have a plastic bracelet on your wrist,
you're plugged into a drip and you're probably not wearing underpants.
Dead giveaways. Are you sure they didn't give you a lobotomy?'

Ethan looked at Alison, who'd made herself comfortable on the
edge of his bed. A scatter of freckles dusted her nose; her eyes were
the same colour as her hair. They were exceptionally big eyes; her iris
looked like a small island surrounded by a sea of white. Alison wouldn't
have been any older than Ethan – her feet didn't even touch the floor.
She let them swing from the end of the bed. Her toenails were painted
bright pink.

'So, what's wrong with you?' she asked. 'What's your diagnosis, as
they say here?'

'I don't know. I don't even know how I got here.'

'That happens to me all the time,' said Alison. 'Just retrace your
steps. What's the last thing you remember?'

Ethan thumbed the corner of the blanket; the word 'hospital'
was printed in blue ink. He remembered fire in the balls of his feet,
a wrinkled sky, air dancing above hot pavement like on a summer day,
the rainbow. 'I think I was running.'

He'd run through the rainbow like it was a mirage, a trick of the
light. Pieces started to come together. The meeting at school. Mum
being late. Will. Will's mother. Jail. His father? He pulled up the
blanket to cover his arms.

Ethan glanced out the window behind Alison's bed, overlooking
the hospital driveway. Outside it was dark, but he couldn't tell if it was
late night or early morning. The street was empty: no pedestrians, no
cars. His eyes unfocused and his chest ached. He wanted his mum.

'What's on your head?' Ethan pointed to the swimming cap.

Alison touched the cap's wires with her fingertips. 'My hat? Latest fashion. Everyone will be wearing these soon.' She paused. 'I have to wear this because I have epilepsy. Lately I've been having a lot of seizures.'

Ethan sat up straight in his bed. 'Why?'

'Weird electrical activity in my brain.'

'Wow,' he said. 'Does the hat fix it?'

'Nope.' Alison looked down at her pink toenails. 'It connects electrodes to my head and records what's happening in my brain. Have you ever seen a lie detector on TV? With all the squiggly lines? Electrical activity in the brain looks like that. Like waves. Or mountains.'

'That's cool.'

'Not really.' She wrinkled her nose, like something in the room smelled bad.

'Sorry.' Ethan kept saying the wrong thing. 'How long have you had epilepsy?'

'Forever,' Alison said dramatically. 'As long as I can remember.'

'So are you okay?'

'Most of the time. Sometimes it gets bad and I end up here again. But I'm used to it.' Alison shuffled closer to Ethan and widened her eyes. 'Have you ever had a seizure?'

'I don't think so. What does it feel like?'

'Hard to explain,' she said, tilting her head and thinking about it. 'Have you ever read *Alice in Wonderland*?'

'I've seen the movie.'

'You need to read it. It's my favourite book,' Alison said. 'You know the rabbit hole? Having a seizure is like falling down that. You disappear. It's scary. Usually I feel terrible afterwards. But sometimes it opens up a whole other world. Sometimes you get to go to Wonderland.'

Ethan pressed his lips together. 'Do you know what the time is?'

'Ten minutes past five. In the morning.'

'Was anyone else here?'

'Yep.' Alison brushed a curl off her face. 'I wish I had blonde hair like your mum.'

Ethan looked around. 'Where is she?'

'I don't know. She was right there before.' Alison reached over and took the red button on the side of Ethan's bed in her hand. 'By the way, you really should let everyone know you've finally woken up.' She pressed down on the buzzer.

An orange light by the door flashed.

∞

From the other side of the street, Claire had watched Ethan fall. His legs just gave way. She'd sprinted over to him, checked his breathing, his pulse. One-sided spasms, indigo lips. Warm pee spread on the pavement and trickled from Ethan's pants into the cracks. She dialled triple zero, calmly gave an address and listened to the control centre officer on the other end of the line. They told her to try to turn the boy onto his side, make sure he wasn't in respiratory distress. Claire numbly obeyed every instruction.

The ambulance arrived quickly. Blue and red lights lit the concrete; the van glowed reflective orange, a ripple of white and yellow paint. Two paramedics ran out, checked Ethan, said he needed to get to hospital. But in the back of the ambulance, as her child lay unconscious on a stretcher and the siren wailed, Claire started to panic. The murky line between dream and reality, past and present, blurred. Her body flooded with adrenaline, that breathlessness, prickling her skin. She broke out in a cold sweat.

Even though the paramedics assured her that the worst was over now, Claire was convinced her son was about to die. Daylight shrank from the corners of her eyes. Oxygen, Ethan needed more oxygen, fresh air. There wasn't any oxygen in here, just the sticky smell of urine. The paramedic sitting beside her in the back of the ambulance gave her a concerned look.

'I'm fine,' she said, gasping. 'But Ethan —'

'We're getting your son to the hospital as fast as we can.'

Claire blinked, overcome by déjà vu. She had to be hallucinating; this was some reflection of another life. Echoing angles of the ambulance lights – the odd, distinct slant of them – dragged her to the past. She blinked again. Breathe in, breathe out. It's only temporary; this too shall pass. She just had to ride the wave. Claire held Ethan's hand and closed her eyes, blocking her ears from the siren, blocking her thoughts from the spinning world.

The ambulance pulled into the hospital driveway. Usually, Claire did her best to avoid the Sydney Children's Hospital. If she ever needed to drive through Randwick, she'd take another route. The curved blue and yellow canopy over the front entrance made her recoil and she hated the friendly smiling logo, its primary-coloured confection. But as much as being back at the hospital filled her with dread, there was also something soothing about returning. Harrowing memories came from these walls – seeing the 'Emergency' sign made every rib stretch, her lungs turn to concrete – but in the same impulse, it felt like coming home.

Ethan was examined, hooked up to monitors. Unconscious, but not in major distress. Doctors and nurses threw around medical terms Claire didn't know – tonic, clonic, post-ictal – as she watched on, paralysed in the corner. She stared at the ceiling lights – they reminded her of a path of stepping stones in a garden or a rocky causeway in shallow water. The harshness of the magnified lighting stung her eyes like chlorine. She felt weightless – a floating cloud, a hovering ghost – and became unconvinced she was a real and solid person, present in the room. Claire felt separate to her skin.

The doctors asked about Ethan's medical history but Claire couldn't communicate properly, could only absently repeat questions she'd just been asked.

How old is your son? *How old is my son?*

What's his date of birth? *His date of birth?*

Through the thin curtains of the Emergency Department, she listened to other parents speak to the triage nurses, explaining tales of fevers and falls, burns and broken limbs. Another ambulance arrived. Claire overheard it was a six-year-old boy, seriously injured in a fatal car accident. They rushed the little boy to surgery. While Ethan was taken to Radiology, Claire sat in the waiting room, eavesdropping on a woman's phone call with her husband. Their daughter had fallen in a gymnastics class and dislocated her elbow.

Back in Emergency, Ethan was eerily motionless. Claire kept checking on him, making sure blood still moved around his body, that oxygen still made it to his brain. He looked pale and wooden. Tiny blue veins covered his closed eyelids. The nurse practitioner assured her unconsciousness was symptomatic – Ethan wasn't comatose, just in a very deep sleep. Not life-threatening but he'd need to stay for observation overnight.

Even though Ethan was fast asleep, Claire told him the bedtime stories he'd loved hearing since he was little, tales of swans and sugarplums, spinning wheels and dancing ghosts.

It was almost midnight when Ethan was finally admitted to a ward. Claire followed two nurses upstairs as they pushed his bed into an elevator, expertly steering around sharp corners. Ward C1 North.

Claire did a double take. The giant corkboard at reception was still covered in children's artwork, but these were fresh drawings, new pictures, different kids. She stopped to look at them for a moment, wondering what they did with the old pictures by the children she'd known, who'd long been discharged, cured, grown up, died. The nurses wheeled Ethan to an empty partition. He didn't stir as they lifted his limp body into the bed. Claire settled in beside the sleeping boy, keeping vigil in the vinyl chair.

'You need to eat,' a nurse had said. 'There's a vending machine down the hall.'

Claire shook her head. 'I'm not hungry.'

The ward was quiet now, nurses at the station occasionally chatting to each other in whispers. A young girl sat with them, putting together a jigsaw puzzle. Her arms jerked as she placed down each piece. Probably cerebral palsy, Claire thought to herself, reminded that things could be worse. Another little girl was in the bed beside them, wired to a beeping machine. Ethan suddenly exhaled, making Claire sit up straight. She put her face close to his. His breathing was fine. Colour tinted his cheeks again. She smoothed his bedclothes, pulled up the blankets, stroked his sweaty hair.

Slumped in the rigid chair, Claire covered her eyes. Her legs trembled and the floor bulged. Her mouth was dry, her face was hot; her fingers and toes tingled. Shallow breath after breath, she started to choke. The room caved in. One of the nurses heard Claire panting and approached with a glass of water. She drew the curtains closed.

'Take deep breaths,' the nurse said, rubbing Claire's back. 'Breathe in through your nose, out through your mouth.'

'I,' Claire started, gulping the word down. 'I can't.'

'Yes, you can. In the nose, out the mouth. Let's try counting backwards from one hundred in lots of three. We can do it together.

One hundred. Ninety-seven. Ninety-four.'

'Ninety-one,' said Claire, following the breathing pattern: inhale, exhale, inhale, exhale, in the nose, out the mouth. 'Eighty-eight. Eighty-five.'

The nurse gave her an encouraging smile. 'That's right. Eighty-two.'

Eventually, Claire caught her breath. The dizziness stopped and her panic began to shrink. But now she felt like she'd been hit over the head with a blunt object. 'Sorry, I don't know what came over me.'

'You're exhausted,' said the nurse. 'You need to sleep. Even for an hour. There's a Parents Lounge just down the end of the hall.'

'I need to stay here. What if he wakes up?'

'Then we'll come and get you,' the nurse said. 'I promise. Rest up for him, you'll be no help to your son tomorrow if you're sleep-deprived.'

Claire reluctantly agreed. She went to the bathroom and splashed cold water on her face. Her hair looked wild, her eyes bloodshot. Breathe normally, she said to her reflection in the mirror, do not fall apart.

But she couldn't fall asleep. She rolled onto her back and stared at the patterns on the ceiling. Each time a car drove past outside, it distorted the light. Her heart beat loudly; she was sure other parents sleeping nearby could hear it pump and pound.

Back here again. She couldn't believe it. Lying on a narrow foldout bed with its familiar metal frame pressing into her back. It even smelled the same – industrial laundry powder, stale hospital food. But what Claire really couldn't believe was that she was back in this place inside her head. The darkest place with the darkest thoughts and the darkest feelings; she thought she'd come so far. This was all her fault. She knew it was. She could've stopped Ethan being here again. She'd made so many mistakes, kept too many secrets.

Claire pushed the memories aside but now everything was flooding back. She'd seen things she couldn't forget. Years of nightmares, flashbacks, hauntings; there'd been so many sleepless, terror-filled nights. Friends had gently suggested she really ought to talk to somebody about it, get professional help. One psychologist had diagnosed her with post-traumatic stress disorder, but knowing the name for whatever was wrong didn't heal Claire. Her trauma wasn't easily extinguished; it quietly continued to blaze and flare. But looking after herself wasn't a priority. She'd do that later. Ethan always came first. Claire learned to live with the lightning crashes of pain and panic, the sudden stun of suffocation. They were her penance for her mistakes.

Another car drove past, white headlight streaks elongating on the ceiling before the sound of the engine rolled away. Her nightmare revisited, refracted from another angle, fractured by a different light. Claire was drained. After her adrenaline-fuelled high, she could feel her body crash. Shadows crept back again, the blacks and blues of pre-dawn like bruises left by night. Her heavy eyelids started to close.

∞

A tall doctor entered the room. Something about him made Ethan think of a rainforest: trunks for limbs, a beard so thick maybe wildlife lived inside. Behind him was a nurse with straight black hair fixed into a neat ponytail. She smiled at the two children. Alison was still sitting on Ethan's bed. Next to the giant doctor, the nurse seemed like a dwarf.

'Morning, Alison,' the doctor said in a loud voice, pushing his glasses up his nose. 'Remember what you've been told about leaving your bed; you're not allowed to get in with other patients. But looks like you've made a friend.' He smiled. 'How long has he been awake?'

'Only a few minutes. Not long, promise,' Alison said, talking too fast. She waved at Ethan, shuffled back to her partition and closed the curtain.

The doctor stood over the bed. 'How are you feeling, Ethan? A little confused?'

Ethan blinked. 'I guess.'

'You've grown,' the doctor said warmly. 'I'm your neurologist. My name is Dr Saunders.'

'Nice to meet you.'

'Conversing normally. AVPU score is A. Pupillary reflexes look normal,' Dr Saunders said to the nurse as he wrote something on his notepad. He turned back to Ethan. 'We've actually met before. Although you wouldn't remember. I was your doctor when you were a baby.'

'When I was born?'

'Bit after that. How old are you now?'

'Twelve.' Ethan rubbed his arm.

Dr Saunders held the clipboard close to his face and read Ethan's file. 'Twelve already! Doesn't time fly? I'm just going to do a couple of tests to see how you're recovering. You were asleep for quite some time, so we need to make sure everything is all right. Is that okay?'

Ethan nodded.

'This is Lucy.' Dr Saunders turned to the nurse with the ponytail who was busy checking the fluid levels of the drip. 'We need to perform a cranial nerve exam and a potted neurological exam of the upper and lower limbs.'

Lucy winked at Ethan. 'Could you squeeze my hand, please?' The nurse spoke with a Scottish lilt; it made her sound like a fairy.

Ethan squeezed. Lucy's hand was warm. She wore a silver ring on her right hand and small veins covered her skin. Something about her long fingers reminded him of his mum.

Dr Saunders smiled. 'Good boy. Normal movement. Responding to simple instructions, great. Now you're probably a little muddled after what happened. Do you know why you're here?'

Ethan glanced at the drawn curtain on Alison's side of the room. 'Did I maybe have a seizure?'

'Yes, you're right. You had a seizure. Where's your mother?'

'I don't know.'

The doctor hesitated. 'Do you remember what happened just before the seizure or anything like this happening to you before?'

Ethan shook his head.

'While you were sleeping we did some scans,' Dr Saunders said. 'I have them here.'

He flipped through his folder and took out a stiff sheet of paper – rows of electric-blue circles arranged on a black grid, like pictures of sponges in a row. They made Ethan think of pancakes: the way the batter spread roughly in a hot pan; how the edges of the pancake were uneven.

'These are cross-sections of your brain. You have non-specific white matter in the left hemisphere. Scar tissue. Just here.' The doctor pointed to a milky smudge. 'See?'

Ethan leaned in. The scar tissue looked like a ghost. 'That's my brain?'

'Certainly is,' said Dr Saunders. 'I've asked to see your CT and MRI scans from when you were a baby to compare them – Radiology are trying to locate the original images. They'll be around somewhere. I suspect your brain injury from twelve years ago is responsible for this scar tissue in your brain, making you susceptible to seizures like the one you had yesterday.'

The doctor made no sense. Scar tissue inside his brain? Ethan touched his head. It was tender, like he'd lost a layer of skin. He felt hypersensitive to every sound and sight: colours were too bright, voices were too loud. What brain injury? He wanted his mum.

Lucy placed a thermometer in the side of Ethan's mouth.

'But I don't think I've ever had seizures before,' he said, the thermometer muffling his voice.

'Not since the original injury,' the doctor said.

Lucy removed the thermometer from Ethan's mouth and gave it a vigorous shake.

Spit had collected under his tongue. 'Injury?'

'The bleeding in your brain,' Dr Saunders said, still looking down at his clipboard.

'Thirty-seven degrees,' Lucy said, squinting as she read the numbers marked on the side of the glass.

'Good.' The doctor continued taking notes in the folder, the pen scratching as he wrote.

Bleeding in his brain. Ethan felt dizzy and tried to centre himself by looking out the window. The sun was coming up, morning illuminating the pavement outside. It made his eyes burn. 'Dr Saunders,' he said, flinching as the doctor placed a cold stethoscope against his chest. 'Why was there blood in my brain?'

'Breathe in. Typically babies with non-accidental head injury present with what we call a constellation of symptoms. A subdural haematoma, retinal haemorrhages and cerebral oedema. Breathe out. In other words, bleeding in the brain, bleeding in the eyes and swelling in the brain. You had all three symptoms when you were admitted here twelve years ago,' Dr Saunders said, adjusting the stethoscope's rubber earpiece. 'Let's take your blood pressure. Lucy?'

Ethan shut his eyes for a moment. Haematoma, haemorrhages, swelling. The doctor must be reading the wrong file, there had to be some mistake. They'd obviously confused him with some other kid. Ethan didn't remember any of this. And babies with a head injury? He wasn't a baby. But he would have been twelve years ago.

The nurse wrapped a plastic cuff around his upper arm, securing it with velcro. The band inflated suddenly with air, then deflated again. His eyes started to water.

Lucy put her stethoscope down, noticing Ethan's tears, and placed her hand on his shoulder. 'Dr Saunders . . .' she began.

The doctor ripped the velcro open. 'Blood pressure is normal, excellent. Just one more test. I'm going to shine this torch quickly into your eyes.'

Ethan nodded absently. Bleached light pierced his cornea.

'Hmm.' Dr Saunders frowned. 'That isn't normal. He isn't reacting to the light. Lucy, can you check this?'

She pointed the torch into Ethan's eyes, shifting it from left to right. 'Strange. Excessive dilation. Looks like a blown pupil.'

'Mydriasis,' Dr Saunders said. 'We'll need to investigate raised ICP. Place a call to the neurosurgeons to give them a heads up.'

'Sorry, Dr Saunders, I think I made a mistake. Pupil reactivity appears normal; I'm observing constriction in the light. Could you check?'

The doctor looked carefully into Ethan's eyes. 'You're right. NPI of 5. Let's make sure there's no apparent loss of visual fields.'

'Ethan, could you please let me know when you see the pencil?' Lucy asked in her fairy voice. She slowly moved her arm closer to Ethan's face. 'Try to keep your eyes focused on my nose.'

'Now.'

She splayed her hand open. 'How many fingers am I holding up?'

'Four. Plus your thumb, which technically isn't a finger.'

'Very clever.' Lucy gave him a half-smile. She shone the torch in

Ethan's eyes again; it made his eyeballs feel itchy. 'What can you see when I shine the light in your eyes?'

'Light.'

'Patient's pupillary response normal and vision unimpaired, ruling out orbital trauma,' Dr Saunders muttered to himself as he took down more notes. 'Conscious state isn't changing, no loss of acuity. Ruling out raised ICP.'

'And it turns red then blue,' Ethan said.

Dr Saunders put his clipboard down. 'What does?'

'The light. As it moves from one side to the other, it changes colour. Red then blue then red again.'

Dr Saunders took the torch to his own eyes. 'Ethan,' he said slowly. 'You shouldn't be able to see that. Lucy, you try.' The doctor repeated the back-and-forth movement in the nurse's eyes.

'No,' Lucy said. 'No colours.'

'Are you sure that's what you can see, Ethan?'

'Positive. Red and blue.'

'I don't know how that's possible.' Dr Saunders removed his glasses and rubbed his eyes. 'We still need to run some more tests then. Get an ophthalmologist to examine you too.' He gathered his notes and stacked them into a neat pile. 'I'll come back later. Come on, Lucy. Let's go.'

Ethan watched the nurse and doctor walk away to another room in the ward. People were waking up now; children yelled further down the hall. Some of the voices seemed happy, other kids wailed. One child within earshot was screaming at the top of their lungs – begging with their parents, maybe a doctor, a nurse, no, please, not another needle.

A small voice called out from behind the curtain. 'Ethan?'

He'd forgotten she was there.

'I didn't mean to eavesdrop.' Alison pulled open the curtain and stood there with fabric half-covering her face.

'It's okay,' Ethan said, lying on his back. Around him, everything in the room swirled but his body was completely still.

Breakfast arrived on beige trays. Alison didn't touch her soggy cornflakes and watery scrambled eggs. Ethan was starving – he couldn't remember the last time he'd eaten – and devoured his meal, then ate Alison's too. Nurses came in and out of the room, inspecting Ethan's chart. Another neurologist hooked the electrodes on Alison's cap to wires on some recording device.

'Hey, Ethan,' she said, trying to cheer him up. 'Want to watch *The Alison Show*?' She pointed to the screen and smiled at him. It was like she was plugged into a television and was broadcasting her mind. 'It's unmissable viewing. If you watch any EEG today, make it this one.'

'You look like a spider,' Ethan said.

Alison stuck out her tongue.

They played poker on her bed, using latex gloves they'd found in the ward to wager their bets. The EEG recording machine jumped every time Alison won another hand.

∞

Claire woke up with a jolt. Her neck clicked as she stretched her back. The bright room was disorienting; she wasn't sure where she was. She sat up too quickly, making her head spin. Then she remembered. Hospital. It was daytime now and the ward hummed with activity. How long had she been asleep? Claire pulled the white blanket off her body. She had to get back to him.

Across the ward, Claire heard Ethan giggle, his throaty, boyish laugh. Relief washed over her; he was laughing, he was awake. She followed the laughter to his room.

Ethan spotted her immediately. 'Mum!' He jumped into his mother's arms.

'Pumpkin, I was so worried. But you look so much better. How do you feel? Are you okay?' Claire held her son close. His skin smelled like butter and bandaids.

'My head hurts a bit. And I have a big scratch on my knee. Mum, this is Alison.' Ethan gestured at the girl in the next bed, who gave Claire a spirited wave. 'Alison, this is my mum.'

'Hi, Alison. Lovely to meet you. Thanks for keeping Ethan company. Do you mind if I speak to him —' Claire pointed at the curtain rail.

'Oh! I was going to beat him anyway; he's not very good at poker. I'll even listen to music. My brother let me borrow his headphones.'

Claire wheeled Ethan's drip back to his cubicle and helped him climb into his bed. She tucked him in and fixed his sheets.

'Where did you go?' Ethan asked.

'The night nurse,' she started. 'She said she'd wake me up. I was up all night then fell asleep in the Parents Lounge. I shouldn't have left you. I'm so sorry.'

He frowned. 'I didn't know where you went. And then the doctor came in and said there's a scar in my brain. From a non-accidental head injury. And that my brain was bleeding. And now the scar is making me have seizures, and that's why I blacked out.' Ethan blurted it out so quickly he had to stop to catch his breath.

'Hold on, you spoke to a doctor? Which doctor?'

'His name was Dr Saunders. He showed me some pictures of my brain.'

Claire's stomach dropped. The doctor still worked here, after all these years.

Non-accidental head injury. She'd worked their lives around

a secret, forever swerving away from the truth. There had been something calculated about it, but never cold; her secrecy came from a place of warmth. It was easy enough to hide – Ethan's brain was locked away inside his skull. He didn't remember. Claire did, though. She was enveloped in her grief, shaped by it, and needed to keep her son safe from its disfiguring effects. But secrets were like scars: they faded and softened, but as much as you tried to camouflage them, they didn't completely disappear. Damage had lasting impact. His scar was still there, the secrets were too.

'So the doctor told you that you had a seizure because of the scar tissue?'

'From twelve years ago.' He swallowed. 'Mum, why did he say non-accidental head injury?'

Claire should have rehearsed this, had a plan. She didn't. 'Ethan, when you were four months old —'

'It happened to me,' he said quietly. He sank into his pillow and looked at the ceiling. 'But a non-accident means it wasn't an accident.'

'Another name for it is shaken baby syndrome.'

'And I was the baby.' Ethan took a sharp breath and turned to face her. Their eyes met. 'Is this something to do with my father? Is that why he went to jail?'

She nodded. His face immobilised Claire: his trembling chin, his glassy stare. She'd always wanted to shield him from the precise distress she saw now in his eyes, spare her child the circumstances of his injury. Protection was primal, a piercing instinct deep inside her bones, as automatic as breathing. There'd been moments when Claire had considered telling Ethan the truth, but it was never the right moment. Never the right words.

'Mum, why did he do that to me?'

'Ethan, I still don't understand it myself. Sometimes having a small baby is stressful. They're always crying, some parents get overwhelmed and can't handle it. They snap.' Claire paused. She'd asked herself why this had happened for years, tried to make sense of something so senseless, explain the inexplicable. Everything coming out of her mouth sounded like a platitude. An excuse. 'Maybe that's what happened to him.'

'But you didn't snap. Was it my fault? Did I cry too much?'

'You didn't do anything wrong.' Claire moved closer and wrapped her hands around his. There was dirt under his fingernails. 'You were just a baby. He should have been taking care of you.'

'He did it on purpose?'

'That's not what I meant.'

'Why didn't you ever tell me? Why did you keep it a secret?'

'I don't know. I love you so much. I didn't want to hurt you.'

'He didn't want me,' Ethan whispered, looking away.

'I promise it wasn't your fault.' Claire would have told him the Earth was flat if it meant Ethan wouldn't ever feel sadness. All she'd ever wanted was to stop every blow, fix every sting, scratch every itch. She'd watched him experience so much pain as a baby – rupturing vessels, spasm of seizure, prick of a cannula into his newborn skin – that she couldn't cope with more of his distress. 'It wasn't your fault,' she said again.

'Mum, I feel really sleepy.'

'Do you want me to get a doctor?'

'Just don't leave again.'

Ethan fell asleep. His eyes shut and his lips parted. Claire looked at her son's face with a saturated wonder, that same awe she'd felt on seeing him for the first time. Doctors came and went. On the other side of the curtain, Alison's parents spoke at length to another neurologist.

Claire felt light-headed; her stomach creaked. It suddenly occurred to her that she hadn't eaten for over a day. Downstairs, she bought a sandwich from the cafeteria in the main building of the hospital campus. Two bites was all she could stomach; its texture was difficult to swallow, the tasteless bread felt like paste stuck inside her mouth.

Across the cafeteria, dozens of faces were lit blue by tiny screens. Claire took her mobile out of her handbag, switched it back on and glanced quickly at her unanswered emails. As she scrolled, the screen went black; the phone began to vibrate in her hand. She dismissed the call and flicked her mobile onto silent. She couldn't deal with speaking to anyone right now. But they rang again. And again. Unknown number. She answered.

'Hello?'

For a second, Claire couldn't identify the voice, couldn't place that tone or pitch. She knew it – it was familiar like a radio presenter, an old forgotten friend – but her ears couldn't decode the sounds.

'Claire,' the caller said. 'It's me.'

The way he said her name provoked a physical reaction, like lightning striking her nerves. Claire couldn't feel her skin. Maybe she was sleep-deprived, hallucinating. This was impossible; his timing was unbearable. After all these years, why now?

'Mark?'

'Please don't hang up. I really need to talk to you, Claire. I've been trying to get in touch with you for weeks. Figured you were probably ignoring me.' His voice was rushed and strained.

'What do you want?'

'Did you get my letter?'

She spoke softly into the phone. 'I didn't read it.'

'Right,' he said. 'Of course not. Well, I wanted to speak to you because my father has stage-four cancer.'

She waited for Mark to continue but the other end of the line went dead. 'Hello? Are you still there?'

'Claire, Dad's asked to see him.'

'Ethan?' She stood up and walked her cafeteria tray to the bin. What if he'd woken up again and she wasn't by his bedside? She'd promised her son she wouldn't leave again; she needed to go back upstairs. 'This isn't a good time. I can't talk now.'

'Wait, just hear me out for a second. Dad doesn't have much time left. Couple of weeks, at best. So I'm here, I'm back in Sydney. Maybe we should talk about this in person.'

'Mark, I don't know.' Claire threw the rest of her sandwich away. She hadn't seen him for almost a decade and wanted to keep it that way. After never hearing from him again, she'd assumed Mark wanted that too. Exposing herself, following years of quarantine, had the potential to destroy her immunity to him. 'Anyway, I have to go.'

'How about Monday? Tuesday? Claire, please. All this time, I've left you alone because I thought that's what you needed. I've never asked you for anything before.'

She heard the urgency in his voice; it sparked an unwanted flash of sympathy. If only Claire felt nothing for Mark, if only she'd figured out how to be impartial, detached. She wished speaking to him was insignificant, that listening to his voice left her unmoved. Her sensitivity was disappointing; she hoped that by now she'd have grown more callous and cold. Despite the pain Mark caused, Claire couldn't bring herself to be cruel to him.

'Maybe Tuesday.'

'Thank you. Just let me know the time and place.'

'Now, I really need to go.' Claire switched her mobile off without saying goodbye, and buried it in her bag. Her head felt tender, her vision sharpening as she collected herself again. She closed her eyes and sighed. It was the deepest sigh, which seemed to contain a universe, releasing twelve years in one breath.

∞

'What's your star sign?' Alison asked. She was reading a glossy magazine, lying on her stomach on her bed, legs swinging in the air.

'I don't know,' Ethan whispered, not wanting to wake his mum who was asleep in the chair beside his bed.

'When's your birthday?'

'Didn't you already memorise my clipboard?'

'Oh yeah!' Alison said brightly. 'You're a Leo. See?' She showed him an image of a roaring lion. 'Leos are energetic but opinionated. I'm an Aquarius. My horoscope says the sun's move through my chart means I need to take it slow.'

Ethan laughed. 'That's stupid. It doesn't mean anything. Doesn't make sense.'

Alison looked up from the magazine. 'Typical Leo,' she said, narrowing her eyes. 'Come on, it's just a bit of fun. Want me to read yours?'

'I guess.'

'Leo, you are bursting with positive energy today. You need to shake things up to ensure that you're in the right place. Tonight, you're the ultimate wingman for a friend who will need cheering up. Help them get back out there again.' She looked up. 'That must be me.'

Ethan was quiet. Horoscopes were silly. He hauled himself out of bed; the floor felt cold on his feet. He walked towards the wide hospital window and looked out at the sky. It was a clear night, almost black. Alison put the magazine down and joined him.

'Star signs are constellations,' Ethan said.

'Constellations?' Alison repeated.

'Groups of stars that make a picture. See those stars over there? In the shape of a kite? Just below those brighter ones?'

Alison searched the night sky. 'Yeah.'

'That's the Southern Cross.'

'Like on the flag.'

'It's the smallest constellation. People used to use it for navigating because it points south. There are eighty-eight official constellations altogether. Signs of the zodiac are pictures in the sky like that too. Leo and Aquarius are constellations.'

Alison squinted at him. 'Why do you know so much about stars?'

'My mum bought me a star map. I think they're interesting.'

'Tell me something else about them.' She put her palm against the window.

'Did you know that the heavier a star is, the more brightly it will shine?'

'Really?' Alison widened her eyes. 'That's beautiful.'

'Can you see that really bright star over there? That's Sirius, the dog star. The brightest in the whole sky. It's nearly twice as heavy as the sun and twenty-five times brighter.' Ethan tilted his head. 'They're all so far away. I wish we were up there. Light years from here.'

Alison stared at Sirius. 'Light years?'

'How fast light travels in a year. So if a star is one hundred light years away then it takes one hundred years for the light to reach us on Earth. Delta Crucis, the faintest star in the Southern Cross, is 364 light years away.'

'Wow, 364 years,' she whispered. 'The light we're looking at now is so old.'

'Yeah, really old.'

In that one sky, Ethan realised that he could see all of history connected to right now; ancient light from time and spaces he couldn't ever visit. Suddenly he felt really small. How could he ever understand what was happening now when the universe was so big it took hundreds and thousands of years for something as simple as light to get here?

Alison took Ethan by the hand. Her palm was soft and warm. They stood there together by the hospital window and Ethan pointed out the patterns of constellations in the sky. Perseus, Pegasus, Canis Major, Cetus. They all made a picture, told a story. Pinpricks of light united by their mythology: distant balls of gas fused into a sea monster, a giant dog and a flying horse – the astral sum of their parts.

Nothing was as beautiful to Ethan as the constellations. A single star was difficult to find, but when they were grouped together they shined brighter. Each star reached out to the others, wanted to be part of a bigger group, a constellation. Every star ached to belong.

Dr Saunders had said non-accidental head injury had a constellation of symptoms but that word didn't fit. Ethan gazed up at that infinite stretch of space – the fixed and wandering stars, the galaxies, the known universe – searching for something. But he wasn't sure what it was.

Then he saw it. The reflection of his face in the window, mirrored against the luminous stars. The constellation Ethan. Made up of his symptoms, his ancient stars: subdural haematoma, retinal haemorrhages, cerebral oedema. All those things had happened to him. They made a picture, told a story. His story.

Alison squeezed his hand as Ethan started to cry.

7

INERTIA

Ethan woke up to find his mum asleep beside him. The elevated hospital bed was just wide enough to support them both. She was having dark-blue dreams – Ethan could see them – like bubbles of midnight floating above her head. He stuck out a finger and popped one. The dream burst. Mum opened her eyes. They were exactly the same colour as the sky, clear and bright; Ethan's eyes were the same. Except, like the sky, they didn't have a real colour: no blue pigment, just a trick of the scattering light.

After breakfast, the doctors did their rounds. Dr Saunders entered the room, holding a pile of x-rays and scans. He held one up to the overhead light and pointed. 'Ethan, this is your brain.'

It reminded Ethan of a piece of lettuce, with its thick stem, crinkly texture and irregular shape – salad tossed inside his head. Dark and shiny on the transparent paper, his brain looked faraway. It didn't feel like part of his body.

Ethan waved. 'Hi, brain.'

'This is the axial view. You can see both hemispheres from this angle. There's the area of white matter, the scar on the right side. Based on your latest MRI, there doesn't seem to be any swelling, which is good news.' The doctor put the scan down. 'It also looks as though you had what we call a partial seizure. That means it arose from only one area in your brain, not both sides. And partial seizure activity only sometimes causes the sort of attack you had the other day. A generalised convulsion.'

Alison chimed in. 'I have those too,' she said enthusiastically. 'They're called *grand mal* seizures. They're French.' She placed her finger below her nose like a moustache and put on a fake French accent. '*Excusez-moi, doctor, but I'ad zee big bad seizure.*'

Ethan smiled. It was nice to see Alison be silly again. The previous night, she'd had a fit in her bed – freezing suddenly, hips raised, wailing like an injured animal – and he'd never seen anything like that before. It looked like a horror movie, like Alison was possessed. When she finally woke up, she forgot where she was and yelled wildly at her father. Ethan had pretended to be asleep until she'd calmed down.

'In Alison's case,' Dr Saunders said, 'she has abnormal electrical activity in both halves of her brain. Left and right. We call that primary generalised epilepsy. What you experienced, Ethan, was a secondary generalised seizure immediately following a partial seizure. A burst of electrical activity in this focal area spread throughout the entire brain.'

Mum stared at the small picture of Ethan's brain, surveying every twist and turn in his grey matter. She looked like she might cry. 'Is it going to happen again?' she asked the doctor. 'How do we stop the seizures from coming back?'

'I can't make any guarantees that they won't recur,' Dr Saunders said. 'But I want to try two things as part of his treatment. Firstly, Ethan needs to continue taking the anticonvulsants we've been administering here in hospital. One tablet in the morning and another at night.' The doctor turned to face Ethan. 'Do you think you can do that?'

Ethan looked at his mum for reassurance. 'Okay.'

'Good,' Dr Saunders said. 'It might make you feel queasy for a while, but we'll keep an eye on it. I've written a prescription that your mother can collect from the hospital pharmacist before you leave.'

'What's the other thing?' Ethan asked.

'I want you to come see me in my clinic. Once a week. This is the phone number,' the doctor said, handing Mum a business card. 'Call my secretary and she'll make an appointment for you. Mention that you're an outpatient here and we can get you in sooner. There's usually a bit of a wait for appointments at this time of year.'

'Once a week?'

'Something unusual seems to be happening in your brain, Ethan. I'm not entirely sure what it is yet, but I'd like to find out. As I'm sure you would too.'

Mum tensed up. 'Unusual? What's wrong?'

'To be honest, I don't know,' Dr Saunders said. 'Because Ethan's brain was injured so early in his life, his neurological development has been unconventional. From the diagnostics we've done here, it looks as though Ethan rewired his brain. He's using areas that aren't usually activated, probably to compensate for the injury to this lobe. Storing information in new places. It's because of something called neuroplasticity, the brain's ability to fix itself, and it's nothing short of extraordinary. It could take some time to figure out the long-term effects of all this rewiring.'

Ethan raised his hand to his forehead. Something was wrong back there, behind the cushioning of his skin and hardness of his skull. He imagined his brain wired like a house, long cables running behind its walls. Circuits and switches, outlets and meters. But his wiring was faulty. Live wires dangling hazardously – sparking and crackling – overloaded with voltage and amps. Ethan knew unusual really meant abnormal. Weird. Even inside his body, in his cells and neurons, he was a freak.

'The good news,' Dr Saunders said, 'is that Ethan hasn't had any more seizures since he was admitted. I'm going to place you under observation for the night, but if everything goes well, I'd be happy to discharge you in the morning.'

Ethan smiled. 'Really?'

'Thank God,' Mum said, putting her hand on his knee. It always struck Ethan as a funny thing for his mum to say; she didn't believe in God but kept expressing gratitude to him. She stood up. 'Dr Saunders, can I have a quick word with you? In private?'

Dr Saunders nodded.

As Ethan watched his mum and the doctor speak on the other side of the glass, he wished he could lip-read. Sometimes he could read his mum's eyes – happiness swelling her irises, the sad shine of her cornea, anger tapering her eyelids – but he didn't know all these movements of her mouth. Round vowels and puckered shapes, nodding, wrinkling, frowns. They were talking too fast. Syllables, words, sentences, phrases tumbled too quickly from their lips. Ethan felt dizzy trying to keep up.

Then the room froze.

Dr Saunders stopped speaking mid-sentence. His arms and face went stiff. His gaping mouth reminded Ethan of those laughing clowns at the Royal Easter Show, their heads swivelling back and forth. Mum was rigid too, pressing her lips together like she had no teeth. It made her look like an old lady. Every particle of dust in the room was still, every atom motionless. The air had crystallised into solid mist, hardened fog.

Ethan turned to Alison. She'd frozen too, stuck halfway through turning a magazine page. It was like somebody had pressed pause on real life. Or like being inside the static world of a photograph. Only Ethan could move. He waved his arms around in the air and started yelling. He jumped on the bed. Nobody reacted.

But he could hear soft noises, a distant rumbling, slowly getting louder like an approaching train. The sound was closer now, thundering, rushing towards him like wind. He heard his name.

'Ethan,' Alison said. She raised her voice. 'Ethan!'

He blinked. The room was normal again.

'They're letting you go home?' She sat upright in her bed. Under her eyes, her skin was dark and hollow. Ethan was reminded of Will's black eye. Her seizures had beat her up, punched her in the face.

'Yeah, in the morning.'

Alison lay back down on her mattress.

'What's wrong?' Ethan asked.

'Nothing.'

'How much longer will you need to stay here?'

'I'm not responding to my medicine this time. I'm not getting better.'

Ethan felt guilty for a second. He was better; he was going home. That wasn't fair. Although now that he thought about it, going back home also meant going back to school and he didn't really want to do that. Maybe it would be better to stay in hospital forever. From the corner of his eye, Ethan noticed his mum still talking to Dr Saunders. She was wiping tears away with the back of her hand.

'I could visit you?' Ethan offered. 'On the weekend. Or even after school?'

'Really? Would you SOOF?' Alison asked.

'SOOF?'

'Swear on our friendship. SOOF. You'll need to spit-swear,' Alison said, getting out of bed. 'I've never had a visitor who wasn't a member of my family before. This is a big deal.'

Ethan grimaced. 'With real spit?'

Alison spat on her hand and gave him a solemn nod. 'An oath

bound in saliva,' she said theatrically, as she held out her wet palm. 'Sealed with spit.'

He tried to collect saliva inside his mouth. Spit pooled under his tongue made him want to gag. He spat. The slimy mucus cooled quickly in the middle of his palm.

Alison grabbed Ethan's hand, the surfaces of their skin clapping together. She gripped her fingers around his and looked straight into his eyes. Their saliva blended – squelching, fusing, moist palm against palm – as they steadily shook hands. 'Spit, shake, swear,' she said with a serious tone.

'Spit, shake, swear,' Ethan repeated, returning her steely look. He had to stop himself from laughing as Alison maintained her earnest, unsmiling face. She took everything so seriously. Ethan pulled his wet hand back, wiped spit on her nightgown and grinned.

Alison screamed. 'Yuck!' she said, running away from him. 'Stop it! Ethan! That's disgusting.'

'And spit-swearing isn't?'

They chased each other around the room with their sticky hands, laughing and shrieking, pretending for a sacred moment that they weren't in a hospital. Alison wiped her hand on Ethan's back, whooping with victory. Their blended spit dried into the lines of his hands, his palm coated in white flakes of drool. It should've been gross, but it wasn't.

The morning nurse peeked her head into the room. 'Alison! Ethan! Back in your beds right away. You both should know better than to overstimulate each other. Especially you, Alison.'

The children did as they were told, giggling and sharing mischievous glances when the nurse wasn't looking, as they climbed into their beds and under the covers again.

Alison gave Ethan a weak smile. 'I don't feel so good. Maybe you could read to me?' She picked up the book that was on her bedside table. 'Will you read me *Alice in Wonderland*?'

Ethan got up and took the book from Alison's hands. He sat at the end of her bed. From under her blanket, she kicked his thigh and snickered. But even her smile couldn't conceal the cloud of illness forming in her eyes. Ethan opened her book to a random page and read aloud. Alison was asleep before he reached the end of the chapter.

∞

Mark had the hands of a pianist, long fingers bowed like the neck of a swan. He tapped them on his knee, each movement striking notes of a nervous sonata of the fingertips. But this was a deceptive elegance. His body was all angles, sharp corners and hard lines. Sweat beads collected in the tide of his brow. There was no softness there.

The train came to a stop and with a myopic squint he read the station name. Circular Quay. Not yet. He removed his jacket and wiped the sweat off his face with the back of his hand. He was dressed in shades of neutral – slate, charcoal, asphalt, stone – and, if put against the Sydney cityscape, he might disappear. Mark worked in ore lodes, inside a lab inside a pit; he wasn't used to dressing up. His leather shoes lacked creases, his laces without the frays of regular wear. The passenger sitting opposite looked at him and their eyes met. They both smiled, but Mark had the sort of downward smile that was actually a frown.

From the pocket of his jacket he pulled out a present, green paper tied with a pink bow. With a swan finger, he touched the edges taped into precise corners. The train stopped again. St James. This was it. He followed the tiled tunnels, up the stairs to the vintage neon sign. *Chateau Tanunda, the Brandy of Distinction*. The blue and orange sign had been there for as long as he could remember. His mother used to take him to the city, past St James station, to have soup and sandwiches at the cafe on the highest floor of David Jones.

Claire was waiting for him at the station exit, leaning against a wall. The afternoon sun lit her hair, but she had such high cheekbones that even on the brightest day a shadow always fell on her face. She wore an old white sundress – Mark remembered it – that had somehow managed to stay impossibly clean.

'You're late,' Claire said.

'Yeah, I know, sorry, the train.'

She looked at her watch. 'I don't have much time.'

This wasn't the greeting Mark had expected. 'Let's just grab a quick coffee then.'

'There's a coffee shop around the corner,' Claire said, leading the way. As they walked, she kept a wide gap between their bodies. When Mark stepped closer, Claire moved back. They were like two kids learning to waltz as they renegotiated the space between them.

The coffee shop was crowded when they arrived, the queue almost out the door.

'Long black with a splash of full-cream milk, no sugar?' Mark asked.

She nodded.

He smiled. 'You haven't changed.'

Claire smiled back, but immediately looked away. 'I'll wait out here.'

Mark went inside. The line wasn't moving and he kept glancing backwards to see if she was still there. He rubbed the back of his neck. It was loud – roar of the coffee grinder, whistle of frothing milk, staff yelling – so Mark couldn't organise his thoughts. The barista was listless, working leisurely: grind, dose, level, tamp. Mark ordered and tapped his foot, wanting to run behind the counter and make the coffees himself. Finally, they called his name.

'Thanks,' Claire said as he handed her the paper cup. 'Let's sit in the park.'

Mark hadn't been back to Hyde Park for years. He used to study on the steps of the Anzac War Memorial, occasionally looking up from his books to stare into the grey water of the Pool of Reflection. Nothing much had changed. Elderly men still played chess with the giant pieces in the Japanese Garden. Office workers still sat on the grass during their lunchbreaks, sprawled on the lawn, turning their faces towards the sun. Down the fig-lined avenue, Mark could see the spraying jets of the Archibald Fountain.

One drunken night in the height of a Sydney summer, many Januaries ago when the balmy late night felt as hot as noon and the humidity soared, Claire had persuaded Mark to jump into the fountain. He liked how impulsive she could be, how uninhibited, except when she tried to make him act recklessly too. But as Claire climbed the marble plinth and bronze statues – wet dress clinging to her body, hair slicked back, her magnetic face glistening in the fountain's mist – Mark reflexively followed her into the water.

'Diana, goddess of the hunt, of purity and the moon,' he said, pointing at the statue. He'd studied Classics at school, knew all about ancient Greek and Roman mythology. 'The Greeks called her Artemis.'

'Show-off.' Claire splashed him and gestured to the bronze man in the middle of the fountain. 'Who's he?' she asked, drops of water dripping off her chin, the fountain's floodlight igniting her face.

'That's Apollo. Diana's twin brother. God of the sun, of beauty, music and light. He was the god of healing too. The ancient Greeks thought the twins shooting arrows at people caused illness and death.

So they prayed to Apollo to cure disease.' At the statue's feet was a horse head; water spilled from its flaring nostrils. 'I guess he was a multi-tasking god.'

Claire laughed and waded through the water to the other side of the basin, lifting the hem of her dress. Tortoises shot water from their mouths at her feet. She had the most beautiful legs. Mark saw the ballet training in her walk – her turned-out hips, her pointing feet – that elegant gait engraved into her body by years of bending at the barre.

She lifted herself onto another statue and smacked its bronzed behind. The metal had oxidised, turned slightly green. 'And this guy?' she asked. 'What's his story?'

'Theseus,' Mark said. 'Slaying the Minotaur.'

'Theseus was a bit of a hunk,' Claire said as she mounted the basin at the centre of the fountain and stood below Apollo. 'Look at his arse.'

In the shadow of St Mary's Cathedral, under the fan of spraying water, Claire looked more striking than any neoclassical sculpture. Mark wanted to touch her. Carved into clay, forged and wrought, cast with molten metal: she belonged in a museum. But she was greater than any statue – animated, fearless, determined, painfully stubborn – and she'd pulled Mark out from his hard shell, taught him how to feel truly alive.

'And look at this ancient mythical creature here,' she said, mimicking his voice as she placed her hand on a water-sprouting bronze fish. 'His name was Trouteus, and he was the god of swimming in forbidden fountains at two in the morning.' She pouted, curling her lips to resemble the fish. 'And he represents vomiting when you've had too much to drink.'

Mark came after her, scaling the granite slabs, sliding on the slippery polished stones. 'Claire, I love you,' he blurted out. He'd never said it to her before and suddenly felt self-conscious, hyper-aware of his sticky wet clothes.

Claire stood there for a moment, wobbling in the pool of water, her mouth agape. 'I love you too,' she'd said, a little breathless.

Crescents of water shot over their heads as they kissed in the moonlit fountain, before they lost their balance and slipped in the basin. Mark had loved the languor of those warm evenings of their careless youth. Laughing hysterically, their bodies submerged, they kissed again in the hexagonal pool. Above them, the bronze mythological figures looked into the distance.

Season following season, year after inevitable year, Diana, Apollo and Theseus hadn't moved. The lifeless statues still held their poses; the jets still sprayed their streams. Mark wondered if Claire remembered jumping into the water as they overlooked the fountain now. Had she forgotten that night? She carefully brushed leaves off the bench before sitting down.

He studied Claire's face. A little more worn than the last time he'd seen her, her eyes a little older but unsettlingly familiar.

'You look beautiful,' he said.

Claire crossed her arms. 'Don't you remember? You used to tell me I wasn't beautiful, I was symmetrical.'

'Oh,' he said, staggered by her comment. It was never meant as an insult; symmetry wasn't subjective, it was absolute. Her beauty could be quantified by mathematics, by divine measurements and ratios. 'I've got something for you.' Mark reached into his pocket and handed Claire the wrapped present.

She barely glanced at it before putting it straight into her handbag.

'About our conversation on the phone. What do you think?' he asked.

Claire looked at her lap; she couldn't seem to look him in the eye. She was different now, even her hair had changed; she'd cut it shorter. Back when they'd met, her long wavy hair almost came down to her waist. But at this new length, Mark saw it still had a natural tendency towards the wild.

'I don't think it's a good idea,' she said.

'Not a good idea for him? Or for you?'

'For him.'

Mark had anticipated this but felt his neck muscles tense. If he was honest with himself, he hadn't come all the way back to Sydney for nothing. It wasn't just for his father, and he wasn't interested in climbing the Harbour Bridge, touring the Opera House. There was something here more monumental than all of those things. 'But Ethan —'

'Ethan doesn't know what's best for him,' Claire interrupted. 'He's a twelve-year-old boy.'

'Maybe you don't know what's best for him either.'

'I don't need this,' she said, still looking down. 'Do you honestly think you can tell me I don't know what's best for Ethan? You don't know him. What's the name of the toy he's slept with every night since he was a baby? What was his first word? When did he take his first steps? You have no idea.'

'I want to know those things. I wanted to be there.'

'Well, you weren't.' Her tone was hard and matter-of-fact now. 'You have no idea what we've been through.'

Mark stared blankly at the fountain. 'You have no idea what I've been through either.'

Claire looked up from her lap and directly into Mark's eyes. 'You deserved that.'

'Dad's dying,' he said. 'It would mean so much to him to see his grandson.'

'I'm sorry about your father,' Claire said. 'I've always liked John. But I have to put Ethan's needs first. It'd be traumatic for him to meet his grandfather for the first time on his deathbed.'

'He can hardly speak but says Ethan's name over and over. I don't know what to do. I feel like I owe it to him to . . .' His voice trailed off. Mark fixed his eyes on the cathedral's stained-glass windows. 'I don't have to be there. If that makes it easier for you. For you both.'

'Don't you think you owe Ethan too? I don't think you understand how upsetting that would be for him.'

'Claire, I think about him all the time.'

'No, I mean his feelings? His best interests?'

'Of course I do.'

Claire tucked some loose strands of hair behind her ear. 'No, I have to put my foot down. It's not a good idea.'

Both of them looked away, staring at people passing by: runners wearing shorts and sunglasses, jogging through the shafts of light; old women walking from mass at the cathedral across to the department stores; school students on an excursion marshalled into a line by their militant teacher.

Mark broke the silence. 'Can I ask a question? He's normal, right? No permanent, you know, damage? Everything is okay?'

'I can't believe you just asked me that,' Claire said. 'Yes, he's fine. But do you seriously think that just because he's relatively fine now, that he's okay? He doesn't have a dad. And you didn't live through not knowing whether or not he'd ever stand up, walk or talk. I spent the first years of Ethan's life holding my breath.'

Mark sighed. 'But he does have a dad.' He wanted to show her every moment he'd experienced since they'd last seen each other, how he'd had no choice but to become somebody else, but how could he make her understand?

'It's not enough. It's just too late.' Her voice fractured. 'It's been so hard.'

'Claire, it's been hard for me too.'

That icy stare. 'You deserved that,' she said again.

A tour group walked past, a flock of tourists led by a guide holding an umbrella high and shouting in German. The crowd shifted their gaze from the fountain to another attraction developing on the bench.

'I'll always love you,' Mark said softly. The words slipped out of his mouth before he'd thought about it, before he'd run it through the filter he knew he should have.

'Mark, you broke my heart.' Claire was almost in tears. She covered her face for a second; he knew she didn't want him to see her cry. Her posture changed as she tried to regain some semblance of composure. 'I shouldn't have come. I have to go.'

'But Claire —'

'Mark, don't.'

'But what about my father? What about —'

Claire stood up and gathered her things.

Mark watched her walk away, the sharp rectangular outline of the wrapped present visible through the leather of her handbag. Will she even open it? he wondered. Would she ever give him the present he wanted most?

∞

Claire walked along Hyde Park's central avenue, hurrying down the garden's spine. Under the cool shade of the leafy canopy – towering arch upon arch of figs – she struggled to take several deep breaths. Do not cry. Do not look back. Just cross the road. She regretted that coffee;

she felt its acidic burn in her empty stomach, milky phlegm in the back of her mouth.

In the late spring light, the park's colours were painfully vivid: bright mazes of manicured flower beds, walls of orange and pink azaleas. Jasmine drenched the air. Jacaranda season's explosion of purple was almost over for the year – the last of the November mauve flowers still clung to the branches. Claire stepped carefully over the dead flowers at her feet.

She pushed on towards Museum station, almost breaking into a run. Surely he wouldn't follow, chase after her. But Claire knew Mark was too indolent for that, he'd always suffered from immobilising pride. Agreeing to meet him had been a mistake. In a moment of weakness, she'd taken pity on him. Yes, his father was dying, but she couldn't expose Ethan to that. She needed to get back home to him. Pedestrians kept standing in front of her, blocking her path. They walked slowly, stopped suddenly, clogged the breadth of the footpath. Why wouldn't they get out of the way?

The arterial paths of south Hyde Park led to the Anzac War Memorial at its heart – a concrete tower, clad in pink stone. The memorial reminded Claire of a miniature New York Art Deco skyscraper, as though the top of the Empire State Building had been sliced off and dropped in the middle of Sydney. She walked along the edge of the Pool of Reflection.

Claire had never been inside the war memorial until the middle of Mark's criminal trial. During the ambulance officer's testimony, she'd stepped out of the court to get some fresh air but ended up finding hundreds of thousands of gold stars.

They were called the stars of memory: a dome of 120 000 golden stars that covered the memorial ceiling, a single star to honour each person from New South Wales who fought in the First World War. Claire had entered the war memorial by accident. What was unfolding in the courtroom was too much to process; she'd needed to disappear. In the cavernous white marble room bathed in amber light, she finally found somewhere to vanish. The crust of stars soared thirty metres above her head – countless gilded heroes and nameless deaths. Stepping inside the memorial and standing under the stars of memory became Claire's daily retreat. It helped her put things into perspective. Her problems weren't the end of the world. She was just one star in an entire galaxy.

Diagonally opposite the war memorial was the Downing Centre. Ornate, with a turreted roof and white, yellow and green exterior. The 'Mark Foy's Department Store' original signage was still above the awning – laces, gloves, silks and millinery – funny words to read along the façade of Sydney's district court. Inside was a grand piazza with marble floors and a spiral staircase. That criminal trial had seemed so long: twelve days, twelve-person jury. Claire spent two days in cross-examination, summoned as a witness for the Crown.

White wigs and black gowns, prosecution and defence rolling their suitcases of files, solid wooden panels of the stands, metal scanners at the entrance. Everything was unreal, surreal, like living in a television court drama. The days fused; she didn't remember every detail now. But she remembered admiring the slate and terracotta tiling of the former department store's beautiful floors.

Grievous bodily harm. Child abuse. Those were the charges. Articles ran in the newspaper about the trial, but thankfully nobody was named. Disclosing their identities was prohibited: the victim was a child. Her child. Throughout those inert days, those long hours of hearing clinical evidence from expert witnesses – specialist doctors, surgeons, police, ambulance officers – Claire sat comatose in her seat.

It felt like living inside a recurring nightmare, listening again to the atrocity of that day.

She didn't cry during the trial, though; Claire didn't have any tears left. It was Mark who broke down. She was taken aback by it; she'd only ever seen him cry a handful of times, but not like this. Guilty, said the juror. Beyond reasonable doubt. His body crumpled behind that stand and he let out a guttural moan. The sound wasn't human. It shocked Claire to her core.

But she didn't see what happened next; she was ushered out of the room and into the hall. The Crown prosecutor was thrilled, threw her wig off triumphantly, but Claire didn't feel like celebrating. She'd focused for so long on this verdict and, now that it was delivered, she didn't know what to think. A definitive answer – guilty – should have made her feel better. Instead, she just felt numb. Could Mark really have done that? Uncertainty still swirled inside her head. She tried to quiet it with the verdict – guilty, guilty, guilty – repeating it like an incantation until its persistent rhythm eventually eroded her doubts.

Five years after the trial ended, Claire was on Liverpool Street for a meeting. She had an appointment with a prospective donor who worked for the Director of Public Prosecutions, a distinguished barrister known for his love of the arts. The meeting went well – he pledged to make an annual contribution to the ballet company – so Claire was in a good mood. She walked away from his office with a spring in her step.

But as she waited at the intersection, Claire looked down at her shoes. She was standing on the Downing Centre tiles of glazed diamonds and Greek frets, wound around the building's edge. Suddenly, the ground fell away. She lost her balance, her vision skewed. A fearful sound came out of her mouth – that same primal cry she'd heard Mark make during his trial. Claire collapsed by the court stairs.

A young solicitor ran over to her and asked if she was hurt. Claire assured him she was fine but tears were streaming down her face. Some strange wall had broken; her numbness finally gave way. Patterns on the tiled floor brought it all back, made her feel everything. It took her a while to compose herself before Claire stood up and left.

She was at Museum station now, making her way down to the platform. A blast of cool air surged through the station, metal squeaks, skid of breaks. Claire boarded the train, sat down and opened her handbag. Automatic doors closed. Then the train sped out of the station. Colourful advertisements for chicken burgers and insurance policies stuck to the platform's wall blended into the blur of the underground tunnels.

Mark looked like Ethan. Claire knew it should be the other way around, that sons resembled their fathers. Ethan was made from Mark's chromosomes, was a copy of his unzipping molecules, their dividing cells. But it was the little boy who was far more present in her life; she'd passed many more hours studying her son's face. Claire and Mark were only together for five years, but now she'd spent twelve with Ethan.

It almost knocked her sideways when she'd seen Mark walk up the station stairs: a sudden smack of similarity. She hadn't expected it – the two of them existed in separate parts of her mind and memory, compartmentalised into different chambers of her heart. His face disoriented Claire. She could have been looking at her son in the future, not at her past in the now.

Hints in the chin, echoes in the nose; something about their bearing was identical. Claire couldn't put her finger on it. The way they held their heads, maybe. Same rigid posture, same inward-pointing feet. Seeing traces of Ethan in Mark made Claire want to be nice to him. She'd forced herself to be hard when her instinct was to be soft.

Under the carriage's fluorescent lights, she caught a glimpse of her reflection in the train's wide window. She looked tired. But still symmetrical. Mark was as insensitive as he'd always been. Her friends used to joke that he was autistic. Maybe he was. Back then, she'd fixated on his remark. Gardens were symmetrical; poems had symmetry. Not people. It was such a back-handed compliment. All he saw was proportion and geometry, not Claire. She was reminded how Mark valued impossible ideas like symmetry more than what was real.

Now the train was emerging from underground, surfacing into the daylight. She looked at her watch. It would take another half an hour to get home. Claire untied the ribbon of the present and placed it on the seat. The tape was difficult to unstick as she began to unwrap one side. She made shallow breaths; her hands shook. But her fingertips resisted. Some invisible force stopped her from peeling the paper away from whatever was inside. She taped the corner back. As the train slowed, Claire set the present down on the seat and stood up. She didn't look back as she stepped onto the platform. The doors closed.

8

VELOCITY

Ethan sat at the front of the bus with a plastic bag on his lap. Constant motion felt exactly like sitting still. If he was going at the same speed as the bus, and in the same direction, then it didn't feel like he was moving. The bus stopped, then started again. Ethan jerked backwards. These streets were unfamiliar. He looked for markers, worried he'd come too far.

That morning he'd walked to school, even made it all the way to the other side of the road opposite the front gate. But the bell's sharp clang, the high-pitched shriek of it, made him hesitate. He couldn't go back to school, not after that meeting with Will's parents, not after everybody heard how his father went to jail. Everyone already thought he was weird; now they'd think he was weirder. Ethan turned around and walked in the other direction. He felt thuds of shame beat in his chest. Every student at his school probably knew all his secrets.

The bus turned around the corner and onto High Street. Ethan recognised the chemist on the corner. This was his stop. He pressed the bell and stood up.

From the outside coming in, the Sydney Children's Hospital looked different. Brighter colours, higher walls, overcrowded atrium: doctors running into nurses, visiting family members and friends looking lost, patients strolling down the hall with their drips on wheels. Music played in the cafe and the coffee machine hissed.

Ethan walked up the stairs and over to Ward C1 North. Alison was still in the same bed. She was wearing the red and yellow cap again, although she wasn't hooked to the EEG machine. Looking up briefly, Alison must have seen Ethan at the door, but she kept her head down in the pages of *Dolly* magazine and frowned.

'Alison,' Ethan said slowly.

She turned the page of her magazine in a dramatic way but didn't respond.

'I know I said I'd come on the weekend, but I wasn't allowed.'

Alison snapped the pages shut. 'What do you want?'

'To see you.'

'You could've called. Maybe I was busy today.' A smile surfaced from the corners of Alison's mouth but she straightened her face and opened the magazine again. 'I almost forgot you were ever here,' she said coolly.

'Really?'

Alison laughed. 'No, I'm totally trolling you. I nearly went crazy when you left. Last week, there was this girl in your bed who kept talking to herself. So weird. Luckily she checked out yesterday.'

He perched on the edge of her bed. 'How are you?'

'I don't understand why they won't let me go home. It's only epilepsy. I'm not dying. The problem is I'm taking heaps of medicine and it's not doing anything. They have to let me out of here soon. I think I'm getting bedsores,' she said, scratching her leg.

'Gross,' Ethan said.

Alison laughed again. 'You're the most gullible person I've ever met.' She lifted her nightie up. 'See? No sores. Hey, shouldn't you be at school?'

'I have an appointment with Dr Saunders,' Ethan said, although the appointment actually wasn't until tomorrow. 'Oh! I almost forgot. I brought you something.' He lifted the plastic bag onto the bed and pulled out a bundle of styrofoam balls, each a different size and colour – greys, greens, browns, reds, blues and whites. Wires attached to the balls were in loose knots and Ethan started to untangle them.

Alison looked at the balls. 'What are they?'

'Wait,' Ethan said, as he stood on the bed and fixed wires to the light fitting. It took a couple of minutes to arrange – he nearly lost his balance and stepped on Alison's leg twice – but when he was done, he pulled her up by the hand so she could stand beside him.

'It's pretty,' Alison said, staring at the dangling spheres. 'But what is it?'

'The solar system.' He pointed to the styrofoam planets. 'This little one is Mercury, the yellow one is Venus, obviously that's Earth, this red one is Mars, and Jupiter is the biggest. Saturn has the rings, I made them with an old CD. Uranus is light blue.' Ethan paused; Alison was giggling. 'Then this dark-blue one is Neptune. And that's Pluto, although it's technically not a planet any more. And that's the sun in the middle. I just thought since you can't go out, I'd bring the solar system to you.'

Alison touched Ethan's elbow. 'That's really sweet.'

'It's nothing,' he said, sitting down again. 'I made it for a school project last year. It's not even to scale.'

She pulled up her striped socks and crossed her legs. 'I wish I could go outside. Feel the sun. What's it like being back in the real world?'

'Boring. But Mum let me have pizza for dinner four times this week.'

'Did you ever talk to your mum about . . .' Alison trailed off. 'You know.'

Ethan tipped his head back to look at the solar system. Jupiter, the largest of the styrofoam balls, swayed from side to side like a pendulum. It was hypnotic. But in the real solar system, Jupiter wouldn't swing. It would rotate on its axis faster than all the other planets. So fast that Jupiter had ten-hour days.

'I don't want to talk about it.'

'You can talk to me,' Alison said.

'If you mean talk about my father,' he said, not taking his eyes off Jupiter, 'then there's not really anything to say.'

'It was just an idea. I thought it might make you feel better.'

Ethan lay down on Alison's bed. At the moment, nothing really made him feel better. Especially talking. He felt like he was carrying something rotten inside him – food poisoning, a tumour – and he couldn't make it disappear. It was a feeling he didn't know, couldn't name. Lodged in a formless place between anger and pain, somewhere between discomfort and sadness. Thinking about his father made him feel weird.

Both of them were quiet. They lay on their backs, eyes fixed to the ceiling, as the planets gently rocked back and forth above their heads.

Quark was eating an umbrella by the door when Ethan arrived home. He put his keys on the shelf in the hall and stooped to take the umbrella out of the rabbit's teeth. Quark turned his back to Ethan and hopped off down the hall. Ethan opened the umbrella; there were now several small holes in its blue fabric. He pulled the broken canopy over his head, shafts of light from the ceiling lamp spilling out from the holes and onto the floor.

'That's bad luck,' Mum said.

Her voice startled Ethan. She shouldn't be home this early. 'What is?'

'Opening those inside.'

Ethan shut the umbrella. 'Bad luck is actually just a statistical probability.'

Mum raised an eyebrow. 'So, how was school?'

'Fine.'

'That's interesting, because Mr Thompson called me to ask why you weren't at school today. Which was news to me, because this morning you were wearing your uniform. Do you have any idea how worried I was? I didn't know where you were. What if something happened to you? You could have been dead!' She was talking too fast. 'And skipping school? Did you think I wouldn't find out? I wasn't born yesterday. I was honestly just about to call the police. I can't believe you'd do something so stupid. Ethan Forsythe, I've never been so worried in my life.'

'But I'm not dead.'

'It's not funny, Ethan. You're in serious trouble, don't you dare act like it's a joke. Why didn't you go to school? Where have you been all day?'

'Nowhere,' he said, focusing on his shoes. He couldn't look at her when she was angry. Her face lost its warmth; her eyes changed. They were supposed to be a team; she was supposed to be on his side.

'Nowhere isn't an answer. You were somewhere. Tell me.' Mum raised her voice. 'Where were you? Don't lie to me.'

You lied to me, Ethan wanted to say. You kept a secret from me for twelve years. But he didn't. He said nothing. He couldn't even look at his mum as she kept yelling and scolding him. Going on and on about hypothetical gutters he could've collapsed in, alternate universes where he was hit by a bus.

Ethan knew that parallel universes might exist. It was mathematically inevitable. Inside an infinite universe, everything must repeat at some point. There were only a finite number of ways particles could be arranged, so every possible configuration of particles in space might happen multiple times. Maybe one day we'd figure out how to visit these alternate universes. Quantum-jump from world to world. Pause time, slow down seconds, speed them up. Go back in time and change the past.

Maybe Ethan could rewind to this morning, decide to go to school, and in that parallel universe he wouldn't be in trouble. Or he could go even further back, along the stretching elastic paths of time, and change his destiny. What if quantum mechanics meant that Ethan could stop his father from shaking him? Perhaps in some parallel universe the three of them were the happiest family, laughing and chatting, about to sit down to dinner together.

'Are you even listening to me?' Mum asked.

Ethan blinked, rushing back to the present. He nodded at his mum. But in his head he was calculating the exponential expansion of the Big Bang and the statistical probabilities that might exist in the chaos of an inflationary universe.

At the doctor's office, the waiting room was crowded. Mum took an empty seat, but Ethan studied the posters of candy-coloured brains stuck on the walls. They looked like maps. Walled cities of the mind with winding roads, valleys, rivers: the topography of the brain plotted like a street directory. Pink highway of the cerebellum, blue suburbs of the frontal lobe, green hills of the temporal lobe. Ethan touched the back of his head. Could all of that – this complex cartography, an entire city – really exist inside his head?

Ethan looked around the waiting room at the other patients. It was the right word for the sick: patients needed patience. Always waiting – for the doctor, a bed, a cure. A little girl sat on her mother's lap. The woman combed her daughter's hair to cover what looked like a large scar on the right side of her skull. Near Ethan's feet, a boy was playing on the floor, driving toy cars in circles and crashing them into each other. He yelled during every collision.

'Crash!' the boy said. 'Boom!'

An orange race car struck Ethan's shoe. He kneeled down and picked it up.

'Here you go,' Ethan said, handing the car back.

'Fanks,' said the boy. He had a strong lisp.

'What's your name?'

'Steve,' the boy stuttered. He fought with his tongue, couldn't command the sounds in his name. They came too thickly and fast.

'My name's Ethan. How old are you?'

Steve held up his fingers. 'Four.'

'Are you waiting to see the doctor too?'

'Yes,' Steve lisped. He offered Ethan a car and they played together. Streaks in the carpet became roads, bumps in the floor were ramps, other people's legs were mountains to climb. Steve was excited by roadside accidents. Driving too fast and crashing into furniture made him giggle. He didn't seem brainsick and Ethan wondered what was wrong. Did a problem with his brain cause Steve's lisp?

At four, Ethan hadn't spoken clearly either. Maybe his brain injury was responsible, it made sense now. He remembered seeing a speech pathologist: imitating the strange noises she made – rounded and unrounded vowels, hard and soft consonants – learning how to transform these strangled sounds into actual words. Maybe something bad had happened to Steve's brain. Maybe he'd been shaken too. Perhaps it was actually a normal thing that happened to lots of other kids.

Steve crashed his car into the coffee table. 'Boom!'

'Ethan Forsythe,' the receptionist called out. 'The doctor will see you now.'

They sat on the other side of the desk, facing Dr Saunders. On their left sat a glazed porcelain bust; it made Ethan think of a head-shaped teapot. Its brain was divided into segments, sliced into rooms in a house, or apartments in a building. Each brain-room had its own name, painted on the shiny white surface in dark-blue ink.

'How are you feeling, Ethan?' The doctor opened his file.

'Much better,' Mum said immediately. 'His appetite still isn't back to normal yet, but he seems more like himself.'

'And what about the medication?'

'The only side effect he's been having is drowsiness. Otherwise he's doing just fine.' Mum touched Ethan's hair and he squirmed in his seat.

That wasn't true; he hated the medicine. It changed the speed of things, made the world slow down. Like whoever was in charge of the soundtrack to his life had altered the tempo – its chemical music wasn't fast enough for Ethan's regular pace.

Dr Saunders gave her a delicate smile. 'Claire, would you mind if I spoke to Ethan alone?'

Mum gripped the strap of her handbag; her knuckles went mottled white. 'Why? What's wrong? Why can't I be here?'

'Don't worry,' the doctor said. 'He'll be fine. I want to talk to Ethan about his brain. It's standard procedure. We won't be long.'

She paused for a defiant moment, unflinching and wary. Mum leaned over to Ethan and whispered, 'Come outside and get me anytime, if you feel unsure or scared, okay?'

He nodded.

Then Mum stalled by the door before reluctantly leaving the office.

Ethan pointed to the porcelain bust. 'What's that?'

'This is Phil,' said Dr Saunders, introducing the head. 'He comes from an old branch of medicine, now obsolete, called Phrenology. People used to believe certain areas of your brain were responsible for character traits. Phrenologists felt the bumps on your head to determine what sort of person you were. There were twenty-seven different parts, what they called brain organs. For example,' he said, pointing to a section of Phil's head, 'this part of your brain was thought to indicate whether or not you were evil. Nonsense, though. Not real science. The brain doesn't actually work like that.'

Ethan examined the head, noting the different slices marked on the glossy brain. The words were painted by hand. Spirituality. Calculation. Time. Memory. Secretiveness. Hope.

'Let me show you how the brain really works.' Dr Saunders opened a drawer in his desk and pulled out another model – plastic like a child's toy, a colour-coded and chunky puzzle. 'I want to talk to you about the cerebral cortex. That's the big outer area of the brain, what we call the grey matter. With all the folds and bumps.'

'Okay,' Ethan said.

'Just under your forehead,' Dr Saunders continued, 'is the frontal lobe. Basically, where our personality lives. The frontal lobe controls motor function, problem-solving, judgement, decision-making, and social interaction. Back here, at the top of our head, is the parietal lobe. This area integrates sensory information from various parts of the body and helps us navigate. Are you following?'

Ethan nodded.

'Now over here, just above your neck, is the occipital lobe. Your visual processing centre. And the last part of the cerebral cortex is the temporal lobe, just above your ears. It's responsible for several functions including auditory and visual perception, memory storage, speech and our emotions. And it's in your left anterior temporal lobe, Ethan, where you have the most damage. This was the area where you had the subdural haematoma when you were four months old. You presented with bilateral temporal lobe contusions. That's where the scarring is now. And, according to your more recent scans, this is also where you had your ictal seizure.'

Ethan touched his head again. On the model, the temporal lobe was tiny. It didn't seem possible that this small part of his body could do so much damage. 'Can I hold it?' he asked, reaching for the plastic brain.

'Take it apart if you like.' Dr Saunders paused, regarding his notes with a frown. 'Ethan, do you remember when I shone the torch into your eyes?'

'Yeah?'

'Do you remember what you said?' The doctor pushed his glasses down his nose and read from a piece of paper. 'You said when the torch was in your eyes, you saw the light move from red to blue. Red to blue to red again. Can you explain what you meant by that?'

Ethan sat back in his chair. 'That was just what I saw.' He fiddled with the plastic lobes on the desk. Dr Saunders had said his pupils weren't something; he couldn't recall the word. But he remembered the torch sting his eyes, the glaring light that changed from red to blue.

'Your mother told me you like physics,' Dr Saunders said.

'Yeah, I do.'

'I suppose you've heard of the Doppler effect? Could you explain it to me?'

'Okay. Say you hear a fire engine coming towards you. At first, the pitch of the siren is really high. And then when it passes you, the pitch is lower. That's why it sounds different when it's moving to you and when it's moving away from you.'

Dr Saunders smiled and reached into his shirt pocket to find a pen. 'Do you know why it sounds different?'

Ethan nodded. 'The distances between the waves. I see them all the time. Especially near ambulances. First they're short waves when the ambulance is coming closer. And longer waves when it drives away.'

'You've seen them?'

'Yeah.'

Dr Saunders wrote in the file. 'What do they look like?'

Ethan wasn't sure how to describe them. Ripples that rushed through the wind, bending and crashing in the atmosphere. He saw them everywhere. Sometimes it looked like an earthquake in the sky; the air shook and trembled. Like sitting on the beach and watching the ocean rise and fall, undulating from blue water to white foam. 'I don't know,' he said finally. 'They're just waves.'

'Do you know how the Doppler effect works with light?'

Ethan scratched his ear. 'The same way. High- and low-frequency waves.'

'It's called red shift and blue shift,' Dr Saunders said. 'The light wavelength changes. Red shift for one side of the visible light spectrum, blue shift for the other. But it's not something you can see with your naked eye. You can't see it with a torch.'

Ethan shifted his weight from one side of his body to the other, wondering how much longer this appointment would take. He leaned forward and tried to read the doctor's notes. His name was written all over the page.

Dr Saunders closed the file. 'I think that's all for today then, Ethan. See you next week?'

'Okay then, bye.' Ethan stepped into the hallway outside the doctor's office and stared into the overhead light. He turned his head one way, then the other, trying to catch the frequency of the electromagnetic waves. Nothing. No scrunching or spreading, no shift. As he walked away from the light, he glimpsed the tiniest flash of red. Ethan blinked before heading back to the waiting room to find his mum.

9

ACCELERATION

Claire set off towards the hospital during her lunchbreak, trying her best not to contemplate why. In one hand, she clutched a framed photograph, in the other a bottle of Baileys Irish Cream. She kept thinking about John. Mark's father was about to die and wanted to see Ethan before it was too late. Her categorical refusal to grant that wish made her feel like a monster, even though she knew it was right.

When Claire was still married to Mark, her loyalty was to him. He'd been whittled down by his father – minimised to a shell – and although Mark didn't often talk about his feelings, he was clearly hurt. Speaking about his family made Mark's voice tremble. His wounds were deep; she wanted to mend them. Put him back together again. Before she'd met John for the first time, Claire had pictured a tyrant: oppressive, controlling, violent. But he wasn't. John seemed benign, just a widowed old man.

She'd lost her own father more than fifteen years ago. Frank had a stroke in his sleep. It was so sudden, so unexpected, that it took a long time for Claire to accept that her dad was really gone. There'd been countless things she'd wanted to tell him and never had the chance. Ethan never got to meet him. She still thought of her father every afternoon, when shafts of sunlight beamed through the trees. Between the leafy shadows, in a few fragile scraps of light.

When Claire was a little girl, her father would lift her onto his shoulders whenever they went for walks outside. 'Careful of the branches!' he'd say and Claire ducked to make sure twigs and leaves didn't brush across her face. Speckled light on green lawns, the smell of eucalyptus, magpies singing duets to each other across the cricket pitch at Burwood Park – a pristine world, her suburban childhood. Up there on her father's shoulders, Claire felt on top of the world. She saw everything in a way she couldn't from down on the ground. That was what her dad did best: made her feel like she truly was on top of the world, showed her a different perspective.

Frank used to sing a Joni Mitchell song to put her to sleep – about ice-cream castles, moons, ferris wheels, and not really knowing love at all – but now Claire understood that couldn't be further from the truth. She'd never known anybody who knew love so much; her dad taught her how to love, made it a verb, not just a noun. Remembering sitting on her father's shoulders seized Claire with sadness, with a dullness that drummed in her chest. Her father was still gone; soon John would be too.

Midday sun drenched the concrete courtyard outside the hospital. No cheerful murals here, no colourful handprints or comic-book smiles – the palliative-care wing was stark. Over the years, John had tried to contact Claire numerous times. He'd invite them both to Christmas lunch, send presents to his grandson on his birthday, but Claire never changed her mind. Better for Ethan to keep Mark's family out of his life; it might confuse him, cause him unnecessary distress. Convenient excuses – it was better for Claire too.

Sometimes when she picked Ethan up from school, she'd spot John standing across the road. He never approached them, never tried to make his presence known. All the old man ever did was look on from afar, hoping to catch a brief glimpse of his grandson. Seeing him wait there, helpless and forlorn, made Claire feel like the real tyrant. She'd alienated Ethan's only living grandfather. None of this was John's fault.

Claire stood at the reception desk and asked for directions. But by the time she reached John's room, her mind had finally caught up with her body. What was she doing here? John wasn't her dad. Seeing him wouldn't raise her father from his grave. Her heartbeat escalated – what if Mark was here, visiting too? Claire opened the door, relieved to find John alone. He was awake, propped up by pillows, looking at the wall with a fixed stare.

'Hi John, it's Claire.' She took a seat beside the bed, holding up the bottle of Baileys. 'Not sure if you can still drink this, but I brought you something. Your favourite.'

The old man turned his head to face her. 'You remembered.' His voice was more faint than a whisper, his eyes were bloodshot and gold. Mottled skin discoloured his hands and neck, purple and grey, patterned like veins on a leaf. John reached for Claire. 'Ethan,' he said hopefully.

She placed the bottle down on his bedside table. 'I'm sorry. Just me. Ethan's at school.'

He cast his eyes back to the wall and nodded.

Monitors attached to his chest filled the room with a mechanical hum. Claire looked around. There were some photographs – Tom's kids, she guessed, pretty girls with shiny dark hair and gap-toothed smiles – behind a row of hand-drawn cards saying, 'Get Well Soon, Pop!' She picked up one of the frames. For a moment, Claire remembered Tom's daughters were also Ethan's first cousins. But they didn't know him; she'd made Ethan an outsider in his own family. How ashamed she felt, how selfish and self-absorbed, looking at the innocent smiles of the three little girls. Ethan's cousins didn't deserve to be boycotted. These children hadn't done anything wrong.

'Your granddaughters are lovely,' Claire said, putting the picture frame down.

'Tell me,' John rasped. 'About him.'

'About Ethan?' She exhaled. 'I don't know where to start. He's brilliant. Curious. Really articulate. Bit of a perfectionist. Has a photographic memory. Such an intelligent boy. Probably smarter than me. When I think about how sick he was as a baby . . .' Claire trailed off for a second before collecting herself again. 'Even though he's only twelve, Ethan is the most determined person I know. He has no idea just how brave he is. How brave he's always been.'

The old man lay still and smiled. His pale lips were the same colour as the rest of his skin.

Claire took the framed photograph of Ethan out of her handbag. 'Here, it's his most recent school photo, only taken a few months ago. Can you imagine, Ethan's about to finish primary school. High school next year. I can't believe how quickly he's growing up.'

She looked at her son in the picture, smiling sweetly at the camera. Sometimes Claire forgot exactly how objectively handsome he was. Normally she saw him through the biased lens of a mother's subjective gaze. But mounted in a silver frame, under a shiny sheet of glass, Ethan was undeniably striking. One day he was going to break thousands of hearts.

John ran a crooked finger over the photograph. 'Mark,' he said softly.

Was the old man confused, disoriented to the point where he couldn't tell the difference? Claire wasn't sure and didn't want to correct him.

'Mark,' he said again. John hugged the photograph to his chest, the way a child cuddles their favourite toy. His eyes watered. As he sank back into his pillows, he tried to tell her something else, but his voice was so weak Claire couldn't hear what he said.

She leaned into him. 'Sorry, John, I didn't hear that.'

John wet his lips with his coated tongue. His speech was strained and slow. 'Claire, I'm dying. I know I'm an old bastard. A bully. Angry. Mean. Terrible father. Boys should hate me. But they don't. Not sure why. They visit every day. Stay for hours. I don't deserve it.' His breathing became ragged.

'Don't be silly,' Claire said, touching his shoulder. His body felt cold. 'They're your sons. They love you unconditionally.'

'Blood, thicker than water.' John shrugged. 'I'm a ratbag. Didn't deserve a second chance.' He held out the photograph of Ethan again, studying it for a while, before tucking the frame under his blanket. 'Never set a good example for them. Mark was always so impressionable; I was too hard on him, too rough. I've always known I'm to blame for what happened too.' John inhaled loudly and exhaled deeply, until the air in his lungs slowly petered out.

Claire looked out the window at the paperbark trees, with their cream bottlebrush blossoms and peeling trunks. She thought of her own father, wondering what he might've said with the chiselled clarity that seemed to accompany imminent death. But she wasn't sure. She couldn't imagine what final laments he'd need to articulate, if he had any sins to confess. Her dad didn't have time to think about it. And she'd never know.

The old man coughed. 'Next time, bring Ethan.'

Claire didn't have the heart to say she probably wouldn't, although now she wasn't so sure. 'It was good to see you, John.'

He closed his eyes. 'Ethan,' he whispered.

As Claire closed the door, she noticed her eyes were wet, although she didn't remember crying. There was a smell in the air, curdled and sweet, that reminded Claire of breastmilk, and a vague sense of being needed, of that phase in her life when she'd been indispensable but didn't yet understand it was only a phase. John's words – perhaps inadvertently – had left her with an insoluble burden. Blood, thicker than water. Didn't deserve a second chance. Immediately, Claire thought of Mark.

She was struck momentarily by an uneasy feeling, some abstract glimpse of what it might mean to forgive and forget. Of the way children love their parents – irrationally, uncritically, blindly – without needing proof that their parents were worthy of love. Claire understood she had the power to give, and also to take away. She could bring Ethan to meet his grandfather. Who would it hurt? Ultimately, this was her choice to make.

But her heart intervened, quickly overriding those thoughts. Exposing Ethan to further distress wasn't a risk she wanted to take. Best to keep that door locked. Claire rushed away from the palliative-care wing and out into the car park. John could voice his deep regrets, reflect on his mistakes, but that had nothing to do with Mark. How did she even draw that parallel? Ballet had taught her that on the stage, you only had one opportunity to get it right. Claire felt narrowed to a ruthless pinpoint of quickening regret. Because it was denial – not remorse or mistakes – that ruled out second chances.

∞

Ethan was discovering his body in the bathroom mirror. He wiped the layer of shower mist off the glass surface and looked at himself in the nude. Popping and flexing, tensing and bending; he found new muscles every day. With a clenched jaw and serious expression, Ethan tightened his deltoids, biceps, major pectorals. He was getting a sharpness about him now – angles, corners, nooks – and he didn't know where these beginnings of definition came from. How he might look one day when he was fully cooked. Change was exciting, but he was also terrified of his future body, his metamorphosis into the unknown.

He held an arm straight up in the air and carefully examined the reflection of the darkening skin of his armpit. No hair grew under there yet. His eyebrows were thicker; maybe he was getting his first pimple on his chin. He took a secret delight in his transformation. Posing like a bodybuilder – taut shoulders, bulked-up neck, groin thrust upward to the ceiling – Ethan imagined he was a grown man. He relaxed his muscles. Although puberty was speeding up, he still had the body of a little boy, a bit doughy and sweet.

Ethan had never seen a naked man in the flesh. He'd seen his mum without clothes on before, but there was a strange, soft hairlessness about her – white thighs, smooth arms, small pointy elbows and knees – and he was never going to have a body like that. Most of the girls in Ethan's class were taller than the boys now. Budding breasts, curving hips, tampons and pads; their accelerated development wasn't just physical. The Year 6 girls posed and preened, spent their lunchtimes sitting in conspiratorial circles. On the opposite side of the playground, the Year 6 boys still played with sticks.

But a mature male body, an adult penis, a hairy ball sack: he'd never seen those things with his eyes. Ethan could search the internet for images of 'naked men' but he didn't want to do that, that'd make him a pervert. If anyone ever found out, he'd be called a homo for sure. He wasn't. Ethan just wanted to know everything about becoming a man. Needed to study it, understand it, master it. Men had their own language – foreskins, beards, erections – but he knew his mum couldn't be his translator. Masculinity was another tongue.

'We need to leave in five minutes.' Mum knocked on the bathroom door.

'Hold on.' Ethan took one last look at his naked body in the mirror, dried his hair and pulled on his school uniform.

At school, his mum accompanied him to the classroom. Ethan didn't let her kiss him goodbye. She stood at the door and watched him walk into class, her eyes on him as he entered the room. Ethan felt everyone's stares. Not everybody was there yet, the morning bell hadn't rung, but a hush came over the room. One girl smiled at him hastily. He hung up his bag and rummaged through it slowly, delaying any interaction. Everybody knew. About his brain. About his father. His pulse raced.

Mr Thompson talked to his mum outside the classroom door. She wore her worried face; she'd worry about being worried if she could. It was a face Ethan noticed her sporting a lot at the moment: crushed forehead, red eyes. This face made her look one hundred years old. If only Ethan were less weird, less sick, not a freak: that face she made was his fault. Mr Thompson nodded thoughtfully at Mum, but Ethan couldn't hear what they were saying. Not that it mattered. Obviously, they were talking about him.

At nine o'clock the school bell rang. Children poured in and filled the empty seats in the classroom, stopping mid-sentence or doing a double take when they noticed Ethan was back. Some of the kids said hello but most avoided him. A loud group of boys walked through the door – Daniel, Will and the rest of their gang. Will's black eye looked better now. His skin had healed; the eyepatch was off.

Daniel whispered behind him. 'Stephen Hawking's back, check it out. E equals M C squared!'

Ethan kept his eyes on the whiteboard at the front of the class. That wasn't actually Hawking's equation.

Mr Thompson explained the new project for the week. The children were going to break up into small groups to make a stop-motion animation, using cameras and clay to trick the eye. 'Animation relies on persistence of vision,' he said. 'The eye can retain an image for a fraction of a second. So if your film has a speed of about ten images per second, the motion in your sequence of different pictures will look seamless.'

Kids broke off into pairs and brainstormed about their movies. Mr Thompson took Ethan aside. 'How do you feel? You okay to do this?'

Ethan nodded. 'Sounds like fun.'

'Your mother explained your condition. Let me know if you get fatigued. Everyone will be taking lots of photos, using a flash. So just give us a yell if you're not feeling great.'

Ethan was partnered with Nathan Nguyen. The boys drew their storyboard and started to mould plasticine characters. It was nice to do something with his hands, and Ethan let himself get lost in the details of the activity – sculpting, embossing, shaping, reshaping. Nathan arranged the first shot against their background and took a photo. Ethan moved a soldier's plasticine arm. Nathan took another photo. Ethan adjusted the arm's angle again. Click. Flash. Change. Click. Flash. Change. Before Ethan knew it, two hours had passed. The bell for morning tea was ringing.

Out in the playground, kids ran and screamed. Ethan knew nobody wanted to play with him so he took his apple and muesli bar from his schoolbag and locked himself in the furthest cubicle of the boys' bathroom. He felt light-headed and lonely, longed to be back home. Everything will be okay, he told himself. It's just school. Not the end of the universe. Sure, since it could be expanding indefinitely at an accelerated rate, the end of the universe was probably inevitable. But it wasn't going to happen today.

Ethan sat on the toilet seat and chewed his muesli bar. Sticky oats got caught in his throat. When he was finished, he shoved the wrapper into his pocket. Something was in his shorts. He pulled a crumpled piece of paper out of his uniform.

The letter. His father's letter.

He read it again. Ethan still didn't understand what his father wanted, what this letter was trying to say. Each paragraph was more cryptic than the next. His dad was somewhere in the same city, right now, maybe only minutes away. But Ethan didn't know if his father wanted to see him. The letter wasn't clear; it didn't say yes or no. Everything took on a new meaning now that he knew about his injuries.

He's my son, but I don't know anything about him. Maybe I should've sent him birthday cards, called him at Christmas. I don't know. I wasn't sure if you wanted to hear from me. And I needed to focus on getting my own life back on track. I often wonder what you've told Ethan about me and about what happened. I'm his father. How have you explained the fact that I'm not around?

Ethan took a slow bite of his apple and read the words again.

The bathroom door creaked open.

'Stephen Hawking! We know you're here,' Daniel cooed. 'We're going to find you, freak.'

Ethan held his breath. He quietly stood up on the toilet seat so the boys couldn't see his feet under the door.

Bang! They started to kick the cubicles. *Bang! Bang! Bang!*

In the furthest cubicle, Ethan's knees quivered. He might wet his pants. They were going to beat him to a pulp; he knew it. Yeah, that was definitely the plan. An eye for a black eye. Ethan probably had to pay some price for what he'd done to Will's face. Physics wanted balance. Equilibrium.

Bang! The noises were closer and louder now. *Bang!*

With the slightest twitch of his finger, the letter fell out of Ethan's hand. It floated upwards for a moment, before slipping under the door of the stall and into the main area of the bathroom. Stupid air resistance, Ethan thought, as the paper flew out of the cubicle.

'Dan,' one of the boys said. 'Come here, check it out.'

'What's this? A love letter from Stephen Hawking?' Daniel read the letter in a girlish voice. 'Dear Claire, I'm sorry to get in touch out of the blue like this but I urgently need to speak with you.' He paused for a moment; Ethan's skin burned. 'Gold,' Daniel said. 'This is fucking gold.'

'Let me see!' Will snatched the letter from Daniel's hands. 'I sent a letter to your office but I'm not sure you received it. Your old phone number is disconnected. Hopefully this is still your address.' Will read the whole letter aloud. At first the boys sniggered but the more he read, the quieter they grew. 'Maybe you could give me a call? Mark.'

Nobody said anything for a little while. Pipes clanged below their feet. Ethan wobbled, scared he might slip off the bending plastic toilet seat.

'I know you're in here, freak,' Will said to the door of his cubicle. 'I can see you through the cracks. Come out, Stephen Hawking, or we'll knock down the door.'

Ethan closed his eyes. He wished the Big Crunch would start right now, that the real end of the universe would begin. Then these boys would just get swallowed into a black hole and disappear. Ethan would get sucked in too, but right now he didn't really care.

'Come out.' Daniel raised his voice. He punched the door with his fist and the metal hinge of the lock clattered.

Ethan made a suffocated whimper.

'Come on, Stephen Hawking. You can't hide forever. I've got another secret to tell you. Want to know what it is?' Daniel sounded a little deranged. 'You think you're so smart and special, but you're just a piece of shit.'

Ethan's legs buckled. These boys didn't know any secret he didn't already now know himself.

'Stephen Hawking's mum is a slut!' Daniel said gleefully.

Heat rushed through Ethan's body. Those boys could say whatever they wanted about him, call him a freak, but they couldn't insult his mum. His nostrils flared; he bared his teeth. Ethan stepped off the toilet seat and onto the bathroom tiles. He pushed the cubicle door open.

'What did you say?'

Daniel looked delighted. 'Hello, Stephen Hawking! Your mum,' he said slowly, 'is a slut.'

'Take it back,' Ethan said. 'That's not true.'

Will took a step forward, pushing Daniel aside. 'Yeah, it is. Your mum is a slut.'

Ethan shook his head. 'No, you're lying.'

'You don't know, do you?' Will looked torn for a moment. 'Your mum had sex with my dad. Ask her. It's true.'

'Shut up,' Ethan cried. His ribs squeezed the air out of his lungs. The bathroom started to warp. Some unknown force pushed Ethan's body against the wall. His shoulder hit the hand dryer. Warm air burst out of the dryer's metal vent, heating millions of particles of air. 'Shut up. Shut up, shut up.'

Hot particles rose to the top of the room. Cold particles sank to the floor. Suddenly, Ethan saw all the particles in the room collide. Bouncing, crashing, dancing; travelling at thousands of kilometres an hour, they ricocheted off every surface of the boys' bathroom. Atoms smashed into other atoms, creating the tiniest explosions of light. Microscopic fireworks filled the air.

It took Ethan's breath away. He bent his head up to the ceiling and stretched his arms wide. He let out a cry, a combustive groan like starting an engine's ignition. With a swish of his arms, Ethan controlled the army of particles, pushing them towards Will and Daniel and the rest of the boys. The particles crashed over their heads like an atomic tsunami.

'What the fuck?' Daniel looked at Ethan with wide eyes.

Will stepped back. 'Let's get out of there.'

'What's wrong with him?'

'I dunno. Let's go.' Will grabbed the corner of Daniel's school shirt and led him towards the door.

As the boys bolted out of the toilets, Ethan slumped against the wall. The particles made themselves invisible again, dissolved back into the other side of the unseeable air. But Ethan knew the others had seen them; they'd felt them too. They saw him make the particle wave with his hands. Will and Daniel were scared of his powers. He wasn't a piece of shit. They were wrong; they were liars. In his fingertips, Ethan had a unique gift. He could split open the hidden mysteries of the universe. See them with his eyes.

∞

After a promising day – of returning appetite, lucid conversation, sudden surges of energy – death felt far away. John's blood pressure and breathing were normal, his condition had stabilised. Tom went home and Mark relaxed into the night. It was an uneventful evening. Nurses checked on John from sunset to sunrise; the old man slept and ate. Mark eventually drifted off in the chair beside his father's bed.

Orange light cracked the dawn horizon and filled the hospital room. Mark stirred. He stood to shut the curtain, didn't want the light to disturb his dad. When he sat down again, he noticed John's face. His father looked pensive, that limp expression of being at peace: loose jaw, tension-free mouth. He wasn't moving, wasn't breathing. Softened muscles, hollow eyes. No, not yet. Mark had seen this before with his mother. He touched his father's hands. They were slightly warm, but too cold to still have life.

'Dad,' Mark said to his father's body. He wasn't sure why he felt the urge to speak to him. John wouldn't answer but Mark wasn't entirely convinced. 'Dad?'

The air conditioner rattled overhead. His mind went blank. As he watched his father's face drain of colour, Mark slowly became aware of the antiseptic finality of this moment. The thud of the end. His father was dead. That was it. No eleventh-hour declarations of unconditional love, no ultimate exoneration. Mark hadn't said everything he needed to say, done all the things he needed to do. There'd be no closure. Too late to cling on to that irrational splinter of hope, that perhaps this would end without any regrets. Time had run out.

Mark sat there for a while, unsure what to do next. Finally, he left the room to find someone. The hospital staff would know. He was startled but relieved, nauseous but light-headed as he approached reception. At least it was over. Terminal illness had the same dragged and driven inevitability as terminal velocity: a final speed we're all destined to ultimately reach. John wasn't in pain any more, but Mark felt winded. He hadn't anticipated sadness with such depth, this puncturing grief that excavated him, left a hole. As he tried to tell the staff about his father, Mark was incoherent with tears. Nurses gave him comforting smiles, offered consoling words. He went outside and called Tom.

Back in his father's room, the doctor pronounced John dead. He handed Mark the certificate in a sealed envelope, gave him a pat on the shoulder. Two nurses laid John's body out and asked about funeral arrangements. Mark had no idea. Tom knew all that stuff. They lifted his floppy arms and carefully wiped his creases, treating the old man's body with reverence. Under John's blankets, one nurse discovered a framed picture. She handed it to Mark.

The smiling face was a strange amalgamation of features he knew well. Ethan – it had to be. But the boy looked older than Mark expected. The last photograph he had of his son was taken over a decade ago. A baby on a red picnic blanket, with a toy tiger in his mouth, staring straight into the camera. Each time Mark looked at the picture, it felt like looking at Claire. Those blue eyes were hers; it was dislocating. He kept the photo in his wallet, but instead of proudly displaying it in the plastic window, it lived crumpled in a hidden compartment. Often he forgot it was there, tucked away behind old receipts.

Mark took the photograph out of the frame and put it into his pocket.

Tom arrived at the hospital before John's body was taken down to the mortuary. He carried several folders – colour-coded, labelled *Funeral, Important Documents, Will*. He'd also brought one of his daughters. Her dark eyes were red, her fists clutching damp wads of tissues.

'Angela loved her grandfather,' Tom said. 'They were very close.'

The little girl brushed her hair out of her eyes. She wore red leather shoes that made Mark think of his mother; Eleanor would've loved to buy her granddaughters beautiful shoes. Angela's fine hair was the most unusual colour: golden black. Inky until it hit the light, revealing accents of ashy-yellow.

'Is that really him?' she asked her father in a quiet voice.

Tom nodded. 'He looks different now that he's passed away, but that's Pop.'

Angela pulled on Tom's sleeve. 'No, is that my Uncle Mark?' She peeked up at Mark quickly, before looking at her red shoes.

Tom was distracted by paperwork. 'I forgot you haven't met him before. That's my brother.' He opened the folders and handed a piece of paper to the nurses. 'I'm his next of kin. When can I get the medical certificate of cause of death?'

The younger nurse pointed at Mark. 'It's already been prepared. We gave it to your brother.'

'No,' Tom said. 'All official documents must be given to me. I've been appointed the executor of my father's estate. I have it here, in writing. I need it for the funeral director.'

'It's just on the table, Tom,' Mark said, gesturing to the white envelope. Did his brother really think he'd hide the death certificate? 'Just there.'

Angela gave Mark an understanding smile. The clarity of her genes cheered and saddened him; she'd inherited Eleanor's pretty mouth.

'It's really nice to finally meet you, Angela,' Mark said, crouching down to speak to her eye to eye. She had perfect skin, powdery smooth. 'How old are you?'

'Eight and a half,' Angela whispered. She was missing a front tooth. 'How old are you, Uncle Mark?'

'Thirty-eight and a half. I guess you were born around the time of my thirtieth birthday.' Mark had spent his thirtieth birthday in Cessnock Correctional Centre. Three birthdays inside but he didn't celebrate one; it was never a good idea to draw attention to yourself. Although he wasn't treated as badly as the sex offenders, Mark had trouble making himself invisible. There weren't many other men like him behind those bars. The worst inmates were savvy, knew precisely how much Mark was displaced.

Tom pulled his daughter away. 'Come and say goodbye to Pop. Didn't you want to read him your letter? Then if you're a good girl, you can sit here and play on my phone while Daddy sorts some things out.'

The little girl nodded, tears swelling in her eyes. She took a piece of paper from her pocket and unfolded it carefully. Mark noticed Angela's handwriting; she wrote in clear cursive script, not like a child.

'Go on,' Tom said.

Angela nodded and took a deep breath. 'Dear Pop, I am very sorry to hear that you are dead. Our cat Toby is dead too, so maybe now that you are both dead, you can play with him. He was a nice cat, and I think he will be a nice cat for you in Heaven too. I will miss you and the stories you read to me and I will also miss the chocolate biscuits you always gave me at your house. I hope you won't forget me. I will never forget you. Goodbye, Pop. Love from your second-oldest granddaughter, Angela Olivia Lim Hall.'

Mark shed an unexpected tear, wiping it away quickly. The little girl loved her grandfather. In death, he saw a side of his father he hadn't known. Mark imagined those snatched moments of tenderness, of chocolate biscuits and reading books, and felt a strange yearning for the safe mask of childhood. But being a grandparent was different to being a parent. Angela would never grow up to know John as a flawed human being. Only as the kind, old man who she'd always miss.

'Beautiful,' Tom said. He handed Angela his smartphone. 'Here.'

She took it from her father's hands, swiping and tapping herself into some form of amusement. They waited outside the room as the nurses finished preparing John's body. His name had been rubbed off the whiteboard outside. Already erased.

'I managed to secure Friday afternoon for the funeral,' Tom said. 'The order of service and readings are already decided. I'll print the booklets later today, but I was hoping you'd help me choose a photo for the cover now so we could get it off to the printer. I've already sent the death notice to the newspaper.'

'Jesus, he's only been dead for a few hours,' Mark said.

'Dad and I planned everything before you arrived.' Tom took out a draft copy of the funeral booklet. 'So I'll give the first, more personal eulogy, and we've also asked his old colleague, Craig Brooks. You remember him. Actually, I think he's your godfather.' Tom paused for a moment. 'Do you want to be a pallbearer?'

Mark shrugged. 'Sure.'

'In that case, you won't be able to do the processional or recession. But that's okay, you can still go after the eulogies.'

'Go where?' Mark hated public speaking but was touched to be included in the service.

'Music,' Tom said. 'You'll play the violin. Like you did at Mum's.'

Mark hardly remembered their mother's funeral. That day was a heavy cloud of white wreaths, dark suits, strangers offering to keep him in their thoughts. Sitting through the service was like being in a vacuum. Airless, soundless, thoughtless – he couldn't remember how to breathe, hear or think. But his mother loved to hear him play the violin and he'd promised. She'd chosen the music herself, morbidly excited about deciding her funerary score.

The only vivid memory Mark had of her funeral was watching the steel strings of his violin vibrate as he pulled the bow against them. Bridge to nut harmonics of its friction force, wave velocity on a taut string. Music made from stress, beauty from tension. Mark was only nineteen years old then, and that soaring wonder of chasing mastery was effortless. He didn't yet know how easily that feeling could be lost.

'That was different,' Mark said. 'I can't play like that any more.'

'Just use the same piece. Nobody will notice.'

'No.' He hadn't touched his violin for years but that wasn't the point. 'It was for Mum. I played it for her.'

Tom gave him a weary look. 'Choose something. Anything. Just take some initiative, Mark. You're a grown-up. I shouldn't still need to give you directions, tell you what to do.'

Mark glanced at Angela, sitting in a plastic chair. Although she was looking down at the screen of the smartphone, the little girl was clearly listening to their conversation. She sat up straight and quickly glanced at the adults. As he caught her eye, Mark winked. She tried to wink back but didn't have full control of her facial muscles, making it look like a sneeze.

'Listen, I wanted to talk to you about the guest list too,' Tom said. 'Claire and Ethan —'

'No,' Mark said immediately. 'No way.'

'Dad wanted us to at least extend an invitation.'

'You can, if you want. Claire will say no. Guaranteed.'

'She got along with Dad.' His older brother spoke with certainty but Mark knew Tom had no idea. Claire tolerated John at best – ignoring his lewd jokes about how flexible she must be.

'She won't come.'

Tom ran a hand over his face. He looked uncannily like John when he did this. Mark was reminded of nights their father worked into the early morning at his desk – swearing, sighing, stressed – and loud classical music playing from downstairs as the children tried to fall asleep.

'Bach. I think Dad liked Bach,' Mark offered. 'Tom, I really need to get some sleep. I've been here all night. Let's talk later about booklets and photos. Great to meet you, Angela,' he said, waving at his niece.

And before Tom could bark any more instructions at him, Mark left. Turned his back to the palliative bays and post-war bricks.

Marched away from his father's body. His thoughts returned to Ethan. He took the photograph out of his pocket and looked at his son's face. In the boy's eyes, Mark saw something bright, something hopeful – thousands of volts of potential.

His every wrong turn was behind him now, fixed in the map of the past. Ahead, there was only the future. Mark didn't want to end up like John; he'd already lost enough time. For the first time in years, Mark felt optimistic. Perhaps his fate wasn't sealed. He was convalescent now, thrilled to see the last of this wretched hospital, sliding happily past people sitting in wheelchairs at the front gate and into the busy street.

I O

MASS

The morning was bright and hot; Ethan woke up sweating. It was a Saturday but he had another appointment with Dr Saunders. As his mum drove towards Randwick, warm breeze in their faces, they sang along to music on the radio together. Mum was a terrible singer. Instead of holding a tune, she yelled – she was always off-key and off-pitch. Her loud voice competed with the stereo, jumbling the vibrating frequencies in the air. Tangled waves of noise filled the car.

Ethan put his fingers in his ears. 'Mum! Stop! It hurts.'

She continued to sing, one hand tapping on the steering wheel.

'Hey, did you get my joke?' he asked. 'It hurts. Hertz is the unit for measuring frequency of sound. So in your case, bad singing.'

'Very funny.' His mum smiled. 'You're too clever for your own good.'

At the hospital, Dr Saunders had set up a dark-blue ping-pong table in the middle of his office. He bounced a ball on a paddle. 'Good morning, Ethan,' he said, keeping his eyes trained on the rebounding orange ball. 'Have you ever played ping-pong before?'

'Couple of times.' Ethan replied, squinting one eye.

'Good, we're going to play right now. Usually this table lives in my garage.' He handed Ethan a tired-looking paddle; its red rubber coat was peeling at the edges, its handle was discoloured and scuffed. 'I should warn you, I was a ping-pong champion at university. Won the Table Tennis Tournament three years in a row. Bit rusty these days, but watch out. You're in for a thumping.'

Ethan grinned. This was going to be fun, although he couldn't figure out what this had to do with his brain. Dr Saunders served and Ethan returned the ball with a gentle tap. They hit the ball to each other a few times like this – back and forth, tap to tap – until the ball rolled on the floor.

'Okay,' Dr Saunders said, kneeling down and reaching for the ball. 'So far, I've been going easy on you. Ready to step this up a notch?'

'Yep!' Ethan widened his stance and prepared his paddle.

The doctor took out a bowl full of orange ping-pong balls and put it on his side of the table. One by one with a snap of the wrist and paddle, he served the balls to Ethan. Now Ethan missed every shot. The balls were curving and spinning – bending erratically in sudden twists and turns – so even though they looked aimed in his direction, they flew off at another angle.

Ethan studied the balls carefully, the way they veered away on unexpected paths. Eventually he saw it: their trajectories. They were deviating, and he was almost sure he knew why. Dr Saunders hit another ping-pong ball. As it crossed the net, it swerved to the left. Ethan held his paddle out. Tap. He struck the ball.

'Wonderful!' Dr Saunders said. 'How did you figure it out?'

'Figure what out?'

'I was serving you curveballs.'

Ethan paused for a moment to consider his answer. 'Air. It was happening because of the air.'

'Go on,' Dr Saunders urged.

'Well,' Ethan began. 'Ping-pong balls are light, so they have a small mass and low density. So air has more of an effect on them.'

'But why does that make them curve?' The doctor held his paddle out to serve another ball. 'Would you like to see again? I'll do a topspin serve this time. Tell me what you see.'

Dr Saunders served another ball. The rubber paddle grazed its surface. Ethan watched the ball glide over the table. It was spinning on an axis. The top of the ball was going in the same direction as the ball, but the bottom of the ball was moving in the opposite direction to the motion of the ball.

'Air pressure,' Ethan said quickly. 'It's because of the air pressure. Gravity and spin work together to make the ball drop. Because the air pressure below the ball is lower, topspin reduces lift and that makes the ball dip downward.'

Dr Saunders held out another orange ball. 'What about with backspin?' He hit the ball. This time the top went in the opposite direction to the movement of the ball, while the base moved in the same direction as the motion of the ball. It gave the ball lift, sent it upwards unexpectedly.

'Lift and drag,' Ethan said. 'When you did the topspin, the air pressure at the top of the ball was high and at the bottom, the air pressure was low. So at the top, the ball's velocity is low and at the bottom, it's high. It drags the ball downwards.'

'Exactly!' Dr Saunders held his paddle triumphantly in the air. 'And backspin?'

'The opposite,' Ethan said, breathless with enthusiasm. 'Gravity and backspin work against each other. High velocity and low air pressure at the top, and low velocity and high air pressure at the bottom. So it lifts the ball up.'

'And you could see it, couldn't you?' Dr Saunders put his paddle down. 'You could see the air pressure and the velocity. With your eyes.'

Ethan gave him a cautious nod. 'It looked like a comet.'

'It's called the Magnus effect. You described it perfectly. People have taken photos of the Magnus effect on a golf ball underwater, and it did look like a comet. Come take a seat, Ethan,' Dr Saunders said. 'There's something important I need to tell you.'

Ethan sat down. Behind the doctor's chair were lots of certificates: degrees, honours, certifications with gold embossing and his name written in ink.

'I've been thinking a lot about what you said, how you saw the red–blue shift. At first I thought maybe you were suffering from synaesthesia, but I think it might actually be far more complex and exciting than that.'

'What's that?' Ethan asked. He tried to repeat the word but struggled to pronounce it correctly. '*Sin-ess-thee-sia?*'

'A neurological condition. Synaesthesists mix up their senses. Someone might see the number one and think it's green, or see smells and sounds as colours. Taste a roast dinner when they read a map. Do you remember when I spoke to you in the hospital about how the brain rewires itself?' Dr Saunders asked. 'About neuroplasticity?'

'Yeah.' Ethan's foot jiggled involuntarily. He pressed his palm hard against his knee to keep himself still.

'While we don't know exactly what causes it, when someone has synaesthesia their brain gets cross-wired. So if the neural pathways between the area in the brain associated with numbers and the area associated with space get cross-activated, then it might cause a synaesthesist to see numbers as shapes. But I don't think you have synaesthesia. Your symptoms aren't consistent with it. What I suspect you may have is extremely rare. You can see waves and pressure and velocity – the forces of physics. Stuff nobody else can see with the naked eye.'

'Like how mass causes inertia? How it looks the same as energy?'

Dr Saunders opened his notebook and wrote on a blank page. 'Can you really see all that? Have you always been able to see these sorts of things?'

Ethan thought back. There'd always been something: a shimmering line, bursts of light, electricity powering light bulbs, the clarity of distance between stars in the night sky. Flashes that sharpened over time – Ethan learned to understand them – like how squiggling lines of sound were wavelengths, how the fireworks he could see were just forces doing their job.

'For as long as I can remember,' he said.

Dr Saunders hesitated. 'Newborn brains are remarkable. They've already formed millions and millions of neurons in the womb. At birth, most of these neurons aren't connected yet. So when babies see or taste something for the first time, it creates a little burst of electrical activity that connects their neurons. That connection is called a synapse, and during the first two years of an infant's life they form twice as many synapses as they'll have as an adult.'

Ethan imagined bolts of lightning flashing inside his grey brain, connecting neuron to neuron. Electrical storms in his mind. 'What happens to the other synapses?'

'Some of the weak connections die off, while the frequently used synapses get stronger.' Dr Saunders paused. 'How old are you again, Ethan?'

'Twelve.'

'When you had your brain injury, you were still forming synapses at an astounding rate. The cerebral contusion in your cortical tissue – like a bruise inside your brain – meant that instead of forming synapses in that particular region, you were forced to make them somewhere else. So these connections developed in other parts of your brain.

I think your brain injury has uncovered something latent in unexplored regions of the brain. And these connections have strengthened over time.'

Ethan was confused. 'What does latent mean?'

'Something hiding. Let me tell you about a similar case. A ten-year-old boy was hit hard in the head with a baseball. It knocked him unconscious, fractured his skull and caused a haemorrhage. The boy went to hospital, recovered and then went back to his normal life. But he was different after his brain injury. Suddenly saw equations and numbers everywhere. He became a mathematical genius overnight. He could calculate impossible sums in his mind in a flash, recite pi up to twenty thousand decimals.'

'But how'd he know how to do those calculations?'

'That's what I meant by something hiding. All this information might have already been hardwired into his brain – we call that "genetic memory". Turned out, the boy had distant ancestors who'd studied mathematics and the brain injury made him able to access this hidden treasure trove imprinted inside his brain. He even saw equations as fractals.'

'Me too,' Ethan said. 'I can see fractals too.'

'Could you draw one for me?' The doctor handed Ethan a sheet of paper and a pen. 'This boy who was hit in the head was diagnosed as an acquired savant. Do you know what a savant is?'

Ethan shook his head. He'd never heard that word before. But the existence of a word that might describe him was brightening, immediately made him feel less alone. He wasn't imagining it. He wasn't a freak. The pencil trembled in his hand. Ethan drew a rough image of the geometry inside his head. Sweeping patterns of recurring line after line; unravelling labyrinths of snowflaked galaxies; knotted angles that crystallised into the tiniest chaos.

'A savant is someone with extraordinary skill. Like being able to memorise the phone book. Calendar savants can tell you the day of the week when you mention any date. Often people with savant syndrome are autistic,' Dr Saunders explained. 'They sit somewhere on the spectrum. Some of them can't even tie their shoe but can recite every prime number. Extraordinary skill is sometimes compensation for an extraordinary deficiency.'

Sitting on the spectrum made Ethan think of a row of chairs running along a rainbow. 'Newton's third law states that every action has an equal and opposite reaction,' he said, not looking up from the paper.

Dr Saunders looked at Ethan's fractal drawing. 'You're left-handed, how interesting. Anyway, because you had such severe developmental delays as an infant, we kept a close eye on you. Did a lot of diagnostic testing when you were small. You didn't meet the criteria for autism.'

'Okay,' Ethan said. Testing, lots of testing. He didn't recall any of that.

'On the other hand, acquired savant syndrome happens when these savant skills emerge after a brain injury or sometimes because of disease. Like the boy who got hit with a baseball. He wasn't born with it, but something made his brain change. It's exceptionally rare. There are only fifty cases in the world and none yet in Australia. If you have this, Ethan, it would be groundbreaking to say the least. You're the most interesting brain-injury case I've ever seen. You can see physics! Neurologists all over the world will want to meet you.' The doctor looked at Ethan intently for a moment, as if he'd forgotten how to blink.

'Einstein said it wasn't that he was so smart, he just stayed with problems longer,' Ethan said.

The doctor spoke hurriedly. 'Of course, we'll need to do some more

tests before I write anything conclusive. But this is potentially very
exciting stuff. You'll be in journals, maybe the subject of documentaries,
and mentioned in books. Physicists will want to speak to you as well.'

Ethan looked up from his drawing. 'Like Stephen Hawking?' He
imagined flying to Cambridge to shake his hero's hand; that would be
huge. But Stephen Hawking was getting old now. How much longer
would he still be alive? Newton's third law – it always made Ethan
feel sad. Every action had an equal and opposite reaction for famous
cosmologists too. As Hawking's mind advanced, his body declined.

'May I keep this drawing? Remarkable.' Dr Saunders studied the
fractal for a moment, then glanced at the clock on his wall. 'We'll
have to continue this next week. I need to show this picture to my
colleagues. Thanks for the game of ping-pong.'

'Can I have this ball?'

'Of course,' Dr Saunders said absent-mindedly. He didn't look up
from the drawing, lost in the centre of the fractal's topography.

Ethan put the ping-pong ball into his pocket and returned to his
mum.

'Everything okay?' she asked.

He nodded.

They walked out of the doctor's office and into the blue day.
Summer was almost here and even though it was only morning, the
warmth of ultraviolet rays pierced Ethan's tingling skin. Frangipanis
had fallen on the footpath. He looked up at the white burst of the
cancerous sun, felt its retina-burn, before looking to his mum.

'Mum, the sun has 99.8 per cent of our solar system's total mass.'

His mum looked ahead. 'I didn't know it was so heavy.'

'Yeah.' Ethan held his arms out in front of him. He looked at
the sun's chaotic mix of hot plasma and magnetic fields; the weight
of its dense cocktail of hydrogen, helium, oxygen, carbon, neon, iron;

the fractal geometry of raging solar winds and flares. Up there, he knew space-time warped. The sun's huge mass bent radio and light waves nearby.

Ethan threw the ping-pong ball in the air. The orange ball hovered for a moment in front of the sun – like the corona of a solar eclipse – but on the way back down, the ball didn't fall in a straight line. Its trajectory warped. The ball landed in his hand. Ethan knew it. Even though Earth's mass was only 0.0003 per cent of the solar system, he could see space-time curve down here too.

∞

Mark and Tom caught the train to Circular Quay to meet the lawyer. His firm's office building had won design and innovation awards; spaceship-like with curved cosmic steels, cylinder-shaped with a glass façade. One of those five-star, green, sustainable buildings – low emissions, recycled water system, zero waste. Sydney loved a trend and sustainability was its current craze. Mark found it weird. The city he'd known was built on excess and now conservation was the hottest thing. Sure, the science of climate change was solid. But all the hysteria about environmental equilibrium? The laws of physics didn't work like that; you couldn't have simultaneous balance and change.

They were early for their appointment and quietly drank a coffee in the forecourt cafe before heading inside. Tom handed Mark a temporary name-tag and they followed a security guard to the burnished lift door. The building's interior core had a ring of glass elevators – crystal capsules whooshing up, plunging down – like transparent rockets launching into space. Mark staggered as their lift rushed up the shaft. People in the lobby looked as small as ants and the drop gave him vertigo chills. His eyes went out of focus. Walls closed in; he felt strangled by the tight space. Everything swirled and multiplied – three copies of Tom's face, three pairs of his shoes. Mark turned his back to the elevator window, looking away from the building's abyss.

'You okay?' Tom asked.

Mark wiped his forehead. 'Yeah.'

With a sudden suck of air, the doors opened on the twenty-first floor. Their father's lawyer was there to greet them, shaking their hands before they'd stepped out of the lift.

'Boys,' the lawyer said. 'Good to see you again.'

Mark raised an eyebrow at Tom; they clearly weren't boys any longer. Richard Townsend was an old friend of John's – they went to school together, were on the same rowing team more than fifty years ago. Richard had always been their father's lawyer. And even though he wasn't qualified – he practised business law, not criminal – he'd represented Mark at his trial. Qualifications didn't always matter in this city. What mattered was if you were a member of an exclusive old boy's club.

Mark hated this side of privileged Sydney. It was ugly and claustrophobic, but he'd bought into it once, was seduced by the idea of belonging. There was something easy about its durable membership. Sydney's most elite boys educational institutions were members of what were called the Great Public Schools. GPS for short. Being an old boy of a certain school was its own global positioning system – grown men still used their alma mater as a tracking device, how they positioned themselves within a tiny world.

'Please,' said Richard. 'Take a seat.'

He opened the door to his office suite, revealing a curved floor-to-ceiling window. The harbour view was spectacular: frothy whites and deep teals of Port Jackson, yellows and greens of the catamaran ferries navigating the harbour basin. Mark shut one eye, the glare of the midday sun reflecting off the water. His mother had once told him that several of Sydney's ferries were named after ships of the First Fleet: *Alexander, Borrowdale, Charlotte, Fishburn, Friendship, Golden Grove, Scarborough, Sirius, Supply*. Mark liked this baptism, how the First Fleet was given a second life. He liked to think the original ships – still driving and heeling, sailing upwind into eternity – haunted the deepest waters of Sydney Harbour.

'Great funeral, boys,' Richard said. 'Really great. Best I've been to for a long time. And I'm an old bastard, I go to a lot of funerals these days.'

'Thanks,' Tom said. 'Dad would've been really happy with it.'

Mark laughed uncomfortably. 'I don't know. He probably found at least one thing that wasn't up to scratch. During the service, I kept imagining him opening his coffin and yelling at us to start again.' Mark imitated his father's voice. 'Get it right, boys!'

Tom looked embarrassed but it was true. They were still seeking their father's approval even though he was dead.

'Let's talk about the estate,' Richard said. 'You've both seen and read the will by now, I believe?'

'Not yet,' said Mark.

Tom and Richard exchanged a look. All week, Tom had badgered his brother about the will; Mark kept putting it off. Luckily, in the days since their father's death, there was a lot to keep him busy. Arrangement of affairs, paperwork, packing up. Legal documents could wait. And Mark didn't really want to know what was in the will. His gut told him it'd probably be another blow.

'Your father was an organised man. John certainly had a mind for business. Didn't want his money lost to the tax office. Tom has assets in his name already,' Richard explained. 'Like John's superannuation fund, so it wouldn't be taxed on his death. It's 16.5 per cent. Robbery.'

'Okay,' Mark said. 'So everything goes to Tom, right? I'm sure that's how Dad wanted to play it.'

'Not exactly. Tom isn't the only beneficiary.' He opened a folder and took out a stapled document. Richard's wrinkled hands shook as he offered the papers to Mark. 'Here, have a look.'

Revoke, appoint, declare, bequeath – its legal jargon was another tongue. Mark already had an inkling his father had written him out of the will. There was no financial compensation for breaking the rules. When Mark needed to go to court, the family paid his legal fees. Thousands of dollars, top barristers, the best solicitors, billed hour after hour; John knew they were investing in the fight for the truth. But there was no justice for his wallet in a guilty verdict, in the hefty bills left over after proceedings had ended. So John made it clear, years ago: Mark didn't deserve his inheritance. Eleanor might have fought for him, if she was still alive. But she wasn't. He didn't have anyone else on his side.

'What am I looking at?' Mark asked.

Richard flipped to the next page and pointed. 'Here.'

Mark squinted. He read the paragraph aloud. 'I give the sum of $10000 to Guide Dogs Australia. That's nice of him. I give my book collection to my granddaughters, Angela Hall, Amy Hall and Alice Hall. I give my Rolex Oyster Perpetual watch to my youngest son, Mark Halley Hall.' He paused and looked up at Richard. 'Is this why we're here? Because he left me his Rolex. How generous of you, Dad.'

Richard frowned. 'Keep going.'

'I appoint my son Thomas Anthony Hall my sole executor,' Mark continued. 'No surprises there. I give a 50 per cent share of my property both real and personal to my son, Thomas Anthony Hall.' His eyes darted over the text and his voice slowed down. 'I give the remaining

50 per cent share of my estate both real and personal unto my trustee upon trust for my grandson, Ethan Francis Forsythe, until he should come of age.'

Mark read the section again, repeating it to himself. It was disjointing to read Ethan's name on paper, see it in print. Claire had legally changed the child's surname to hers but when the baby was born – when they'd filled out the official forms for his birth certificate together – Ethan had been a Hall. 'Wow,' Mark said finally. 'Look at that.'

Tom leaned forward in his chair. 'Please don't be upset.'

'I'm not.'

'This was just what Dad wanted.'

'And you've known about this all along?'

Richard removed his glasses and cleaned them with a small cloth. 'Tom needs to apply for a grant of probate from the Supreme Court. Before John's assets can be released and distributed.' He fogged up his lenses with a few warm breaths then continued to wipe the glasses. 'And we've been concerned that you might contest the will.'

Mark narrowed his eyes. 'What do you mean?'

'Under certain grounds, when someone has been excluded from a will, they can contest it. Make a claim for a larger share of the estate than what's been specified,' Richard said. 'You're eligible. As a child of the deceased.'

'And go back to court?' Mark imagined more solicitors, affidavits, summons. Just the thought of the Supreme Court made his blood congeal. 'No, thanks.'

'Not necessarily,' Richard said. 'We could negotiate, arrange something that makes everyone happy through mediation. The matter doesn't necessarily need to go to court. You're more than welcome to seek your own legal advice about this.'

The office was quiet for a moment. Mark looked out the window at the sparkling harbour, its diamonds of salt bright on the surface. It was that precise angle of the day when the sun caught the water – when their star turned the waves into light. He looked down at the paper in his hands again. His father's instructions. Still hurting him from the grave. But there was something liberating about not being included. He knew he didn't need his family's money to survive.

'I did always love that watch,' Mark said brightly.

'You won't contest?' Tom asked. 'Are you sure?'

Richard gave them both a stern look. 'Perhaps you should speak to another lawyer before making this decision, Mark. I could give you some names. Once probate is granted, it'll be too late to make a claim.'

'No,' Mark said. 'I don't want to.'

His brother looked at him kindly; it was an expression he hadn't seen on Tom's face for years. 'I need to get in touch with Claire about this,' Tom said. 'Ethan's share will go into a trust until he turns eighteen, but if she wants to release any funds early to pay for school fees or something, we can negotiate a plan.'

'I can do it. We've been in touch. I'll speak with her.'

'You have?'

Mark shrugged. 'We had coffee.'

Richard stood up. 'Well, we can make an application for probate as soon as possible then. I'll get my assistant to put a draft together for you to approve. And Tom, let's look into opening an account to consolidate the assets. Maybe start making some enquiries about selling the house.' He stretched out an arm and shook their hands. 'Boys. Good to see you both. I'll walk you out.'

'Thank you, Rick,' Tom said. 'I'll call you later.'

As they waited for the lift, Mark turned to Tom. 'I didn't realise you planned to sell the house.'

'Of course, no point keeping it now Dad's gone. We'll need to start packing everything up. Giving stuff away.'

Mark was silent. That was their mother's house and their mother's stuff. He didn't want to give anything of hers away.

'You can still stay there,' Tom said. 'Until we're ready to go to auction.'

'Thanks.' Mark stepped into the lift and pressed the button. Then they were free-falling back to Earth, plummeting to the ground floor. G-force emptied his lungs, pulled blood away from his head. With the indistinguishable forces of the equivalence principle – gravity felt like acceleration, acceleration like gravity – Mark momentarily realised that whatever he felt, looking down the building's atrium, also felt exactly like pain.

∞

Claire waited for the doctor in his consulting room. Several framed photographs cluttered his desk but faced the other way; she couldn't see who was in the pictures. Today's newspaper was spread across the table, the crossword almost complete. Claire tilted her head as she tried to read the upside-down clues.

The door opened. Dr Saunders smiled, before taking a seat at his desk. 'I have Ethan's test results here. I wanted to talk to you about them.'

'Is something wrong?'

'No, not exactly.' He handed her some sheets of paper. 'Let's go over the neuropsychologist's assessment first. Ethan took an IQ test, the Wechsler Intelligence Scale for Children. Pretty standard for kids under sixteen. But we had Ethan take it twice.' The doctor paused. 'To say he aced it both times would be an understatement. Ethan's IQ is high genius level, around 170. Our neuropsych has never seen anything like it.'

Claire cast her eyes over the report. Her son's results were on the furthest side of the bell curve, in the top 1 per cent. 'I don't understand. When Ethan was five and assessed before, here in this very hospital, I was told his development was well below average. That he had a significant receptive and expressive language disorder. I've always known he was bright and never believed those assessments. Now you're telling me you think Ethan is a genius?'

'Genius isn't always expressed as solidly as you might think. Asynchronicity in early cognitive development does happen. Late talking is quite common in gifted people. Einstein himself didn't speak until he was four. Based on Ethan's results in the various intelligence and memory tests, and taking into account his brain injury, I think his abilities actually go beyond genius. Ethan isn't just a child prodigy. I think your son may be a savant.'

'Like *Rain Man*?' She shook her head. 'I don't think so. Ethan's not autistic.'

'Claire, I understand your hesitation. Most people hear that word and think idiot savant. Not all people with savant syndrome have autism, just as not all autistic people are savants. Ethan's what we call an acquired savant. It's a very rare phenomenon, where savant skills emerge after a traumatic brain injury. Where the injury itself rewires the brain.'

'You mean he's been a savant since he was a baby?'

'Exactly. Primary damage in Ethan's brain is concentrated in the left anterior temporal lobe, where the associative memory system is normally located. But when higher regions in the cortex fail, older parts of the brain – like the basal ganglia in the subcortex – take over. His healthy right hemisphere compensated for damage to the left.

Ethan has a remarkable memory; his skills were above the ceiling in every memory test. But I don't think it's a question of the boy simply having good recall. Ethan stores memories in the ancient, more primitive parts of the brain. Like the memory that never forgets how to ride a bike. His brain is very sticky. He actually can't forget.'

'His memory isn't so great when I remind him to clean his room.'

Dr Saunders showed her another piece of paper. 'Typically, the memory of a savant is very narrow but infinitely deep. Memory aside, I want to talk to you about his remarkable splinter skill. As I'm sure you know, Ethan has a remarkably intuitive understanding of physics.'

'He always has,' Claire said. She looked at the picture – hand-drawn lines that spiralled like a cobweb. 'Did Ethan draw that?'

'I showed this drawing to a physicist friend of mine. Apparently, this is a perfect schematic of a black hole warping space-time.'

'Really? Ethan draws pictures like that all the time.'

'Has he displayed any other special skills?'

'Ethan just knows things, I suppose. He could count before he knew numbers. I think he was calculating inside his head before he could talk. When he was a baby, he liked mirrors and shadows. He studied his toys instead of played with them. He used to make sundials in the backyard from paddle-pop sticks. He's always loved looking at stars.'

Dr Saunders removed his glasses. 'This might sound a little crazy, but I think Ethan can see physics. Complex things the rest of us hardly understand.'

Claire frowned. 'But how? Ethan hasn't studied the theories, he doesn't have any formal training in physics. Besides reading some textbooks and watching documentaries. He's just a little boy.'

'Some neurologists believe that when we're born, the brain isn't a blank slate. It comes loaded with factory-installed software. What's called "genetic memory". Like when an elderly woman with dementia, who's never painted before, suddenly becomes a prodigious artist. With acquired savant syndrome, these dormant skills emerge after illness or injury. Genetic memory might explain why Ethan knows things he's never learned, why he has an innate, perhaps inherited, knowledge of the complex rules of theoretical physics. Correct me if I'm wrong, but I recall his father was . . .'

'A theoretical physicist.' She looked down at her lap.

'Prodigious savants are extremely rare, Claire. Less than one hundred known savants exist in the world. You should be proud of yourself too. Ethan's talents are more than just genes and circuits. I'm sure they've also been propelled along by your love and support.'

She nodded, unsure what to say.

The doctor continued. 'With your consent, I'd like Ethan to meet with some professors from the physics department at the university. They're very interested to meet Ethan. Despite the odds against him, Ethan is a remarkably gifted child.'

As she listened to Dr Saunders, Claire felt like she was walking underwater. She knew what it was like to be called gifted, understood the danger of that word. Talent didn't mean anything; natural ability only got you so far. Hard work, perseverance, sweat, tears, blood – that was what real dreams were made from. She'd surrendered to ballet, completely sacrificed herself to it, before being given the gift of performing on stage. But for Claire, that gift had come wrapped in a tainted double-bind.

Her mother enrolled her in ballet classes at the local dance school when Claire was six years old. Rose had always wanted to be a performer; all her life she'd been told she belonged on stage. But Claire wasn't the sort of child who enjoyed being noticed. Attention was terrifying: she'd hide behind her mother's skirts to avoid it and squeeze her eyes shut, pretending she was invisible.

Before classes began, they caught the train into the city to shop at the Strand Arcade. Strong coffee smells filled the tiled promenade, white light spilled from the glass ceiling. Claire gripped her mother's hand as they climbed the winding cedar staircase. Upstairs in the dance store, Rose grabbed handfuls of black leotards and pink tights, ribbons and ballet slippers, and pushed the little girl into a dressing room.

Claire stood in front of the mirror and looked at her reflection. Wearing the clinging leotard made her feel naked; the stockings were itchy and skin-tight. She pulled at her underpants, bunched uncomfortably between her legs.

'Stop that, Claire,' Rose said. 'It's not very elegant.'

A shop assistant approached them. 'What a beautiful little girl you have! Look at that pretty blonde hair. That size looks good. Do a little spin for us, love.'

Claire twirled across the store in the new pink slippers and took a small bow. Other customers and the shop assistants clapped. Her mother blinked, surprised.

'Good sense of rhythm. Natural. She's got the body for it too,' one saleswoman said. 'Right proportions.'

'Thank you,' Rose said, her eyes lighting up.

In the beginning, Claire found ballet akin to torture: blistered feet, her hair pulled into buns so tight they made her eyes water, bobby pins stabbing her scalp, hairspray stinging her eyeballs. But she did it for her mum; it made her happy. Every afternoon she drove Claire to lessons and rehearsals; every evening was a drill of stretches to improve her flexibility. Rose held her daughter's legs over her head, pulled her heels off the floor, pushed Claire's body down – degree by excruciating degree – until she could do the splits.

After being cast in her first lead role, there was praise: 'You're my shining star,' her mother said. 'I love you so much.' But when the girl fell or tripped, she was punished. So Claire learned how to be perfect – perfect posture, perfect balance, perfect technique – to earn her mother's love.

Eventually, Claire found her own joy in dancing. With every lesson, her passion bloomed. But there was something sour about it, that each jump and pirouette had to feed her mother's ego. Rose's dream of her daughter as a prima ballerina was so vivid that she lost sight of her child. No matter how hard she practised, Claire still felt invisible, like the little girl hiding behind her mother's legs.

Rose recorded each recital then forced Claire to watch the videos, making note of every wrong step, often pushing her daughter to tears. But Claire found refuge from the pressure in ballet itself. By the time she was twelve, she was taking fifteen lessons a week. At the barre, she decompressed; in the studio, she felt lighter than air. She enjoyed the hard work, the sense of accomplishment, the firmness of purpose.

As Claire's stamina and strength grew, her mother's currencies – beauty, elegance, grace – stopped having value. Claire discovered that her achievements were her own. Her ballet teacher recognised her talent, telling Rose that girls like her daughter made her job worthwhile. That if she got to teach one student like Claire in her entire career, she was extremely lucky.

When she was fifteen, Claire auditioned for full-time training at the Sydney Ballet School. On the day that the letter of offer arrived, Rose wept uncontrollably. Claire assumed they were happy tears but a few weeks later, her mother left. Moved interstate to live with another man. Claire watched Rose push her face creams and make-up off the dressing table and into a suitcase, before walking out the door. This didn't make sense, hadn't Claire done everything right, everything her mother ever wanted? She was meticulous, constantly evaluating and re-evaluating her turnout, making sure her alignment was always correct. She'd been dedicated, focused, flawless, every step of the way.

So Claire channelled that confusion into ballet, practised six days a week. She'd always had good technique and the right body – small head, long neck, long legs – so physically, she was a machine. But after her mother moved away, something inside Claire transformed. Emotions spilled from her fingertips and pointed toes, her eyes projected every feeling, there was a new intensity behind every *frappe* and *développé*. She wasn't just dancing any more; Claire was performing. Sweating and panting, the weight inside her chest would lift. Now when Claire stepped on stage, she no longer wanted to hide. It felt powerful – moving the audience, telling a story, turning her body into art. Suddenly she had presence and commanded attention. Claire wasn't invisible. Performing felt like being loved.

Sometimes she'd speak to her mother on the phone – exchange clicks, switchboard songs, that dilated silence before the call connected over border-crossing wires. Rose never asked questions about ballet, and never came to see her daughter dance again. Long after her mother hung up, Claire would keep the receiver against her ear and listen to the binary music of the signals and tones.

It took becoming a parent for Claire to understand why Rose left. How motherhood could easily annihilate whatever came before it. Basking in reflected applause wasn't enough; Claire's success threw Rose's lost dreams into sharp relief. They'd danced a dangerous pas de deux: she needed her mother's love, but fighting to win it drove Rose further away. Parenting a shining star meant being overshadowed.

Without realising, Claire had eclipsed her mother but her mother couldn't live without the light.

For a moment, Claire was lost staring into Ethan's drawing of a black hole. She blinked and looked up at the doctor. 'Dr Saunders,' she began. 'This might be a stupid question. Are there any other ways people can become savants?'

'Besides autism, there's always some underlying brain disorder. Developmental disabilities, meningitis, brain damage following premature births, stroke, seizure disorders. And of course, brain injury.'

'But is it possible that Ethan wasn't actually a victim of shaken baby syndrome? That he had another underlying brain disorder?'

'Over the last few years, I've read reports that claim SBS was a fad diagnosis. I'll be honest; we understand it better now than we did twelve years ago. Back when Ethan was a baby, we knew much less.'

'So you're not 100 per cent sure Ethan was shaken?'

Dr Saunders stared at the wall. 'There are lots of sceptics who say it's impossible to shake a baby without breaking their neck. That SBS doesn't exist, that the triad of symptoms is caused by something else. But I've worked at this hospital for thirty years. I've seen babies die from non-accidental head injuries. There's no question it's real. Even with Ethan, though, I can never be completely certain of a diagnosis like that; I wasn't in the room. I'm never 100 per cent sure.'

Claire cleared her throat. 'But mostly.'

'Oh yes, mostly. Besides, brain injury almost always impairs rather than enhances. Even with Ethan's abilities, he's still been a very sick child.'

All Claire wanted was a normal childhood for her son, but it was already too late for that. It was true: Ethan had been a very sick child. And genius? Savant syndrome? That was loaded with more potential stress. Claire hated the idea of Ethan being under the enormous pressure she'd felt – to be gifted, to perform. But what if she held him back? What if Ethan really could see physics? Maybe his gift could make some difference to the world.

'So, what do you think about Ethan meeting these professors?' Dr Saunders asked.

'Sure, he can speak to the physicists,' Claire said. 'Let's find out what's going on.'

11

ENERGY

After school, Mum took Ethan to a meeting at Sydney Uni. They walked along Carillon Avenue, under the Moreton Bay fig trees, and through the sandstone gate. Across the campus, some students were playing rugby on the oval. As they threw the ball at each other, Ethan noticed how their hands sparked with kinetic energy.

'Mum, look!' He pointed at a street sign. 'Physics Road. Can we please live here?'

'We need to find the Slade Lecture Theatre.'

They stood under the sandstone archway of a long white building. Above the wooden door was a sign that said 'School of Physics'. His mum led the way; she seemed stressed, fiddling with the strap of her handbag.

In the lecture theatre, Dr Saunders was waiting for them. He stood beside a woman and a man. The room had a high ceiling, rows of wooden benches and desks, and chalk-covered blackboards that reached all the way up to the roof.

'Awesome,' Ethan said, admiring the equations written in chalk.

'This is Professor Skinner,' Dr Saunders said, gesturing to the woman beside him. 'She's a lecturer here; her speciality is astrophysics. And this is Dr Thorp, he's a cosmologist.'

The boy shook both their hands. 'Cosmologist, cool. Like Stephen Hawking.'

'And this is Ethan, who I've been telling you about. He's twelve years old. And his mother, Claire.'

'Hello.' Mum's voice was small. She pointed at the benches. 'Should I just take a seat back here?'

'I'll join you,' the doctor said. 'Let's watch.'

Professor Skinner switched off the lights and turned on a projector. Pictures of planets were cast onto a huge screen. 'Ethan, I thought we'd talk about the solar system today. Do you know much about it?'

He shrugged. 'I guess.'

'Great. Let's start with Mercury.' The professor changed the slide. 'What can you tell me about this planet?'

Ethan straightened his back. 'Um, Mercury is only a little bit bigger than the moon. It doesn't have an atmosphere; it has an exosphere instead. That's why it's hotter on Venus, even though Mercury is closer to the sun, because Venus has an atmosphere even thicker than Earth does. And a year on Mercury is eighty-eight days, but a Mercury day is fifty-eight days and fifteen hours on Earth.'

The professor smiled. 'Why do you think days on Mercury are so long?'

'It rotates on its axis slowly because it orbits the sun quickly. So from sunrise to sunset it's already orbited the sun twice.'

'Anything else about its orbit?'

'Mercury's orbit is elliptical but it moves slightly, it's kinda weird. As it orbits the sun, the ellipse rotates. That's because gravity bends space-time, and there's more of it near the sun, so obviously that makes the perihelion shift.'

Dr Thorp and Professor Skinner gave each other a strange look. They showed him more slides, of other planets and distant dwarfs, comets and asteroid belts. As they asked questions, Ethan rattled off everything he knew about the solar system, planet by planet: how seasons on Uranus last only twenty days, how Jupiter is like a cosmic vacuum cleaner and sucks things up, how asteroids can have their own moons, how Saturn would float.

After an hour, Dr Thorp turned the lights in the lecture theatre back on.

Ethan let his eyes adjust. 'So, how did I do?'

Dr Saunders came down from the wooden benches. 'It wasn't a test, Ethan. But I must admit, I'm sure everyone is pretty impressed with your very comprehensive knowledge of space. How come you know all this?'

'I read some textbooks in the library. But it all just makes sense to me. I don't know.'

Professor Skinner smiled. 'You know much more about how the solar system works off the top of your head than most of my students, even the postgrads.'

'Fascinating,' Dr Saunders said. 'Your brain is certainly very special. They do say there are as many neurons in the brain as there are stars in the Milky Way.'

'More than one hundred billion?' Ethan asked.

'I must admit I've never counted personally. Did you see anything interesting today? Like what happened with the ping-pong ball? Anything like that.'

Ethan shook his head. 'Excuse me but I'm busting. I really need to use the toilet.'

'Hold on, I'll go with you.' Mum came out to the hallway with him. 'There's a bathroom just around this corner.'

He gave her a funny look. 'How do you know? Have you been here before?'

'No, never,' she said quickly.

But Ethan knew that even though those words had just come out of her mouth, the rest of her face was really saying yes.

∞

Claire raised her face to the sun. Office workers spilled from buildings and into the city streets. Rush hour crowded the footpaths; pedestrians elbowed each other along the sidewalk as they hurried home. She walked from her office to her bus stop, through the narrow alleys of The Rocks. This old part of Sydney always reminded Claire of Ruth Park's *Playing Beatie Bow*, how any moment she might wander down a cobblestone path and walk into the past. Follow the little furry girl along Argyle Street and travel back in time. The Harbour Bridge would vanish; the Opera House would melt away.

Claire walked down to Dawe's Point Battery. Across Lavender Bay, the rosy-cheeked face of Luna Park smiled. She stood beside the chalky grey pylon and looked up at the arching iron of the bridge. Sea breeze hit her face. Traffic bellowed overhead, powering along the towering alloy. Her phone rang. She glanced at it vacantly, expecting it to be the office – she'd left a little early – or maybe Ethan's school. But it wasn't. It was Mark.

Claire held the phone to her ear and waited for him to speak. He didn't say anything. She heard him breathe and hesitate; she could almost hear him think.

'Hi,' Mark said finally.

'Hi,' she replied.

'I just wanted to let you know my dad passed away. Early last week.'

'Mark, I'm so sorry.' She took a deep breath. 'How are you doing?'

'I don't know. I'm okay, I guess. Sorry, I probably should've told you sooner. Meant to invite you to the funeral. It was on Friday. I'd planned to get in touch. There was so much to deal with and I just blanked out about it.'

'Don't worry, it's fine. It doesn't matter. Remember when my father died? I was a wreck.'

'You almost wore your pyjamas to his funeral. You were literally about to walk out the door in your slippers.'

Claire smiled. 'I'd forgotten about that.'

'What are you doing right now? Do you want to get a drink?'

'Oh, I can't. I should go home.' She paused, thinking back to when her own dad had passed away. Of how supportive Mark was then, how caring and attentive – literally slipping her dress over her head, putting shoes on her feet – while she was immobilised by grief. But that was the past; she knew better than to be mindlessly sentimental. 'Mark, I'm not sure it's a good idea.'

'Yeah, you're right. I've just felt really lost this last week. Thought it might be nice to see a familiar face but, like you said, it's not a good idea.'

His voice was strained; he sounded upset. His father had died days ago; of course Mark felt lost. Claire chastised herself for being insensitive. Perhaps he didn't have anyone else to talk to about it, Mark was only trying to express his feelings. She felt a small twinge of pity. After all, he'd helped her through her grief years ago. One drink wouldn't hurt. 'Mark, I'm sorry. Let's have a drink.'

He relaxed. 'Where are you?'

'The Rocks.'

'Does the Lord Nelson still exist?'

'I think so,' she said.

'See you there soon.'

Claire hung up the phone. She wasn't far from the pub and walked up the hill towards Argyle Place. The Lord Nelson's façade had been renovated and stripped back, revealing chisel marks made by convicts on harbour-quarried stone. The pub had its own brewery and the heavy smell of malt and yeast filled the air. She examined the grey wall for a moment, thinking about the convicts who'd carved those grooves in the rock.

Inside the pub, Claire went to the bathroom and tried to fix her hair. In the mirror, under the tungsten lights, she looked so much older than she remembered – exhausted, with dark circles under her eyes. Mark hadn't arrived yet so she ordered a glass of wine and sat at an available table.

'Sorry to keep you waiting.' Mark tapped her on the shoulder and she quickly stood up. He leaned in to give her a kiss but Claire twisted away. Their cheeks touched awkwardly. 'Let me just grab a beer,' he said.

She found herself staring at him while he stood at the bar, admiring the shape of his back. He'd aged well, she thought idly. Men were lucky like that. As he returned to the table with his drink, Claire pretended to look for something in her bag.

Mark sat down and pulled his chair in. 'Thanks for coming to see me.' He smiled.

Claire looked across the table at his hands – rough skin, bare fingers – and wondered what he'd done with his wedding ring. Her own rings were hidden somewhere in the furthest corner of a closed drawer. When she'd stopped wearing them, smooth white lines lingered on her ring finger for a long time – two ghosts who haunted her hands.

'You work near here?' he asked.

'Just down the road. At the Sydney Ballet Company.'

He sipped his beer. 'You're still dancing?'

Claire shook her head. 'Haven't danced since . . . well, since Ethan, I suppose. I'm philanthropy manager. A professional beggar, essentially.'

'Oh, I'm sad you quit. You were an extraordinary dancer; you worked so hard.'

'It's fine,' she said, quickly grabbing her wine glass. 'What about you, what are you doing over in Kalgoorlie?'

'Bit north of there. I work at a mine. Not actually in the mine, in a lab. Metallurgical research.'

'Mining? You're kidding.'

'Money is okay, I guess.' Mark looked at her, amused. 'That's right, I forgot about your angry environmentalist phase. How you went to those Jabiluka action-group meetings. Whenever we walked past any fast-food chain or bank you'd stop at the door and scream, "*Capitalists!*"'

'Come on, I wasn't that angry,' Claire said, feeling a flush creep across her cheeks. 'And it wasn't a phase, I still care about the environment.'

'Bet you're a stickler for composting and recycling.'

'Maybe.' She suppressed a smile. 'So you really didn't go back to physics. What about your PhD?'

'Got derailed, like everything else.'

'Yeah, I know what you mean. Well, cheers to us!' She raised her glass. 'To approaching forty with unrealised dreams.'

Their glasses clinked. Claire felt a rush of fondness for him again; perhaps she'd demonised him too much inside her head. They'd had an overpowering connection once, been so in love. As she swallowed her wine, she forced herself to remember that this connection was only a memory.

Mark cleared his throat. 'Claire, I wanted to ask you something. Since Dad died, I've been thinking about Ethan a lot. About family.

How Dad never got to see him again before he passed away. While I'm back in town, it would be nice to see Ethan. I don't want my relationship with my son to be like the one I had with my father.'

She frowned. 'Your father didn't give you brain damage.'

'Ethan has brain damage? You said he was fine. Normal.'

'He is fine. Actually, that's not entirely true. He's been in hospital recently. A few weeks ago, Ethan had a seizure. Apparently triggered by scar tissue in his brain.'

'Why didn't you tell me?'

Claire shrugged.

'Has this happened before?'

'Not since he was a baby. But those seizures were caused by his injuries and the blood in his brain. Because of shaken baby syndrome.'

'Right.' Mark laughed, with an edge in his voice. 'You still believe that. Shaken baby syndrome is a hoax, you know. It's been proven now that it's based on hypothesis and faulty science. The laws of physics don't work like that, never did. Did you know bio-mechanical studies have shown the syndrome doesn't exist?'

'I don't know about that,' Claire began.

'There's lots of new research from the past few years. You wouldn't believe how often it's incorrectly diagnosed. SBS mimics Menkes disease, brittle bones, vitamin K deficiency – hundreds of other conditions. Was Ethan ever tested for those?'

'He had the constellation of symptoms.'

Mark took a pen from his pocket and started to draw dots on a cardboard coaster. He pointed. 'What's this?'

'The Southern Cross.'

'Yeah,' he said. 'But this is only a two-dimensional view. It's how it looks from Earth. What about the distances between all these stars? You can't tell when you look at the sky, but all constellations have three dimensions. If you looked at the Southern Cross from anywhere else in the universe, it'd appear completely different. Not in this shape at all. So much for constellations.'

She shook her head. 'Don't go off on some astrophysics tangent.'

'My point is, if you only looked at Ethan's symptoms from one narrow view, you'd only draw one conclusion. But if you reorient yourself, they mean nothing. If Ethan is still having seizures now, maybe he's always had some neurological disorder. Maybe he had a febrile seizure when he was a baby?'

Claire pushed her wine glass away. 'Then how do you explain what happened to him?'

'I don't know, but I don't think the doctors did a differential diagnosis. Bleeding in the brain is common in babies. Besides, you can't medically diagnose abuse. It was all assumption and mythology. These days, the diagnostic criteria for SBS are completely different. Doctors don't even call it shaken baby syndrome any more. That diagnosis broke our family, destroyed us. I loved that child and he was taken from me. Claire, I couldn't even come near you. The police put out an AVO.'

She turned her body away from him; she couldn't listen to more of his lies.

'Doesn't matter,' Mark muttered. 'You've already made up your mind.'

'What else was I supposed to do?'

He shifted on his chair. 'You were supposed to believe me.'

'I really wanted to,' Claire said. 'I wanted to believe that you weren't capable of such a thing. But seven doctors testified that you shook my baby. A jury found you guilty. You went to prison!'

'So you trusted the legal system more than me? In the last few years, tons of people found guilty by a jury of shaken baby syndrome have been exonerated. They've had their names cleared because the evidence was wrong. A guilty verdict didn't mean that I was guilty. Once people think you've hurt a baby, you're as good as guilty anyway. After I was accused, I never stood a chance. Stigma always stays there.' He stared into his empty beer glass.

'There was a huge pile of evidence, enough to put you in jail. So I had to reconcile the Mark I loved with this other version, this criminal. Accept things I didn't want to accept. But it's been twelve years, I've accepted you hurt Ethan. Just tell me you did it, I've already dealt with it. You can tell me the truth now.'

'You want the truth?'

'I really need to hear you say it.'

He looked into her eyes. 'Claire, I don't know how many times I have to tell you. I didn't hurt him.'

Claire studied him carefully; she couldn't read his face. She wished she could see a flash of something on it – guilt, sadness, remorse – but Mark's expression was stony. All he had to do was admit it. Confess. It wouldn't change anything now except finally quiet her doubts. She felt agitated by his empty protests of innocence, after all these years.

'I can't be here,' she said.

'What do you want? You'll never be happy, no matter what I say. I did it, I didn't, I'm guilty, I'm innocent. What does it matter? You've already accepted your own version of the truth.'

'Don't you dare do this to me again.'

'Claire . . .' he began.

'No, stop.' She cut him off and raised her voice. 'I've wrestled with uncertainty for too long. It's all over. It's in the past. Just tell me the truth.'

'I'm not going to admit that because you want to hear it.'

'Do you think I ever wanted to hear that you hurt Ethan? That he stopped breathing and had a brain haemorrhage. He was so tiny; he was only four months old.'

'I know.' He closed his eyes. 'I know all that.'

'Babies don't stop breathing for no reason, Mark. Don't you understand the pain you've put him through, put me through? And for what, to save your neck? After everything, you still have the audacity to say you didn't do it.'

'But I didn't do it!' Mark threw his hands up in the air.

Claire felt the seed of doubt sprouting the smallest stalk. He wasn't going to do this to her again. She threw her crumpled napkin on the table. 'You should never have contacted us. You should have left us alone.'

'I only wanted to make things right,' he said quietly. 'I served time for nothing, lost years of my life, and now I don't want to lose any more.'

'Things will never be right. You voided any chance of that a long time ago.'

'But Ethan is my son,' he began.

Claire stood up. 'He's my son. And I really need to go.' Her chair grated against the floor as she pushed it away. She couldn't look at Mark and turned away from him before walking quickly towards the exit.

Outside, some old men sat at a small table – schooners of beer and lit cigarettes in their hands – arguing about the future of the Labor Party. Swearing and slurring, spilling their beers on the newspaper, they squabbled about factions and leadership spills.

'Come join us, love!' one of the men called out, winking.

'No, thanks.' Claire looked away.

'We'll buy you a drink,' said another man. 'What do you want, legs? It's on us.'

There was something unforgiving about natural light: the men looked disfigured; the sun highlighted every ugly wrinkle and groove. Further along Kent Street, a taxi approached the pub. Claire held her hand out and hailed it. 'Sorry,' she said to the men. 'I have to go home.' She got into the taxi, slammed the door and drove away.

∞

Mark took another swig of beer. It left a biscuity aftertaste in his mouth. He'd finished his third drink now and his stomach flushed with warmth. One minute they were laughing, the next Claire stormed away. She'd always been capricious – there was a genuine need for a branch of science like meteorology to predict her moods – but he knew it wasn't to be cruel. Confidence was her problem. Claire never trusted her decisions; she'd always ignore her gut and regret it later. At least, that's what she was like twelve years ago.

An old man sat a couple of stools down at the bar, matching Mark drink for drink. 'Waiting for someone?'

'More like recovering from someone. What about you?'

'Just enjoying my own company.' The old man smiled. 'A woman?'

'My ex-wife.'

'Better have another beer then. It's on me.'

The old man ordered and Mark watched the bartender pour two more amber beers from the tap, white froth spilling carelessly from the rims.

The old man raised his glass. 'Cheers. To ex-wives – may they stay that way.'

Mark laughed. 'Thanks, mate.'

Inside the pub, the air was dense and thick with a fermented tang. Happy hour had just begun and the after-work crowd were seeping in – loosening their ties, rolling up the sleeves of their shirts – clouds of conversation filling the room.

The old man pulled his seat closer. 'So, what did you do wrong?'

Mark looked into his beer. 'She thinks I did something I didn't do.'

'That's a tricky one. Once a woman's made her mind up about something, it's tough to persuade her otherwise.'

'Tell me about it,' said Mark. He'd carried the weight of blame on his shoulders for so long that he couldn't imagine having it lifted. What it might be like to feel free.

Mark never expected that he'd go to jail. The guilty verdict was a shock. Just that morning as he'd waited for the jury's decision, he'd joked to a friend about how happy he was that it was the last day. That all this stress – trials, charges, court – was finally over, and now he could just get on with the rest of his life.

He didn't remember much of those fourteen days behind the dock. Long days, filled with evidence and experts, prosecution sparring with defence. Child-abuse allegations made people stop thinking straight, they let their feelings override common sense. Jurors stared him down. Mark's fate was in their imprecise hands; he had to trust these strangers. These days, if he passed one of the members of the jury in the street, he wouldn't be able to identify them. But Mark was the defendant, the accused, the prisoner; they'd definitely recognise his face.

That trial was an out-of-body experience. Floating in the court-room, Mark watched himself from above. Listening to the witnesses, disagreeing with their evidence in his head, but making sure he kept his feelings hidden.

Prison life had crossed his mind; he'd normalised the idea, thought maybe it wouldn't be that bad. Lots of time, few responsibilities. How terrible could it be? He could study. Read lots of books. Not worry about paying bills or cooking meals. But going to jail wasn't a likely scenario. His legal team said there wasn't enough evidence for a conviction; his case was impossible to lose. Guilty beyond reasonable doubt with no witnesses? Reasonable doubts were easy to find.

When the verdict was read – we find the defendant guilty – Mark hadn't believed it at first. His ears were playing tricks on him; this verdict was wrong. But he could see the verdict on the faces of everyone else in the court. He'd been found guilty. Some people seemed surprised; others seemed pleased. Guilty. It wasn't possible. He felt like he'd just received the heaviest blow to the head. Guilty. Before Mark knew it, he was on the floor. He was crying; he was a mess. Friends and family rushed over to the dock, climbing over seats before the guards took Mark away. When he finally stood up, Claire had already left the court.

'We'll appeal,' his barrister said. 'We'll make sure the sentence is light.'

But after three years of court, Mark didn't have any strength left. Three years of subpoenas, matters and statements. Three years of waiting and putting his future on hold. This was supposed to be the end, the beginning, the first day of the rest of his life. Now he'd been robbed of that and it destroyed him. Guilty. All it took to break him was that single word.

That afternoon, Mark sat for hours in the courtroom cell-block waiting for whatever happened next. It was freezing inside the cells, dry air reddening his eyes. He wished the jacket of his suit wasn't so light; its satin lining didn't keep him warm. Later that evening, he was taken to Silverwater Correctional Complex. Incarceration limbo, where he'd be received, before getting transferred to another prison.

Mark handed over the essential pieces of his life, his self: his wallet and driver's licence, his shoes and suit, his keys, his mobile phone. At Silverwater, he was given a six-digit Master Index Number, his new identity: 251429.

'That's a prime number,' Mark told the correctional officer.

'Down the hall for the strip search.' The officer handed him his prison greens and toiletries.

Standing naked in the bright concrete room, Mark closed his eyes. His cheeks were hot but the room was arctic. Cold palms on his thighs, running along the hairs of his legs, pushing his butt cheeks apart. Latex hands pulled on his skin, stuck to his body hair, explored deep inside his mouth. The gloves left bitter powder on his gums and his stale tongue clicked from dehydration. It was humiliating, being treated like this; indignity sank into the cavity of his chest.

As the male officer attentively checked every hole of his body, Mark went to another place in his head. He played violin solos in the concert hall of his mind and listed the next prime numbers: 251 431, 251 437, 251 443. Medical and psychological checks were done next. Then they watched a 'Welcome to Prison' video and were sent to bed. On that first night, he barely slept.

Two days later, Mark was put into segregation. Segro, they called it on the inside. Stupidly, he'd told one of the guys in his pod about the trial. He'd sounded concerned – interested in the case – but the bastard didn't keep the details to himself. Out of the blue, a group of men attacked Mark in the empty gym.

Fucking monster, they'd called him. Baby-shaker piece of shit. You're a fucking disgrace. They held Mark to the wall and pushed his face against the concrete slab. He hadn't known crimes against children were worse than murder within these walls. He hadn't known he'd be a target. With a sharpened fingernail, they sliced the flesh on his cheek open. Said they were going to rape him. So Mark punched one of them right in the head. He hadn't meant to hit him that hard, but it was self-defence.

Mark enjoyed the isolation of segro. Some people couldn't handle their own company, went mad after long hours alone trapped under the shame of fluorescent lights. But he'd never had trouble being on his own; he could relax, he could think. During those secluded days, he'd listen to the distant sounds of keys turning in locks, the clicks and twists of cuffs and latches, soft voices behind solid brick slabs speaking indecipherable words.

The screws kept him under protection orders for fourteen days. Day and night dissolved at the edges until they were one single knot of time. But this brief dalliance with incarceration would be over soon. Mark's lawyers assured him the sentence would probably be light; he was young, he was smart. There was no way he'd get the max.

His sentencing hearing was set for two months later. The legal team got his hopes up, said they'd probably let Mark go home right away, since he'd already done time on remand. A white van drove him back to town. Behind the van's caged windows, Sydney looked like a foreign city.

In the court, Mark was made to wear handcuffs. He tried to hide them under his sleeves, but it was impossible to conceal the metal chain that linked his wrists. Some of his friends were there, his father and brother. They shouldn't see him shackled like this.

At that sentencing hearing, the judge gave him four years. Two years non-parole. The prisoner displayed no remorse, was the judge's comment. The prisoner won't acknowledge that his actions caused the crime. Mark wanted to yell and scream at the judge – you're wrong, Your Honour, you have no idea – but he wasn't allowed his voice. His barrister made him keep his mouth shut. Said making any statement or remark would just make it worse.

After the hearing, the same miserable white van – heavy sliding doors, mesh steel walls, stained upholstery – drove Mark back to his new home. To the next two years of his life.

Eventually, he was moved to a minimum-security complex in country New South Wales, with other C-class inmates. Mark was put in protection again, but this time he didn't say a word about his supposed crime. He fell into a routine. Cornflakes for breakfast, ham sandwiches for lunch, bland spaghetti bolognese every Wednesday. For the first few months he lost himself, became just another head to count during muster and lockdown.

In the summers, the inmates could smell the eucalyptus smoke of the nearby bushfires. Winters were so cold they saw their breath billow inside their cells. Mark learned a new life and new language: buy-ups, cell ramping, shanghais, rock spiders, numbing out. He hid his books from the screws; they'd kick them out of his hands if they saw them, reminding him he wasn't there to learn, he was there to do his time. After the incident at Silverwater, Mark made sure he kept a low profile. He did his job, kept to himself and worked out in the prison gym.

Exercise became an addiction, the daily release of endorphins after lifting weights Mark's sole comfort behind bars. That single moment of the day when he felt pleasure's spark. With his newly carved muscles, he took on another identity: tough, mysterious, intimidating, shrewd. After several weeks of weight training – bench presses, barbells, dumbbells, sets and reps – his body was re-sculpted into one Mark didn't recognise in the mirror. He looked like a proper crim.

After one year inside, Mark was contacted by an investigative journalist. In her letter, she explained that she was researching shaken baby syndrome and wanted to speak with him about his case. Mark declined. He didn't want to talk about it. The woman – her name was Kate Levy – wrote to him again. The doctors were wrong, she'd said. New evidence proved shaken baby syndrome was a dangerously common misdiagnosis, that parents were falsely accused of abusing their children all over the world. Mass hysteria was putting innocent people behind bars.

During his trial, Mark was struck by the methodological shortcomings of shaken baby syndrome. There were so many inconsistencies and weaknesses in the scientific evidence. Diagnostic goalposts kept moving. He knew he was sent to prison on this imperfect paradigm. According to Kate, there'd even been stories about how vaccination might cause infant subdural haematoma, that half of all newborns had bleeds in their brains from birth.

What forensic doctors claimed happened to these babies was unproven, she wrote. With a pointed finger, they ruined lives. Called themselves expert witnesses when they didn't witness anything; their evidence was just faulty science. And Mark was versed in the iterative cycle of scientific method: question, gather information, hypothesise, test, experiment, analyse, interpret, retest. Physicians weren't physicists. Their hypothesis about shaken baby syndrome, Kate said in her letter, was showing to be inconsistent with the anatomy and physiology of infant brains.

Kate Levy believed Mark was innocent. He didn't fit the profile. She came to visit him at the correctional centre over the course of several months, brought him reports on other causes of cranial bleeding in infants. The so-called constellation of symptoms wasn't enough; intracranial pressure caused all of them. Shaken baby syndrome couldn't be tested by experiment, so it could never be proven. Every visit, she'd buy a can of soft drink from the vending machine and sip it through a straw. Kate found him attractive, Mark could tell. But she seemed like a complicated woman, too composed and polished, no vulnerability and all veneer.

She cited other incidents overseas where the clinical judgement of the medical professionals was completely wrong. Once shaken baby syndrome was put on the diagnostic table, of course Mark was treated like scum. He was guilty until proven innocent. In Kate's view, the baby's diagnosis wasn't evidence based, so the testimony of these expert witnesses was admissible. Breaking this story would be a huge exposé. She was going to get her hands on a copy of the court transcript and see what they could do.

Then one day, out of the blue, Kate stopped visiting. Stood him up on a rainy Sunday afternoon. Mark waited for two hours, staring at the vending machine. The following week he waited for her again. The screws smirked, made him feel like a fool. Months passed. In a frenzy of frustration, Mark wrote to her several times, an angry letter at first, but then eventually only wanting an explanation for the sudden silence. She'd disappeared. Why had she gone to all this effort to help him, and then never followed through with it? The exposé was never published. His side of the story never got told. Kate Levy never wrote back.

The crowd inside the Lord Nelson was thinning now. Mark decided it was time to head back home. The old man was drunk, ranting about various women who'd broken his heart over the years – the bitches, the beauties, the ones who got away. Mark knew he probably sounded just as bitter. But Claire should have believed him, stood by him. At least considered another view. Treated him with respect.

Mark didn't want to admit that it hurt, so pushed it to the back of his head with beer. She wasn't using her head; she was irrational. He'd tell her about his father's will some other time.

∞

There were three things Ethan needed to ask his mum and they were keeping him awake. Noisy questions that thrashed around inside his head like the thunder of rough surf breaking on rocks. He stared at the dark patch of mould on his bedroom ceiling.

The first question was whether or not he could sleep over at Alison's house, because yesterday she'd sent him a text message asking if he could this weekend. She'd been out of the hospital for over a week now. The second question was about what Will said at school. Ethan needed to confirm that the boys were liars, that obviously she wasn't actually a slut.

Ethan needed an answer for the third question the most, but it seemed the trickiest to ask. Why was Mark's phone number saved in her phone?

His parents were speaking to each other; they'd spoken to each other today. Ethan looked at her call history, then saw his father's name. He blinked repeatedly to make sure it wasn't a mirage. In the last month, they'd spoken to each other exactly five times for call durations of 11:02, 0:30, 2:41, 6:29, 2:08, making a total of exactly twenty-two minutes and fifty seconds of conversation between his parents, or 0.38 hours, or 1370 seconds. Mark had called her three times. She'd called him twice.

But the problem was Mum's force field. It wasn't exactly invisible – Ethan could just make out the buzzing plasma of its energy shield – but nobody else could see it. Maybe not even Mum. Her force field only materialised sometimes, usually when she was sad. This made scientific sense. After all, a body's amount of energy was directly proportional to its mass, so logically the mass–energy equivalence concept applied to his mum too. When his mum was feeling heavy, that increased the energy, and that strengthened the force field's barrier. Sometimes she vibrated on a frequency he couldn't understand, and all he could do was watch, and wonder, and notice.

In the middle of the night, Ethan was woken by a loud sob. He lay still for a moment to analyse the sound. At first he thought maybe it was a wounded possum outside the house, possibly the neighbour's cats fighting again, but as he listened more carefully he recognised it – his mum was crying.

He pushed her bedroom door open. 'Mum?'

'Ethan, why are you still awake?' Her eyes were red and her face was wet. She sat up in her bed. The room was mostly dark, but his mum's bedside table lamp was on. It lit her up from the left, casting a weird shadow across half her face.

'Can't sleep.'

'Neither.' She looked at him carefully for a moment. 'Do you want to sleep in my bed tonight?'

He nodded.

'You need a haircut,' his mum said, handing over one of her pillows.

Ethan couldn't wait any more – the questions screamed to be let out. 'Mum, can I ask you something?' He stalled. Her deflector shields were up; this force field was strong. To break down the energy barrier, he'd need to start with the easiest question.

'Can I sleep over at Alison's on Saturday night?'

'Is it okay with her parents?'

'I think so.'

'Maybe,' she said, nodding absently. She placed her head on her pillow; they were now looking at each other face to face. 'Was that it?'

Something about her expression snapped Ethan's resolve. He didn't want to upset her more. 'Yeah, that's it.'

She pulled the blanket up. 'Come here,' she said, throwing an arm over him. 'Ethan, I love you so much. I used to yell it at you when you were in the womb.'

'I know, weirdo. But I love you more.'

'Goodnight, pumpkin.'

'Goodnight, Mum.'

She kissed the top of his head and switched off the lamp. Ethan rolled over to face the wall.

Neither of them fell asleep right away. Mum thrashed about, adjusting her pillow, rolling from her back to her side to her stomach. Ethan could still taste the leftover questions lingering inside his mouth. He waited until his mum was perfectly still – for her breathing to slow down, for her temperature to drop, for her muscles to relax – but by the time she finally drifted off, he was already dreaming.

I 2

ELECTRICITY

'Come and see my room!' Alison said, excited. She wore a grey beanie on her head that had knitted ears. It made her look like a koala.

'Don't overstimulate yourself, Al!' her mother called out.

Ethan followed Alison upstairs. Along the hallway, there were several framed family photos displayed on the walls, all similar – studio shots, neutral backdrops, kids stiffly wearing their best clothes. There weren't photographs like this in Ethan's house; he'd never posed for a family portrait. In one of the pictures, Alison's hair was combed to one side, covering an eye and making her lopsided.

Ethan laughed. 'This one is great,' he said, pointing at her asymmetrical hair.

'Shut up,' she said, grinning. 'I hate that picture so much. Mum did my hair like that to hide a huge bruise on my forehead. Two days before that photo was taken, I fell down those stairs and hit my head.'

Ethan lowered his eyes. He shouldn't have teased her but Alison shrugged it off. She opened the door to her bedroom. Posters covered every centimetre of her walls, kaleidoscopic jumbles of clothes were piled all over the floor, teetering towers of books stacked by the bed. Her room was a mess; it didn't look like it belonged to this tidy house.

She pushed some magazines off a chair and onto the carpet. 'Make yourself at home.'

'You have a lot of stuff,' he said, looking at the tubs of nail polish on her desk. He put his overnight bag down on one of the few uncovered patches of carpet.

'Let's paint your nails!' Alison picked up two little jewel-coloured bottles and read their labels. 'Which colour do you like best, Holiday or Nouvelle Vague?'

'Nail polish is for girls.'

'If you let me paint your nails, I'll tell you a secret?'

'Nope, no way.' Ethan shook his head. But a really good secret had a power of its own. 'Maybe the blue one.'

'That's not blue, it's Nouvelle Vague. It means "new wave" in French. Okay, spread your fingers out on the table like this. No, like this.' Alison demonstrated how to perfectly splay a hand and Ethan tried to copy her. 'Good. Don't move.'

The nail-polish fumes had a chemical punch; Ethan felt light-headed. Alison poked out her tongue as she dipped the brush in the little pot, painting his short nails in slow strokes. Her concentration made Ethan smile; he'd never had a friend who was a girl before. Alison was different, but she got him, she understood. Somehow, somewhere, something between them had fused: the misfiring of their neurons, the misshapen cartilage of their faulty skulls, their abnormal synaptic activity.

He looked at the polish drying on his fingernails. 'What's the secret?'

'Before I can tell you,' Alison began, 'you have to promise me you won't tell anyone. Cross your heart and hope to die.'

'Stick a needle in my eye.' He passed his hand over his chest as he made the oath.

'Careful not to smudge the top coat!' She grabbed his hand and blew on his finger. 'Remember how I was still having seizures and needed to stay in hospital for a really long time?'

Ethan nodded.

'Okay.' Alison took a deep breath and carefully removed her beanie. She lifted a section of her hair and winced. 'I had a lobotomy.'

One side of her head was bald. There was a long curved scar around her ear – the shape of the letter C. Metal staples held her skin together; the area around the cut was puffy and pink.

He sat forward in his chair. 'Seriously? Why'd they do that?'

'Because the anti-seizure medicine stopped working. They've put me on at least eight different kinds. So the surgeon removed the part of my brain where the seizures were happening. To make them stop.'

'Does it hurt?'

Alison squinted at him. 'What do you think? They cut open my head and took out a piece of my brain. Not exactly a trip to Disneyland.'

'Do you feel different?' Ethan asked.

'I guess. I haven't had another seizure.'

'Can I touch it?'

Alison hesitated and straightened her posture. 'Only for a second. It's still pretty sore.' She pulled her hair back and closed her eyes.

'Gross.' Her skin felt hot; the stitches were lumpy. Ethan quickly retracted his hand.

They both stared at the floor for a while, not sure what else there was to say.

Ethan perked up suddenly. 'I have a secret too. I haven't told anyone. Well, except my mum. I'm an acquired savant.' He explained what Dr Saunders told him about savants: how he could see physics because of his brain injury, how that was unusual, how there were only around fifty acquired savants in the whole world.

She looked at him, stunned. 'Fifty, out of seven billion! That's amazing. You're one of the most special people on the planet.'

'No, I'm not. Maybe. I guess so. I'm one in 140 million. That's like six times the population of Australia. So savants like me are only 0.000000714285714 per cent of the total world population. I never thought about it like that.'

'It's huge!' Alison stood up. 'You just calculated that number in your head, didn't you? Ethan, you could be famous. You could even go on my favourite talk show and do physics tricks. Once, I saw some kid say the whole periodic table backwards. Please show me. Show me something you can see?'

Ethan thought really hard then shook his head. 'I can't. It doesn't work like that. I can't just make it happen whenever I want. I don't know how it works. Sometimes when I listen to music I see sound waves. There are lots of things we can't see with our eyes everywhere. Like the internet. Websites and emails are all floating around us right now.' He pointed at the empty space in front of their faces, where data shot wirelessly through the air.

'You're right,' Alison said, looking intently at nothing in particular. 'I can't see anything, but there is stuff in the air. It's like you have microscopes inside your eyes. So you can see this stuff because of your brain injury from when you were a baby?'

'I suppose so.'

Alison smiled. 'You know what that means? You don't need to be sad about it any more. Maybe it was actually a good thing that your father hurt you, if it made you special.'

Ethan stared at his painted fingernails, thinking carefully about this. 'Then why did he go to jail?'

'Yeah,' Alison said, considering it for a moment. 'I don't know.'

'Maybe you're right. My mum has been talking to him on the

phone. If he were really a bad person, she wouldn't ever speak to him again. And look!' Ethan took a piece of paper out from his backpack. 'I have his phone number.'

'Do you want to call him? You could use my mobile.'

Ethan imagined dialling, listening to the ringing phone, hearing his father's voice on the other end of the call, saying hello to him. 'No,' he said finally. 'I don't want to talk to him.'

Alison put her beanie back on and grabbed his hand. 'Let's go outside. We're going to camp in the garden. Have you ever slept in a tent?'

That night, as the moon peeked through the boughs and branches of the acacia tree in Alison's back garden, black clouds gathered overhead. A dark storm front broke into torrents of rain. Water smacked the tent's fabric, cascading down its thin walls. Lightning lit the nylon white. Claps of thunder followed, shaking the ground.

Alison screamed and collected bedclothes in her arms. 'Ethan, I'm not going to get struck by lightning. We have to go inside.'

The children ran back into the house, shielding themselves from the rain with pillows on their heads and sheets over their shoulders.

Ethan looked up at the electric lightning firing across the purple sky. From Alison's place, they could see the outline of Sydney's skyscrapers dotted on the horizon. Electrostatic charge was building up inside the clouds – positive charge to the top, negative charge to the bottom. A brilliant blue flash of electricity surged suddenly from cloud to earth. Thunder rumbled in the distance. Ethan traced the lightning's jagged path with his finger on the fogged-up kitchen window.

'It's the air,' he said, pushing wet hair off his face. 'That's the sound of the thunder. Lightning heats the air really quickly, and that makes a sonic shock wave. It gets so hot the air expands and then nearby air gets compressed. That bolt of lightning was five times as hot as the surface of the sun. Did you see those sonic waves that came from the lightning? They were bubbles of sound. They looked a little like cartwheels.'

Alison's eyes were bright, lit by the electric storm. 'Nope,' she said, grinning. 'I didn't see any sonic waves. But you did.'

∞

Claire's eyes struggled to focus on the road. The sky had suddenly darkened. Her head felt light. She knew this spinning feeling, this loss of balance – the vertigo of ambivalence. Years ago, she'd felt the same whirling confusion before.

In the hours, days, weeks and months after Ethan was hurt, Claire had still loved Mark. She couldn't make that go away overnight. Rational parts of her mind knew that was the end: Ethan came first. So Claire needed to make an impossible choice. She'd wanted to support her husband but how could she, when the victim was her son?

Cricket commentators on the radio yelled – another wicket had fallen. She switched the car stereo off. Back then, Claire was angrier with herself than with Mark. What kind of person still loved the man accused of shaking her baby? Must be something wrong with her; she was faulty, deranged. Secretly, she held on to a small piece of hope that Mark hadn't done it, that everybody else had made a colossal mistake.

An unspeakable amount of time passed before Claire let that hope go. Time wore it down: medical diagnosis, Family Court, revoking Mark's rights, stripping him of parental responsibility. An apprehended violence order and a criminal investigation. Officers apparently knocked on his new door, arrested him, and then took him to the police station. Fingerprints, charges laid, trial date set. Mark had a new identity: the accused.

Heavy rain started to fall and Claire turned on her windscreen wipers; the rubber of the blades squeaked against the glass. But it was still innocent until proven guilty. Mark pleaded not guilty; Claire wished his plea were true. Finally, the jury's verdict: guilty beyond reasonable doubt. She'd always thought her doubts were reasonable but apparently they weren't. Without the safety net of doubt, Claire had no reason to keep clutching on to her hope that he was innocent. She had to open her palm, loosen her grip, and let those last particles of empty hope evaporate into the air.

Oxford Street was covered in rainwater; traffic lights lit the shining road green. As she drove past Centennial Park, her tyres hissed in the rain. She was almost there, surprised by how automatically she'd remembered the route. Claire thought of what Dr Saunders had said, about how he could never be completely certain of his diagnosis. If what Mark said was true about shaken baby syndrome – if it didn't exist – that would mean Ethan was never a shaken baby.

She was outside Mark's house now. Claire parked the car and loosened her grip on the steering wheel.

Inside her palm, the hope was back.

∞

Mark had forgotten about the electrical storms that rolled over Sydney after a hot summer day. Dark clouds that clustered over the horizon, the sinking front of mammatus formations – patterns of pouches, hanging low in the sky like black balloons about to burst. Kookaburras sang, sensing the rain. That sudden cool change, that shifting wind. Day became night before lightning cracked through the thick canopy of clouds.

As a child, storms terrified Mark. He used to hide in his mother's arms and block his ears. Now he enjoyed the charged drama of a thunderstorm – flash, clap, rumble – as static discharge turned into light, sound and heat. He lay in his bed listening to the weather change, a crisp breeze coming in through the open window. Water spilled down the roof and passing cars splashed puddles onto the sidewalk.

It was a shock when the doorbell rang. Mark looked through the peephole and there – distorted by the rounded glass – was her face, her blonde hair. He opened the door.

'Claire? What are you doing here?'

Her clothes were transparent from the rain; her pale skin looked translucent. In the golden beam of sodium streetlight, Mark could almost see right through her. Claire's hair fell flatly around her face and her fingers trembled.

'Hi,' she said.

Mark opened the door a little wider. 'Would you like to come in? You're all wet.'

'I'm sorry, I don't know why I'm here.'

'Please come inside.'

The rain continued to pelt down.

'Just for a minute.' Claire wiped her feet on the doormat and removed her shoes. Mark remembered how she'd always looked so funny barefoot, walking on tiptoe with her high dancer arches.

Inside the house, the television was the only source of light. Mark liked its company when he was alone. After prison, absolute silence unnerved him. White noise helped. Mark led Claire to the lounge room and switched on a lamp. She stood there in her soaking clothes. Her vulnerability made Mark feel custodial; he wanted to dry her wet skin and wrap her cold body in blankets.

'Would you like a drink?' he asked.

Claire shook her head. 'I shouldn't stay.'

Mark poured a glass of red wine. She reluctantly accepted and nursed the glass in both hands. It looked like a bowl between her fingers; he'd forgotten how delicate she was. Outside, a flash of lightning illuminated the sky. Thunder rumbled in the distance.

'Can I get you a towel?'

'No, thanks. I'm all right.' Claire sat down and took a small sip of the wine.

'How about some dry clothes?' Mark didn't know what to offer her – none of his clothes would fit, his mother's clothes were gone – but he went to look in his suitcase. He still hadn't unpacked properly although he'd been in Sydney for almost a month. Finally, he found an old t-shirt. It was huge but it was clean, albeit slightly crumpled. He handed it to her.

Claire held the t-shirt up. 'The Big Banana?'

'Best I could do.'

She finished the wine in a single gulp and stood up. 'I'll go change.'

Mark tapped his fingers on his knees as he waited, and looked around the room. It wasn't exactly untidy but there were a few dirty mugs lying around. He turned on another lamp, then turned it off again. Then he returned to his seat and continued to tap his knees. Hopefully there wasn't anything embarrassing in the bathroom.

Claire came back, wearing only the shirt, and sat beside him on the sofa. Mark couldn't help but notice the lines of her legs underneath the shirt. A little heavier now, some visible veins, but he was hardly a young man himself. Her skin was pale but flawless; she'd never liked sitting in the sun. He found her fragility beautiful.

'Are you okay?' Mark asked.

'Yes,' she said, holding out her empty wine glass.

He filled it again. 'After our conversation the other day, I'm confused why you're here.'

Claire didn't respond, but slowly sipped the wine. She kept pulling the bottom of the t-shirt down, trying to cover her legs. Mark looked away, embarrassed that she might have caught him looking at her thighs, that she might get the wrong idea. She bent her legs up to her chest and stretched the fabric of the shirt so that it formed a small tent over her knees.

'I wanted to talk to you about that night,' Claire said finally.

'I wanted to tell you something too.'

'You really upset me, saying all those things. It's like you think this is a game, toying with my feelings like that.' She paused as she took another swig of wine. 'I really hate you, Mark.'

Her words stung but he made sure it didn't show on his face. 'If you've come here just to tell me that, to yell at me or get angry, then you should go home.' He finished his glass of wine. He'd half-expected her to say something bitter like that, to be deliberately hurtful, and perhaps it was inevitable that she hate him. She'd never believed him, after all. But he wasn't trying to play a game and toy with her feelings; he hoped she knew that. The last thing he wanted to do was seduce her or rekindle their relationship.

Claire's head was in her hands. 'I'm sorry. I don't know why I said that.'

'Because you hate me?' Mark offered.

'No, I don't think I do. Hate is too strong a word. I wish I were indifferent to you. The opposite of love is indifference, so they say.' Her voice wavered; she didn't sound convinced. Claire stared into her glass. 'I don't have anyone else to talk to about this. About Ethan. Nobody else understands how I feel.'

Welcome to my world, Mark thought. No old friends related to him any more, no-one connected to his past. He'd made some new mates in Kalgoorlie but they were superficial friendships – drinking companions, workmates who might share a joke – and they didn't really know him. Whenever anyone asked about his life in Sydney, Mark always changed the subject. His mates probably thought he was trying to be mysterious so they let it slide, but Mark knew they'd think differently of him if they heard his real life story. Not many people gave you the benefit of the doubt; everyone always assumed the worst.

In prison, Mark had paid an unmentionable price for letting his guard down – he was beaten, bullied, worse. When he was released on that freezing August day, crammed into old clothes that no longer fitted, he needed to put all that behind him. Erase those incarcerated years. After his parole period, Mark left the state. Ran away and started afresh. But nobody truly knew him; nobody scratched the surface. He suppressed himself, internalised all his thoughts. It was a dangerous way to live.

Clean slates had invisible consequences. Mark worried that his unconscious feelings were slowly poisoning him. Like radiation – ionising him into decay – his secrecy had a subatomic instability. Just like the law of conservation of energy: energy couldn't be created or destroyed, but it could change form. Mark worried that he'd combusted like an exploding bomb – chemical energy converting to kinetic energy – and the detonation of prison life had altered his molecules.

'Claire, I get it,' Mark said quietly. 'I don't have anyone to talk to about what happened either. You're the only person who'll ever understand how I feel. And maybe I'm the only one who really understands you.'

She ran a hand through her hair. 'I don't know about that. I wasn't the one who —'

Mark cut her off. 'We already had that conversation.'

'Fine. You said you had something to tell me too.'

Mark didn't know where to begin. Half this house they were sitting in right now belonged to Ethan, but those words wouldn't come out of his mouth. In the back of his mind, he didn't want her to know. Mark wanted to punish her like she'd punished him. And he was jealous. Claire got to play the victim to his villain, the good to his bad. She had the relationship with their son; he had nothing. In his darkest fantasies, Mark would imagine how close they were, inseparable, bound by an unbreakable cord. She knew their child intimately, at his best and worse. She gave Ethan her unconditional love.

Mark didn't know what that felt like. Conditions were placed on his love; he wasn't allowed to love his own son. Only in abstraction, at a distance – the way people love a football team, celebrities, worship from afar. Completely unlike the messy love that should exist between members of a family. Whatever he felt for his child was intangible, lacked complexity. Mark had spent more than a decade trying to pretend Ethan and Claire didn't exist. A good policy most days, and a lot of the time he hadn't given them a passing thought. Days, weeks, even months went by when the two of them didn't enter his mind. But there were always reminders – their wedding anniversary, Ethan's birthday, Christmas – inflaming the memories and making them rush back.

'I wanted to tell you . . .' He paused. 'My father wrote me out of his will.'

'Mark, that's awful. I'm sorry to hear that.' She gave him a genuinely sympathetic look. He'd forgotten the precise colour of her eyes.

'No big deal,' he said. 'Wasn't a surprise.' Something about Claire's expression made Mark want to touch her but he knew it was a bad idea. She was so angry with him and he didn't want to confuse himself. He'd moved on too, made progress. Forgotten all about her. The last thing he should do for his own sake was touch his ex-wife.

The rain was heavier now. She shuffled closer to him and rested her head on his shoulder. 'How did we end up like this? What did we do wrong?'

Mark didn't know what to say but began to stroke her hair on instinct. It was still damp in places but alarmingly soft where it was dry. He smelled the top of her head. How peculiar that after all these years she still smelled the same, how strangely reassuring. It disarmed him – the familiar musk of her scalp – but it was wonderful. He wrapped his other arm around her; it felt awkward at first, then effortless. Claire craned her head up and before Mark could register what was happening, she kissed him.

She tasted the same too. They kissed; the curves of each other's faces slowly remembering how they once fitted together; the warmth of both bodies transferring heat. Lightning struck outside again.

'I can't do this,' she said, suddenly pushing him away.

Mark wiped his mouth. 'It's a really bad idea.' He knew this wasn't the right thing to do; he was serious.

Claire hugged her legs and looked around the lounge room. 'Do you remember when we used to meet here in the afternoons between my rehearsals?'

Mark nodded. How could he forget? When they'd first started seeing each other, he still lived at home. Used to sneak her into the house in the afternoon before his father came back from work. They'd spent hours in bed in this house – talking and fucking and laughing – and Claire would fall asleep in his arms, their noses touching and her sweet breath on his face. Mark loved watching her snooze; her eyelashes were so pale they looked see-through; her mouth, red from kissing, slightly open as she drifted off. It was always a struggle to wake her up so she wouldn't miss her evening dance rehearsal. But that was so long ago, when they'd been so young and uncomplicated. Suddenly it felt like it was yesterday. A strong wind outside rattled the window.

Claire looked at Mark's face. 'I hate you,' she said softly and she cupped his cheek with her hand. She leaned forward and pulled off the Big Banana t-shirt. 'I hate you,' she said again as she sat on his lap. She was only wearing her underpants now.

'I know,' Mark whispered. His mouth brushed against Claire's chin as her arms went up around his neck. Her torso pressed against his own and he exhaled, trying to unknot his stomach and not look at her exposed breasts. But her touch felt soft and familiar, and as Claire lifted his shirt up over his head and her bare skin came into contact with his, Mark felt a shock run through his body. Some sort of electric current passing between them.

'I hate you,' Claire whispered into his ear as he ran a hand over her breast and started to kiss her neck. 'I hate you. I hate you. I hate you.'

∞

All those years of an empty bed, of waking up without the consolation of a morning reunion, had not gone unnoticed by Claire. The warmth of another body under the sheets as she woke up in the middle of the night made her feel safe – tangle of limbs, head of hair on another pillow, the symphony of other lungs. Since her marriage ended, Claire had never had many boyfriends. A few brief indiscretions, yes, that stupid affair, but never anything serious. She didn't fall in love again.

Not because of Mark or because she'd never got over him. She knew she had. Claire simply wasn't interested in the currency of love; its exchanges carried a price she didn't want to pay. Men chased her but she never let them get close. She built necessary barricades, fortified her heart, and wasn't interested in ever tearing down those walls. They were easy, safe and strong. Over time, Claire calcified; she grew emotionally insoluble. Nobody would ever hurt her again that badly. It wasn't possible anyway.

The cocoon of night was slipping away from them, ephemeral as the storm. So while it rained outside and Mark lifted his leg over hers, Claire drowsily catalogued him: the way his lips felt against her lips; the way his skin pressed against hers. She recorded the rhythm of his breath and the cadence of his sighs as if they were music, committed to memory the sweaty smell of his body as if it were perfume. Muscles melted, cartilage softened, joints unhinged.

Their fingers brushed together and Claire closed her eyes. They still had that indefinable thing, that fiery intensity. The spark. In the midnight throes of it, that spark was still there. She'd forgotten what it felt like to be electrocuted. Through the night, Mark made her sweat, smile and laugh, but more than that. He made her believe in energy.

Claire was woken again by the unexpected dawn chorus of birdsong – currawongs, magpies, galahs – as the sun was coming up. Mark rolled over and rested his arm on her hip. His touch felt wonderful but she quickly experienced a sickening unease. Slowly, the room came into focus. Clarity shocked her back to real life. She was in bed with Mark, in his childhood bedroom. His clothes strewn across the floor, her underwear hanging off the end of the bed. What had she done? Claire tried to deaden her feelings of guilt, shake off her conscience, and buried her face into the pillow. Maybe this was a dream.

Mark was still asleep, purring in a contented snore. He looked childlike, like Ethan. Absent-mindedly, she ran her fingers up and down his back. A layer of sweat clung to his skin and Claire felt it transfer to the tips of her fingers. He was more muscular now than when he was younger; his skin was brown and smooth. Maybe he worked out these days and spent more time in the sun. Goosebumps formed on the downy areas of his lower back.

'Good morning,' Mark said, roused from his sleep.

'Hi.' Skin-to-skin contact was like a drug and she needed another fix. She wanted to resist him, but her body had other plans. Claire pressed her face into his back and kissed his skin. Whatever she felt was just driven by pheromones, she reminded herself. What happened here was only sex.

Mark rolled over to face her, his breath on her cheek. Claire remembered how cute she found him in the mornings, squinty-faced with messed-up hair. She'd forgotten these little things, edited them out of her revisionist history. He pulled their bodies closer together. Claire felt his erection brush up against her stomach and she sank into the mattress. She closed her eyes.

'Look at me,' said Mark.

She kept her eyes shut and pressed her skin against his erection again.

He moved away. 'Look me in the eyes. It's not that difficult.'

Claire squirmed; his pupils were dark and dilated. Mark was the only person who'd ever looked at her this way. Staring at him made her uncomfortable; she couldn't wait to look somewhere else. She'd already clawed her way out of that labyrinth – stopped being lost in the vortex of his dark eyes – and now she'd found the exit, Claire didn't want to go back. She blinked and looked away.

Mark ran his hand through her hair. 'They're still there. Those galaxies in your eyes.'

'Please don't.'

'You used to love it when I said that to you.'

Claire sat up in the bed. Once, that was the most romantic thing anybody had ever told her. She remembered the first time Mark said it. They'd only been going out for a few weeks, and after her admission she'd never seen any of the *Star Wars* movies, Mark forced her to watch the trilogy in one sitting. She fidgeted on the sofa, trying to work out what was going on. The storyline was difficult to follow and the dialogue was terrible. Mark apparently knew the script off by heart but he was watching Claire instead. They were his favourite movies and he couldn't take his eyes off her. She noticed him staring, somewhere in the middle of *The Empire Strikes Back*, and shot him a look.

'What's wrong?'

'You have galaxies in your eyes,' he said.

It was the closest Claire had ever come to melting. Now it felt like a cheap line.

The bedroom felt stuffy suddenly. Sweat, bodies, unwashed sheets: the smell in the air made her feel sick. She put her feet on the floor. 'I need to go.'

'Why are you here?' he asked.

She could tell by the tone of his voice that he was upset; she recognised the cadence.

Mark continued. 'What are you doing? Why did you sleep with me? Are you so miserable that you need to fuck people for comfort?'

'Why did you sleep with me?' she shot back.

He shrugged. 'Long time since I'd had sex and you were up for it.'

Claire tore the sheet off the bed and wrapped it around her body. 'You don't mean that. You're just being cruel.'

'What do you want me to say? That I still love you and want to be with you? Even if I did, you wouldn't want to hear it anyway.'

There was nothing to say in response. 'I'm going to have a shower,' she said.

After closing the bathroom door, Claire ran cold water in the sink and put her mouth to the tap. Gulp after gulp, she drank until she was almost choking. She washed her face and watched the running water spiral down the drain. His smell was on her body; she had to wash off last night. She didn't understand how all of a sudden they were kissing, touching, undressing, making their way into bed. But she recalled vivid flashes of it: his hand running along the bare skin on her back, her lips making their way down his chest.

How had she let this happen? How had Mark? Both of them should have known better. Or maybe it wasn't a mistake in his eyes, maybe this was his plan all along. To get Claire back into bed, manipulate her into having sex with him. Fuck his way to atonement. Would this make him feel better about himself, as though he hadn't done anything wrong? He was disgusting. Worse. It made her insides curdle. He'd sucked her into his fantasy world where he was blameless. Where he could play the victim when he'd committed the crime. After all these years, she'd thought maybe he'd show just a speck of remorse for what had happened to their son. Be a human being.

Claire stood under the shower and caught her breath. The sound of running water made her calm down. She thought she hated him; she'd felt it in her blood. But she carried something else in her blood too – some involuntary pull, poisonously locking her body towards his, like a mutual blood-borne disease or virus. She wondered if she did still love him, if she could possibly be that stupid. Maybe with the vague affection everyone has for their former loves. Even the bluest veins continued to flow but the blood pumping through them was oxygen-starved. Her heart had that same starved duality, broken into chambers; Mark split Claire in half.

She lathered her body with soap. But what if he was innocent? Or shaken baby syndrome didn't exist? Mark's words from the other day weighed heavily on her mind – it broke our family, destroyed us, he'd loved that child and he was taken away. What if there'd really been a misunderstanding, some horrible misinterpretation of medical evidence? The shower floor felt like it was giving way under her feet.

'Claire?' He knocked on the door. 'You okay in there?'

She let out a sob. 'Mark.'

He came into the bathroom, wearing only his underpants. 'What's wrong?'

'I don't . . . what if,' she said, choking on water. It was a struggle to articulate this tangle of binary feelings: love and hate, trust and doubt. Fallen scaffolding, fractured framework; she'd believed their lives were built around facts, but perhaps those facts were actually lies? She'd lost her bearings and felt swept away by an avalanche of uncertainty. Claire leaned against the tiles and cried.

Mark opened the shower door and turned off the tap. He tightly encircled her wet body. Claire didn't want to be held like this. Inside, she refused to be contained, but on the outside she fell into his embrace. His arms felt safe; his touch felt dangerous. Frightened by blurred boundaries, she shivered; her sense of definition was as clouded as the bathroom filled with steam. Claire was a single heartbeat away from believing him.

'It's okay,' he said, as he reached for a towel and carefully wrapped it around her body.

Claire shook her head. 'No, it's not okay.' Her mind focused on a question – how could somebody this tender hurt a baby? 'Mark, I need to tell you something about Ethan.'

'What is it?'

'The doctors did all this diagnostic testing on him recently. They think he's a genius; his IQ is ridiculously high.'

Mark took a step back. 'Why are you telling me this?'

'Because,' she said. 'I don't understand how something violent could cause something so positive and good. Maybe there's some other issue inside Ethan's brain, maybe there's always been. I was completely convinced it was shaken baby syndrome. But people used to believe the world was flat. I suppose you can convince yourself of anything. Now, I'm not so sure what I think.'

He looked stunned.

Claire got dressed. Her head was full of contradictions, as though each hemisphere of her brain were battling some civil war. Confusion left her with a strong desire for solitude, to be left alone with her conflicting thoughts. She felt completely disoriented, questioning her entire life. What if her heart had reshaped itself around a lie? Part of her was angry, at the doctors who gave evidence at Mark's trial, at the prosecution – for being too quick to point the finger, for maybe making a mistake. Another part of her was utterly distraught. If they'd been wrong, the consequences were devastating. Mark was right – it had broken their family.

Across the room, Mark was rubbing his face with his hands. She thought immediately of Ethan; it was a mannerism they shared.

'I need to go,' she said.

'Sure.' Mark still wasn't dressed but he suddenly seemed guarded. 'Let's talk later.'

His distance made her skin flush with self-conscious heat. She wasn't sure how to say goodbye to him now. One moment they'd been intimate, then arguing, then intimate again. Claire was exhausted; she felt nauseous as she contemplated what had happened between them last night. But her shame was coupled with this persistent exhilaration. She let herself out of the house.

Outside, the monochromatic sky slipped into morning. The storm was over and although the rain had stopped, the streets were covered in puddles. Claire walked through them, not caring if her feet got wet, as she made her way to the end of the road to find her parked car.

∞

Ethan woke suddenly, covered in sweat. He'd dreamed of Albert Einstein. Universes had bent around them like a cosmic grid – time and space intersected, galaxies swirled. They'd shot across the dark sky, riding motorcycles and chasing beams of light. Then the white-haired man vanished, splintering himself into the shining beam of another time and out of Ethan's dream.

Ethan's t-shirt was stuck to his chest; he felt breathless and disoriented. He pulled the sleeping bag off his shoulders and wiped sweat off his face. Alison was in her bed on the other side of the room making sleeping noises – the sighs and snores of a body at rest – and while Ethan wanted to wake her up, he thought it was probably too early.

Dr Saunders had said something about genetic memory, something about how – inside Ethan's brain – a hidden gift had been uncovered. But if physics was really hardwired into his brain, how did it even get there in the first place? Where'd Ethan get his genetic memory? And from who?

Outside the window, the washed-out sky brushed up against tomorrow. That vague unbroken moment between late night and morning: now the storm was melting away and the clouds had cleared. Silver light shone onto Alison's bedroom floor.

Ethan lay back down on the carpet, thinking about Einstein and the speed of light. The dream seemed real; he could still feel the motorcycle handlebar in his palm as they'd driven so fast that time had slowed down. He rolled over, pressing his cheek into his pillow, and sighed heavily.

'Hey,' Alison said, opening one eye. 'What's wrong?'

'Time is the biggest illusion.'

'Did you take drugs while I was asleep?'

'I was just thinking about the way time slows down as we travel fast. And how if we travel at the speed of light, we could really go to the future. Einstein's theory of relativity says that's possible. But only in one direction: forward. I'm not sure how to travel back to the past.' Ethan's voice was throaty. 'I wonder if we can change things that have already happened.'

She opened her other eye. 'Okay, Time Lord. So worrying about time travel is keeping you awake at night?'

'If only there was some kind of space-time highway,' Ethan said. 'Or a shortcut.'

'Like a rabbit hole?' Alison suggested.

'Exactly. Or a wormhole! It's hard to travel at the speed of light when you're heavy, so mass is still a problem. But to compensate for that you'd just need lots of energy. $E=mc^2$. Energy is proportional to mass.' There was a long pause. 'Alison, reckon it's possible to make a time machine?'

She rubbed her eyes. 'Totally possible. I've seen *Dr Who*. Why?'

'I'm going to build one.'

'Cool,' she said, unfazed. 'I guess if anybody could make a working time machine, it would be you. Will it be dangerous? Can I help?'

'Yeah,' Ethan said, rolling onto his back. 'Probably really dangerous. I'm not sure how to do it yet. Something about energy.'

'Let's talk about it tomorrow?' She closed her eyes again. 'Goodnight, Ethan.'

'Goodnight. See you in the future.'

Alison smiled but kept her eyes shut. 'You're such a dork,' she said.

13

MAGNETISM

She was gone now but Mark could smell Claire in the air. He searched the room for something more concrete, some solid proof of her presence. But the house was unaltered, a museum of his usual masculine artefacts – canisters of shaving cream, woody aftershave, dirty clothes hanging limply on a chair – it looked like any other day. That blossom-infused scent of her skin struck a nerve, though, triggering a string of excruciating memories. Strands of pale hair were stuck to the sofa; whispers of the previous night still rustled inside his head.

They'd made love twice: slowly the first time, then with a quickening greed as they rediscovered each other's bodies, navigating through the sweet animal landscapes of familiar skin and bone. Could Mark call it making love? Was that love or just ease, like a body's sigh after slipping on an old pair of well-worn jeans? The two of them were a good fit.

But something about Claire had hardened and callused. The intensity of their fused bodies bothered Mark. Surely that radio-activity meant something; he tried his best to push it out of his mind but it kept rushing back in hot waves, flushing his face hypertension pink. Last night had fried his circuits: he couldn't think straight but couldn't stop thinking about it.

Downstairs in the kitchen, Mark fixed himself breakfast. He made an instant coffee, watched the brown lumps dissolve into the water as he lazily stirred, and considered calling Claire. But there wasn't a reason to ring, just the vague desire to hear her voice. Stupid idea. He sipped the bitter coffee and brushed the impulse aside.

He opened his laptop and glanced over the subject lines of his emails. There was one from his boss, asking when he'd be coming back. Mark needed to return to work soon. Back to Kalgoorlie, back west to the dust, back to the middle of nowhere. He'd been gone three weeks already, used up all his compassionate and personal leave – now he was eating into his annual holiday. Not that it really mattered. Nobody to go on holidays with anyway; nowhere he really wanted to see. His criminal conviction made it hard to leave Australia and freely explore the rest of the world.

Last year, Mark had driven up to Darwin by himself – almost eight thousand kilometres round-trip, fourteen days there and back – just him and the asphalt belt of the Great Northern Highway. He travelled through the white deserts of the Western Australian salt lakes, up to Newman and Broome, and into the ancient limestone reef of Geikie Gorge National Park in the Kimberleys.

On the night Mark finally arrived in Darwin, he parked his car near the beach and stretched his stiff legs. On the crowded sands of Mindil Beach – a skewer of satay chicken in one hand, a can of sweating beer in the other – he watched the evening sky change from coral to red. Purple waves lapped gently at the shore; children chased each other down the smooth stretches of wet sand. He'd never been this far north before. As the orange sun disappeared over the horizon and into the gulf, Mark was suddenly overcome with loss. He'd wasted so many years of his life, been robbed of so much time. This was the closest to the equator he'd ever come, the furthest from the two poles he'd ever ventured.

On the dining table, his mobile phone vibrated, jerking sideways along the varnished wood. Mark picked it up and read the screen. Claire. He wanted to answer immediately and started to sweat lightly as he stared at the phone. But he hesitated; just let it ring in his hand. What would he say? These days, he was systematic in his dealings with women and treated flirting or dalliances as simple transactions. But this was his ex-wife, not some casual fuck. Mark didn't know which tone to take with Claire – could he even modulate his voice to sound cool, casual, warm? Without a guaranteed strategy to cut through the tension, he felt exposed.

With a lucid jolt, Mark suddenly remembered the way last night Claire had reached for his cock, how she'd maintained eye contact as she rubbed his erection against her inner thigh, quickly thrusting herself onto him with an unbroken focus. He'd let out an involuntary groan.

The phone stopped ringing.

Don't overthink this, Mark thought to himself. He brushed a hand across his eyes. Claire had called him; she'd dialled his number. She'd obviously felt the same urge he'd felt and acted on it instead of shrugging it off. There was nothing to lose by calling her back. But in the shapeless years since Mark had lost everything – lost Claire, lost his son, lost his former life, lost his freedom – he'd at least tried to save his dignity. Preserve some pride. Risk was best avoided; vulnerability was pathetic. He recoiled from even the slightest chance of failure. He'd felt enough defeat.

Mark returned Claire's call. His mind went blank as he listened to her phone ring. He wanted to see her again, but wanted her to suggest it. His stomach muscles tightened. The call connected with a click.

'Hey,' Mark said. 'Sorry I missed you before.'

The other end of the line was silent.

'Claire? Can you hear me?' Mark stood up and walked towards the front of the house; the phone reception was patchy out the back. 'Claire?' he repeated. Down the line, he heard the softest breaths.

'Hi,' said a small voice. 'It's not Claire.'

Now Mark was silent. This was a child's voice, silvery and clear. Once he'd sounded like that himself, before testosterone flooded his prepubescent body, elongating his vocal cords and enlarging his larynx, causing his voice to break. He coughed, and felt a sharp clang in his chest. Coffee rushed up his oesophagus.

'Ethan? Is that you?'

∞

After breakfast, Mum picked Ethan up from Alison's house. Her hair was wet when she arrived; she smelled like shampoo. Ethan told her about the storm, how they hadn't been able to camp outside, but his mum's eyes were fixed on the road. She yawned and pushed her sunglasses up her nose. Maybe the lightning and thunder kept her awake last night, lying in her bed, scared to be home alone.

'Mum, can I ask you a question?'

'Shoot.'

He groped for the right words. 'Did my father ever study physics?'

She sucked in her cheeks. 'Why do you want to know?'

'I dunno,' he said, rolling down the car window. Outside, the air smelled fresh and rich. Ethan could see that the rain had brought ozone molecules down from the upper atmosphere. 'Just wanted to know if I was like him. Figure out how all these tesseracts and geodesics got inside my brain.'

They stopped at a traffic light and she turned to face him. 'Ethan, they're inside your brain because you're you. Are you worried about what Dr Saunders said? All that stuff about being an acquired savant?'

Ethan nodded.

The red light changed to green. His mum put her foot on the accelerator and directed her eyes back to the road.

'You didn't answer my question,' he said.

Mum leaned forward in the driver's seat and pressed her lips together. She turned the steering wheel as they took a sharp corner. 'Your father was a theoretical physicist.'

Back at home, Ethan tried to draw a picture of a wormhole: a tunnel bridging two pieces of time and space. How could he make one? Nobody had ever seen a real wormhole; they only existed in theory. Wormholes were probably everywhere but they'd be too tiny to see. He imagined stretching one to fit the size of his body, jumping inside it, and travelling across to the unreachable past.

But no matter how hard Ethan thought about it, he couldn't see the solution. Backwards time travel was full of paradoxes and problems. He didn't know how to get enough energy, how he could remove mass from matter, how to travel at the speed of light. It was impossible; he'd get swallowed or shattered as the wormhole collapsed.

Ethan pushed his notes away and put his head into his hands. He felt stupid. He was stupid. Wasn't he meant to be special, a savant? Some genius; he couldn't even figure out how to convert a wormhole traversing space into one traversing time. Ethan hadn't really talked to Einstein; that was a dream.

If only he had somebody to help him, who could explain all the mathematics he didn't understand. Ethan's muscles went rigid. He felt a strange fluttering inside his belly. If only he knew a physicist.

From the other side of her bedroom door, he heard his mum

breathing deeply. It was weird she was asleep in the middle of the day. Why was she so tired? Ethan took her phone out of her handbag, went to the other side of the house and unlocked the screen of her mobile. He scrolled through her contacts until he found the number. Ethan let his finger fall on the button to dial.

But his father didn't answer. The call rang out and went to voicemail.

Ethan swallowed hard; his finger touched his parted lips. He was listening to his father's voice.

'Hi, you've called Mark Hall. Please leave a message and I'll call you back.'

The recording was only fourteen words long, but those words were the acoustic vibration of his father's voice, speaking to him across signals carried through the radio frequency in the air. Ethan didn't leave a message.

Immediately, the phone trembled in his hands; Mark was returning the call. Ethan quickly flicked it to silent and stared blankly at the name on the screen. His face felt cold. He wanted to answer but was paralysed with fear. Yet his desire to speak to his father – years of building layer upon layer of curiosity – outweighed whether or not answering the phone was the right thing to do. He held it to his ear and listened.

'Hey, sorry I missed you before. Claire? Can you hear me? Claire?'

'Hi.' Ethan drew in his breath. 'It's not Claire.'

The line was quiet. Ethan could see currents crackle through the air. This was a bad idea, a huge mistake. His father obviously didn't want to speak to him; he wanted Mum.

'Ethan? Is that you?'

He nodded then remembered he was on the phone. 'Yes, it's me.'

'It's nice to hear your voice,' his father said.

Ethan laughed. 'It's nice to hear your voice.'

Mark laughed too. 'I've imagined this moment so many times, and now I don't know what to say.'

'Same.'

'How are you?'

'Good.'

'That's great.'

Ethan shuffled his feet on the floor. 'Cool.'

'Listen, I know your mother doesn't want us to meet. And if you don't want to, I understand. But I'm in Sydney at the moment and I'd really like to see you. Maybe we could have lunch or something?'

'Okay,' Ethan said without hesitating.

'Do you think you could meet me at Circular Quay? Are you okay to get the train?'

'I could catch the bus. I catch the bus by myself all the time.'

'One o'clock?'

Now Ethan felt panicky. His father meant today. That was in less than two hours. He wasn't sure which bus went all the way down to Circular Quay or how long it would take to get there. Usually he was only allowed to catch the bus to school and had never gone into the city alone on the weekend. And he couldn't just leave the house while Mum was sleeping, not without telling her where he was going or who he'd be with. That was against the rules.

'Yep,' Ethan said, ignoring his head. 'See you at one o'clock.'

Mark paused. 'Thanks for calling me, mate.'

'It's nothing,' Ethan said quickly and hung up the phone.

But it wasn't nothing. Ethan didn't know why he'd said that. Blood rushed to his face, his eyes felt full; he'd said lots of wrong things on the phone. Ethan thought about all those times he'd walked along busy streets, staring at strangers and wondering if they were his dad.

All those nights when he'd asked himself questions about his father to lull himself to sleep: what's his favourite colour, what's his favourite book, what's his favourite song?

Maybe Ethan didn't want answers to those questions. It was far easier to have his father only exist inside his head. That abstract figure – who didn't have a voice, a face or a phone number – had done a bad thing. Ethan wasn't sure how to feel about the real person, about the voice he'd just spoken with. Should he love Mark because he was his dad? Should he hate him for what he did? This wasn't nothing. It was everything.

Ethan had often daydreamed about finally meeting his dad. In the dreams, his father stepped out of an unfolding wall of smoke. It was always epic, as they looked at each other for the first time – one of those moments where everything explodes. The Big Bang. It made something inside Ethan stop feeling empty and broken; the white noise that buzzed constantly inside his brain disappeared.

He opened the door of his wardrobe and considered what to wear. All his clothes seemed kind of wrong, childish. Nothing was right. Eventually, he chose jeans and a black t-shirt and studied his reflection in the mirror. He wondered if his father would know it was him, if Mark would recognise his own son's face.

But Ethan's fantasies of epic explosions now seemed inappropriate. This was more complicated – his father had hurt him, committed a crime. It was reassuring that Mark sounded nice on the phone, but he might still be a bad person. Ethan's formless dreams hadn't updated to take those unpleasant things into account as the mythical father figure emerged from the fog. He felt scared for a second but pushed the fear out of his mind. His father wasn't going to shake him; he wasn't a baby any more.

Maybe Mum was really sick and wouldn't notice if he left. Ethan peeked into her bedroom. She'd be furious he was going to the city by himself without permission – he'd be grounded forever – and she'd go absolutely berserk if she knew Ethan was going to meet his dad. But he'd have to deal with that later, he didn't want to be late. Ethan trembled as he sneaked out the front door and hurried down the hill to the bus stop.

∞

Mark stood under the glass shelter outside Circular Quay train station. He carefully watched people step off every bus across the road. Traces of the last night's storm remained; the pavement was coated in a slick of dirty water and the crisp smell of rain hung in the air. Mark's stomach rumbled. He glanced up across the road at the red and yellow signage of McDonald's on the corner, and contemplated grabbing something quick to eat. Ethan needed lunch too, and he'd probably be happy with a burger. Twelve-year-old boys loved fast food. Didn't they?

As Mark queued and stared at the colourful backlit menus, it dawned on him that he didn't know what his son liked to eat. Did Ethan have allergies? Was he vegetarian? Mark had no idea. When it was his turn to order, he panicked and bought almost everything on the menu. Cheeseburgers, Quarter Pounders, nuggets with every flavour of sauce, salad wraps – enough for twelve people, not two. He carried the heavy brown bags back to the bus stop, the greasy smell of French fries sticking to his clothes. It was too much food.

Passengers poured out of blue buses.

He opened his wallet and looked at the old photograph of Ethan. He wouldn't look like that now: not even a year old, round and dribbling. Mark was this boy's father, but he felt like an interloper.

What sort of father knew nothing about their only child? Didn't even know what Ethan looked like. He scratched the back of his head and thought fleetingly of his own dad – how John had begged for this meeting, how this encounter was happening too late.

Mark looked up from his wallet. From the corner of his eye, he recognised the hair first. He'd fought with a comb every morning to control those exact waves. At school they'd teased him, said he looked like a mental patient, called him Young Einstein. Since then, he'd always slicked his hair to the side with gel. And there it was, that unruly black hair on another head.

Ethan looked across the road, his eyes darting back and forth. He was taller than Mark had expected, much older looking. Mark couldn't remember how tall twelve-year-olds should be; he hadn't been that age for a long time. Ethan crossed the street. Their eyes met. Mark immediately noticed the shape and colour of the boy's eyes – that piece of Claire transplanted onto someone else's face. It dislocated him.

Mark waved with his free hand.

The boy stumbled up to him, his mouth slightly open. 'Excuse me, sir,' he said softly. 'Is your name Mark Hall?'

Mark nodded, speechless.

'I'm Ethan. I'm, um, your son.' Then the boy quickly looked away.

Mechanically, Mark held out his arm to shake Ethan's hand. Suddenly it seemed a peculiar thing to do, an unnatural ritual. The boy didn't seem to understand immediately; he tilted his head, confused by this offering of an arm in the air. Then he grasped Mark's hand and looked cautiously into his eyes.

Mark tried to make sure his handshake was gentle.

Ethan let go first.

'It's nice to meet you,' Mark said.

'It's nice to meet you,' the boy repeated, with stiff politeness.

He's shy, Mark thought to himself, examining his son's face. He tried to fill in the gaps – how Ethan had grown from a chubby baby into this almost adolescent boy – because now he had bone structure, thick eyebrows. Mark felt an affinity with him and recognised his awkwardness: he'd been painfully shy at this age too, always wary of new people, overanalysing everything. Replaying conversations in his head and wincing at all the pathetic things that came out of his mouth. He hoped his son didn't suffer from that same gnawing self-consciousness he'd once felt too.

Ethan kept his eyes on the ground, tightly holding his arms to his body. The boy was quiet and watchful, evaluating his father's every move. It made Mark feel like an experiment, like a scientist was observing him in a lab while he conducted research. Occasionally, Ethan shot glances at him but never for more than a second. Mark realised he'd have to work hard to get the boy's guard down. He had to find a way to connect and figure out how to gain his son's trust.

'I've brought lunch,' Mark said shakily. He hadn't expected to feel so nervous. His stomach was in knots. 'I thought we could eat in the park.'

Ethan looked at the bulging paper bags. 'Is someone else coming too?'

'Nope, just us. Let's walk down this way.'

They headed towards the narrow stairs that led to a tunnel, through the cobblestoned laneways of The Rocks. As they waited at the intersection, an old woman looked at them both and smiled. Mark felt a burst of pride and smiled back. Yes, this was his son, thank you for noticing. But as the traffic light changed from red to green, Mark couldn't meet her eyes again. He didn't deserve that smile; he was an impostor, a fraud. But Ethan didn't notice the exchange.

They stood for a moment and listened to the didgeridoo player sitting in front of the Museum of Contemporary Art. Tourists crowded around him and threw coins into a bucket. The music rumbled and purred.

'Look,' Ethan said. 'That sounds funny. The resonances occur at frequencies that aren't harmonically spaced.'

'You can hear that?' Mark raised an eyebrow. 'It's because the didgeridoo is an open-closed pipe, so we hear that low drone plus the acoustics of the player's mouth. And because of the shape of the tube. Termites ate the wood, so the inside has irregular contours.'

'Yeah, that makes sense. They're low-frequency waves.'

Mark shook his head in disbelief and stared openly at Ethan. How on earth did he know that? Claire was right. Their son was some kind of genius – his kind of genius. Mark could talk the talk, but he couldn't distinguish harmonic spacing of frequencies.

'So, do you like school?' he asked.

'Nobody likes school.' Ethan put his hands in his pockets.

'What's your favourite subject?'

'Science, obviously.' Ethan shrugged. There was something in the way he moved his face, his nonchalant expressions, that seemed exactly like Claire. But Mark's genetic information was stamped all over this boy and he couldn't believe how much he saw of himself, his father, his brother. He couldn't take his eyes off him.

'Me too,' Mark said. 'I used to be a scientist. Particle physicist, actually.'

They walked up the incline to Observatory Hill Park.

'I knew that. Well, not about the particles. How come you're not one now?'

'Didn't finish my thesis,' Mark said, looking at the white rotunda in front of them. 'So never got my PhD. Ended up working in a different field. Do you want to sit over here?' He pointed to a picnic table that was covered in scraps of rain.

'Okay. So do you have a job?'

'I work near Kalgoorlie at a mine, although not down the mine. In a lab.' Mark dried the wet seat with a McDonald's napkin and offered Ethan the paper bag full of food.

Ethan looked gingerly into the bag and took the cheeseburger. 'I'm not allowed to eat McDonald's. Mum says the meat comes from factory farms and processed food gives you cancer.'

It took a moment for Mark to process who Ethan was talking about. Mum – that was what he called Claire. He noticed the methodical way the boy's hands unwrapped the yellow paper from the burger. Those were Mark's fingers, only smaller, more youthful. It was confusing to see a piece of himself transposed onto somebody else. Mark felt curiously impelled to touch them, like a magnet seeking metal. 'Well,' he said, taking a bite from a burger. 'Lunch will have to be our little secret.'

'My rabbit is named Quark,' Ethan said proudly.

It made Mark laugh. 'That's a wonderful name for a rabbit.'

'Yeah, I know. When I grow up, I want to get a PhD. I'm not sure what about yet, but definitely in physics. What was yours about?' Ethan stuffed a handful of fries into his mouth.

Mark paused. He hadn't thought much about his thesis for years. Remembering his abandoned research left a bitter taste in his mouth, like recalling a relationship turned sour, a painful memory that still stings. 'My research topic was anomalous parity asymmetry in the Cosmic Microwave Background.'

'What's that?'

'Right after the Big Bang, lots of antimatter was destroyed. The known universe is basically the leftovers of the fight between matter and antimatter. And what antimatter left behind was electromagnetic radiation. What we call the Cosmic Microwave Background. Because matter won the fight, antimatter lost. So my thesis was about that asymmetry. Why there's more matter than antimatter in the universe.'

Ethan stopped eating and looked up. 'Like particles and anti-particles.'

'Exactly. Electrons and positrons. Do you know anything about Paul Dirac?'

'*The Principles of Quantum Mechanics*,' Ethan said quickly. 'Dirac worked at Cambridge. Just like Stephen Hawking.'

Mark blinked, impressed. 'So you know Dirac predicted the positron. Let's say this cheeseburger is an atom. And the pickle inside is an electron. From what we know about the laws of quantum mechanics, electrons are restricted to a few paths called quantum states. In other words, the pickle is stuck to the cheese. Quantum theory says electrons are like pickles, and two pickles in one cheeseburger are too many. Dirac called this the exclusion principle: no two electrons in a collection can occupy the same quantum state. Which implies that electrons can have negative energy.'

'Negative energy,' Ethan repeated.

Mark took a sip of soft drink. He was probably boring the kid. Everyone hated when Mark started talking in scientific analogy like this. Let's say this cheeseburger is an atom! Electrons are like pickles! No wonder Ethan was looking away, his eyes fixed blankly on something in the distance.

Neither of them said anything for a while.

Ethan broke the silence. 'Did you get the Father's Day cards?' he asked.

'Yes, I did. Thank you.' Mark hadn't meant to sound so wooden.

'Yeah, you're welcome.'

Both of them finished their lunch quietly. Ethan ate a second burger, peeling the sticky orange cheese off the waxy wrapper and rolling it into tiny balls before putting them in his mouth. Crumbs lured the seagulls and ibises; with piping cries they fought over dropped chips, jousting with their black beaks like swords.

'Look, there's a sandpiper.' Mark pointed at the speckled brown bird, poking its bill into the soil. 'You only see them in Sydney a couple of months a year.'

Ethan threw the bird a cold chip. 'How come?'

'Sandpipers are migratory birds; they're always chasing summer. When it's winter down here, they fly to Europe and Asia where it's warm.'

'No way. But it's tiny. How can it fly all the way across the world and know where to go?'

'Apparently migratory birds can see Earth's magnetism and orient themselves in the right direction. Like an internal compass.'

Ethan crouched down near the sandpiper, carefully observing it move. The bird bobbed its head. 'They can really see magnetic fields? With their eyes?'

'Might be with their eyes, maybe their beaks. Nobody knows exactly how they detect variations in the Earth's magnetic field.'

'Awesome.'

The boy watched the sandpiper forage in the earth, poking and probing, stiff-winged and dark-eyed. With his lips slightly parted and attentive gaze, Ethan was the clearest distillation of his parents: Mark could see the best of himself in his son's curious face; he saw Claire in his focus. He was sad he'd lost something Ethan still had – curiosity, the naive wonder of a child. To be able to marvel at the smallest miracles, to look at a sandpiper and stand in awe at the beauty of nature's mysteries.

As they watched the bird fly away, Ethan smiled at Mark. The smile threw him. Mark wanted to explain to his son where he'd been all this time, how he'd wanted to watch him grow up, would've loved to be his dad. Things just hadn't gone exactly to plan.

But as they stood there on Observatory Hill, an ibis pecking at their feet, it turned out to be far easier to not say anything at all. They shared the silence and watched the traffic together, lanes of cars roaring from the city towards the yawning iron mouth of the Sydney Harbour Bridge.

∞

Ethan couldn't look at his father for more than two seconds in a row. Not just because he didn't want Mark to catch him staring – discover the confused state of flux written on his face – but mostly because whenever they made eye contact, it hurt Ethan's eyes. It felt like looking directly at the sun, how exposure to its ultraviolet light caused damage to the retina. Then Ethan remembered his retinas had already been damaged once. This man had done something to hurt his brain. Thinking about that made Ethan feel scared but he wasn't sure if it was a real reason to be afraid of Mark.

As a small child, Ethan had a crippling fear of the dark. He wouldn't walk down dark hallways alone; his night-light stayed on until sunrise the following day. Mum would hold his hand, always promised there were no monsters under the bed. He didn't know why he'd been scared, he just knew something terrifying lurked in the shadows. But whenever Ethan switched the light on, there was never anything there. His fear of nothing made him feel silly. There weren't any monsters hiding in the dark.

Mark's knee knocked against Ethan's leg under the table. He didn't feel very prepared to meet his dad. Prepared was the wrong word anyway. You prepared a cake: followed a recipe, measured the ingredients, baked it in the oven. You'd know when the cake was ready – its sweet aroma would fill the air, its batter would solidify. But Ethan couldn't smell the air and know he was ready like a cake. He felt raw and unprepared. This meeting wasn't playing out like he'd imagined inside his head. Everything he said to Mark sounded dumb. And he thought he should be more afraid of his father but something about Mark put him at ease. Ethan felt silly, like when the light came on and nothing was there after all.

They overdosed on McDonald's and Ethan's stomach ached. Talking to his father made him nervous. So instead of speaking, Ethan took mouthful after mouthful of food. Mark smiled at him and Ethan wondered how that smile should make him feel; it didn't feel the same as a smile from his mum. He gulped, trying to digest his feelings.

'Have you had enough?' Mark asked, turning to face him. There was a thin scar on the side of his face.

'Yeah, I'm full,' Ethan said. He wanted to ask about the scar but didn't.

'This park hasn't changed much since I was a kid.' His father stood up and brushed crumbs off his jeans. 'Want to go for a walk?'

Ethan nodded.

'My mum used to bring me here. I sprained my ankle in this park. Twice.'

'I've sprained my ankle too. Running along Narrawallee Beach.'

It was a vivid memory. Ethan and his mum visited that beach one freezing July day as they drove back up the South Coast from Melbourne to Sydney. The swell was huge, the surf was wild; she wouldn't let him swim. Ethan ran towards the shore and into the sea breeze – salt in his mouth, cheeks turned pink from the cold – but Mum stayed behind. She sat on the dunes, wind blowing through her hair, and looked out at the waves. Damp sand crumbled at his feet as Ethan ran and he rolled his ankle in a ditch. Ligaments tore; he wailed. Mum ran over to him and carried him back to the car. She bought him a rainbow Paddle Pop from the local shop.

'Narrawallee,' Mark said. 'I've been there with your mother too.'

That was weird. Mum hadn't said anything about that. Ethan never really thought much about his parents having a life together before he existed. But they must have. Was Mum thinking about his father while she sat on the dunes and looked at the water? Maybe his parents were happy back then, before he'd been born. Maybe they ate rainbow Paddle Pops on the beach and ran across the sand without spraining their ankles.

Mark walked towards the play equipment. 'Follow me.'

Ethan watched his father stride ahead. He could see clear panels enveloping them – fields of positive and negative currents and charges, attracting and repelling each other – but he didn't say anything about the electromagnetic field hanging in the air to Mark.

'Hold this for me?' Mark handed Ethan his jumper. He climbed over a maze of blue plastic and red ropes and over to the swings.

Ethan made sure his dad wasn't looking and held the jumper up to his nose. He inhaled quickly. This was his father's smell – soap, wool, wood – which was different to Mum's. He tried to store the scent in his memory.

Mark sat on the swing seat. The black rubber band distorted around his backside. 'You've played on the swings before, right?'

'Yeah, obviously,' Ethan replied, half-offended and half-confused by his question. 'I'm twelve. I might even be too old to play on the swings now, you know.'

Mark's hands gripped the rusty chains. He seemed puzzled by Ethan's reaction but continued anyway. 'Do you know what's happening to your body when you're on a swing?'

Ethan hesitated; he wasn't sure what his father wanted to know. You push against the ground, point your feet towards the sky and swing. There wasn't much more to it than that.

'Come sit next to me. I want to show you something.' Mark grabbed the chains of the swing beside him and offered them to Ethan.

Ethan positioned himself on the seat of the swing, careful not to place his body too far forward or backwards. He curled his fingers around each chain; the metal rings were cold in his hands. With his feet, he pulled his body back before he pushed himself into the air, pumping his legs until he was in full flight, swinging back and forth in a steady trajectory.

'I'm oscillating,' he said.

Mark laughed. 'That's right. Now stop moving your legs.'

Ethan pulled his feet in and he started to slow down. Eventually, he came to a halt. His feet slid along the ground; gravel flew into the air.

'I'm not sure what you were trying to show me.'

'Let me try and explain.' Mark tilted his body back and started to swing. Feet tucked in. Feet turned out. Feet tucked in. Feet turned out. 'The swing pushes on me, and I'm pushing on the swing too. You try. Tell me what you can feel.'

The warm air hit Ethan's face as he swung back and forth. 'Torque, angular momentum and gravity. Obviously.'

'Wow,' Mark said as he swung his own body higher. 'But to make sure you keep swinging higher, you need to apply a little bit of force at the end of each swing. Know what I mean?'

'Yeah.' That last-minute pump of the legs.

Mark yelled across the swing set. 'And when you're in that in-between place, where you're not going up and you're not going down, something amazing happens.'

'What?'

'For a tiny moment, you're weightless.'

'Technically that's wrong,' said Ethan. 'I weigh forty-one kilograms.'

'But for a fraction of a second – between swinging forwards and backwards – the forces of gravity, friction and air resistance bring the velocity of the swing to zero. At that moment, you feel no centrifugal force. Weightlessness. Just like you're in space. You're flying. That's what I wanted to explain.' Mark smiled at him. 'Ethan, I know I'm a little bit late, but if you give me a chance now, I could teach you to fly.'

Even though Ethan knew he shouldn't believe it, even though it all sounded a little lame, this man knew how to talk to him. Mark spoke Ethan's language; they were the same. A magnetic thrill leaped from his chest. As Ethan swung up into the sky with his father beside him, he'd never felt higher in his life.

A thick lump lodged in the back of his throat. Ethan tried to suppress it, but suddenly his eyes were swollen with tears. He started to cry. *No, stop it.* Crying was against the rules.

Growing up, Ethan tried his best to be a boyish boy. He played with trucks and rockets and trains, he kicked balls and scuffed his shoes, he collected rocks and sticks. Although Ethan liked those things anyway, he also knew he was obeying the rules. Rules for being a boy. And if he followed these rules, people wouldn't notice that something was missing.

He'd heard a teacher once say that you could tell when a boy doesn't have a father; young boys always needed a strong male role model. Ethan knew he didn't have either of those. Nobody taught him any curriculum for how to be a man. At school, he listened to friends' stories about weekends fishing with their dads, building furniture together, watching footy. He longed for that alliance, man to man, more than anything else. Ethan wanted it so much that what he already had – the person who loved him, his mum, who didn't care about the rules for being a boy – sometimes wasn't enough.

Mark stopped swinging. 'What's wrong?'

Ethan wiped his eyes with his sleeve. 'Nothing.' He pushed his voice an octave lower than it really was.

'Did I say something to upset you?'

Ethan shook his head. He was so embarrassed and couldn't look at his father again; crying wasn't tough. What would his dad think of him now? He'd find out his son was a wimp. A freak. Ethan kicked the gravel. 'It's just,' he began. The words sat, congealed, in the back of his mouth. 'It's just you seem like a really nice person.'

Mark looked away.

'I mean, you are a nice person.' Ethan backtracked. That came out wrong, he needed to reverse those words. Great, now he'd upset his father plus made himself look like a crybaby. 'I don't know. I guess I don't understand. It doesn't make sense to me. That since you're such a nice person, you did that really bad thing.'

His father didn't respond. Maybe Mark hadn't heard anything Ethan said; maybe Ethan hadn't said his thoughts out loud.

Mark stood up. 'Have you ever been to the Observatory?'

'No, never.'

'I used to go all the time when I was just a bit older than you, when I was in high school. Someday I'll bring you here at night so we can look at the stars.'

'Really? I'd like that.'

'Anyway, I once spoke to an astronomer at the Observatory who was writing down the coordinates of stars and galaxies. But I noticed he used a formula to correct the positions, so I asked him why. He told me that because of gravity's effect on the electromagnetic spectrum, mass bends light. So through the telescope, it looks as though a star is in a different place to its actual position.'

'Yeah, I know. That's the gravitational deflection of light.'

'Ethan, you're a very smart boy,' Mark said. 'Way smarter than I was at your age. I really wanted to be a good father to you. And I haven't been, and that's my fault. But not everything was my fault. I'm not sure what your mother has told you, but I never hurt you. The doctors were wrong. I didn't do it.'

Ethan looked at the Observatory's green dome and thought about the hardened lies of bending light. Einstein showed that the sun's gravity distorted the entire sky, proving that gravity wasn't really a force at all. Before that, nobody questioned Newton – things that went up had to come down – but Newton was wrong, things bent.

Theories were disproven all the time, Ethan thought, sometimes everything we thought we knew turned out to be a colossal mistake. Indivisible and indestructible atoms, that light came from our eyes, a heliocentric universe – all those theories were incorrect and superseded by something else. There were no universal truths, just views of the world yet to be proven wrong.

'I have to go home,' Ethan said. 'Before it gets too late.'

'I didn't mean to upset you.'

'You didn't. Physics is figuring out how to ask the right questions. Einstein had to prove the ether didn't exist to figure out that the speed of light was constant.'

Mark scratched at his temple. 'I'll walk you back to the bus stop.'

Back at Circular Quay, they said goodbye and attempted a clumsy hug. Neither of them knew how to navigate the other's arms. Seagulls clogged the footpath. The bus arrived and Ethan boarded. He waved at Mark from the window. After the second traffic light, his father disappeared from sight.

Ethan buzzed for the rest of his journey home. He felt like he'd drunk every litre in every river and lake after spending years dying of thirst, like he'd just solved an impossible mathematical problem. Discovered some kind of grand unification theory. Now he knew the truth. His father had never hurt him. Everything – about who Ethan was, where he came from – finally made sense. Now he just had to figure out how to prove it to everyone else.

He carefully opened the gate and then quietly unlocked the front door. Mum was still asleep in bed. She finally woke later that afternoon and wandered into the lounge room where Ethan was playing *Minecraft* on the computer.

'Sorry, sweetheart, I think I've come down with the flu.' She pulled her hair off her face and into a ponytail. 'You must be starving.'

'Not really, Mum.' Ethan shook his head. 'I'm fine.'

14

BLACK HOLES

Dr Saunders set up a pair of large speakers in two corners of his office: black cylinders, like thick pipes covered in dark mesh. On top of his desk, there was a stereo and subwoofer. The set-up made Ethan think of a city skyline – hard angles along the horizon, as tops of the buildings tried to scratch the atmosphere, skyscraper to sky.

'My son is an audiophile,' Dr Saunders said. 'These speakers create 360-degree sound.'

Ethan sat down at the desk. 'What are they for?'

'I've been thinking about what you said about seeing waves.' Dr Saunders bent down to check the power point of the stereo. 'So, I'm going to play you some music and I want you to draw what you see. Stand right back on the other side of the room, opposite the speakers.'

Ethan positioned himself against the back wall.

Dr Saunders switched the stereo on. Black speakers emitted white noise. He pressed some buttons and music began, although Ethan didn't recognise it. Dr Saunders turned the volume up. It was so loud that Ethan almost felt his eardrum straining, his jaw vibrating.

'What can you see?' The doctor shouted from the other side of the room.

Piano music, just a solo pianist. There was solidity to the sound, its notes were firm and grounding. Ethan felt the music inside his body – striking ivory keys resonating down his spine, reverberating deep through the minerals of his bones. He closed his eyes. Notes sent tiny impulses through his nerves. He opened his eyes again.

But Ethan couldn't see anything. No waves. Nothing at all. He stared at the speakers, unsure whether or not he was imagining them quiver slightly. Then, from behind the piano, an orchestra started to play.

Waves radiated from each of the speakers in concentric circles – rings of a bullseye, ripples that encircle a rock dropped in a lake. The waves had identical crests and troughs. Layers of loops, one after the next, surrounded each speaker. But when the two bullseyes of waves met in the middle of the room, they created a pattern. The geometry of the sound reshaped itself. Rings turned into diamonds.

As the textured music swept across the room, Ethan felt dizzy. Lines formed where the music collided; interference changed the wavefront angles, making the waves uneven. In some parts of the room, sound stood still. In other parts, it blasted.

Dr Saunders stood beside Ethan. 'Can you see the sound waves?'

'Yes.'

'What's happening?'

'They're coming out from each of the speakers in circles. Then the circles get bigger, like expanding hoops. When the waves meet in the middle, it looks a bit like a weird round chessboard,' Ethan said. It was difficult to describe. 'Can you see them too?'

'No, I can't see anything.'

As he watched the ripples of sound, Ethan thought about his father. He wanted to talk to someone about finally meeting him. Maybe Dr Saunders would understand. But Ethan was worried he'd get in trouble or that the doctor might tell Mum. Alison was the only person who knew. She'd made him tell her everything – hidden in his bedroom, speaking in whispers – about where they'd gone and what they'd said.

The halos of music were bigger and brighter now, round waves propagating outwards with thickening clarity. Ethan's eyes stiffened; he didn't blink. Sound waves were invisible to everyone else but he could see them. This was his secret world. Entirely his own, his private experience of the universe.

Dr Saunders handed him a sheet of paper. 'Ethan, do you think you could draw the waves for me?'

'Sure,' Ethan said. He made a diagram of the concentric circles and their crosshatched pattern.

'Interesting,' the doctor said. 'Could I keep this?'

Ethan nodded. 'Dr Saunders? I was wondering about something. Are there other ways to become a savant? Without having a brain injury, I mean. Maybe I was just born like this, able to see this stuff?'

Dr Saunders raised his eyebrows. 'Brain injury seems the most likely explanation for your savant abilities, Ethan. Cognitive scientists who specialise in savant syndrome believe it's caused by abnormal cross-communication between different brain regions. Hyper-connectivity. Your pattern-recognition and numeracy skills are highly developed, and the regions responsible for those skills sit beside each other on the left side of your parietal lobe. But yes, there are other ways to develop savant abilities. Although your brain injury rewired your brain, cross-communication can also be caused by other neurological conditions. Autism. Schizophrenia. Epilepsy.'

'Seizures?'

'Your seizures could be a contributing factor. But it's safe to say they were triggered by the subdural haematoma. So no, I don't think you were born with your abilities. Savant abilities are always caused by some form of disorder.'

Ethan looked at his feet. Safe to say wasn't the same as certain; it wasn't conclusive proof. Trusting cognitive science sounded like believing theoretical physics. Quantum mechanics, black holes, dark matter and dark energy: they all floated tied to theory's anchor. Ethan didn't need to look into the spinning chasm of a black hole to know that they existed. But just like the exact mechanics of Ethan's brain, black holes hadn't yet been directly observed.

So the doctor spoke in speculation, not fact. Shaken baby syndrome couldn't be the reason he'd had a brain haemorrhage if Ethan hadn't actually been shaken. There must still be lots of unknowns inside the brain, stuff doctors hadn't figured out yet. Whatever had happened to his synapses and neurons, it made him special.

'Are you okay?' Dr Saunders asked. 'You seem a little distracted.'

'What?' Ethan sat up straight and pulled himself out of his thoughts. 'Yeah, I'm okay.'

∞

Ethan stared into his blueprints. Words and numbers leaped off the pages; equations moved around like cartoons. Lines on the plotted graphs bulged and curled. It was going to be difficult to calculate the exact energy requirements. He redid the Einstein field equations from scratch. A rotating black hole possesses angular momentum. Getting out of the wormhole would be the biggest problem.

'Building a time machine is boring!' Alison complained.

Ethan didn't look up. He scribbled something out on the page. What would Stephen Hawking do, he wondered; how did he figure out black holes weren't completely black, but actually emitted radiation?

Alison peered over his shoulder at the sheets of paper – sketches of the time machine, pages and pages of equations, numbers and diagrams – and pointed at the blueprints.

'That's a lot of drawings of doughnuts,' she said.

'They're not doughnuts.'

'Now I'm hungry. What are they then?'

'Closed time-like curves. Gravitational fields bend the fabric of space-time and it makes something that looks like a doughnut. In geometry, it's called a torus. So to go backwards in time, I just race around the doughnut, going further back into the past with each lap.'

'That made zero sense. You're going to race around a doughnut?'

'Yeah, kinda. We just need to warp the fabric of space-time, so it loops back on itself.' Ethan took a piece of paper and folded it in half. 'Imagine this is space-time. The top half of the paper is the present, and the bottom half is the past. Then, if I poke this pencil through the top to the bottom, there's my shortcut. That's the traversable wormhole.'

'Wait, but why the doughnut?'

'Pay attention. It leads back in time. Like a looping door. Obviously I'll need to do a few laps to go back twelve years. Follow me!' Ethan led Alison to the laundry where he'd hidden at least twenty power boards in a garbage bag.

'We'll need lots of energy to power the time machine,' he said. 'All the energy in the house.'

'Ethan, isn't that dangerous?' she asked.

'Maybe. It only needs to work for a second. Before the circuits get overloaded. But I still need to figure out exactly how much electrical current will open the wormhole.'

She wrinkled her nose. 'What do you mean, open the wormhole?'

'Alison, I told you this already. Wormholes let you go backwards in time, and enough energy will bend space so they open. There's a rule in physics that lets you borrow a huge amount of energy – as long as you pay it back quickly. It's called the Heisenberg uncertainty principle.'

'Like a loan? How will you pay it back?'

'In particles, of course. With negative energy.'

Alison gave a hesitant nod. 'Ethan, I know you have a special gift and everything. You definitely know what you're talking about. But are you sure this'll work?'

'Yeah, I've figured it all out. It has to,' he said. 'Now, one problem will be getting the wormhole to exit in the right place in time. I need to go back to the exact moment I got sick when I was a baby. Twelve years ago. So I can prove my father didn't hurt me.'

'What happens if you get stuck?'

'That's where quantum mechanics comes in,' Ethan explained. 'At the centre of the black hole is a singularity. Where every law of physics breaks down and everything gets squished. I'd get squished in there.'

'Squished in a bad way?'

'Really bad. So I'm going to quantum teleport. Black holes emit tiny bits of radiation, made of entangled pairs of particles. Negative energy particles fall into the hole and positive energy particles escape. So inside the hole I'll take a measurement of myself together with the incoming Hawking radiation, and then I'll send the results back to you. Then that information can re-create me out of the outgoing Hawking radiation. Get it?'

Alison shook her head. 'Ethan, this sounds really risky.'

'That's why we need the doughnut. Time travel is risky, but the closed time-like curve makes it safe. They did it once in Canada, using entangled photons. Don't worry, the photons were fine. I won't get hurt.' He paused and muttered to himself. 'Wait. I almost forgot!' Ethan went to the bathroom and came back with a pastel-green can of women's shaving cream.

Alison laughed. 'You're going to shave your legs? Suppose it'd make you more aerodynamic, so you'd go faster. Like an Olympic swimmer.'

'No, silly. It's the quantum foam.' Ethan shook the pressurised can and sprayed gel into his hand. It turned into a creamy lather, like a cloud sitting on his palm. 'Quantum foam is the foundation of the fabric of the universe. It's subatomic space-time turbulence. And the Heisenberg uncertainty principle lets energy briefly decay into particles and antiparticles, and then annihilate without violating physical conservation laws.'

'Speak English,' Alison said. She poked the wobbling shaving cream and put some on Ethan's nose.

'According to Einstein's theory of general relativity, energy curves space-time,' he said, wiping his face. 'On a small scale, space-time is foamy. On a bigger scale, it's fabric. There's still one problem, though. I need to connect the energy so it becomes a single source. Like a little explosion. How can I make it all explode?'

'Ethan, I don't know.' Alison sounded annoyed. 'You're not going to start a fire, are you?'

'I know what I'm doing. All I need is something really flammable that will merge the energy. Only for a nanosecond, like a fireball. Just trust me, okay?'

'Flammable sounds like starting a fire to me,' she said under her breath. She inspected the ends of her hair. 'Flammable,' she repeated. She opened up her backpack and produced three little candy-coloured jars. 'Nail polish is flammable. If we pour it on the time machine, that might make the energy combine.'

'Alison! You're a genius!' Ethan grinned.

She shrugged. 'I know. But it's quick-dry nail polish so the wormhole better open in under three minutes.'

'That'll be okay.'

'So how long until we can actually use the time machine?'

'I think we're almost ready. But I still don't know how much energy we need. The mathematics is really complicated. I need help with these equations.'

She sat down on the sofa and crossed her arms. 'This would be way easier if we just had a flux capacitor and DeLorean.'

Ethan leaped to his feet. 'You're right! The flux capacitor! That's the energy that sends them backwards in time. We need to watch *Back to the Future.*'

'Finally!' Alison rolled her eyes. 'Watching you do maths is not my idea of fun. Hey, before we start the movie, can we go to the shops and get some doughnuts?'

∞

Ever since he was a teenager, Mark had suffered from migraines. Sometimes they made him throw up; pressure that crushed his brain until it squeezed his stomach dry. Flashes of light and auras appeared; his pulse throbbed through his skull. Once the pain was so bad, he punched a hole in a wall. Not much helped – painkillers, dark rooms, glasses of water – usually he just needed to wait and see it through. Ride the wave, while the migraine slammed him against rocks, eventually washing him up on the shore of the following day.

Inside the dark pit of a migraine, Mark remembered things. Things he couldn't erase, memories he'd suppressed. Bright flashes of old feelings: the claustrophobic confinement of a cell; the monotony of endless white walls, white floors and white ceilings; the humiliation of sweeping the dull concrete floors of the prison block. Ticking clocks, empty hours, infinite days. Cheek pressed against a cinderblock wall, his hands pinned to his back. Mark was never a religious person, but sometimes he dropped down to his knees and prayed those memories would go away.

He'd need to wait until it was dark before he dared venture up the road to the shops. Even though he was a grown man, in some ways he still couldn't take care of himself. Ethan seemed to ground him, though. For the first time in years, Mark felt like himself. He didn't have to follow orders or be at another's command; he didn't feel trapped. His son appreciated him. Something flickered behind Ethan's eyes as he hung on to Mark's every word.

It was still a surprise to see him suddenly appear at his door.

'Ethan, what are you doing here?'

The boy was carrying a heavy backpack. 'I'm on school holidays. Are you busy?'

'I was just going to the shops.'

'Can I come?' Ethan smiled.

Mark noticed how perfect his son's teeth were. 'Yeah, all right,' he said, massaging his temples.

'What's wrong?'

'Just have a little headache.'

'How come?'

Ethan asked a lot of questions. He asked questions about physics, about how the stars were formed and if time travel were possible, how you might make a wormhole. Thankfully, he'd stopped asking personal questions. It was for the best: Mark's past was a gyre; nobody ever went down there.

'What are you going to buy?' Ethan asked as they entered the supermarket.

'Aspirin.' The migraine had intensified. Brutal supermarket fluorescence made it worse. He closed his eyes for a moment. It always reminded him of prison, this bright artificial light.

Ethan picked up a basket. 'What's your favourite food?'

Mark opened his eyes again. 'I don't think I've been asked that question for a while,' he said. He stopped to think about it for a second. 'Mexican food, I think.'

'Me too! Have you ever been to Mexico?'

'No, I haven't.'

Ethan looked over at the breakfast cereals. 'Neither. Maybe we could go together one day?'

Mark didn't even stop to consider how realistic the possibility of that was. 'Definitely.'

'I know how to make fajitas,' Ethan said. 'I could make them for you.' He took a kit in his hands and started to read the back of the yellow box. 'We need chicken breast and some vegetables and maybe cheese.'

Mark followed him to the next aisle. His vision was clouded by scintillating scotoma; he couldn't focus from one moment to the next.

'Can you help?' Ethan asked, trying to reach the sour cream.

Mark grabbed it from the top shelf.

'What's that?' The boy leaned in. He touched Mark's upper arm, lifted up his t-shirt and poked his skin.

The tattoo. Mark put his hand over it, covering its lines. 'Problem with tattoos, isn't it? Can't get rid of them.'

Ethan stepped back. 'Did you get it in prison?'

'No,' Mark said quickly. 'I got it a very long time ago.'

'It looks like —' Ethan pushed his father's hand off the tattoo and took a moment to inspect it. That tattoo had been on his skin for almost thirteen years; the black ink had faded to navy blue, the crisp lines softer now, where the pigment bled into his flesh.

'It's an equation,' Ethan said, excited. 'It's $E=mc^2$. But what does that mean?'

'Well, c is the speed of light,' Mark began. 'And —'

'No, I know that. E is energy, m is mass. I mean, what does it mean?

When adults get tattoos they usually mean something. Why do you have a tattoo of that? What does it stand for?'

Mark pulled his sleeve down. 'Nothing. It doesn't stand for anything.'

'So you just really like Einstein's mass–energy equivalence equation?'

'It's silly, really. I got this tattoo when you were born. It's us. You were the product of us. $E=mc^2$ – E for Ethan, M for Mark, C for Claire. She was my constant.' Mark trailed off. 'Not any more.'

Ethan looked away.

Mark wondered what he was thinking. He'd said too much. The boy was only twelve; he wouldn't understand. That stupid tattoo. It reminded him there'd been so much optimism once. Before other things forced themselves in the way, Mark believed their little family could survive anything.

Now the only constants he believed in were mathematical, scientific: the gravitational constant G, Planck's constant h, the electric constant ke, and the elementary charge e. These were, for Mark, the only things that he could rely on to be universally true. Nothing else was truly constant – not family, not people, not love. Not even himself.

Ethan tapped Mark's shoulder. 'You wouldn't happen to know anything about Einstein's field equations, would you?'

∞

According to his calculations, Ethan needed to be back home in one hour and fifty-two minutes. Mum was working late – another ballet opening; this time he wasn't allowed to come – and the show finished at 8.30 p.m. Ethan and Mark finished eating dinner and were watching television. The fajitas were a little overcooked but his father hadn't really noticed. In fact, he hadn't noticed much. Mark seemed agitated and upset, massaging his forehead and shutting his eyes. Ethan hoped he hadn't done anything to annoy his father.

Ethan looked around the house; it was massive and unfriendly. Even though it was full of stuff – old family pictures in dusty golden frames, glass paperweights trapping butterflies, faded portraits of frowning saints – it felt empty and abandoned. More like a museum, not like a home.

The long corridors asphyxiated light; Ethan couldn't even see the other end of the hall. Whispers and creaks echoed from behind closed doors, like secrets and ghosts hid inside locked rooms. Ethan stared at the family photographs, curious about the people who'd lived here once. His grandparents, both dead. Their unfamiliar faces made him ache for his own home.

'It's getting late,' Ethan said.

Mark opened his eyes. 'You're right. I'd give you a lift but I don't think I'm in any state to drive. But I don't want you to catch the bus home alone at this hour. How about I give you some money for a taxi?'

'I'm not allowed. Mum says never get in cars with people you don't know.'

'Even taxi drivers?'

Ethan was wringing his hands. 'I've never caught a taxi alone. And I don't want to break any other rules. Maybe you could ride in the taxi with me?' His voice shook a little; he didn't know why.

Mark nodded. 'Sure, I could do that.'

The taxi drove from Sydney's east to its west: climbing up to Edgecliff's peak where the darkening city horizon shifted to dusk; through the Bayswater tunnel and into the neon reds and pinks of Kings Cross; weaving around the traffic-choked blocks of the CBD where pedestrians jaywalked, stumbling off the pavement at busy intersections; past Chinatown's flickering signs for noodle houses and light-flooded frozen yoghurt shops; briefly stopping behind swarms of blue and grey buses collecting passengers at Railway Square.

'Dad, did you study at UTS?' Ethan asked as the taxi drove past the tower.

'Nope, Sydney Uni.' Mark pointed towards Broadway.

'Oh yeah? Physics Road.' Ethan stared out the window. Mark obviously hadn't heard. Ethan had never called him Dad before; he'd never actually called anyone Dad. It felt nice to hold that word in his mouth – Dad – the cluck of the syllable rolling effortlessly off his tongue.

He changed the subject. 'Is there such a thing as the opposite of a black hole?'

'Sort of. Some people call that a white hole,' Mark said. 'Whatever black holes do, white holes do in reverse. But they've never been observed. In fact, there's only been one proposed white hole singularity in the history of the universe. At the heart of the Big Bang.'

They drove along Parramatta Road, past the petrol station and antique furniture warehouse.

Ethan sat up straight. 'But they're not totally impossible?'

'White holes don't agree with the second law of thermodynamics. Entropy is supposed to increase over time, but in a white hole the entropy is low.'

'Oh,' Ethan said, sinking back into the seat. 'That sucks.'

'But the second law of thermodynamics only applies to closed systems. To balance out the entropy problem, a white hole could draw its energy from somewhere outside the system. But that would require an awful lot of energy.'

'What if you borrowed lots of energy but paid it back quickly?

Then do you think it's possible to make a traversable wormhole with a black hole and a white —'

The brakes squeaked as the taxi stopped in front of the house.

Mark stared. 'This is where you live?'

Ethan looked at the narrow entrance of his front gate and suddenly felt embarrassed. It was bigger than other places they'd lived – a castle compared to their studio apartment back when he was still in preschool – but it wasn't fancy like the Woollahra house. Ethan saw his home through his father's eyes. 'We have a garden out the back,' he said. 'Quark is scared of the garden, though.'

The taxi's engine was still running, headlights illuminating the quiet street. Another car pulled up behind them and beeped its horn. Inside the dark house, someone switched on a light.

Ethan's stomach sank. 'Oh no. Mum.'

'She's home? I can come inside with you. Do you want me to talk to her?'

'No, that'd just make it worse.' Ethan slowly opened the door and climbed out of the taxi.

Mark held the car door ajar with his hand. 'Ethan, you can call me later if you'd like.'

'Thanks, Dad.'

Mark's face stiffened and he blinked. That time Ethan knew that he'd noticed; that time he'd definitely heard.

Inside the house, Mum sat on Ethan's bed. Her eyes were blank and she looked like a ghost in the half-lit room. Ethan felt truly scared of his mum for the first time. Other times – when he'd been badly behaved, hadn't done well at school, a couple of occasions when he'd disappointed her – Ethan was scolded. But she'd never been scary. Now there was an absence in his mum's eyes that terrified him. He couldn't tell how angry she was; her face gave him no hints.

'Mum?' He felt himself shrink back into his body. His limbs grew shorter, his rib cage narrowed, his internal organs contracted. 'Mum, I'm really sorry.'

'I missed a phone call this afternoon at work. So I opened up my recent call history. And I was surprised to see several phone calls on that list that I didn't make myself.'

Ethan knew where this was going. 'Mum, I can explain —'

She cut him off. 'When I saw who the calls were made to, I became quite concerned. I came straight home so I could talk to you about it. But you weren't home when I got back. I had no idea where you were! And it was getting later and later. Do you think maybe I was worried out of my mind, Ethan?' Mum didn't wait for a reply. 'I was going to call the police. I came into your bedroom trying to see if you'd left any clues about where you might be, a note or something. And then I found this.' A crumpled piece of paper was in her hand. She unfolded it, offering it to Ethan. The letter from Dad.

'Mum, it's not what you —'

She spoke over him. 'Is that where you went tonight? To see him?'

All Ethan could do was give a small nod.

'I see,' she said, her voice flat. 'Thank you for being honest with me.'

'That's it?' Ethan searched her face. He needed her to explode, to cry, to behave like his mum. But all she did was give him a stony stare. 'Am I in trouble? Am I grounded?'

'No, you're not. You've just really hurt my feelings, Ethan. And the thing that hurts the most,' Mum said, taking a small breath, 'is that you hid this from me. For how long? Weeks? Months? You knew your father was back but you never said a word. Since when do we keep secrets like that from each other?'

Now Ethan was hurt. 'Mum, you kept a really big secret from me.

And you didn't tell me he was in Sydney when you knew.'

She closed her eyes. 'Ethan, that's very different. I was trying to protect you.'

'He isn't going to hurt me. He isn't dangerous.'

It was the truth. They'd met twice now – had spent precisely six and a quarter hours together – and Ethan knew that his father wasn't a dangerous man. He was gentle and generous. Always explaining things to Ethan, just wanting him to learn. Mark knew so much about everything – physics, music, architecture. He was like an audio guide; he made life a museum. Ethan could take him anywhere and he'd explain anything.

Mum wasn't like that. She didn't know the answers to Ethan's questions – what happens at an event horizon, what's the escape velocity of Mars? They were universes apart. She lived behind a force field. But his father, in the space of six and a quarter hours, had allowed Ethan to totally enter his world.

'He's my dad,' Ethan said.

'I'm your mother!'

'But you lied to me about him. And you made my father leave.'

'Ethan, that's not true. You had a serious brain injury, it's much more complicated than that. You almost died.'

'But I didn't die. I'm fine. Better than fine. Dr Saunders said my brain injury gave me a special gift.' Ethan held his chest high. 'I can see physics. Nobody else can do that. Just my brain. Dr Saunders said so. Only me. I'm special.'

'You think your brain injury made you special? You're special because that's who you are. Your injury and your father had nothing to do with it.'

'That's not true.' Ethan was getting angry now. She wasn't listening to him and he was right. 'You don't understand.'

'It's not that I don't understand, I just don't agree with you.'

'Then you really don't understand. Anyway, you called him too. You're not allowed to be angry with me. I know you did. I saw it on your phone. You've been speaking to my father for weeks.'

'That's different,' Mum said. 'That was —'

'And I know everything about Will's dad too. That's why Will's mum was so angry. That's why she said those mean things.' Ethan knew he was twisting the knife now but he couldn't stop. 'Everybody knows what you did. All the boys at school called you a slut.'

Mum didn't react straight away. She became very still, so still it didn't look like she was breathing. Her eyes narrowed. Suddenly, she didn't look like his mum any more.

'Go to bed, Ethan.' There was a wildness in her voice now, something primitive, close to a growl. 'I don't want to look at you. I can't even be in the same room as you right now.'

Ethan watched her storm off, shielding her face to hide that she was crying. Good. She deserved to cry. It wasn't fair Mum was angry with him for things she'd done wrong. She was meant to be the grown-up but she was acting like a child. Keeping secrets. Telling him lies.

He put on his pyjamas and returned to the time-machine plans. Ethan knew he'd hurt her feelings, said things that made Mum sad. But she'd made herself that way; it wasn't his fault. She was trapped, collapsing under her own weight. Only Mum could drag herself out of the darkness. He couldn't believe anything she said any more. Once he travelled back in time and could prove Mark was innocent, she'd realise Ethan was right.

15

RELATIVITY

The ingredients were almost ready now: a dash of energy, a sprinkle of time. Ethan had carefully picked steps from every recipe – general relativity for mixing the batter of space-time; special relativity to whip tachyons faster than light; quantum theory to chop particles into the past.

The time machine would fix everything: a wormhole leading to a critical moment outside the present's mess. But after what had happened last night, Ethan needed to push the schedule forward. He needed to go back now.

Ethan picked up the phone. 'The plan's changed,' he said. 'It has to happen today.'

'Why? What happened?' Alison asked.

'Mum knows that I've met . . . you know.'

'How? Did you tell her? Oh my gosh, did he tell her? He totally told her, I bet it was him.' She took a deep breath. 'What does she know?'

'Not everything. She doesn't know about the time machine. She only saw the phone calls. Anyway, it'll take too long to explain right now. Come to my place. We're pushing the schedule forward.'

'But you haven't finished the design yet! Do we have everything we need?'

'Almost. We'll figure it out. But you need to come over right now.'

'Ethan, I don't know if I'm allowed,' Alison whispered. 'Mum won't let me if there's no parental supervision. She'd freak out.'

'Make something up. Try and get here as soon as you can. I can't do this without you but time is running out. It needs to happen today.'

It would take at least 1.21 gigawatts to travel back in time, according to the flux capacitor. Ethan needed to collect all that power and channel it into one place – energy. $E=mc^2$. His father's tattoo. E for Ethan. M for Mark. C for Claire. Ethan had to get this right, so he could fix everything.

He closed his eyes and pictured the glimmering black hole. He'd be able to enter it from any direction, so he pointed the time machine at the back garden. Mathematically, the white hole was just a black hole under inverted time. All he needed to do now was find the right light-cone coordinates. Ethan sat up straight and stretched his arms.

Alison arrived, dressed in a navy-blue jumpsuit that was far too big, and plastic goggles on her forehead. 'Okay, let's travel back in time!'

'What are you wearing?'

'These are my dad's King Gees. If I've learned anything from watching all those time-travel movies, it's that you need to wear a onesie to be protected from radiation. Safety first.' She put the goggles on her eyes.

Ethan scratched his head. 'I'll need to record a video for proof. Can I borrow your mobile?'

Alison took her phone out of her pocket and rubbed the screen on the coveralls. 'It was my birthday present. I'll be in so much trouble if I lose it, so you have to be really careful. What if you accidentally leave it in the past?'

'I promise I won't. I'll be super careful. But I have to show everyone that my father didn't actually shake me. I need to collect evidence.'

'Wait a sec,' Alison said. 'What if my mum calls you when you're in the wormhole? Or in the past?'

'Then I won't answer. Maybe I'll send her a text message? To be honest, I don't think there'll be good reception inside a wormhole. But I promise I'll take really good care of your phone. We SOOFed, remember? Our oath bound in spit.'

Alison handed the phone to Ethan. 'Okay. Only because we SOOFed.'

She pointed at the time machine. At least a dozen extension cords ran from the machine to different power sockets at the wall. Ethan had put a blanket on the top of the machine. 'What's that, the fabric of the cosmos?'

He frowned. 'It's really called the fabric of space-time.'

'Sorry,' Alison said sarcastically, putting a hand on her hip.

'We'll be able to open the wormhole right here. But before we can power up the time machine, I need to find the rabbit.'

Quark was hiding in a cardboard box in the kitchen, chewing on a parsley stem. He looked up at the children, twitched his nose and turned away. His tail wiggled briefly. Then the grey rabbit licked his paws and pulled his ears down across his face, carefully cleaning his fur.

Ethan tapped his fingers on the ground. 'Quark. Come on, come out here.' He offered the rabbit a tiny piece of biscuit. After a while, Quark sniffed the crumbs and hopped towards them.

Alison kneeled on the floor and scooped the bunny into her arms. The rabbit quivered for a moment, before relaxing into her embrace. 'Good boy,' she said, nuzzling her nose into the top of Quark's head. 'What does the rabbit have to do with time travel?'

'Quark is the final ingredient.'

'You're not going to hurt him, are you?' She held the bunny protectively, pulling him closer to her chest.

'No! He's my pet. I need to send Quark to the past first. According to quantum theory, during the time-travel process quarks are decomposed and then duplicated. If he gets out of the wormhole in one piece, then it's safe for me to do it too.'

'That's horrible. It's basically animal testing.'

Ethan took the bunny from Alison's arms. 'Quark will be fine. You can only destroy a quark with an antiquark. Quark just needs to keep rotating.' He took a deep breath and tried to calm himself down. 'I think we're ready.'

Alison nodded. 'Good luck.'

Ethan held Quark in his hands and took his position at the gate of the wormhole. Excitement surged through him – he was moments away from confirming the truth. This was going to change everything. He felt that pulse-quickening thrill of anticipation, like opening presents on a Christmas morning, pushing the paper back to see what's been wrapped up inside.

He looked at the time machine. This was a big deal. Ethan wasn't just about to change his life, he was about to change the universe, change the laws of physics. With the truth of the past, he could take right now and bend it back into its intended shape.

'Now,' he said. 'Turn the power on.'

Alison flicked the switches. Electricity surged through the wires. Motors started to run, blades rotated, fans whirled. The vacuum cleaner sucked in air, creating vacuum energy and strengthening the quantum field. Its Casimir effect would stabilise the wormhole, allowing Ethan to travel faster than light.

A deafening roar reverberated through the room – 1.21 gigawatts of energy amalgamating to crack space-time apart. Normally Ethan could feel time, but now he saw it too. It was right in front of him; he could touch it. Time was a grid, an intricate web, an elastic sheet spreading before his eyes.

Suddenly, time opened up and rippled through his skin. Ethan saw lengths of time warping and looping towards him. Seconds flew at him and bruised his skin, tiny moments that ripped his veins apart. Ethan's muscles contracted and his teeth clenched. Collagen and calcium buzzed inside his bones. Sparks flew from the time machine and then a big bang sounded, echoing through the floor. Quark wriggled in his arms.

A crease of light appeared, underneath the fabric of space-time. He drew in his breath and felt a rush of heat through his body. Negative energy was pulling him into the tunnel through time. This was it.

Ethan looked up.

The mouth of the wormhole opened above him in a blinding flash of white.

∞

Claire ran up the sidewalk and hailed a taxi, jumped inside, and told the driver to hurry. She crossed her arms over her chest; she needed to stop her internal organs from falling out and onto the floor. Her mouth was dry and her throat felt blocked. Her lungs didn't want to stay inside her ribs; her heart wanted to leap out of her skin. She rolled down the window and stuck her head into the wind, seeking the sustenance of air.

She dialled Mark's number. 'What happened? Tell me what happened.'

'Claire, what are you talking about?'

'Ethan's in hospital.'

'What?'

'In Emergency. You didn't know?'

'Of course not, what's wrong?'

'But I thought . . . Mark, could you meet me there?'

'I'm leaving now,' he said.

In the hospital foyer, a mother was breastfeeding her baby, her face down and shirt lifted to one side. The baby ran her pink tiny fingers up and down her mother's arm. Each time someone walked through the automatic doors, the mother looked up, protective and alert. Plastic butterflies dangled from the foyer ceiling. Claire felt a pain in her chest. She longed for that unparalleled intimacy with Ethan again, when he'd needed her more than anyone else.

Claire thought she knew every hallway and wing of the Sydney Children's Hospital but in her rush, she'd walked the wrong way. There was a new extension that made the old orange columns of the original hospital look rundown. She found Emergency and the nurses took her to Ethan's bed. Hot-air balloons were painted on the wall of his cubicle. Her son was unconscious but breathing. He was hooked up to several monitors; their screens flashed and beeped.

When Ethan was in hospital when he was a baby, Claire remembered staring at the machines that kept track of his heart, his breath, his life. As long as they kept the same rhythm and sang the same tune, she could convince herself he was okay. Now, the nurse reassured Claire that Ethan's condition wasn't critical and his life wasn't under threat. But the colour had drained from his face and his hands were cold. Claire leaned over her son and kissed the top of his head. His hair smelled of smoke and chemical fumes.

'What happened to him?' she asked, stroking his forehead.

'Your son suffered an electric shock. We've been monitoring his heart rate and everything seems stable so far. From the sounds of it, it could have been much worse.'

'What do you mean? How did he get here?'

The nurse flicked through Ethan's chart. 'His friend called the ambulance. There was an electric surge, according to the ambulance officers. She said they'd switched on every electrical appliance in the house.'

Claire looked down at Ethan's closed eyes. 'Is his friend still here?'

'She's in the waiting room.'

'Thanks, I'll be right back.'

The Emergency Department waiting room was full of kids with makeshift slings made from tea towels, others who groaned with stomach-aches, and their panic-stricken parents flicking their eyes across the room.

Alison sat by the window, rubbing her hands up and down her thighs. She was wearing a blue jumpsuit but her hands were stained black. She looked up. 'Mrs Forsythe, I'm so sorry.'

'Alison, are you all right? Please call me Claire.'

The little girl shifted the weight of her body to one side. 'Claire, we didn't mean to hurt anyone. I promise. It was an accident. I didn't think Ethan would . . . He said he knew what he was doing. That it wasn't that dangerous. He told me it was safe, that he wasn't going to get hurt.'

'It's okay,' Claire said. She put a hand on the girl's trembling knee. 'You did the right thing. Thank you for calling an ambulance and getting Ethan here.'

Alison bit a fingernail. 'It really was an accident, I swear. When we turned it on there were all these sparks. Then all the power went out and Ethan was thrown across the room and was shaking on the floor. I thought he'd stopped breathing. I was so scared.'

'Tell me what happened.'

'We were only trying to open the wormhole. Ethan made a time machine. He's been planning it for weeks. He said that if we generated enough energy he could create a wormhole in a doughnut and then he'd be able to travel backwards into the past.'

'Time machine?'

Alison nodded. 'We plugged every electrical appliance in the house onto different power boards and then we plugged those onto a single power board. Ethan said that if he collected all that energy, the wormhole would take him back in time.'

'What do you mean?'

'He was going back to prove that he wasn't shaken when he was a baby. And I honestly thought he'd be able to do it. Because of his special gift. Because he's a savant. Claire, I'm really sorry. I never thought he'd —' The little girl's voice choked, unable to finish her sentence.

Claire rocked the girl in her arms. 'Shh, everything's okay. It's not your fault.'

'And the bunny. Oh no, I'm so sorry about the rabbit. I think he's dead.'

'Quark?'

The child gave a hesitant nod. 'He was in Ethan's arms. He said that quarks don't experience time because of quantum flux. But then we turned the power on and . . . Poor Quark.' Alison paused and wiped her nose. 'Are you going to tell my mum?'

'She doesn't know you're here?'

'No, I'm going to be in so much trouble.'

'Don't worry, I'll talk to your mother and explain. You really did the right thing. You saved my son's life.' Claire looked into her wide eyes; she could see glimpses of the woman Alison would one day become in the girl's face. Like Ethan, she was quickly growing up. But they were both still so young and had already been through so much – seizures, hospital, surgery – it saddened Claire. 'Are you okay to stay here for bit longer? I really need to get back to Ethan.'

'Are you kidding? I feel more at home here than in my own house. I know everyone.' She pointed at the triage nurses, who waved back. 'I'll be fine.'

'I promise I won't be long.' Claire stood up.

Loud footsteps followed her down the linoleum corridor. Mark tapped her shoulder, sending a shiver down her spine. There was warmth in his wrinkled brow that Claire found comforting but she quickly disregarded the thought. His concern was too clear on his face; it made her feel uneasy.

Mark immediately took her in his arms. 'Is Ethan okay? Are you okay?'

Claire took a moment to untangle herself from the pull of his embrace. 'He was nearly electrocuted. I'm not sure what happened. He was trying to build a —'

Mark spoke over her. 'Time machine.'

'Did you have something to do with this? Was this one of your stupid plans? He's only twelve years old; he's very impressionable. You can't go and tell Ethan that time travel is possible. This is the real world. It's not science fiction.'

'It is actually possible,' Mark said. 'In theory. But no, of course this wasn't my idea. Ethan asked questions about time travel, black holes and negative energy, but I had no idea he was building a time machine. Now it all makes sense.'

'Apparently he wanted to go back in time to prove that you didn't shake him.' They were now standing in front of Ethan's cubicle. She lowered her voice. 'He thinks he has some special gift. He thinks he can see physics.'

'He can?' Mark looked into the distance.

Claire pulled back the curtain. 'I don't know.'

Ethan was still asleep.

16

MATTER

Both his parents stood over him, speaking a garbled language that Ethan didn't understand. Their words sounded broken and strange, their voices muffled like they were underwater. It was weird to watch them talk: he'd never seen them together before. Now they were in the same room. His mum whispered odd sounds; his father gave a jumbled reply.

Ethan squinted. His eyelids felt too heavy to lift; his muscles were tender and sore. But it had worked. The time machine had worked. He was really in the past; he'd really gone backwards in time. Of course he couldn't understand them – he was a baby. Ethan didn't know how to talk.

But looking around the room, this version of the past didn't seem right. Bars on the bed frame, scratchy sheets, an oxygen tank – they were in hospital. The room smelled like saliva and bleach. This was the wrong destination; this wasn't where Ethan wanted to be. His calculations must've been wrong. Unless he'd gone back too far and was in hospital because he'd just been born.

But if he was a newborn baby, then how did he know already about quantum mechanics inside his head? Maybe travelling through the wormhole had caused baby Ethan to be mind-melded with older

Ethan. Although that sounded like a temporal paradox, turning causality on its head, and that would close the time loop. His head hurt just thinking about it.

Ethan groaned.

'Pumpkin.' Mum leaned over him, her hair falling into his face. 'I'm so glad you're awake. How are you feeling?'

He blinked. Babies weren't supposed to answer questions so he'd need to keep his mouth shut. It must have been rhetorical; Ethan only understood what she'd said from listening to her voice in the womb.

'Hey, sport,' his father said. He didn't seem that much younger even though they were twelve years in the past.

An ache pulsed down Ethan's spine, stabbing him vertebra by vertebra. He tried to roll onto his side, but his arms didn't feel like his arms, and his legs were really far away. They didn't bend like baby legs but he couldn't lift them.

'Ouch,' he said. Hopefully, it was a word that babies knew.

'Could you get the doctor?' Mum asked Mark. 'I think he's in pain.'

His father disappeared. Mum sat on the bed. She held Ethan's hand and kissed it. 'I'm so sorry, pumpkin. I'm sorry I got so upset with you. This is all my fault. I should've told you the truth from day one.'

Her words confused him. This was wrong. Ethan tried to say something but only a weird croak came out. His mouth was dusty, his tongue prickled. Pins and needles made his whole body tingle. He felt pinned down by some invisible force.

Dr Saunders pushed open the curtain. 'Ethan, you're awake. We urgently need to get you to Radiology. They're expecting us in the Medical Imaging Department in five minutes.'

Mark stood behind him. 'What's going on?'

'The human body conducts electricity,' Dr Saunders said. 'With high-voltage injuries, depending on the length and severity of his electric shock, Ethan is at risk of seizures, aphasia, visual disturbances. Given his previous neurological history, he had a CT scan on arrival but it was inconclusive. I'm sending him to the neuroimaging centre on the other side of the hospital complex for a fMRI to look at blood flow in his brain.'

'Oh my God,' Mum said.

They wheeled his bed out of the bay and into the blazing light of the ward, down corridors and through automatic doors. Ethan stared at the ceiling, counting the grid of flecked fibreglass panels. They looked like sheets of graph paper – curved lines sweeping through coordinates, graphing the inverse of exponential functions. Exactly like the curvature of space-time. His head spun.

Ethan cleared his throat. 'It didn't work, did it? The time machine didn't work.'

The wheels of his bed were grinding. Nobody replied.

In the neuroimaging centre, Ethan was rolled into a dimly lit room. Blue light glowed on the ceiling; on one wall the yellow faces of the Bananas in Pyjamas grinned. He was lifted from the hospital bed onto a strange plank connected to a large white doughnut – just like a closed time-like curve.

Was this a time machine? They strapped Ethan onto the table and secured his body under a plastic frame. Suddenly the plank slid backwards into the hole of the giant doughnut. His legs wobbled as the machine swallowed him. Lights came on inside the cylinder. The giant machine made him feel small, like he was a particle inside the Large Hadron Collider.

Static came out of the speakers. 'Ethan, how you doing in there?' a radiographer said through the intercom. His voice boomed through the tube.

Ethan pulled his hospital robe down, trying to cover his knees; it was freezing in the doughnut. 'Where am I?'

'In the fMRI machine. Last time you had a scan, you were sleeping, so you probably don't remember. Stay very still. Don't move. If you move, it'll ruin the images. Are you ready?'

Ethan gulped and stared at the curved walls. He closed his eyes and tried to stay still.

The machine powered on, loud noises whirling around him. *Boom boom boom boom boom.*

Its sound pulled Ethan down. *Boom boom boom boom boom.* Like a hammer knocking on the side of the round walls, there was something soothing about the rhythmic blows. Loud clicks that were almost musical, that took on a melody of their own. Ethan focused on the noise. *Boom boom boom boom boom.*

He opened his eyes again. Radio waves burst out of the machine. The magnet hummed. The doughnut was a magnet; the hollow of the tube filled with a bright torrent of waves. Flickering waves soared above him, like he'd opened his eyes underwater while light billowed on the surface. He saw spiralling patterns of ripples everywhere. Crashing electromagnetic and radio waves gathered in his field of vision.

'Keep still,' the radiographer said over the intercom.

Ethan's eyes fluttered, hypnotised by the quivering waves. He calmed down and went rigid. Waves crossed paths – danced with each other to the thunderous song of the machine – as the particles inside his body aligned.

∞

'Claire, can I speak to you over here?' Dr Saunders was back, but Ethan wasn't with him.

She stood up and accompanied him into a consultation room, glancing over at Mark. He followed.

Ethan sat on a wide metal table. He fidgeted with the fabric of the hospital gown. Claire noticed how hairy his legs looked; they were no longer the legs of her little boy.

'What's wrong?' she asked.

'Good news is, it looks like the electric shock hasn't done any further damage to Ethan's brain.'

'Does that mean there's bad news?'

The doctor frowned. 'Remember how we spoke about Ethan seeing unusual things? Electromagnetic and sound waves? Particles?'

She put her arm around her son. 'So you think Ethan can really see them?'

'Honestly, I was nearly convinced he could; I got excited about it.' Dr Saunders looked at Ethan. 'Unfortunately, it doesn't seem like that's the case. While Ethan was in the fMRI scanner, the radiologists and I observed him have several small seizures. Partial seizures, in one area of his brain. Because the fMRI measures blood flow, we were able to identify seizure activity as it happened and exactly where in the brain it was focused. When he has these focal partial seizures, Ethan is fully awake and alert. He wouldn't know he was having them.'

'So the waves and particles —?'

'Are hallucinations, caused by temporal lobe seizures,' the doctor said.

Ethan shook his head. 'No, that's wrong. I can see them. They don't feel like a seizure. And the time machine. What about —'

'In cases of symptomatic epilepsy, it's often determined by MRI or other neuroimaging techniques that there's some degree of damage to a large number of neurons. Lesions, or scar tissue, caused by the loss of these neurons can result in groups of them episodically firing abnormally, causing a seizure.' The doctor turned to the boy. 'Did you see anything in the scanner, Ethan?'

'Waves. When the scanner made the clicking noises, the radio waves met the electromagnetic waves, and then particles bounced off each other. The doughnut was a magnet.'

'But isn't that right?' Mark asked. 'That's how the MRI machine works. Ethan must be able to see the physics. How else would he know?'

'They're definitely visual hallucinations caused by focal partial seizures,' the doctor said.

Claire interrupted. 'What's causing this?'

Dr Saunders pushed his glasses up his nose. 'The part of Ethan's brain that was originally damaged is the same area in which we've pinpointed the recent abnormal electrical activity. If you look at this section just here,' he said, holding up a picture of Ethan's brain, 'you'll notice it's a different colour to the rest of the grey matter of his brain. This is a lesion, where the seizure activity is occurring. It's the same place where the original brain haemorrhage was.'

Claire let her eyes linger on the discoloured area of Ethan's brain. A lesion. It was like looking at a painting – a picture that was once a masterpiece – ruined by a thoughtless brushstroke. There was a stain inside her son's head.

Ethan's face brightened. 'Then what happened to me wasn't bad? The brain haemorrhage gave me a gift.'

Dr Saunders looked up from his notes. 'Ethan, I'm sorry; I wish that were the case. But this isn't a gift. You're sick. If you continue to have these seizures, you risk further brain damage.'

'But I can see physics.' Ethan looked at Mark. 'Things nobody else can see.'

'Sadly, what you can see isn't real,' Dr Saunders said. 'You had a severe traumatic brain injury. It caused as much damage to you as a baby as an adult falling off an eight-storey building. It's brain damage.'

This was an analogy Claire remembered. Eight storeys: as much damage as an adult falling off an eight-storey building. Dr Saunders had told her that twelve years ago, when he'd made his initial diagnosis. She once went to the eighth floor of a high-rise office just to look at the window, to see how terrifying that jump must have been. What she wouldn't have given to fall out that window herself instead of Ethan.

'But the red and blue shift of the torch?' Ethan asked. 'What about the ping-pong ball and the Magnus effect?'

'When you've having a seizure, you think you can see them,' Dr Saunders said. 'But they're only inside your brain. They're not there.'

'No, they're real. I saw them.'

'You're seeing with your brain, Ethan. Hallucinating. Remember when I set up the four speakers in my office? How you said the waves made a pattern as a chessboard? You explained wave reflection perfectly. But I didn't realise until today that there was a bass at the front of the room. If you really saw sound waves, your drawing would include the waves the bass made too.' The doctor handed him the picture.

'I was wrong?' Ethan ran a finger over the concentric circles. The little boy's eyes welled up. 'But if I can't see physics, then I'm not special.'

Mark placed his hand on Ethan's shoulder. The gesture made Claire lose her focus.

'Going forward, there are two options,' the doctor said. 'Either Ethan will need to be on anti-seizure medication for the rest of his life. Or surgery. We remove the part of his brain where the legion is, the source of the abnormal electrical activity. This is my recommendation.'

Claire turned to the doctor. 'Isn't that serious, cutting out a piece of his brain?'

'Ethan hasn't responded to aggressive treatment with anti-seizure medications. We need to consider his quality of life. Continued seizures and constant hallucinations would take a huge toll on him, day-to-day. Physically, emotionally and intellectually. Socially too, when he starts high school.'

Ethan's face crumpled. 'But I don't want that. If I have an operation, they'll go away. I won't be able to see physics any more.'

'You're one of the lucky ones, Ethan,' Dr Saunders told him. 'I've seen hundreds of cases of abusive head trauma at this hospital. Most babies with brain injuries as serious as yours either die or become vegetables. It's a miracle that you survived, and even then you've still had significant cognitive and developmental delays. My team needs to have a more extensive look at the scans and speak to the neurosurgeons. The triage nurses might want to transfer Ethan into the surgical unit later this afternoon. I'll come back a little later.' Dr Saunders walked out into the hall.

The three of them were alone in the consultation room now. Claire tried to make eye contact with Ethan, then with Mark, but both of them were distant, faraway in their own worlds.

Mark walked to the window, his hands resting on his hips.

Claire stared at his back and saw the reflection of his face in the glass. She tried to decipher his expression. As clouds passed, Mark looked up at the sky, wide-eyed and bewildered.

She turned to Ethan. His eyes were focused on the floor, trying his best to hold back his tears, but Claire could feel how upset her son was. His disappointment was attached to every atom in the room. She held her hand out to Ethan and he took it, wrapping his fingers around her thumb.

'Mum.' His bottom lip trembled.

'Pumpkin, don't be scared. Everything's going to be okay.' She'd assured him of this so much that Claire doubted Ethan still believed it.

Things hadn't been okay; those were empty words. His palm was sticky in her hand.

'I really need to talk to Dad,' Ethan said, letting go. 'Alone.'

∞

Mark stood at the window. Ethan came up beside him, playing with the plastic tag wrapped around his wrist. His skin was the pearly colour of glue. Looking at the boy was difficult – moist eyes, limp posture like a deflated balloon – so it was easier to keep looking out the window. Those were nimbostratus clouds ahead, Mark could tell by their formless shape, thickening into a dense layer over the sky. Dark blankets of cloud caused by atmospheric instability; the temperature outside must have risen.

'Makes you feel small,' Mark said. 'Doesn't it? The sky.'

'I guess.' Ethan touched the window.

'Did you know that the sun is 108 times wider than Earth and 330 000 times more massive? But there are stars out there that make the sun look like a tiny speck of dust. Crazy, don't you think? The size of the universe is unimaginable. Really puts things into perspective.'

Physics was beautiful like that – it was the most powerful lens to see the universe through. Whenever Mark felt throttled by his own feelings, he knew that he could quickly forget everything by looking at the sky. We were all part of something bigger – massive and infinite – and the sheer size of the universe overshadowed the smallness of our lives. Everyone was made of the same stuff as wandering stars, as interstellar galaxies of gas and dust. Even on the opposite side of the galaxy, our building blocks were identical; we shared the same atoms, molecules and compounds as other planets, suns and moons.

Ethan touched Mark's arm. 'Dad, I know all that. But I don't really care about the size of the universe at the moment. I don't want to talk about physics right now.'

'Only 4 per cent of the observable universe is made of ordinary matter,' Mark continued. 'That's everything we can see and imagine and beyond. We don't understand 96 per cent of what's out there. There are so many big questions that still need answers. How did the universe begin? What's dark matter made from?'

'They're your big questions. I don't think they're mine.'

'Remember what you said at the park? Physics is figuring out how to ask the right questions.'

Ethan frowned. 'Then I asked the wrong ones. The time machine didn't work. I couldn't time-travel. I didn't find out the truth. Now I need to have an operation. So I don't really care about physics any more. Physics is just a stupid bunch of abandoned theories and wrong hypotheses and invisible stuff nobody can see. I couldn't make a wormhole. I'm not special. I'm just a freak.'

'You are special.' Mark looked his son in the eyes.

'I'm not. I'm no different to anyone else. Why'd you tell me time travel was possible?' The boy moved away from the window and sat back down on the metal bed.

'Ethan, I didn't know you were trying to build a time machine.'

'But Dad, I was making it for you,' Ethan said. 'It was supposed to fix everything. The time machine was going to fix us. I wanted to go back to prove that you didn't shake me. Then it would be like you never left. Like we'd always been together. Mum wouldn't have made you go away. We'd be happy. We'd be a family again.'

Mark wanted that too. Happiness, his family: they belonged to each other. They should have been a unit; instead, they were shards of broken china that couldn't be stuck back into a vase. Their family was ruined, wrecked with cracks and faults, shattered by its own entropy.

It was already too late; they were irreparable. Time travel could never set that right.

'There's something wrong with my brain,' Ethan pressed on. 'There's a scar inside my head that's making me sick. Scars form for a reason, so I guess I'm confused. If you didn't shake me when I was a baby, what's wrong with me?'

Mark closed his eyes. 'This was a mistake.'

Ethan looked at the ceiling, his left eye twitching slightly. Mark could tell the boy was trying to hold his feelings in, like a diver clinging to oxygen inside his underwater lungs. His son breathed deeply then started to cry. 'What did I do wrong?'

'You didn't do anything wrong, mate.' But it didn't matter; Mark shouldn't have said that to his son, that anything was a mistake. Now he'd hurt Ethan's feelings. He'd crossed a line.

It always happened so quickly, so abruptly – the crossing of the line. Mark had long forgotten the colour of the baby's towel, erased the order of events of that morning bath, had blanked out the sounds of a dying infant choking for breath in his arms.

Sights, sounds and smells were easily repressed – the senses were fluid, powdery, fleeting – but feelings had solidity. Mark still felt the shape, the density, of that moment of turbulence twelve years ago. It was impossible to forget the power of his animal frustration, during the tiniest second when he'd crossed that uncrossable line.

In prison, several psychological assessments suggested Mark suffered from dissociative amnesia – derealisation, compartment-alising, gaps in his memory. One prison psychologist wrote that the subject's detachment might have interfered with the encoding and storage of his recollection of the crime. Mark's memory was mercurial – large and small details kept shifting and turning inside his head. No, he'd insisted, he didn't do it, it wasn't him. He needed to undo his thinking; the enormity of it crippled him. Mark unravelled reality to protect himself while his mind built false memories on false foundations.

But now love was unravelling him.

Until recently, Mark hadn't known how it felt to truly love his child – this robust selflessness, when whatever the price, Ethan's needs came first. This love was pure and unconditional. But he knew he had to earn it.

'Ethan, I love you.'

'I love you too, Dad.'

Mark took his son in his arms, wishing he could stay there forever. Freeze this moment and stop time. He smelled the top of Ethan's head and wiped hot tears off the boy's soft cheek. From the subatomic – protons, neutrons, quarks and leptons – to massive stars and galaxies, Mark thought about the scale of everything. All 13.7 billion years of the known universe: it carried so many incalculable secrets. Out there, beyond the Milky Way, was an infinity that dwarfed them both.

But their bodies carried their own infinities, composed of billions of tiny particles with secrets of their own. Mark had held on to his secret for over twelve years, had bound it tight around every organ and cell. As he held his son against his body, Mark thought of his mother's embrace. How no matter what he'd done, how badly he'd behaved, Eleanor's love for him never changed.

She'd often joked she'd throw herself under a bus for her children, take a bullet for them; she was selfless to a fault. He knew how much she'd sacrificed: Eleanor was miserable in her marriage, had a universe of talents that were wasted on the roses. And Mark could hit his brother, fail tests, lose his temper, but still the strength of their bond was unbreakable like an electron, indestructible like energy. His mother always loved him unconditionally. That was just what existed between parent and child. He understood that now.

Meeting Ethan had ionised Mark. He'd never be the same. Falling in love with his son had changed him on a molecular level. The boy sobbed into his father's chest and grabbed his hand. Physics might be figuring out how to ask the right questions, but what Ethan deserved were the right answers.

Mark took a deep breath and looked his son in the eyes. 'Ethan, none of this is your fault. It was mine.'

∞

Claire stood outside the hospital with Alison, waiting for her mother. The girl balanced on the curved green brick wall, poking out her tongue and holding her arms apart. With her jumpsuit on, she looked like a tiny plumber. What the doctor had said to Ethan weighed on Claire's mind. His world turned upside down again. Ethan was still sick.

She'd never hallucinated, had never seen things that didn't exist, but Claire knew how it felt to realise your perception was wrong. When your eyes played tricks on you. When what you were convinced was in front of you didn't align with what was real.

'Alison, can I ask you something?'

'Yep.' The girl jumped off the wall.

'What's been the worst thing about being sick?'

She answered without hesitating. 'I never get to swim. I love being in the water. My favourite thing in the world is going to the beach, or the pool. Putting my head underwater and feeling my hair float around me like I'm a mermaid. But my parents never let me. They're always scared I'll have a seizure and drown. Or hit my head on a rock. So I've always felt like I'm missing out on something. Fomo, I guess. It's hard to feel left behind.' The little girl looked at her hands.

'I wonder if that's how Ethan feels.'

Alison pushed her hair behind her ear. 'Why don't you ask him?'

'I wish he wanted to talk to me about it.'

'Yeah, he does.' Alison smiled. 'You're his mum.'

'Ever since his father came back, everything has been such a mess. I've been a mess. Sorry, I don't know why I'm telling you this. I just wish Ethan knew the truth.'

'Have you told him what happened?' Alison asked. 'Your side of the story?'

Claire shook her head. It was too painful and she knew it would hurt him – it hurt her. But now it was too late. She'd been so caught up in her own reaction to Mark's reappearance that she'd overlooked Ethan. Thinking she was protecting him, when what he needed was honesty. Claire knew she could never offer Ethan the whole truth, but she could give him particles of it. Fragments, pieces, scraps: they were all she had.

'Maybe if you'd told Ethan exactly what happened, he wouldn't have needed to make that time machine.'

'You're a smart girl.'

'I know.' She pointed to a silver wagon driving up High Street. 'That's my mum.'

'Thank you, Alison. You saved his life.'

The girl smiled and squinted into the sunlight. 'No big deal. He'd do it for me too.' Alison climbed into the car and waved from the window of the front seat.

Claire waved back as she watched them drive away.

Corridors and faces flashed past as Claire hurried back to the consultation room. In her rush, she almost tripped over a lunch trolley. She pressed the elevator button over and over again. Inside the lift, she glanced briefly at her reflection. Her skin looked weathered and discoloured. When the lift door opened, Claire walked straight into Mark, who was about to step inside.

'Where are you going?' She pulled him back into the corridor.

Mark didn't look at her. 'I can't stay here. This is too much.'

'But Ethan —'

'Claire, I thought I could handle this. You. Ethan. But I can't.'

For the last twelve years, she'd wondered how Mark really felt. Claire knew her pain well but she never understood what was inside his head. In front of her right now, he looked like a lost little boy, left behind by his parents in a crowded place. Even when accusations started flying all those years ago, Mark had seemed totally assured of himself, of his innocence. Now she wasn't so sure.

'You can't just leave —'

'Claire, listen. There are things I went through in prison that you wouldn't understand. I can't ever explain them. But being around you both is worse. It's torture,' he said. 'I can't handle it. I have to go.'

'But what about Ethan?'

Mark looked like he was about to cry. 'Ethan is extraordinary. You know, I've spent almost his entire life convinced I didn't do anything wrong. Twelve years is a really long time. Tell yourself something for twelve years and you'll definitely believe it. But being inside this hospital again, seeing how sick Ethan is . . .'

Claire didn't know what to say.

'I'm sorry.' He placed his hand on her cheek and looked at her face. Then he stepped into the lift and pressed a button.

'Mark, wait.' She reached for the door of the lift as it closed. Mark looked right at her. The elevator shut. Claire rested her forehead against the cool steel door. What was he trying to say?

Ethan was waiting for her in the consultation room. Claire knew he'd been crying; there was a wet patch on the sleeve of his hospital robe and the tip of his nose was pink. He looked small and cold. Light glinted off the metallic table.

'I'm really tired, Mum,' he said.

'Let's get you back to bed.' She kissed his forehead.

Back in the Emergency bay, Claire watched her son fall asleep. She thought of her conversation with Alison, wondered where to find those fragments, those shards of truth. Pieces that could help her put it all together for Ethan. But maybe her word wasn't enough. There was so much more to their story – official records, affidavits, sworn statements, medical reports, scans. Enough concrete evidence to convince a jury. She just had to get her hands on this stuff.

But Claire had forgotten so many of the details. She couldn't even remember the name of the Crown prosecutor, and what was the name of the judge? Who gave evidence? So much of her memory had crumbled and disappeared; there were so many holes and gaps.

But other memories were stubborn, indestructible; they still echoed intact across her mind. Some piece of Claire would always be trapped inside that terrible moment, never able to walk away from the indelible horror of that sun-stippled room.

Abigail. The Crown prosecutor's name was Abigail Kirk. Claire grabbed her mobile and tapped the name into Google. Nothing. She looked up the website of the Office of the Director of Public Prosecutions, wondering if they had a staff directory. Of course they didn't. They weren't going to publish their email addresses for criminal offenders to see.

She tried a combination of the Crown prosecutor's name and surname, hoping to guess the correct email address. She wrote a quick message, asking if Abigail remembered their case and if she recalled the judge's name, knew how to get a court transcript. Ethan is twelve now, she wrote. Claire attached a photo of him and clicked send. The email didn't bounce back.

Within a few minutes, her phone rang – a blocked number. It couldn't possibly be. That was much too fast.

'Claire, it's Abigail Kirk. I just read your email and had to call. I think about your case all the time.'

'Abigail, hello. Really? You do?'

'We don't see shaken baby syndrome cases like that every day. It's stayed with me for the last ten years. Recently, we moved close to your old house. Every time I walk down that street, I think about that scene of the crime, what happened to Ethan. I've often wondered how he is.'

'He's great.' Claire burst into tears. Somebody else remembered, was haunted by it too. 'I'm sorry. I'm getting a bit emotional.'

'So you wanted some help getting the court transcripts? I'll have to look up the name of the judge, but what you need to do is apply to the registrar of the NSW District Court. I wish I had a copy; I'd give it to you if I did.'

'Thank you so much.'

'I think it's an important thing for Ethan to have. Thanks for sending the photo. Ethan's grown up into such a handsome boy. He looks a little bit like the accused,' she said quietly.

'Thanks for calling straight away,' Claire said. 'And thank you for all the hard work you did during the trial. I'm not sure if I ever thanked you properly at the time. I was a bit numb back then. But I'm really very grateful.'

'Being numb is normal. You needed to be, to get through it. To cope. You're welcome, Claire. It's so good to hear from you. I really wish you and Ethan all the best.' Abigail hung up the phone.

A few days later, the District Court registrar sent the entire transcript at no cost. All 387 pages of the trial, plus sentencing remarks. The victim was his child, the judge had said. He was defenceless and looked to the prisoner for protection. Instead, the victim was badly injured by the actions of his father and would have cognitive problems for the rest of his life. The words stung Claire as she read them again.

Claire couldn't believe she'd wiped so many specifics from her memory: ambulance officers, social workers, doctors and nurses. Tiny details she'd sworn on in the witness stand – what the baby was wearing, the sequence of events – rushed back to her as she read about them again. As she turned each page of the transcript, Claire relived that nightmarish day: calling triple zero, riding in the back of the ambulance. The past came back to life. It was like time travel.

There was never any mistake. No misinterpretation of evidence, no misunderstanding, no miscarriage of justice. Every recent article Claire had read about shaken baby syndrome, about its faulty science and wrongful convictions, said that the triad – three symptoms – wasn't enough.

But Ethan's constellation had a few more stars.

Reams of paper, medical reports, stacks of other people's cross-examined words – she gave it all to her son.

'Ethan, it's time I was honest. You need to know exactly what happened to you,' Claire said. 'I promise to tell you the truth. I promise to tell you everything.'

17

ANTIMATTER

For the last two months, Claire had been in denial. She was exhausted, falling asleep everywhere: in her dance classes, during movies, riding on the bus. Overnight, every smell in the world had amplified; she couldn't wear perfume or visit the butcher without wanting to be sick. Food tasted different. Coffee and cigarette addiction disappeared. When she finally went to the doctor, suspecting a case of glandular fever, pregnancy was far from her mind. But Claire couldn't deny it by the time she'd done the third test. Couldn't keep talking herself out of believing those two blue lines.

Positive. Positive. Positive.

'Mark,' she said that night as they prepared dinner. 'There's something I need to tell you.'

A tear ran down Mark's cheek. 'Stupid onions.'

She hesitated. 'How was your day?'

'Quiet. Rewrote the introduction again. How was yours?'

'Busy. Long rehearsals; we have new choreography. Had lunch at that dumpling place in Chinatown. And I'm pregnant,' Claire blurted out. She didn't look at his reaction. They'd been married just over a year, and while they'd talked about having children in the future, right now wasn't ideal. Mark had started the final year of his PhD. Claire couldn't give up ballet. There was no room in their lives for a baby.

'What? How?' Mark stopped slicing the onion and turned to look at her. 'You're taking the pill.'

'Yes, I am.' She paused and cracked an egg on the side of the mixing bowl, separating the yolk and white in her hands. The slippery consistency made her feel nauseous. 'Remember how I had that throat infection and took antibiotics? I didn't realise one cancelled out the other and . . .' Claire started to cry. He was angry with her for being careless; she knew it.

Mark put his arms around her waist and kissed her nose. 'Don't cry, Claire Bear. It's okay.'

'It's not . . . I'm so stupid. I'm sorry,' she managed to say between sobs.

'Don't be sorry.'

'I just got egg all over your clothes.'

Mark smiled. 'No, silly. Don't be sorry for being pregnant. You can't take all the credit; I had a part in this too.'

Claire washed her hands. 'I'll be honest, I don't think I'm ready for a baby. I can't give up my place in the company. You're still writing your thesis. And we're too young. I'm only twenty-five, you're twenty-seven . . .'

'What options do we have?'

'I'm eight weeks along. There's still time to . . . you know . . .' She shut off the tap and dried her hands on her top.

'Claire, I don't know if I'm ready either. And the decision is ultimately up to you. But you know what? I'd like to be a dad. You'd be a wonderful mother. And I'd look after you. I'd look after the baby.' Mark touched Claire's stomach. It was still flat; there were no hints of any bump.

She rested her fingers on top of his hand. Something was growing in there – a baby, the size of a bullet. Claire couldn't feel it, but the baby had already taken control of her body. The body she'd spent her whole life getting into shape.

Claire shook her head. 'Mark, I can't quit ballet.'

'You don't have to quit. You'd have to take some time off, but it'd be like recovering from an injury. You'll bounce back. Once it's born, I'll still be at home writing. I could be a stay-at-home dad. We'll work it out. We always do.'

Claire looked him in the eye. He'd lost his mind. Did he really want to have a baby? There was so much to think about and so much to lose. How would she know which decision was the right one? But she trusted Mark, trusted him with her life, and knew in her heart that he meant it. They loved each other.

'You're right,' she said. 'We'll work it out. I'll look at my contract.'

She rested her face against Mark's chest. He smelled of onion and herbs. This man wanted to be a father, he wanted to look after them; it made her want that too. As Claire imagined her new family, she was seized by the strangest hope. That this was a chance to put right the wrongs of her own childhood, to finally belong to a perfect family. That she could love this baby clearly and completely, exactly the way she'd wanted to be loved herself. Claire looked up at Mark and he kissed her. The half-prepared dinner was forgotten on the kitchen bench.

Her pregnancy was relatively easy. Morning sickness only lasted another month and there were no complications. During the ultra-sound at sixteen weeks, the baby was given a clean bill of health. The ultrasonographer asked if they wanted to know the sex. Mark and Claire had discussed it the previous evening over dinner and decided they wanted to leave it as a surprise.

'What should we name it?' Claire rubbed her belly. It had popped out that week and her clothes didn't fit properly any more. This felt like reality now; she was pregnant. She wasn't living in some bizarre dream.

'I was thinking of Sophie for a girl,' Mark said. 'After my grandmother. It means wisdom.'

'Sophie,' Claire repeated. She gave him a quick kiss. 'You are quite wise yourself, you know.'

Mark swallowed a mouthful of food. 'What about for a boy? I like Adrian.'

Claire scrunched up her nose. 'I don't think so.'

'Do you have any better suggestions?'

She stopped to think for a moment. 'How about Ethan?'

Mark laughed. 'You know I'm a sucker for nineties heartthrobs.'

And even though Claire had often wondered if she'd felt the baby move – small shudders here, a possible bump, maybe indigestion – there was no doubt about it now as she felt the baby kick. It was real. It was there.

Claire persevered with her ballet classes – two hours a day, five days a week – until the seventh month of her pregnancy. She maintained her rigorous stretching routine until the day before she gave birth. But as the baby grew, her body changed – it became a stranger. It spoke a new language of oedema, cellulite and varicose veins. Claire's strong connection with it severed; she lost her precise awareness of the bend of her spine and turn of her feet. This swollen body didn't belong to her any more. When she tried listening to it, it no longer talked back.

When the baby kicked all night and she couldn't sleep, Claire obsessed over pregnancy books – studying diagrams of childbirth as if they were dance notation, poring over the growing size of the foetus as it developed fluidly from first position to fifth. She was fastidious about her diet and avoided every variety of forbidden bacteria. Pregnancy had so many rules, but she enjoyed following them. They gave Claire a sense of purpose, made her feel like she was getting something right.

Ethan was born on a Sunday morning. Claire had expected labour would be worse than it actually was; she'd pictured a slaughter, her imagination ran wild. But she was strong and athletic, and knew how to push herself. She could work through pain, was accustomed to it, understood its brevity. When she held her son for the first time, the brutality of labour was quickly forgotten. Ethan was perfect. Looking at her new baby made Claire feel like she couldn't see anything else in the room. Mark cut the umbilical cord. Three days later, they brought Ethan home.

Those early weeks were full of contradictions. Days went by quickly and in a blur, but were boring and endless. Claire felt displaced but experienced an overwhelming sense of belonging; she'd lost her individuality but felt self-assured. Ethan was brand new and unfamiliar; nonetheless, they were instantly close. The baby frayed Claire at her edges but she was tightly bound to him. When he wailed, she'd be confused yet instinctively understand – his cries were both explicit and a mystery. As she watched him sleep, she felt fearful and fearless. Claire fell in love with Ethan immediately but in an abstract and obsessional way, like he was an object, but it was also the purest love she'd ever known. Theirs was a binary relationship; its complexity split Claire into two.

In the first four months of his life, Ethan didn't sleep for more than ninety minutes in a row. When he wasn't sleeping, he was eating, and the rest of the time he cried. He cried in the morning, he cried throughout the day, he cried in the darkest hours of the night. Ethan cried so much his face was always red. He cried with his entire body, tiny hands shaking and chubby legs kicking, hollering and hollering until he wore himself out.

Claire was the only person who could comfort Ethan. She'd wrap the baby in his bunny rug and dance him around the room. But it didn't soothe him for long – the crying always started again. Sometimes she fed Ethan just to keep him quiet, shoving her breast into his screaming mouth. Was that cruel? Feeding him when he didn't need it, to buy herself five minutes of peace.

Pregnancy was over, but Claire felt more disconnected with her body than ever before. She'd assumed it was elastic, that after childbirth it would simply snap back. But it didn't. Wrinkled skin on her stomach she could grab in handfuls, stretched skin hanging from her arms, padded thighs, engorged breasts. Looking in the mirror made Claire start to panic. Mark wasn't allowed to touch her; he might discover the loose folds around her waist. She found herself repulsive and feared he'd think so too. Although her revulsion had little to do with vanity – it was more about lost control.

She'd seen enough dancers stumble and break: at puberty when they developed the wrong physique, after a fall during an audition, following a serious injury that ended their career. Claire thought back to those defeated faces, that precise moment when they'd realised it was all over. How they crumpled, winced and shrank as their ambition collapsed.

Claire wasn't going to let herself become another casualty to failure, another dancer forced to forfeit their dream. Ambition might be the wrong size for her body right now, but she wasn't going to throw it away – she'd fight to make it fit again. In stolen minutes without the baby, she resumed training. Nightly exercises to stabilise her ankles, stretches to open up her shoulders, routines with resistance weights, until Claire snapped back to her original shape.

∞

Mark was convinced the baby was gifted. He was positive Ethan had smiled two weeks before it was considered normal, and was sure he'd seen him roll over at ten days old. Claire told him this was silly, Ethan could hardly hold up his head, but Mark knew his baby son was advanced. To stimulate Ethan's brain development, Mark made a black-and-white mobile to hang over his cot, and at two months was teaching the baby to crawl. Clearly, the baby was a genius.

He devoured parenting books – detailed manuals for this puzzling new device – trying to keep track of how early Ethan met milestones. One book advised playing newborns classical music, another suggested having meaningful conversations with your baby. So Mark spoke to Ethan like he was an adult, explaining his doctoral thesis to the baby as it wriggled in his arms.

His thesis was about antimatter. Conceptually, it had always intrigued Mark. Quantum theories of corresponding opposites kept him awake at night. He loved the symmetry of antiparticles: same mass as their particle partner but with opposite charge. Electrons and positrons, protons and antiprotons, neutrons and antineutrons – they were all symmetrical. Antimatter's volatility had a lacerating beauty – when it collided with matter, they annihilated each other.

But there was a fundamental problem with antimatter and it irritated Mark. Why had the Big Bang left us with an observable universe made up almost entirely of matter? The standard model of particle physics predicted it should be half and half. So why wasn't the universe symmetrical? And if matter and antimatter destroyed one another, why did the universe even exist? Theoretically, there should be nothing, but something had been left behind.

His thesis topic was anomalous parity asymmetry in the Cosmic Microwave Background. Mark knew his paper wouldn't disprove the standard model, but it was certainly publishable. His research was solid and innovative, but he needed it to be perfect. There'd been talks of getting a job overseas; maybe he'd do a post-doc. His supervisor even hinted at the possibility of working as an academic in the faculty. These were only dreams if he couldn't finish writing the bloody thing, though.

Since Ethan's birth, Mark had felt more and more isolated. He missed Claire. He'd reach drowsily for her in the early hours of the morning, but she'd shift away from his touch. The baby's constant crying formed a barrier between them. Ethan was primally attached to Claire – knew the patterns of her smell, touch and voice – so he'd cling to his mother and want her alone. Her patience with him was monumental. Even though he'd devoured the parenting books, Mark still found parenthood tedious, but Claire never looked bored; he was terrified of Ethan's urgent cries but she seemed unafraid.

But Claire had come back from the hospital altered. Attention and affection she once gave Mark now belonged to somebody else. When Claire breastfed the baby, it made Mark blush – he had to look away. Like he'd intruded on something private and sacred, something he wasn't supposed to see. Like they'd formed a secret alliance that excluded Mark.

They were too tired to speak once they'd finally put Ethan to sleep. Claire sat on the floor and stretched her legs. Mark wanted to touch her, but knew he'd be rebuked. Instead, he sat at his desk and tried to work, stealing furtive glances at her profile as she pulled her body into different shapes.

'So, I have some really good news.' Claire reached for her toes. 'I have an audition.'

Mark kept his eyes on his laptop. 'That's great.'

'Next week. Isn't that great? Problem is, it's in Melbourne. I missed local auditions, but they can squeeze me in there. I'd need to fly down and probably stay overnight.'

'And you'd take Ethan?'

She stepped forward into a lunge. 'I thought he could stay at home with you. I wouldn't be gone long. Forty-eight hours, max.'

'Hold on.' Mark closed his computer. 'You can't go away for two days.'

'Last month, you went to a conference for three days. Ethan and I coped.'

'But that was different. You're still breastfeeding; you can't leave him. And an audition? Isn't this all happening too soon?'

'I'll express enough milk and freeze it before I go. Ethan's started solids anyway. My doctor has cleared it, I'm in great shape.' She looked at him with an expectant expression. 'Haven't you noticed me practising?'

'Slow down, Claire. Can we talk about this first?' His mind darted from possibility to possibility. 'The issue isn't that you'd go away for two days. What if you actually get the role, then what? Daily rehearsals? Touring? Performing several nights a week? You'd be going back to work.'

'Yeah, I think I'm finally ready.' She smiled and crossed her legs. 'My flexibility is back to normal now and I've lost most of the pregnancy weight. I've been training at home every day. I want to get back to work.'

'You don't just make that decision by yourself. We need to talk about it. Decide together. We're a family.' Mark paused for a few seconds and ran his hand over his face. 'I'm not sure you can go back yet. We can't juggle that at the moment.'

Claire stiffened. Her cheeks were flushed from stretching. 'Decide together? Sounds like you're the one making the decision by yourself.'

'Couldn't you put it off a little longer, maybe until my thesis is done? There'll be other auditions.'

'No, I can't,' she said, standing up. 'I've waited long enough. Do you realise I've already lost eight months? My career has an expiration date, unlike yours. You can be a crazy scientist until the day you drop dead. But I don't have all the time in the world to dance professionally.'

'It just makes more sense for me to finish my thesis first.' Mark glanced at the pile of notes on his desk. 'You don't understand the pressure I'm under right now. Let me focus and get this done, then we can talk about your dancing later.'

She pulled at her tights. 'That's not fair. Dancing is my work.'

'Let's be practical.' Mark said. 'Maybe it's not worth it. Financially, I mean. You don't make enough money, at least at the moment. Dancing pays sweet fuck all. Think how expensive it'd be for you to work again. By the time we've covered childcare, plus all your ballet paraphernalia, we'd only just break even. Unless you became some prima-ballerina superstar, it's not sustainable.'

'Like you can talk. Last time I checked, theoretical physicists weren't rolling in cash. You've never even had a real job, Mark. You've spent the last decade at uni. And you should know better than anyone, it's not about money.' Her voice was strained. 'Why do I have to be the one put on hold?'

'You're a mother now, Claire.'

'So what? I'm still me. I still want to dance.'

'Listen to yourself. You sound like a princess. Exactly like a spoiled child. Don't you care about Ethan?'

Claire didn't look at him. 'I can't believe you'd say that. Honestly, I thought you'd be fine with this. You even said you could be a stay-at-home dad so I wouldn't have to give up ballet.'

'When did I say that?'

'Now you can't remember? How convenient! Just like you to rewrite history.' Claire removed her leg warmers and threw them across the room. She raised her voice. 'So much for equality then. So much for thinking you weren't like every other man. Wow, I really thought you got it. But no, let's preserve your identity at all costs, and forget all about me because I'm a mother now. Better step back and embrace my womanly destiny of breastfeeding and sleepless nights. Is this what you assume I'll do with the rest of my life? Raise your children?'

The baby started to cry.

She shook her head. 'Great, now we've woken him up.'

Mark sighed. 'Don't be like this; you're blowing it out of proportion. Please don't act like a victim. You made your own choices. It shouldn't be a surprise that a baby would change our lives. You knew you'd need to give up ballet for a while.'

'I didn't know you were a prick, though,' she said under her breath.

'I'm a prick? You're playing the martyr, Claire. You're not some hard-done-by single mum; I help. Ethan keeps me awake all night too. And now you're demanding I look after him while I finish my research? You don't understand how difficult it is to write a thesis. You don't even understand what it's about. If I don't meet my deadline, they'll cut off my funding. Then we won't have any money to support the baby. Would you like that?'

The baby's wailing grew louder.

'I'm sorry I'm not smart enough for you.' Claire adjusted her nursing bra. 'I'm so sorry you're stuck with this stupid wife and inconvenient child while you're trying to solve scientific problems beyond my understanding.'

'You know what?' Mark yelled so he could be heard over Ethan's cries. 'I knew it was bad timing. We shouldn't have had him now.'

There was a long pause, as Claire baulked at him. 'But you're the one who wanted to have the baby. Practically insisted.'

Mark couldn't believe her; she made his blood pressure surge. Putting this on him. Pretending to be this innocent dupe to shirk her responsibilities. 'And you didn't? I didn't force you, Claire. Great story to tell him when he's older. Sorry, Ethan, Mummy didn't really want you.'

'I'm going to pretend you didn't say that. He's probably hungry again,' she said, throwing her hands up. 'I'd better feed him.'

After she left the room, Mark marched to the kitchen and grabbed a beer. He slammed the fridge door shut – its contents clattered – and swore. Claire was so wilful and manipulative. Complaining about all the sacrifices she'd made, then dictating he make a massive one – all in the same breath. How could she be that inconsiderate? Forget the critical importance of his thesis on top of not noticing his stress.

He sat down at the kitchen table, covered in unpacked groceries. Sure, Mark could admit he'd zeroed in on his research, maybe been oblivious to her training. It was true: the barre was back up, pointe shoes dangled on the banister again. He knew ballet meant a lot to her. Claire was simply being her determined self. And he'd fallen in love with that tenacity – it resonated with him. He took another swig of beer.

When she'd first moved in, they'd both become so immersed in their own work they wouldn't speak all day. Neither felt neglected or ignored, not like Mark's previous girlfriends, who'd pout and sulk, then make him feel guilty about working. Claire got it. She was just as single-minded and industrious as Mark, if not more so. There was something special about it, their solidarity, their tacit agreement to chase big dreams. He'd get lost in quantum theory; she'd fixate on perfecting spins. Preoccupied and tranquil, in unison. Worlds apart, but they were in it together.

In the bedroom, Claire lay on the bed and stared at the ceiling.

Clean laundry was piled behind her, waiting to be folded and put away. The baby had settled in her arms; he'd fallen back asleep.

Mark stood in the doorframe. 'I'm a dickhead. I said a lot of things I didn't mean.'

She kept her eyes on the ceiling. 'I just didn't think this would be so hard. I didn't realise being a parent would be like this.' Her voice was uneven, like she'd been crying.

'I know,' he said, sitting beside her. 'Having a baby is completely shithouse. They're helpless, they smell, they're really bad conversationalists.'

Claire smiled at him. She looked down at Ethan and stroked his downy hair. 'He's pretty cute, though, isn't he?'

'Yeah, I'll give him that.' Mark placed a hand on her shoulder. 'Claire Bear, you're so much better with the baby than me. I'm just scared about being left alone with him for the first time. But we'll be fine. I want you to go to your audition.'

'Really? Are you sure?'

He nodded. 'Just don't literally break a leg.'

∞

Her flight was leaving in three hours, but Claire worried she hadn't expressed enough milk. She held the pump to her breast again, cringing as its rubber mouth sucked at her nipple. It made her eyes water. Even though Mark had agreed to the audition, he still sulked about her leaving. And she was still quietly fuming about their fight. How apparently she was too dumb to understand the stupid thesis. She knew exactly what it was about; he hardly talked about anything else. She could sum it up in a sentence. Who did he think he was, Einstein?

What especially annoyed Claire was how Mark accused her of

playing the martyr and insisting that he gave her lots of help. Friends help, neighbours help – shouldn't he be just as invested as her in the baby? When Claire looked after Ethan, nobody called that helping. Motherhood was full of these uneven expectations and assumptions, an exasperating disjuncture between what was demanded and what was fair.

Ethan sat in his bouncer, his eyes searching the room for his mother. Claire kneeled down and tickled his toes. He seemed to love looking at her face, blinking his glossy eyes, mimicking her expressions. The baby smiled and reached out to grab her hair.

She hid behind his tiny feet, and then surprised him with a silly grin. 'Peekaboo!'

Ethan giggled hysterically. His laughter was the most wonderful noise Claire had ever heard; it filled her with a giddy euphoria. She'd pull strange faces and make weird noises simply to hear the baby laugh, like his chuckles were a drug and she was a junkie craving another fix.

Claire didn't mind being a slave to her oxytocin. Sometimes it made her cry for no reason, or misfired and made her go into raptures over cornflakes, and every time she looked at Ethan, she fell in love with him a little bit more. But it was bigger than simply chemicals and hormones. It was the way the hair on the back of his head smelled sweet. Babbling noises he made, expressions on his face. When he coughed, she jumped. When he grinned, she beamed. It sounded stupid, but she'd never known herself to be capable of this much love. This love was infinite; this love was primal.

She lifted the baby from the bouncer and rested him on her hip. Ethan gurgled happily in her arms. 'This'll be hard for me too,' Claire said to Mark. 'I've never been away from him for more than a few hours.'

'Stay home then.' His voice was at once jokey and serious.

All week, he'd been like that: saying one thing, meaning another;

making sarcastic remarks with underlying intent. Perhaps Mark was right, maybe the timing was off; there'd be other auditions. But her bag was packed, her flight booked and she knew her choreography of the variation she'd dance inside out. Claire brushed the thought aside. Ethan and Mark would survive; so would she. In no time at all, she'd be back home.

She placed the baby back in the bouncer, distracting him with a rattle. The clothes he was wearing were already too small; the press-studs were coming apart. Claire thought to herself how fast he'd grown. Ethan didn't fit in any of the little suits he'd worn fresh out of hospital.

Mark searched frantically through papers on his desk. He exhaled through his nose. 'Great, I can't find the bloody outline again. I can't believe it; my filing system is all out of order. I don't have time for this.'

Claire stood behind Mark's chair and wrapped her arms around his neck. 'Don't worry. You'll be fine,' she said, resting her chin on his shoulder. 'And you've been working so hard lately. You probably need a break.'

'Looking after the baby isn't a break.'

Claire didn't respond. She took out a handwritten list. 'Okay, I'm pretty sure there's more than enough milk in the freezer. You can give him some baby cereal once a day, but make sure it's not too thick. He's due for his nap in about half an hour. There's clean laundry in the dryer and I bought new nappies and wipes yesterday. I'll call before I take off and when I land.'

He gave her a perfunctory nod – she could tell he was tuning out her voice – and continued rummaging through his folders.

A horn outside beeped.

'That's the taxi,' Claire said.

'Already? You really can't reschedule? It's almost Christmas; why are they even holding auditions this week?'

'Please don't make this more difficult than it is already.' Claire picked the baby up again and held him close. Ethan nuzzled into her chest and gripped the sleeve of her shirt. 'See you soon, pumpkin. Be good for Daddy.'

She handed Ethan over to Mark. Immediately, the baby started to scream.

'I know how you feel, buddy. I don't want her to go either.'

'Love you,' she said, quickly giving them both a kiss. Then she grabbed her bag and exchanged a look with Mark. Worry tightened her chest. Ethan's cries turned his face bright pink; his cheeks were covered in a slick of tears. The baby reached for his mother in desperation while Mark tried to hold him back. Claire feigned a reassuring smile and blew them another kiss. The taxi's horn honked again.

She closed the front door. As Claire walked down the atrium stairs, she still heard Ethan screaming from the other side of the building. Hopefully, the neighbours weren't too annoyed. Nobody had knocked on their door and complained yet.

Humidity leaped from the atmosphere; sweat crystallised on her skin. Mark hadn't even wished her luck. She exhaled, deciding to forget about their silly fight, suppress her separation anxiety, and just focus on this audition. Clear her mind.

Claire crossed the street to where the taxi waited. What she didn't realise at the time – walking under the scalding sun, wading through the tropical air – was that Mark's pleas for her to stay and Ethan's desperate cries would haunt her for years to come. That each heated word of their argument would become an obsession. That she'd always wonder if what happened next could have been prevented.

∞

Mark stared at the baby. It continued to holler at the top of its lungs. How could somebody so small produce so much noise? For someone who never stopped crying, Ethan sure had a lot of stamina. What did it want? Babies were such irrational little things. Mark couldn't wait for his son to grow up, so he could finally reason with him. Communicate.

After Claire walked out the door, Ethan didn't stop screaming for two hours. Mark tried to feed him, changed his nappy twice, and then attempted to rock him to sleep awkwardly. By the time it was noon and the baby still wouldn't settle, Mark was already falling apart. He knew Ethan wanted his mother; the baby didn't want him. These were the wrong arms, this was the wrong smell, that was the wrong voice. Holding Ethan as he wailed for Claire – kicking and struggling to escape his father's disappointing embrace – felt like trying to save someone from suffocating inside an airless cell.

'Daddy has to work,' he said, placing the baby back in the bouncer.

At last, Ethan had run out of steam, exhausted from his screaming session. He bobbed in the bouncer, calmly sucking on his fist. Saliva collected between his fingers and the baby went cross-eyed as he tried to examine his wet hand. Ethan's eyes were dark violet when he was born, but recently they'd changed colour. Now they were Claire's eyes: iridescent blue with fractures of yellow.

Mark skimmed over his research but his mind was elsewhere. Claire had deserted him; she needed to stop acting like she was the centre of the universe. Since Ethan was born she'd become deranged, getting cross with Mark for the smallest things and picking fights several times a day. He couldn't understand her frustration. She wasn't writing a thesis; she didn't have a supervisor telling her she wasn't working hard enough or the weight of a deadline hanging over her head.

He'd struggled in the last few months, and Mark couldn't entirely blame it on the baby or Claire. Nothing was clear in his mind – as though it were made out of antimatter itself. His anti-brain only had anti-thoughts. Days were spent at the desk idly pretending to work. Instead of writing, he hesitated, distracting himself with computer games and porn.

All Mark wanted was a single innovative thought, a real idea, but that was like finding a subatomic needle in a quantum haystack. The more he thought about how unattainable that was, the more it clogged his brain – his pursuit of originality was an impossible Möbius strip.

He re-read the paragraph he'd written and rewritten this morning. Lucky he'd completed a whole paragraph at all. The blinking cursor taunted him – demanded another word to follow the last – like it knew Mark had nothing to say. He checked his emails, checked the news, and checked to see that all of his software was up to date. Then, as always, he came back to the white space of the document. The cursor continued to blink.

Afternoon sun burst through the window and onto his laptop; the glare made it impossible to read the screen. Mark stood up to close the blinds. Squinting, he stared briefly at the sun – it seemed to flicker, like solar flares were erupting on its surface – before it irritated his eyes. Mark blinked and looked away. Bright light had left a grey blotch floating across his field of vision. Like an optical illusion, sunlight in reverse: a negative afterimage.

'Negative afterimage,' he whispered to himself. Mark pictured a solar flare. How the sun ejected energy: radiation streaming out, particles accelerating near the speed of light. Magnetic energy would create polarised radiation – high-energy particles, some charged in reverse – so not only electrons, but negative electrons too. Positrons. Particles of antimatter.

He quickly took out a pen and scribbled some notes. Huge amounts of energy with a small mass, travelling at the speed of light – $E=mc^2$. Relativity would apply. Mark drew a diagram of a solar flare releasing magnetic energy. As the particles accelerated, they'd become more and more massive but the nucleus would shrink. They'd melt into their quarks, creating smaller particles. Antiparticles.

Suddenly, he felt a rush of adrenaline, his thoughts beginning to click and align. Mark tapped his feet and wrote more quickly. Something was interfering with the oscillating particles, making fewer of them decay as antimatter. But what? He tilted backwards in his chair. Maybe it had something to do with quarks. An original idea felt within his grasp.

The baby screamed.

Mark's thoughts scattered; now he couldn't hear himself think. Great, his concentration was broken. It'd take him ages to get back into the flow again. He put his pen down and lifted the crying baby into his arms.

∞

Claire lay in bed, thinking she'd relish her first night in months of uninterrupted sleep. But the sheets were rough and she was restless. She ached for her baby; she could physically feel his absence. Like a phantom limb, Claire kept sensing Ethan – reaching for him, expecting to find him there beside her body – but he'd been briefly amputated. She clutched a pillow tightly to her chest and tried to fall asleep.

Her audition played on her mind; this morning, she'd been uncharacteristically jittery. Claire usually never had butterflies. Now her muscles ached, and she had a severe cramp in one foot. Uncertainty about the audition's outcome – and whether it was worth the trip – troubled Claire. Before entering the mirrored studio, she'd strapped down her breasts in the bathroom, just in case they started swelling or leaking milk.

During the interview the artistic director, James Mitchell, asked lots of questions about her new baby. There were already plans to share the lead role of the Swan Queen between two soloists; one of the principals was retiring and the company needed to consider her replacement. But James was concerned that, even with role-sharing, Claire wouldn't be able to handle the demanding rehearsal and touring schedule. That perhaps having a baby was incompatible with dancing a lead. She had to suppress an urge to stamp her foot and scream – why did everyone think motherhood suddenly made her incompetent? Claire quickly assured him of her dedication and promised family wouldn't ever get in the way of work.

Then Claire danced her variation from *Swan Lake*. Her mind had gone blank when the music began, but she couldn't actually recall dancing, whether or not she'd danced well. It was a fluid memory. All she remembered was how she'd felt in the moment: weightless, calm, exhilarated, an ecstatic release of pressure. Like coming home. Normally, Claire had a sharp instinct for gauging an audition's success, but she wasn't sure this time. Based on the company's lack of confidence in her ability to juggle ballet with a baby, she suspected she'd screwed up. Part of her craved consolation from Mark, but after how hard she'd fought to get here, how could she tell him auditioning was a mistake? Claire lay in the darkness nursing her disappointment – in the audition, in herself – in lieu of nursing her son.

When she landed in Sydney the following morning, Claire rushed off the plane and out into the terminal. Mark had promised to pick her up and bring Ethan to the airport. But they weren't there among the crowd; she couldn't find them anywhere. She collected her bag and searched the arrival hall for their faces.

Claire dialled Mark's number but nobody answered. She tried the house phone; it kept ringing too. Perhaps they'd gone out. She tried his mobile again.

'Hey,' he said wearily.

'Hi, it's me. I'm at the airport. Remember you said you'd pick me up?'

Mark exhaled. 'Sorry, I totally lost track of time. Ethan's being really fussy. Nothing makes him happy, he doesn't want to sleep, eat, be touched or left alone. I don't know what to do. He's impossible.'

'Maybe he's overheating,' Claire offered. She heard the baby howl in the background; the sound made her long for him. Ethan's cries were like cryptic signals Claire needed to decode. 'It's boiling today. Give him a bath; it might calm him down. Does he still have that rash under his arms?'

Mark replied but she couldn't hear him over Ethan's loud shrieks.

'I'm coming straight home. See you soon.'

Her right breast had started to leak, and below its curve, she could feel warm milk seep into the creased skin. As if the constant ache of being away from Ethan wasn't enough, her body gave her visceral reminders. Time to get back to him. She waited in the queue for a taxi, the smell of breastmilk sweetening the humid air.

∞

Mark found the rash under the baby's arms. May as well give Ethan that bath; maybe the rash was what had been bothering him. Maybe he'd finally calm down. All night, Ethan had been inconsolable. The baby wailed as if he were being tortured, loud and urgent, like the wail of a siren warning of emergency. Mark's sleep deprivation veered towards madness. He kept trying to return to his thesis – he was so close to grasping antimatter's riddle – but his son kept howling and he couldn't think.

Problem-solving didn't work with babies; Mark couldn't find a solution to Ethan's problems. He consulted the manuals again, every parenting book in the apartment, looking for answers, but nothing fixed the crying. Ethan wailed and screamed, squirmed and writhed. Mark considered calling his father and brother for advice, but knew they'd just laugh at him. Call him out for being pathetic, for asking for help, for allowing Claire to leave him alone with the baby. Overnight, his frustration had made him punch the wall.

Mark picked the baby up and walked to the bathroom. It was the most beautiful room in their apartment, almost bigger than their bedroom, with a large picture window that looked out onto the courtyard. Sun spilled onto the white tiles and reflected off the mirror. He turned on the tap.

With its four legs on wheels, the yellow baby bath looked like a headless giraffe. It didn't take long to fill – it was no bigger than a sink. Claire had bought lots of neutral-coloured items for the baby – mint greens and lemon yellows – as she'd had some idealist notion that their child wasn't going to grow up conforming to gender stereotypes.

Mark laid Ethan down on the change mat. Claire had taught him to check the water temperature and he pulled up his sleeves and dipped his elbow in the bath. Too hot. He cooed absent-mindedly at his son then abruptly stopped. Mark hated baby talk, all that inane babbling and senseless noise. Perhaps it was just the way he was genetically wired to love his child, but there was something about that baby that made Mark forget that he was acting like a fool.

The bath water had cooled now and Mark undressed his son. As his cold hands braced Ethan's body, the baby screamed again. He kicked and fought and wriggled as Mark struggled to lift him up into the tub.

Later, this yellow bath ended up in court. Evidence from the scene of the crime in a criminal trial, standing out of place in the middle of the court, inspected by lawyers and a jury. The tub was probably still kept somewhere with other left-behind evidence, in a room of forgotten things at the storage facility of the courthouse. Nobody ever went back to collect it.

With one hand, Mark held the baby's shoulder to support his head, and tried to wash Ethan's body with the other. But the baby wasn't cooperating. His limbs thrashed, he splashed and shrieked, forcing his own face underwater. Mark breathed out and tried to compose himself. He washed the baby's hair. Ethan pushed his legs against the edge of the tub, spilling water over the floor. The baby's strength was surprising. Claire was wrong; this bath was not calming him down.

Mark lifted Ethan out of the bath and wrapped him in a towel, lemon yellow with an embroidered duck. The baby kept crying. Roaring. Piercing decibels that climbed each time he opened his toothless mouth, rising octave after brutal octave. Mark's eardrums hurt – it felt like they were bleeding – and the pressure inside his head escalated to a crushing throb.

What was wrong with it? Nothing calmed this baby down. Where was Claire? Why wasn't she back yet? He was furious at her for leaving; it was unfair. He felt racked by a dark impulse to settle the score. The baby howled and arched its back. What did it want? Why wouldn't it shut up?

Mark noticed urine running down Ethan's leg. Great, it was everywhere. He'd only just been cleaned. Mark would need to run the bath again, start all over. Fuck.

The baby kicked and yelled. His cries boiled the marrow inside

Mark's bones. His unbroken scream was grating and shrill, like a deafening alarm; it set Mark's nerves close to breaking point. The baby screamed louder. *Stop crying. Stop.*

Mark grasped Ethan, his hands tightly gripping the baby's ribs.

He shook him hard.

The screaming stopped.

Mark couldn't pinpoint the moment he'd lost control; he didn't understand how it happened. It was like standing on a train platform and doing what we all imagine: that universal morbid urge. The train approaches. You look down at the tracks. You think to yourself, I could easily throw myself down there, I could die.

Or you could be standing at the edge of a cliff, looking over the edge. You imagine yourself falling down, your body tumbling towards the earth and breaking against the rocks below. Everyone thinks about it, feels that flickering impulsion. It's like a cognitive itch you shouldn't scratch, the way the brain assesses risk. So you stop yourself. You make a choice. You choose to live.

When Mark was a teenager, he went on a family holiday to Airlie Beach on the Whitsunday Coast. He befriended one of the local boys – Mark had long forgotten his name – who was about his age. One morning, they took the boy's speedboat around the shoreline. In the back woods, by the freshwater cascades, was a line of rugged quartz cliffs.

Mark craned his head up, staring at the tallest cliff. 'Can we go all the way up there?'

'Yeah, sure,' the boy said.

The cliff was about fifteen metres high. Although the climb wasn't hard, Mark grazed his knee against the rocky edge. He wiped the blood off with his palm.

'Do you wanna jump?' the boy asked when they had both reached the top.

'Is it safe?'

'Reckon you'll be right.' The boy ran off the edge of the cliff and jumped into the water.

Mark felt sick to his stomach looking at the drop. He counted backwards. Ten. Nine. He looked down at the water, a slick of black on its surface. Eight. Seven. He took a step backwards. Six. Five. Four. Then a step forward. Three. You only live once, Mark thought to himself. If he did this now, he'd never have to do it again. Two. One. Zero.

Zero.

There's nothing to lose at zero.

Mark stretched his feet and jumped.

The fall was over before he knew it. He landed in the water.

It was over. It was done.

The baby felt light in his arms; Ethan's slack limbs flopped by his sides. His head dangled forward. His eyes were closed. Fingers clenched in a fist just moments before were now splayed out and lifeless. Mark stared at this limp creature in his hands. The baby was almost like a piece of meat. A skinned rabbit. A plucked chicken.

What had he done?

Mark quickly put the baby back into the bath. Ethan tried to open his eyes but immediately closed them again. Then he pooed – an eruption of orange diarrhoea – all over the inside of the bath. Its sour stench made Mark gag. He didn't know what to do. Should he wash Ethan again? Did he need mouth-to-mouth resuscitation? Surely it wasn't that serious. He moved his ear to Ethan's mouth to listen to his breath. Was he breathing? Mark wasn't sure.

'Claire?' he called out, then remembered she wasn't home.

When something terrible happens in a film, the world suddenly exists in sinister slow motion. Light intensifies; we want to shield our eyes from the glare. Voices drop, background sounds muffle, and the camera moves in and out of focus. As Mark held the stiff, cold baby in his arms, he realised this wasn't a movie. It was real life. But he felt sedated and calm. Like he was inside the eye of the storm, as the hurricane of reality swirled and warped around him.

His thoughts wandered to the violin, to what music might best accompany this unfocused moment. Something slow, with low tones. Mark could almost hear the string's vibrations inside his mind fill the air.

But crucial seconds were slipping out of his fingers, faster than oxygen was disappearing from the baby's lungs and brain. Time played tricks on him. He was trapped in some liminal space, frozen, unable to respond or react. By the time Mark heard Claire's keys in the door, he didn't know how many minutes had passed since the baby's chest stopped moving.

∞

When Claire arrived back at the front door, she was relieved by the silence. Maybe the baby was asleep. Or if he wasn't sleeping yet, she could feed Ethan and settle him on the bed and they could have a nap together. She was careful to be quiet when she turned her keys in the lock and removed her shoes before walking down the hallway.

'Claire?'

Mark's voice was off.

Something was wrong. She dropped her bag.

Before Claire heard the words, she heard the panic – an irregularity of breath, a strain of vocal cords, a cry, a gasp. Panic existed on a frequency of its own. Air into air, particle by particle, it vibrated through the elastic atmosphere faster than the speed of sound. The most sudden and terrible thing, it pierced the calm and propelled her towards the worst place. Before the words came out, the anxiety was there, roaring on the other side of silence. Before her brain registered what she was being told, she knew that something was wrong. And before she could respond it was already too late. Because once she'd heard those words, an event was set in motion and everything had already changed.

'Help,' Mark said. 'He's not breathing.'

They were only four words, delivered calmly, considering. Four words, five syllables, nineteen letters, six vowels, thirteen consonants. Practically nothing. But it's often the sentences with few words that land the hardest punches. I love you. I hate you. Will you marry me? I'm pregnant. Words that turn your world upside down. But they are in most people's vocabularies, common exchanges in the trajectory of love.

Claire screamed.

She didn't remember doing it at the time, only when she had to recount it later for the police. She didn't hear the sound that came from her throat, but Claire never forgot the glimpse she caught of herself in the hallway mirror. Her contorted mouth. Terror in her eyes. She could still to this day see the reflection of her face as she had let out that long, loud piercing cry.

What happened next played out in a blur. Ethan wasn't breathing. Claire heard her pulse pound against her temples. Her chest tightened. She needed to find the phone, she had to get help. She didn't know what to do by herself; someone needed to give her instructions. Where was the phone? She had to find it now. Was he dead? Claire dialled triple zero, her body on automatic pilot. She clutched her throat and held the phone up to her ear. Her breathing was louder than the phone ringing on the other end of the line. Hurry up. Come on.

'Emergency Services. Police, Fire or Ambulance?'

'Ambulance.'

'Ambulance Service. How can I help you?'

'My baby isn't breathing. Please, I need an ambulance right away.' Claire almost yelled into the receiver.

'What is the address?'

She repeated their address several times. 'Please hurry,' she pleaded.

'We're sending one to you right now. How old is the child?'

'Four months. You have to hurry!'

'Please try to stay calm. What's your name? Would you like to speak to an ambulance officer?'

'Okay. Yes. Claire.'

She hadn't seen Ethan yet. Claire didn't know if he was alive or dead. Her first instinct had been to get help but now she was frantic to see him. As she walked up the hallway to the bathroom, her legs fought to carry her weight. While Claire desperately wanted to be with her baby, at that very moment she dreaded what she might see when she opened that door.

It looked like an overexposed photograph, a washed-out summer day. The bathroom was full of white light: reflections, mirrors and the shiny plastic of the baby bath. Scattered smells of baby shampoo and talcum powder clung to the air. The only shock of colour in the room was the inside of the bath, a vivid smear of bright-orange runny poo. Mark hovered by the side of the bath. He was pale and pacing; Claire had never seen him look so scared. Lying on the change mat was Ethan.

For her eighth birthday, Claire was given a gift of seventy-two Derwent pencils, the entire rainbow boxed in a tin. She loved their names, they sounded like poetry. Prussian Blue. Burnt Sienna. Vandyke Brown. She'd recognise the seventy-two colours of the box in reality, like it was her superpower, the Derwent spectrum her index to the real colours of the world. Milk was No. 72, Chinese White. Lemon Curd was No. 6, Deep Cadmium Yellow. Claire put her hand over her mouth as she looked at the colour in Ethan's face.

No. 69, Gunmetal.

A very pale grey with a tiny trace of blue: the colour of death. When Claire drew pictures as a child, she used Gunmetal only for silvery ghosts, shading them to eerie perfection with a very soft touch. It wasn't a colour that she wanted to see in the face of her own baby.

'He just . . .' Mark trailed off and looked at Claire.

She started to cry. 'Is he alive?'

When Claire was pregnant, she had recurring nightmares about her unborn baby fighting for life. Details were never the same. Sometimes the baby was drowning, sometimes it was deformed; other times the baby fell and fell into a measureless void. According to parenting magazines and books, these nightmares were perfectly normal so Claire put it down to the anxiety any mother-to-be feels. But those dreams always bent themselves towards abstraction.

This, there – right in front of her – was too real, too tactile. Chill of the bathroom tiles against the soles of her feet. Layer of sweat on her hands making the plastic casing of the phone slippery. Claire handed it to Mark. He spoke with the ambulance officer but she couldn't hear a word they said. All she could do was look at her baby.

Ethan was very still. He was partially wrapped in a yellow towel, its embroidered duck looking inappropriately cheery. His body was unrecognisable. Podgy arms with bracelets of fat around the wrists motionless at his sides. His chubby cheeks, which Claire had kissed so many times before, were sunken and sallow. He didn't open his eyes. Without any signs of life, Ethan looked like a broken doll, cast aside.

She reached out and touched Ethan's hand. It was freezing; she lurched back. Claire put her ear up to his mouth. Nothing. She wanted to pick Ethan up and hold him in her arms, but what if she made it worse? Mark was still speaking to the ambulance officer on the phone and started trying to resuscitate Ethan. Claire couldn't watch. She ran outside to wait for the ambulance, looking at the vanishing point at the end of the street, listening for a siren.

It was only five minutes between Claire's call and the ambulance arriving at their front door. She'd never experienced five longer minutes than those. Five minutes for her heart to break, for her nightmares to come to life. Five minutes of thinking she'd lost her Ethan. Five minutes without enough oxygen. Babies took an average of forty-four breaths per minute, two hundred and twenty in five. One hundred and twenty litres of air. Five minutes without breath was too long.

She heard the siren. It grew louder, lights flashing, its brakes screeching as the van arrived. Two ambulance officers hurried to the baby. Claire ran upstairs with them. One was blonde and tall; the other had brown hair and a more solid build. They brought a tank, a bag full of instruments and the tiniest oxygen mask.

'What's his name?'

'Ethan.' Claire hugged her stomach.

'Okay, Ethan, hang in there for us, mate,' said the blonde as he fitted the mask over the baby's head.

'GCS 3,' said the other ambulance officer, 'shallow breaths, respiratory rate forty.'

'He's alive?' She almost didn't believe it.

Mark paced behind them, staring at the tiles on the floor. 'Do we need to go to the hospital?'

The blonde ambulance officer turned around. 'We need to stabilise his breathing first. Once he has a regular breathing pattern again we can make the trip.'

'He's going to be okay?' Claire asked.

'We'll do our best.'

Colour hadn't returned to the baby's face yet. Claire held her breath, hoping it would leave more oxygen in the atmosphere for Ethan. She reached for Mark's hand and together they watched the naked baby fight for air.

Within a minute, mask on mouth, Ethan found his lungs again. He strained to open his eyes. But they weren't his eyes – they were black and empty, no iris, all pupil. The baby was too sick to cry. Silence wasn't natural. Claire wondered if Ethan knew what was happening, if he was in any pain. She knew babies felt pain, but how much? When did consciousness begin? It felt like the baby was begging her to save him with his dark glassy eyes.

With the mask still anchoring the baby to the oxygen tank, the two men took him out to the ambulance on a tiny stretcher. Claire stayed in the back with Ethan and the blonde ambulance officer while Mark rode with the driver. They attached a heartbeat monitor to Ethan's toe; it chirped irregular beeps. He was barely alive. Claire stroked his mottled arm as the ambulance raced through red lights to the Sydney Children's Hospital.

By the time they arrived, the siren was drowned out by the long monotonous tone of the heartbeat monitor – of Ethan's small life flat-lining to an end.

∞

In the resuscitation area of the Emergency Room, a door led straight from the ambulance driveway to an operating theatre. Red tinsel dangled from the violet walls. Nine nurses and doctors – all in white coats except for one – waited for Ethan. Immediately after the ambulance pulled in, the baby was placed onto a metal table.

Medical staff swooped over Ethan. Attached him to another tank. Poked him with syringes and drew his blood. Checked his pulse, held a light to his eyes. Inserted a catheter directly into his bladder by injecting a needle straight into the skin just above his groin. Ethan didn't cry or flinch.

'Would you be able to tell me what happened?' A female doctor asked the parents. 'Who was with him when he went into respiratory distress?'

Mark took control. 'I was giving him a bath and then he just stopped breathing.'

'Was he submerged underwater?' the doctor asked.

'No.'

'Did he fall off any high surfaces?'

'No.'

'When did he stop breathing exactly?'

Mark looked over at Ethan's catheter. 'After the bath.'

He didn't know what to say. What had happened in that bathroom gave him aftershocks, had left him with earthquakes in the tips of his fingers. That strange sensation of the baby's body shaking backwards and forwards, snapping at the neck. But that couldn't have led to this. It was nothing; Mark hadn't done anything. Something else was wrong, the baby was sick. 'He just stopped breathing.'

'Normal birth, no complications?'

Claire nodded vacantly but looked away. Her face was pale, her eyes pink. She was pulling on a necklace, a gift Mark had given for

Mother's Day, when she was six months pregnant. He reached his hand out to hers and their fingers interlocked. Two linked lives; there was no way Mark could tell her that maybe this was his fault.

On the operating table, they were losing Ethan. He slipped in and out of consciousness. His breathing was unsteady and his left foot twitched. Mark stared at his own feet. Some nameless shame, deep in the core of his body, crushed him as he watched on. It was in the family of guilt, but it was different. The feeling was repulsive – darker than shame – like a dense pool of mercury collecting in his heart. He couldn't explain this to those doctors or to Claire. As Ethan fought for his life, the thought of losing her too was unendurable.

'Seizure,' a male nurse said to another doctor. This doctor had a big brown beard and examined the baby's jerking foot. Ethan's eyes rolled into the back of his head and he stretched out his neck. His tiny tendons reminded Mark of the roots of a mangrove.

A female doctor ran her fingers over the baby's head. She paused when she touched the fontanelle. Ethan was still small enough to have that empty space between the bones of his skull, it hadn't fused yet. It was taut and bulging.

'Intracranial swelling through the fontanelle,' she said.

'Haematoma?' a bearded doctor asked.

The female doctor addressed Mark again. 'Did anything happen to the baby's head? Did he knock it against anything?'

'No. Maybe when he kicked in the bath, he hit his head against the side?'

'You were the only one with him?'

Mark nodded.

Saliva spilled from the side of Ethan's mouth and he started convulsing violently. Ripples of the heart monitor fluctuated, crashing then subsiding until the beats of the baby's heart quieted completely, like the still waters of a waveless beach.

Claire became hysterical, pushing her way to the operating table. 'What's happening?'

'Did the baby hit his head against the bath?' The bearded doctor now looked back at Mark.

'Maybe,' he said. 'I think that was what happened. He hit his head against the side of the bath.'

'Please,' Claire pleaded. 'What's wrong with Ethan? Why is he shaking like that?'

The baby's eyes closed and his spasm stopped. He was flatlining again. More nurses came into the operating theatre, obscuring Claire's view of her son. She tried to look through the wall of doctors but could only catch glimpses of Ethan, a small foot here, a flash of torso there. The baby's heartbeat came back.

Mark exhaled and put his hand on Claire's shoulder. He pulled her back from the table. Mark buried his face in Claire's neck. He didn't want to look at Ethan any more.

'He's still naked,' Claire said to Mark. 'Don't you think he's cold? Can't they find something to keep him warm?'

'Don't worry. They know what they're doing.'

Another female doctor stood over Ethan. 'His retinas. Take a look.'

Claire was frantic now. She broke free of Mark's embrace, trying to monitor any movement that Ethan made. The baby still wasn't breathing properly; his rib cage stayed motionless for a moment too long. Finally, Ethan's leg stopped jerking. It took another five minutes for his breathing to stabilise once more.

'We need to take him to Radiology,' the bearded doctor said.

'X-ray and MRI?'

'Maybe EEG too.'

Mark couldn't follow what the doctors said, but he didn't want the baby to have an x-ray. Had it left marks inside Ethan? Could they see what happened in his bones? No, that wasn't possible. Whatever it was Mark had done, it wasn't that harmful. If he'd done anything at all. Nothing more than a light nudge. Or a small bump. It couldn't have done enough damage to leave traces of itself inside Ethan's body.

'I don't understand what's happening,' Claire said.

Mark feigned a smile. 'Ethan must be okay now if they're going to take him to have an x-ray, right?'

The doctors moved Ethan to an elevated stretcher. He didn't look like a baby any more – he was more like some toy robot – with the oxygen mask covering his face, and intravenous cords of the drip and monitors extending from his body.

'Where are you taking him?' Claire asked. 'Can I come?'

The female doctor with the red hair nodded. 'We're taking him to Radiology. He needs some scans so we can figure out what's wrong.'

Claire put her hand on the stretcher. 'You don't know yet?'

'He's just had a seizure,' the red-haired doctor said, adjusting the baby's oxygen mask. 'Looks like something's up with his brain.'

Ethan's brain? Mark stared at his hands. They were big, but not big enough to cause significant harm. Just a small . . . shudder. Jiggle. Knock. Mark couldn't find a word for it. How had anything happened to the baby's brain?

That split second in the bathroom played out again and again, vague snapshots dissolving like smoke inside Mark's head. He needed to reorder and rearrange the memory, warp it back to the right shape. The memory he'd pulled out must be wrong. Mark's antimatter self – identical but oppositely charged – had hurt the baby. But that wasn't him. It wasn't.

The medical staff were ready to move the baby now. Claire shadowed the stretcher as the female doctor and two nurses opened the double doors to exit the theatre. Mark tried to follow them, but the bearded doctor stopped him before he could step out of the room.

'I'm Dr Saunders. I'd like to ask you more questions about what happened to the baby.'

Mark nodded. He calmly followed the doctor out of the resuscitation area, walking away from his son.

∞

Claire stood behind a glass screen. She watched her baby travel down the white tunnel of the MRI. Ethan was tiny and the massive equipment overwhelmed him; he looked like the smallest babushka doll nestled inside the biggest. Radiographers flipped switches. The machine hummed.

When Ethan was born, he was perfect. Perfect weight, perfect height, perfect health, perfect Apgar score. They'd been to the baby health centre twice; the midwife told Claire that everything was progressing normally. Ethan was gaining weight and reaching his milestones. He fed well. Nothing to signal that he was sick. Did he have a congenital disease? Was he born with some dormant poison, waiting to erupt? What did the doctors say about knocking his head? His brain? Claire jumped, startled by the machine's sudden loud whirling boom.

On the opposite side of the room was another window where the medical staff looked on. Pictures appeared on the monitors. The radiologists were talking to the red-haired doctor but Claire couldn't hear what they said. She only saw their mouths move, exchanges of serious looks, frowns and nodding heads. What could they see inside Ethan? Claire couldn't see her son so kept her eyes on the heart monitor, making sure he didn't skip a single beat.

Her breasts were full; her nipples ached. She called out to the nurse. 'Could I feed him? He must be hungry.'

The nurse shook her head. 'He'll be in the scanner for a while longer. Don't worry, your baby has a drip.'

Claire snorted quietly. Don't worry? Her son was the colour of a corpse. There was nothing to do but worry, nothing to do but fill her head with fear. Maybe this was her fault; maybe she'd done something detrimental during her pregnancy. Or had taken Ethan for an afternoon stroll in the cold for too long. She'd smoked during the first weeks of her first trimester, before she knew she was pregnant. And she'd continued to dance until close to the end of the third trimester; maybe each *pas de chat*, *soubresaut* and *tour jeté* had hurt him in the womb. Everything Claire had eaten, drunk, thought flicked through her mind as she searched for the root of the problem.

Where was Mark? Claire needed him. She was starting to break, felt dizzy and terrified. Why wasn't he here? She leaned back to support her weight on the wall, listening to the jingling bells of Christmas carols that blared through the hospital speakers, behind the bangs and clicks of the MRI coils.

∞

Mark sat in a plastic chair on one side of a desk, the two doctors opposite staring him down. With the glaring lights, incessant questions and taking of notes, it felt like a police interrogation. He stretched his legs; he'd left sweaty marks on the chair. This would have to be over soon. Mark exhaled. Everything was going to be fine. Nobody had seen it; nobody could prove anything.

'Can I see my son now?'

'Soon,' Dr Saunders said.

'I have a few more questions,' the other doctor said. His name was Dr Gibson, director of forensic paediatrics. No wonder Mark felt treated like a criminal – this doctor was looking for a crime. 'At what point did the infant stop breathing? Was it before he did the poo? Or afterwards?'

'After.'

'And how long did you wait before you called for help?'

'Claire called the ambulance.'

'But she wasn't present when Ethan stopped breathing?'

'No.'

Dr Gibson wrote some notes. 'How long, approximately, do you think it was between the child going into respiratory distress and the ambulance arriving?'

Whatever happened grew increasingly clouded. Mark's memory had a hazy underwater quality now. Before the ambulance arrived, each thought, each movement, every word exchanged were now clustered together into chaos. Mark had no clear concept of how much time had actually elapsed between one point and another. Like an impressionistic smudge, time and space were an incoherent tangle. But there remained a stubborn darkness that split him in two.

'I'm not sure. Maybe fifteen minutes?'

Mark felt a singular awareness as he watched the doctors; he knew exactly what they were trying to do. They wanted to catch him out somehow, find an inconsistency. But it would be impossible for them to prove anything. Mark was smart enough to keep his story straight. Nobody else had been there. No witnesses. No-one but the baby, and the baby couldn't tell his side of the tale.

He felt the heat of a tear run down his cheek. 'I'm sorry,' he said. 'My son . . .'

The doctors were quiet. Mark held his face in his hands; he

couldn't bring himself to say anything else. His knee trembled under the table. As Mark tried to retrieve the violent memory, it corrupted the file, became the memory of a memory. Margins between reality and remade reality began to blur inside his head.

∞

Dr Saunders motioned to a small room down the hall in the Intensive Care Unit. 'Could I speak to you in private?'

Claire felt her stomach drop. One of those little rooms; she felt claustrophobic just thinking about it. Good news was never shared in those little rooms. They were the rooms where you were told your loved one had cancer, a brain tumour, was dead. She didn't want to go there. Mark was still gone. He'd disappeared at the precise moment when Claire needed him more than ever.

The doctor opened the door. 'I need to show you something.'

She followed reluctantly. One wall had a light box that was covered in x-rays. Small skull, baby bones – pieces of her son. A chill went down Claire's spine: it was as though Ethan were a ghost, glowing like phosphorus, who haunted the wall. Shining white skeleton, cross-sections of Ethan's brain – delicately patterned, like the vein structure of a leaf. Claire stared at the x-ray of Ethan's rib cage: thin lines fragmented the bony frame. Something wasn't right.

'What's wrong with him?' Claire asked quietly.

Dr Saunders lifted one scan to the light and pointed at her son's brain. 'See this dark section? It's an acute subdural haematoma, a collection of blood between the skull and the brain. Also notice here how Ethan's brain isn't symmetrical? This hemisphere has been displaced by the blood so it's shifted past its centre line. We call that midline shift. The blood has increased the intracranial pressure, mounting the pressure in his skull and on his brain.'

'Blood?'

'Your son has sustained a severe, high-impact brain injury.'The doctor paused. 'Have you heard of something called shaken baby syndrome?'

Claire gave a feeble nod. Shaken baby syndrome. She didn't know much about it but she'd heard the term before. Read about it in the paper: cases of frustrated babysitters shaking an infant in their care. But surely they didn't think this had happened to her baby. 'That can't be what's wrong with Ethan?'

'His symptoms are consistent with SBS. Infant neck muscles provide little support for their heads. So the violent movement of shaking pitches the infant's brain back and forth within the skull, rupturing blood vessels and nerves throughout the brain and tearing brain tissue. When someone forcefully shakes a baby, the infant's head rotates uncontrollably about the neck, then the brain repeatedly strikes the inside of the skull, causing bleeding in the brain.'

'Forcefully shaken?'

'Quite a lot of force,' Dr Saunders said. 'Enough to cause diffuse axonal injury, the result of shearing forces that occur when the head is rapidly accelerated and decelerated. The force that caused Ethan's injuries is equivalent to the force of an adult falling off an eight-storey building.'

Claire swallowed. No, this was a mistake. Her baby wasn't forcefully shaken. It was illness, not injury; Ethan was sick. There had to be another explanation. Her legs buckled.

Dr Saunders continued. 'These are Ethan's ribs. If you look closely, you'll see small green-stick fractures, conceivably from the baby being gripped tightly around the chest. On Ethan's elbows and knees you'll notice metaphyseal fractures, possibly caused by twisting, pulling, jerking or wringing of a child's arms or legs.'

Claire looked away. Twisting, pulling, jerking, wringing – these were violent words. She saw white spots in her vision. 'This happened to Ethan?'

'All his symptoms are consistent with abusive head trauma. Inside the child's eyes, we found extensive retinal haemorrhages extending to the ora. Further bleeding. Another indicator of shaken baby syndrome.' The doctor's eyes had hardened.

Blood in Ethan's brain and eyes, fractures in his ribs and limbs. Claire didn't want to be in this awful room any more; she wanted to be with her baby. But he was unconscious in the Intensive Care Unit, connected to giant devices with wires and cords. His breathing had stabilised, his heartbeat was regular, but the seizures were now getting worse. She wanted to go home, back to yesterday, when none of this had happened.

'Did you see anything happen to Ethan?' Dr Saunders asked. 'Anything at all?'

'No, I was in Melbourne. I've been there for the past two days. When I spoke to Mark from the airport earlier this morning, Ethan was screaming in the background. But normal screaming, not like he was in pain.'

'So, you went away? Mark was the only person looking after the child?'

It sounded like an accusation, like the doctor disapproved of her absence too. That Claire should never have left her baby or let him out of her sight. 'What are you saying?'

'I only want to establish that Ethan was left in Mark's care.'

She looked at her son's skeleton and asymmetrical brain. 'You don't think that Mark . . .' Her voice trailed off. Ethan was too young to speak, but the scans spoke for themselves.

'There's one more thing I need to show you,' Dr Saunders said quietly. He opened a large brown folder with a number written on its spine: 1435962. Her son was reduced to a number. 'I must warn you, these photographs are upsetting.'

Claire looked at the pictures briefly. 'No,' she said, turning away.

'We took these photos a few hours ago,' the doctor said. 'If you look here, you'll see several bruises on Ethan's neck, just below his chin. Also, he has this bruising on his chest. They weren't visible when Ethan was admitted, leading us to believe the trauma is fairly recent.'

In the photographs, purple marks covered Ethan's pale skin, his eyes looked dead, a sickening pattern of bruises dotted his chest. She squeezed her eyes shut, and then opened them again. Claire could visualise exactly where Ethan was held – the bruises looked like fingerprints.

'I need to get some fresh air.'

'Of course,' Dr Saunders said. 'Take your time. I'll check on Ethan in Intensive Care in the next hour.'

Claire found herself standing outside the hospital. A southerly breeze blew in her face. The cool air gave her goosebumps but she didn't feel cold. What was going on? What had happened to her baby? She didn't want the doctor's conclusion to be the answer – just considering it was an irreconcilable thought. Mark needed to explain that this was some misunderstanding. But he'd abandoned her and left her stranded in waters out of her depth – it was a feeling Claire recognised feeling before.

Summer light shifted to a starless sky. This was the precise moment her life reoriented itself, when Claire began living with a sharp pain. Its sting grew milder over time, muted and transmuted, but whenever she recalled Ethan's scans and x-rays – those photographs – it was like touching the raw skin of an open wound.

Like a bruise, the horizon changed from pink to violet. Nausea swirled at the back of her throat. As the late December sunset stained the pavement magenta, Claire ran over to a tree and vomited on its roots.

∞

That night, Mark went home without speaking to Claire. When he woke up in the morning, he was alone. Their bed felt wide and empty and he reached over to touch her before realising she wasn't there. Mark had slept like a baby that night – a dreamless, cavernous sleep – and it was difficult to resurface into real life. The warm safety of reverie slipped away from him before he opened his eyes.

Police had come to the apartment late the night before. Videotaped his version of events, treated the bathroom as if it were a scene of a crime. They examined the baby bath but he'd wiped it clean before they arrived. Bleach mixed with the sour smell of the dried baby poo. Photographs were taken, objects measured, but Mark remained unruffled by the police. Not one crack in his voice, nor one catch in his story – everything was going to be just fine.

Upon waking, Mark packed his suitcase. He grabbed some clothes, plucked his toothbrush from the holder beside Claire's, and took his dusty violin case out from under the bed. Then he scrubbed the bathroom again, spraying every surface with disinfectant until the harsh chemical fumes burned his eyes. He scoured everything until his knuckles were white and skin peeled off his fingers.

But echoes of memories repeated their shapes on the tiles and inside the tub. No matter how hard Mark scrubbed, they wouldn't disappear and dissolve.

It was Christmas Day. But the lights on the tree they'd decorated together didn't flash, presents beneath it unopened. This was going to be his Ethan's first. Claire had bought an ornament that proclaimed it proudly: 'Baby's First Christmas!' Mark was reminded of the first Christmas he'd spent with Claire. She'd been uncharacteristically shy, rearranging the ham and turkey on her plate. He knew Claire had wanted to impress his family – keep up with their dinner table conversation about politics, philosophy, physics – but she'd floundered. She thought with her body; Mark loved that about Claire. No pretension, no snobbery, she was just herself. She'd thawed him, brought warmth he'd never known before into his frosty life.

Now, inside the home they'd started to build together, Mark saw only objects. Chairs, tables, things. Things that triggered memories; memories he didn't want brought back. Everything was painful to look at. He had to leave. Mark still didn't know whether or not Ethan had survived the night. The baby was in a critical condition when he'd left yesterday. In a way, Mark didn't want to know. Last night, he'd even had the briefest, most rotten thought: he wished the baby would die so that his secret might die with him.

Tom was glazing the Christmas ham in their father's kitchen, crosshatching its skin with a sharp knife, poking cloves into fatty diamonds. After their mother died, Tom took on the responsibility of cooking the family meals. As boys, they watched her prepare dinner – helping to chop vegetables, mix batters, stir broths. But when she passed away, Mark found everything inside the kitchen distressing. Whenever he held a vegetable peeler, he still pictured her soft hands guiding him over the moon-like surface of a potato skin.

'Hey, Santa, what's in the bag?' Tom looked up from the ham.

Mark put the suitcase down. 'Merry Christmas.'

'You're here too early; I told you not to come until later. We won't be ready to eat until at least noon. Does Claire need help with the baby? Is she still outside?'

'Just me.' Mark rubbed the back of his neck. Even though it was a hot day, he was shivering. 'Is Dad around?'

'In his study.' Tom wiped his hands on a tea towel and looked carefully at his younger brother's face – scanning and measuring, his head on an angle like an inquisitive bird. 'You all right?'

Mark stared at the streaked marble of the kitchen counter. Tom had prepared a prawn and mango salad: their mother's favourite Christmas recipe. 'I'm fine. Do you want help with lunch?'

'Not from you,' Tom said, laughing. 'I'll need Claire, though. When will they be here?'

'Not sure yet,' Mark said. Part of him wanted to tell his brother that Claire wasn't going to make it, that Ethan was in hospital, that something awful had happened. But he couldn't break the membrane. That would ruin Christmas; it'd ruin everything. Bad news could wait. He left the kitchen and walked towards the back of the house.

John was at his desk, wrapping a gift. Folding and taping golden paper around a brown stuffed animal. Tongue sticking out, unbroken focus – he looked up only when Mark knocked on the door.

'Wish this bloody thing came with a box,' his father said, struggling with the toy's uneven shape.

'What is it?'

'Got it when I was in Tasmania last month. For the baby. Help me wrap it, will you?'

Mark took the stuffed animal from his father and looked into its shiny plastic eyes. It was a wombat. Warren, according to its name tag. He flattened the wrapping paper and curled it around the toy, methodically creasing the edges before sticking them down.

John frowned. 'Still looks like a mess.'

Mark placed it on the table. 'Ethan is a baby, he doesn't care,' he snapped. He lowered his voice; he'd momentarily forgotten about yesterday. 'Listen, Dad, I need to talk to you. There's something wrong with him. He's sick.'

'What about Christmas lunch?'

'The baby's in hospital.' Mark sat down, pushed the strips of gold and red paper aside, placed his head onto the desk and looked at the floor. His gaze settled on his father's shoes under the table; their feet were the same size. 'There's something wrong with his brain.'

'His brain?' John looked winded.

On the desk was a photograph of Mark's high-school graduation day. He wore his school uniform, held an embossed certificate, his parents stood on either side. One elbow linked through his mother's arm, his father's hand resting proudly on the other shoulder. 'Ethan just stopped breathing. The doctors said he had a brain haemorrhage. They're saying it's something called shaken baby syndrome.'

'I don't know what that is. Was there an accident?' His father was silent for a moment, his breathing made a rattling sound in his chest. 'Did you do something? Did you lose your temper?'

Mark laughed dismissively. 'Dad, you're the one with the temper. And you wouldn't ever . . . You know me, you brought me up. You know I wouldn't hurt my own child.'

He knew lies were coming out of his mouth but lies made more sense than the jarring truth. Mark looked at the framed photograph again: at his hands holding the graduation certificate and awards, at his arm linked with Eleanor. Did those hands grip the baby's ribs, did those arms churn his skull, turn his brain into butter? Maybe, yes, but no. None of that clicked. It was wrong, didn't fit. The real Mark was the smiling boy in the picture.

John stood at his bookshelf and looked at a row of Christmas cards. One of the cards was a picture of Ethan on Santa's lap. 'A brain haemorrhage,' he said quietly.

'Dad, I don't know how it happened.' The more Mark said it, the more it felt like the truth. Perhaps his hands and arms were physically responsible, but he hadn't done anything wrong. Mind over matter, like walking across burning coals. Numb to the scorching fire on the soles of his feet as he'd stepped on the embers. When the baby was shaken, Mark wasn't himself. He wasn't inside his own body. Antimatter over matter.

John turned to face him. 'I'm sorry, you're right. I can lose my temper but I'd still never hurt a baby. Of course you didn't hurt him. You're a good boy.' He touched his son's shoulder and sighed.

Mark saw himself through his father's eyes. He was a good boy. Too sensitive and emotional – but not a thug. Not tough enough to do something so severe.

Other people snapped and shook their babies – not him. Only the most evil parents physically abused their own kids. Monsters, brutes, villains – heartless creeps and lowlife scum – but Mark wasn't psychotic, he wasn't those things. They were bastards; he was different. He was just a normal man. Who came from a good family, went to a good school, got good grades, like good boys did.

'Of course I didn't hurt him,' he repeated. Those words tasted better in his mouth, they matched his real identity. Mark scrubbed his mind of the unspeakable memory, re-encoded it, and reshaped it. Let it oxidise, broke its chemical bonds, like bleaching the stains on the bathroom floor. 'I didn't do it.'

'What are you still doing here then?' John sounded annoyed, but then his voice softened. 'Get back to the hospital. Be with your son. Call us if you have any news.' He put the wrapped wombat in Mark's hands. 'Here, give this to Ethan.'

∞

Claire glanced at the screen on her phone; she hadn't looked at it since the previous morning. Voicemail. Flashing envelope. Maybe it was Mark. She checked yesterday's missed call log, feeling her stomach flip when she saw it was a Victorian phone number. Now, in the wretched light of the hospital ward, her audition felt long ago. Like a day lived in another lifetime, from a life that no longer belonged to her.

Her hands shook as she held the phone to her ear.

'Claire, sorry for calling on Christmas Eve,' the message said. 'It's James Mitchell. I couldn't wait to let you know. We were so impressed by your audition; you completely blew us away. We want to offer you the lead – you're our new Odette. Give me a call back when you can. Merry Christmas. And congratulations. Have a glass of champagne, you deserve it.'

She listened to the message again. There was a sharp taste in her mouth, vinegary and bitter; her stale tongue was coated white. Odette, the lead. She'd actually got the part. Claire swayed on the spot. Ever since she was a little girl, she'd fantasised about this phone call: being told she'd finally made it, offered a starring role. Squealing and jumping, thrilled her hard work ultimately paid off – that was the reaction Claire had pictured in her head.

But beside her, her infant son was hooked to life support. Catheters, feeding tubes, mechanical ventilation. Moments ago, while he was having a turbulent seizure, Ethan's heart had stopped for ten seconds. Doctors and nurses quickly encircled the baby, rushed to resuscitate him, while she stepped back helplessly. For ten seconds, Claire thought Ethan was dead.

She put the phone down. Her stomach muscles caved in, like there was a change in her core, some terrible instability. One of her ballet teachers once told her that ballerinas couldn't be mothers. Both required total dedication and it was impossible to have the discipline for both. It was a comment easily dismissed as a wide-eyed dance student, when Claire thought she was immune to difficulty, a special case, exempt from the pitfalls of ordinary life. How arrogant she'd been then, how foolish and naive.

Across the room, she caught her reflection in the window. There it was: the defeated face. Claire saw herself disintegrate, realising there was no way she could accept that role. Never dance *Swan Lake*, become a star. It was over. She gulped for air.

Right now was her breaking moment, her hour to stumble. To crumple, wince and shrink, like so many other fallen dancers before her. Dream forfeited. Ambition collapsed. All those years, all that unwavering hope, obliterated in an instant. She was another casualty to failure, forced to exit stage left.

Ethan squirmed with discomfort. As she held the baby's limp hand, it dawned on Claire that Mark had been right. Things were different now. She'd made a colossal mistake, she should never have left Ethan. Deserted her son, for what? To go to a stupid audition – it was selfish, she was spoiled, an entitled princess. Claire was a mother now; she couldn't pretend it hadn't changed her shape.

Because next to her was this child, beautiful but blue-lipped and sallow-cheeked, fighting to stay alive. She was his mother but had failed to protect him; she'd exposed him to harm. Let this happen. Exactly the opposite of what mothers should do. Ethan recoiled as a nurse adjusted the tube running down his throat – Claire recoiled with him. This happened because she put herself first. This was all her fault.

After all, Mark had asked Claire to stay, pleaded with her not to go. Why was she so stubborn? Why hadn't she been more concerned?

She still wasn't positive Mark had hurt their son, she'd spent the night wavering between certainty and suspicion. One moment Claire was convinced he'd done it, the next she was filled with doubt. Mark wasn't capable of this – she loved him, he loved her, he loved Ethan – but who else could it have been? His absence, right now, hurt her deeply. But his presence, at the crucial moment the baby was shaken, hurt her more.

Ethan was restless, frowning, but still too weak to cry. Claire tried to soothe him. His eyes couldn't focus or track her movement, as she searched them for signs of background blood. Every one of her senses was heightened. Every minute dragged like an hour. She wanted someone to hold her, tell her everything would be fine. She wanted Mark.

Because even if he'd done it, Claire still secretly knew she was to blame. Mark had warned her against leaving; he'd flared a scrambled chain of beacons to signal his distress. She'd heard them and ignored him. Now she was being punished, and had to punish herself. Quit ballet. Surrender. Ethan needed her – his mother. She'd devote herself entirely to her son and master motherhood's techniques. That was the only role she could accept now, the only lead to dance. She wasn't a star; it was Claire's time to fade. Ethan had to take centre stage.

Trembling, she returned James Mitchell's call.

'Merry Christmas,' Claire said, scarcely audible. Her eyes settled on Ethan. She shook her head and started to cry. 'No, I'm so sorry. I can't accept the part. My son is in hospital. He's really sick.'

∞

At the hospital, Christmas carols played in the foyer. Mark felt like everybody was looking at him – every nurse, doctor and patient, every visitor. He kept his eyes on the floor. Santa Claus sat in a fibreglass sleigh, surrounded by mounds of cotton snow. Sick children lined up to sit on his lap and wish for their Christmas miracle.

Mark didn't know where to go; his son was no longer in Emergency. Asking at reception was humiliating, but he was relieved to hear that Ethan Hall had been admitted to a ward upstairs. He wasn't dead. Mark held his head high, and reminded himself he hadn't done anything wrong.

Claire sat beside Ethan's bed, stroking his cradle-capped head. The baby was still wearing an oxygen mask but he was asleep. Wisps of his fine hair were matted together and purple circles were around his eyes. Ethan was so tiny; Mark had almost forgotten how brand new he was. Only four months old. One hundred and twenty days.

'How is he?' he asked. 'Have a Christmas present for him, from Dad.' Mark put the wrapped wombat on the bedside table. He waited for her to say something. 'Claire?'

The baby stirred and she patted his chest, soothing him back to sleep. Claire didn't look up. She knew. They'd told her. What he'd supposedly done. But she'd never believe that, would she?

Her eyes were anchored on the baby. Mark felt invisible, like light diverted around him, like he was subatomic, unable to be seen with the naked eye. He didn't know how to reach her. She was as far away as the most distant star.

'Claire?'

'Quiet, you'll wake him,' she said firmly. There was a depth to her voice that didn't sound right, like she was possessed. 'Let's go outside. I need to talk to you.'

Finally, she glanced up at him. And in that look, Mark knew that whatever she needed to say would annihilate him.

They left the sleeping baby in the Intensive Care Unit. Santa was ringing a bell in the hospital atrium; hundreds of children shrieked with glee.

Outside the hospital, they sat at the empty bus stop. Their shadows connected on the pavement – silhouette on silhouette – but their bodies didn't touch.

Claire looked into the distance. 'Tell me it's not true. Please.'

Before they met, Mark had seen the world in a particular way. Everything could be stripped back to basics – particles, atoms, forces – and sorted and catalogued by matter or mass. But being with Claire made another dimension of the universe open up to him, shone a light on something new. He saw it with the fiercest clarity, how everything – motion, time, space, energy, gravity – had a relationship. Particles, atoms and forces were never absolute. Their relativity left him breathless. She showed him how everything in the universe existed in proportion to something else.

Changing one side of the equation always changed the other. Mass grew and length shortened as speed increased. Observed time between two events inside a moving body appeared greater to a stationary observer. Vector sums of forces acting on a body were equal to its mass multiplied by its acceleration.

Energy was the product of mass and the square of the speed of light – just like his new tattoo. Mark was one variable of an equation and Claire was the other. He existed in proportion to her, she to him. He wasn't absolute: he was one piece of a single entity.

'It's not true,' he said.

'But —'

Mark put his finger over her lips; the warmth of her mouth made him want to kiss her. 'Claire Bear, you know me. Better than anyone. Do you really think I could have hurt our baby?'

'No,' she said. 'I don't. Last night Ethan almost died. Where were you? He had three seizures, one where he stopped breathing again for almost a minute. The doctors said he might have permanent brain damage. He's been throwing up bright-green vomit and he hasn't eaten anything for a day. And I saw the bruises. I saw —'

Mark interrupted. 'What bruises?'

'On his neck. And ribs. Fractures. Bleeding in his eyes too.' Claire put her arms around him and pressed her face into his chest. 'Mark, how did this happen? I don't understand.'

Could she feel how quickly his heart was beating? Her ribs under his ribs, rising and falling together. Mark rested his chin on the top of Claire's head, smelled her hair, and touched the tangled ends. For a second, the world stopped turning – the moon stopped orbiting the Earth, the Earth stopped orbiting the sun, the universe didn't expand. This was where he wanted to stay, where he wanted to be forever. Capture this eternity and stretch it out to infinity. But this wasn't a static universe.

'I love you,' Mark said, lifting her chin up so their eyes met. Her eyelashes were almost white; she had the most beautiful freckle under her left eye. He didn't know how to prove how much he really loved her, couldn't write a thesis to support how he felt. Words weren't enough. Mark stroked the side of Claire's face with his thumb and they kissed. Their lips, mouths, noses and faces still fitted perfectly together. Equilibrium – there was a perfect balance to their mechanics. None of that had changed. They were still interlocking pieces of one perfect whole.

Claire pulled away. Her face was wet with tears. 'This is my fault. I shouldn't have left. I'll never forgive myself if Ethan dies.'

Mark didn't know what to say. If he tried to convince Claire it wasn't her fault, reassure her that she wasn't to blame, then he'd need to admit where the blame really lay.

'Everyone is saying you did this to him,' she continued. 'That you shook him. The police told me they might press charges. They want me to make a statement.'

He kissed her again. 'Tell them I didn't do anything wrong. It's me. Come on.'

Claire gave him a shattering look. 'I want to believe you. But I don't know what happened, and something terrible clearly happened to Ethan. So maybe I don't know who you really are. Because the only logical explanation is . . .' She stopped, unable to finish the sentence, and suddenly walked away from him.

He chased after her up the footpath. 'Claire!'

'I'm sorry, Mark. But I can't.'

He watched her cross the road. They stared at each other for a moment from opposite sides of the street. Traffic passed between them. This was the woman Mark thought would be his partner for life, had believed was more steadfast than a constant. She was his speed of light. He could still taste her on his lips. Those words rang in his ears – I can't – Mark wished he knew what she'd meant. Talk to him, listen, believe him? Couldn't love him? Even if he had hurt Ethan, that awful minute was the smallest fraction of Mark's entire life. What about every other minute? Why was that tiny instant more important to Claire than all the years they'd spent together?

With her blonde hair saturated with summer light, Mark never forgot how Claire looked at that moment. Something about her was unreachable; they'd been contaminated. The speed of light was constant, if they were together or apart. She didn't believe him. What Mark believed indivisible – their quantum mechanics – had been split; that nameless force that bound them together had ripped apart. Claire had altered her side of the equation.

She rushed back to the hospital entrance, knocking into a man carrying a pile of Christmas presents. Mark lingered for a few minutes, gazing at the empty space where she'd stood, before eventually walking away.

∞

The baby went to the operating theatre the next morning. His condition had deteriorated – high fevers, thunderous seizures that blocked his lungs – and Ethan kept slipping in and out of consciousness. He needed surgery, to drain the blood collecting on the surface of his brain. The bleeding agitated his grey matter; it made his brain swell and shift. The problem was the pressure, a cerebral fizz. They'd give him a cranial burr hole: make an incision along his scalp, then drill an opening into the bone to release the blood.

Before surgery, Ethan wasn't allowed to feed; he was going to have a general anaesthetic. That night, Claire couldn't even hold her baby in her arms – he smelled her milk and went berserk. All she wanted to do was comfort her child but her presence caused Ethan distress. Claire didn't want her baby to feel like she'd abandoned him when he needed her most. She'd carried Ethan inside her for nine months; he felt like part of her body, an extension of herself. But overnight she had to keep her distance so he couldn't pick up her lactic scent.

Anaesthetists and surgeons checked on the baby in the morning. They took his temperature and prepped him for theatre. Claire watched them wheel Ethan away, his small body swathed by the blue operating gown. It went against her every instinct to allow Ethan out of her sight; she didn't trust anyone now. But she had to trust these surgeons. Her son's life was in their hands and without this procedure he might die. There was no other option.

While Ethan was in the operating theatre, Claire went to the cinema.

She couldn't stay in the hospital – she was sick with anxiety, pacing the halls. At the theatre, she bought herself a large tub of popcorn but didn't eat a bite. As the lights of the projector danced over her head, Claire cried. Tears of grief, grief she'd never felt before. She cried silently, but with every fibre of her body and every sac in her lungs. Her sadness was a hellish, unstable place; she felt trapped in its centre. Claire watched the screen but paid no attention to the film. The credits rolled and the lights came back on. Her popcorn had spilled on the carpet.

Back at the hospital, Ethan was brought into the post-operative recovery room. Claire wore a net over her hair and a sterile gown over her clothes. She washed her hands and sat beside his bed, waiting for him to wake up. They'd shaved his head. His fine baby hair – gone. White bandages covered his forehead. Relaxed muscles, shallow breathing; the baby's central nervous system was still asleep. Claire put her ear up to his mouth to listen to him breathe again. Ethan was broken, but he was still perfect.

Eventually, the baby stirred. He stretched his fingers and opened his eyes. Bewildered, he slowly climbed out of the analgesic haze. His pupils were huge, dilated from the anaesthetic.

Claire's heart wouldn't allow her to accept Mark had caused this. He said he hadn't; she wished that were the truth. She didn't think he was capable of it, didn't believe it. Had there been clues? A signpost, some warning? Mark had a temper, yes, but wasn't physically violent. Once, in the heat of the moment, he'd slapped her across the face but it wasn't serious or scary. They'd laughed about it the next day.

The doctors and the police just needed somebody to blame, to condemn and hold liable, to make sense of this. Even though the finger was pointed at Mark, Claire knew ultimately the responsibility fell on her. After all, she was Ethan's mother. She'd let her baby out of her sight.

But there were so many unknowns in the universe, so many unfounded beliefs. Their tiny son – product of the two of them merged together – was the only witness. This was much more than the unthinkable act of hurting an innocent child, it was a crime against the foundation of her life. There wasn't a shoulder Claire could cry on; the shoulder she'd needed was gone.

Claire leaned in and kissed baby Ethan's nose. His skin carried the savage smells of surgery: disinfectant, rubber gloves, the metallic tang of blood. She was reminded of the day he'd been born – his pure shock at being alive – only this time she couldn't touch him. Then, despite the baby's obvious discomfort, his body high on anaesthetic drugs, Ethan looked up at her. He seemed to recognise his mother. His face broke into a smile. The widest gummy grin. She hadn't seen Ethan smile since before all this. Claire cried again but this time she was happy.

A week later, the bandages came off Ethan's head, revealing a thick brown scab along his scalp. By the time his condition stabilised and the seizures stopped, flakes of his scab had fallen off. When he was discharged from the hospital, it was only a pink scratch. As Ethan's hair grew back, the scar stayed smooth and hairless. It grew with him. Claire fell in love with her child more and more every day. But she came to understand that time didn't actually heal wounds. This wound would always be there – constant, unchangeable – like a secret written permanently onto her son's skin.

18

GRAVITY

Ethan looked at his reflection in the hospital mirror. He studied the shape of his skull, tilted his head, combed through his hair with his fingers. Carefully through his nape, ridge and crown. His fingertip fell on a splinter of glossy skin. The scar. There it was – finally, he'd found it – a tiny bald sliver. His lungs opened up, testing their own capacity.

For most of his life it was right there. Ethan couldn't believe he'd never seen it before. Saliva gathered at the back of his mouth as he ran a finger over the smooth hairless line. Hard evidence, a lasting wound; they'd really cut open his head.

His scar was his time machine, a concrete link to the past, recorded on his body. Proof. Ethan ran to the toilet bowl and threw up.

Alkaline green vomit clogged his throat. He gulped for air as his head hovered over the toilet. Thinking about the scar again made his body rise up in disgust. Acidity burned his tastebuds as he vomited until there was nothing left inside. He wiped the sides of his mouth with his sleeves and breathed heavily through his nose.

'Ethan, you okay?' the nurse called out.

It was time to shave him for surgery. Murmuring blades, humming with electricity, echoed through the tiled room. The nurse put the buzzing razor to his hairline. Chunks of black hair fell onto the floor as the blade swept over his scalp. Ethan looked at his reflection again. Now he was bald. He ran his hands over his head; smooth skin but his skull was lumpy. The scar glowed.

'You look like a crazy person,' Mum said, when he was back in the ward.

'Which is fitting, since you're about to have a lobotomy,' Alison joked.

'Shut up.' Ethan grinned. 'Like you can talk. You've had one too.'

'Yeah,' Alison said. 'But at least I made it look good. You just look kinda scary.'

Mum went with Ethan to the operative-care holding bay, where the nurse checked his wrist tag, took his temperature and recorded his weight. Then they were taken to the anaesthetics bay – like walking along a coastline, crossing bay after bay – where the doctor gave everyone a fabric cap to wear on their head.

'You look good in that hat,' Ethan told his mum. He lay back on the bed and reached for her hand. 'Mum, I'm scared.'

'Let's pretend you're time travelling,' she said, stroking his cheek. 'Only this time you're going into the future. And I'll see you there.'

'Time dilation.' He turned to the anaesthetist. 'Can my mum stay for my operation?'

The anaesthetist smiled. 'She can stay in theatre until you fall asleep. You'll see her in recovery very soon.' She tapped on the drip and adjusted the tubes. 'Ethan, could you please count backwards from ten for me?'

He nodded. 'Ten. Nine,' he said drowsily. 'Eight.'

Mum squeezed his hand.

Light ripped Ethan from the deep cavity of general anaesthesia. The steep climb made him dizzy; icy air rushed between his ears.

He woke up in the cool white sunlight of the recovery bay. Slowly, sounds unmuffled, pins and needles prickled his fingers and toes. But Ethan couldn't feel his face. His head was gone. Did the surgeons cut it off? This was a shame; he'd liked having a head. It was going to be inconvenient to live without one.

Mum sat by his bed, still wearing the white shower cap on her head. 'Hi, pumpkin. Welcome back.' She stroked his cheek; her touch made his skin tingle. 'Your poor head.'

'It's okay, Mum. I can feel it again now. I think my head grew back.'

Ethan fell back into a dreamless sleep, where time didn't pass and space didn't expand. When he woke up again, he was in another bed, up in one of the bays of the wards. Comforting sounds and smells of hospital soothed him: sweet powdery custard, rustling magazines, chatter and beeps. Outside the window it was getting dark, but Mum wasn't in her chair.

He sat up and touched his head. It was covered in bandages. His skull felt smashed and tender; his brain throbbed, like it had its own heartbeat; his skin was hot and raw. Ethan wanted to rip the bandages off and scratch his stitches.

Someone pulled the curtain back. 'Hey, sport.'

Ethan did a double take. 'Dad?'

'How are you feeling?' Mark sat on the bed.

'Kinda like I'm missing a piece of my brain.'

His father glanced up at the bandages. Then he shifted over slightly; he'd sat on a stuffed animal. Mark picked up the toy and handed it to Ethan. 'Is this a wombat?'

'His name is Warren,' Ethan said, taking it from his father's hands. The wombat had patches of fur missing, loose stitches, and scratches on his plastic eyes. 'He used to come everywhere with me. He's been my favourite toy since I was a baby.'

'Warren the wombat was your favourite toy,' his father said, smiling. 'Listen, Ethan, I'm going back home. Back to Kalgoorlie. My flight leaves tonight.'

'Oh, okay.' Ethan's voice was flat. He felt a pinch in the nerves of his neck. 'But I don't want you to go.'

Silence fell for a moment, hovering on the linoleum floor. Something compelled them towards each other, but both of them stayed still.

Mark sighed. 'When I was your age, I wanted to be an astronaut. Float around a space shuttle. Visit the moon. I didn't think there was any gravity in space. Remember at the park, when I said the swing made you weightless? That wasn't right. You felt weightless, just like astronauts in orbit do. But gravity still acted while you were on the swing, as it does on the astronauts in orbit. They just don't feel its effect because they're falling with their ships. You can't escape gravity; it's everywhere.

'Sure,' Ethan said. 'But gravity also keeps the moon orbiting around Earth. And Earth orbiting the sun.'

'You blow me away, kid.'

'Then don't leave.'

His father slumped on the edge of the bed. He was close enough for Ethan to smell – Dad smell. 'Ethan, I fucked up,' Mark said. 'I hurt you, and then I lied about it. Can't even offer you an explanation either; I don't actually know why. But I did it. And then it was done. I've hurt the people I love the most, who love me the most. Put you through all this pain. You deserve better than me.'

Ethan shrugged. 'But you're a quantum physicist. Obviously, light behaves like a particle and wave at the same time. Particles can be in two places at once. You understand paradoxes and extreme duality.

Everything that can happen does happen.'

'Schrödinger's cat is both dead and alive.' Mark laughed.

'And you can be a good person and still fuck up.'

'Don't tell your mother I swore in front of you.' His father cleared his throat. 'I'd love it to be that simple, Ethan. I really wish I could stay. But I've made too many mistakes, put too much negativity into the universe.'

'Me too. Really, I make stupid mistakes all the time. I just tried to make a time machine. Once, I even punched my best friend in the face,' Ethan admitted. 'Gave him a black eye, plus he lost a tooth. Making mistakes is normal. And I lose my temper too. We're the same. I'm just like you.'

'No, we're not the same. You're nothing like me.'

'You're my dad.'

Mark wiped his face. 'There's a big difference between being a biological father and being a dad.'

'But you are my dad. I take after you.' Ethan pressed his lips together. They were running out of time. 'Anyway, I don't care that you made a mistake. No wrongs and rights in science, remember? Just theories that need to be disproven.'

His father smiled. 'Uncertainty is at the heart of every discovery.'

Ethan was struck by how much he wanted to touch his father, to have his father touch him. He wanted Mark to pat him on the back, touch his shoulder, and give him a hug. Craved that physical contact, knew he needed it to survive – the way the stamen of a flower reaches for the sun.

'Here's what I've figured out about time machines: it's really hard to change the past. But we can change the future. So I forgive you,' Ethan whispered.

Mark was silent. They briefly looked at each other. Ethan carefully studied his father's face. He wanted to know every wrinkle, every grey hair in his stubble, every mole – memorise them, learn his dad off by heart.

His father looked away first. 'Textbook quantum mechanics says Schrödinger's cat is both dead and alive, until you look inside the box,' Mark said. 'But there's another theory that says the universe divides into two: in one universe the cat is dead, and it's alive in the other. Every action splits the universe. So I'd like to think there's another universe out there where you and I get to stay together. Where I made different choices.'

Ethan thought to himself for a moment. 'Mathematically, I think that's possible. I'd like to think that too.' He smiled at his father. 'And even if you did put some negativity into the universe, it's not the end of the world. There's still more matter than antimatter, right? So the universe must be optimistic. It prefers matter. That's why we exist.'

Outside, the street was tinted with silver light – the full moon had risen, had turned its face to the sun.

'I'd better get going. My flight.'

Ethan nodded. 'Will you ever come back?'

Mark gestured at the moon. 'Doesn't it keep on orbiting around Earth? And doesn't Earth keep orbiting the sun?'

'Yeah, I suppose. At least until the Milky Way collides with Andromeda. But that won't happen for at least four billion years.'

His father tipped his head back and laughed. 'Pretty sure I won't get to see that. You know, according to quantum physics, it's the act of observation that changes the universe. Opening the box. I was so scared to meet you but I'm so happy that I did.'

'Luckily, I wasn't a dead cat.'

Mark smiled, and then put his hand into his pocket, rummaging around like he'd lost something. He pulled out a watch and handed it to Ethan. 'Here, I want you to have this.'

Ethan held the watch in his hands and turned it over. It was heavy: gold, with a black dial. 'Wow, seriously?' He tried to put it on his wrist.

'It belonged to my father,' Mark said, helping him close the clasp. 'But I want you to have it.'

'Thanks. It's awesome.'

His father stood up. 'I should go.'

'Dad, wait.' This was his last chance to tell him, their last chance to make things right. 'I'm happy we opened the box too. When two particles become quantum entangled, they still influence each other even when they're separated at great distances. I promise I'll never stop making you Father's Day cards. I love you.' Ethan had tears in his eyes. He reached for his father and hugged him, held him tight. Thick hair from Mark's forearm brushed against Ethan's skin, tickling his face.

Mark squeezed his son back. 'I love you too, Ethan.'

And then his father loosened his grip and let him go. He stalled for a moment by the curtain and then he was gone.

Ethan wiped his eyes with the hospital blanket and caught his breath. The watch weighed down on his hand. He held his wrist under his bedside light and studied the shiny face. Golden stars covered its dark dial. Below the watch's hands, in the centre, was a frowning moon – this was a moon-phase watch.

In the window, the real moon was bright in the sky. Perfect balance between its orbital velocity and the pull of Earth's gravity kept it spinning around them, stuck in orbit. Ethan smiled. No matter what, the moon always came back.

∞

Claire waited in the corridor, outside Ethan's room. She tried not to eavesdrop on their conversation, but heard Mark laugh. His laughter gave her a vague sense of solidarity: knowing someone else found Ethan hilarious, that another human being recognised precisely how magical that boy truly was. Nobody else had been in on that secret before; she'd never had the opportunity to share it.

Mark pulled the curtain back, quickly walking away from Ethan's bed. His face was flushed; he rubbed at his chin. Claire could tell he was trying to hold back tears.

He gave her a stiff nod. 'Thanks for letting me come and say goodbye.'

'Sure, I think it was important. For Ethan.'

'Ethan is . . . Wow.'

Claire smiled. 'I know, I can't really believe we made him.'

Mark readjusted the strap of his bag and glanced back at the drawn curtain. There was an uneasy silence. 'Claire, I can't really take any credit. You did it all. All I did was contribute a single cell.'

She pretended to laugh off the comment, but it struck a tender nerve. 'Thank you.'

'Look, I need to get to the airport. Would you walk me out?'

'Sure.'

They sat outside at the bus stop, quiet for a while, watching for an available taxi. Claire was suddenly overcome by a strong sense of déjà vu, the way time could wrap itself into a circle when you recognised a familiar place.

'We've sat here before,' she said.

'I remember.' Mark rubbed his hands on his knees; he was having trouble sitting still. 'Listen, about what happened when Ethan was a baby. It only took a few seconds to hurt him,' he whispered. 'But by the time I realised what I'd done, it was too late. I knew I'd hurt you too. I just didn't want to lose you.'

'So why didn't you just —?'

'Because I loved you. Because I was scared. And then I lost you both anyway. Claire, I didn't realise I'd done so much damage.'

'Selective memory is crucial to survival.'

'No,' he said. 'I don't mean that I don't remember. I didn't repress any memories. Maybe just pruned them back. Made it less severe in my head than it was in real life. But when I saw Ethan back in hospital . . .'

'Look, I know I'm to blame too, I should never have left you when —'

He interrupted. 'Last time we sat here, you said that too. And I didn't reply or correct you. That was the moment I made everything worse. What I should've said was you're not to blame. At all. I didn't take responsibility for what I did to Ethan then, but I do now.'

'No, if I hadn't gone to that audition . . .'

'You know, I never even asked you how it went.'

She laughed suddenly. 'They offered me the lead.'

'Jesus, Claire. I had no idea.'

'Dream come true,' she said, waving a hand.

'That's why you stopped dancing, wasn't it?' Mark asked, his eyes scanning her face.

'Problem with dreams, right? They just live inside our heads. Dreams aren't ever real, they're always projections. And when they finally do come true, technically they stop being dreams. Then they're just your life.' Claire was quiet for a moment. 'Anyway, that wasn't the only reason I quit ballet. There's no way I could've looked after Ethan on my own and kept dancing professionally. All of a sudden, I was a single mum.'

A bus approached, stopping in front of them. The doors opened. When the driver eventually realised they weren't boarding, he swore under his breath before quickly driving away.

Mark kept his eyes on the bus. 'That was the thing I loved about you most. How driven you were. Why don't you go back to ballet?'

'Oh, I'm much too old now.' Claire tucked her hair behind her ear. 'Besides, I'm not in touch with that obnoxious, pushy side of myself any more. Thankfully, I chilled out. Learned my limitations.'

'Hey, you were never obnoxious. Take some advice from our son. He is a genius, after all. Don't stop trying to disprove yourself.'

'Yeah, why do we resist doing the thing we love the most? I have been thinking of teaching. There's an opening for a kids' ballet instructor.'

'You'd be great at that.' Mark touched her leg then quickly retracted his hand. 'So, I pretty much ruined your life, didn't I?'

'Don't give yourself too much credit.' She nudged him in the ribs. 'You did ruin it a bit, for a little while. But you also gave me Ethan. He's the best thing in the world.'

'Like I said before, I'm basically a sperm donor. And you're wrong, Ethan's actually the best thing in the universe.' He raised his bag over his shoulder and held out his hand. 'Here comes a cab.'

'Mark, you're not just a sperm donor. Ethan came from a place of love,' she said.

He smiled. 'We were like a supernova. Burned brightly and collapsed, but for a brief moment, we did outshine the rest of the galaxy. Stellar explosions also stream elements from their core and release energy into the universe. So Ethan is a child of the stars.'

Claire laughed. 'That's maybe the nerdiest and most beautiful thing I've ever heard.'

Both of them held each other's gaze until there was nothing else to do but look away.

Mark broke the silence. 'There's something I've been meaning to tell you, Claire. My father left Ethan half his estate. The house in Woollahra is about to go on the market. Obviously, the money from the sale will go into trust until he turns eighteen. Tom's organising everything; I'm sure you can both work it out.'

She stared at him in disbelief. 'Mark, that's crazy. You have to be joking.'

He pulled out a folded document from the pocket of his jacket. 'Not a joke. I have a copy of the will right here.'

'I can't believe your father did this,' Claire said quietly, carefully reading over the words on the page.

The taxi pulled up at the kerb.

Absently, Mark took her hand. 'I'm so sorry, Claire. I'm sorry for all of it.'

She nodded but her mind went blank. She couldn't think of anything to say.

He pointed at the sky. 'You'll always be my constant.'

His smile was bright and hopeful; Claire saw a glimpse of the man she once loved. A recollection of love, rather than love itself.

Mark quickly got into the taxi; the door slammed behind him. As the car made a u-turn in front of the hospital, she wiped away a tear. She could just identify the outline of his head through the tinted window; he looked directly at her but she couldn't see his face. The air was dry; she inhaled sharply. Then Claire watched the car recede into the distance before it turned around the corner, driving away from her sight.

Claire walked back upstairs to the ward. Ethan was snoring, lost in a painkiller-induced deep sleep. Her eyes fell on the skin below his bandages, an arch of stitches that swept around the back of his head: an embroidered rainbow. Outside, rain pelted against the window. Passing cars splashed puddles into the air.

During the night, Ethan had kept crying out in pain. Claire had held his hands to stop him from scratching his stitches. Once he'd calmed down, she drifted off on the armchair by his bed. Claire dreamed she was dancing *en pointe*. In her dream, her body floated effortlessly through the air, surfacing from the chrysalis of skin and bone. When she woke up early the following morning, she suddenly felt lighter than she had in a very long time.

Later, Ethan stirred. He wriggled his legs out of the sheets and stretched his arms before noticing the look on his mum's face. 'Mum, what's wrong? Are you sad because of Quark?' Ethan was silent for a moment. 'Are you still sad because of Dad?'

She shook her head, then nodded.

'I think maybe I'm still sad about Dad too.'

'Pumpkin, of course you are. It's okay to feel sad. But you know what? It gets better, I promise you. I know how sad you feel, because I've felt that sad too. The worst pain you've felt in your life feels the same as the worst pain I've felt. Relativity isn't just about space or time.'

Ethan propped himself up and rested his chin on his mum's shoulder. He smelled of bandage adhesive and disinfectant. 'According to that theory, it works for the best thing too.' He started to play with her hair. 'Mum, I'm sorry about the time machine.'

Claire collected his limbs into her arms, pulling his weight towards her own. He looked so funny without his hair. 'It's okay. Although we don't have a vacuum cleaner or a toaster any more.' She kissed her son's forehead. 'Doesn't matter, I'm just happy you're okay. I love you.'

'I love you more.' Ethan scratched his nose. 'Mum, I'm hungry. Can we get pizza?'

She laughed. 'Maybe later.'

As Claire hugged him, she felt his heart beating. She was reminded of her first ultrasound, the moment she'd first heard the flurry of his heartbeat – that rapid booming song of life growing inside her uterus.

Her baby was only as big as a pear then, a lump, but at that moment, everything else fell away. Nothing was ever going to be as important as that lump. She'd never quite be able to tell Ethan that he was the real love of her life.

The hospital seemed brighter now – its walls relaxed, the ceiling rose, the ward looked fresh and airy instead of antiseptic and stale. Clarity charged through Claire's head. She didn't feel worried any more; this was only a temporary pit stop. Soon she'd be able to take her son home. She tucked him back into bed.

Outside, the sun was blinding; white light fell on her lap. Peak-hour traffic clogged the road. To Claire, High Street in Randwick had always been stained by the past so she'd never seen it properly. Trees along the pavement grew taller, sunlight kept glinting through leaves. Walls were revitalised by fresh coats of paint – cheery greens, buoyant blues, blazing yellows. Shiny new wings were built; new patrons donated their money and time. This place didn't just hold bad news, trauma and pain. It offered people hope. Cured them, fixed them, performed miracles. Brought families closer together.

Because even if Ethan had built a time machine, Claire wouldn't take any of it back. She didn't want to change history or tie her loose ends. Because the past was just a measurement of the person she'd become. Because love – even the most dangerous and volatile love – could become the solid foundation for something else. The most difficult steps in the choreography were always the most memorable of the dance. Sometimes the wake of a broken heart was just the winding path we needed to follow to get to where we ultimately needed to be. Somewhere bigger, massive, thrust forward by the tiniest smashed-up pieces of the building blocks of the universe.

∞

Storm fronts delayed Mark's flight. He sat at the airport bar. Announce-ments boomed over loudspeakers: all flights were grounded until the front had passed. On flat-screen televisions behind the bar, the evening news was showing without sound. He watched the muted faces of reporters, wondering what they were saying about the Prime Minister now. Same shit on every channel: same stories, same faces, same exclusive breaking news.

A woman sitting beside Mark at the bar looked across at him. 'Where are you off to?' she asked. She closed her book. Quite an attractive woman, with olive skin and dark hair. Mark noticed her lips were wet from her drink.

'Home,' he said.

The woman smiled. 'And where's that?'

'Kalgoorlie.'

'Long way.'

Mark nodded. 'What about you?'

She took a sip of her drink. 'Brisbane. Was just here visiting some family.'

'Yeah, me too.'

The woman examined her boarding pass. 'Not easy, is it? Leaving the people you love behind.'

'Nope.' Mark didn't want to continue this conversation; it wouldn't lead anywhere he wanted it to go. What could he say about the people he loved? Not easy was an understatement. He ordered another drink, hoping it would take him further and further away from his thoughts. Drown them out in a pool of shimmering liquor.

'Well,' said the woman as she gathered her things. 'Have a safe flight.'

Mark held up his glass. 'You too.'

Eventually, his flight boarded. He took his seat, over the wing.

As they prepared to take off, Mark closed his eyes and listened to the engines roar. Wheels turned; they reversed out of the gate and headed down the runway. Picking up speed, the plane accelerated towards the tip of the port. Mark worried they weren't going fast enough, but remembered bad weather meant take-off speeds were relative to the motion of the air.

Suddenly, they lifted off the ground. Take-off always made Mark feel triumphant, how this heavy machine could defy fundamental physics – like gravity didn't apply. He shut the blind, blocking out the shrinking view of Sydney as they climbed above the city.

He thought of his father, wondered if coming back home had been a mistake. Had it made any difference? Maybe he should've ignored Tom's call. Dad hadn't wanted Mark, he'd wanted his grandson, he'd wanted Ethan. And Mark just let him down again; John had died without getting his final wish. They'd never resolved their differences or repaired their relationship. Unsettling feelings gnawed at him. Closure was fiction; it didn't exist.

Inside the plane's hull, it was quiet now. Mark wished the cabin crew would make an announcement, or other passengers would wander noisily down the aisle. There were too many thoughts inside his head, too much rarefied air in his lungs. He needed another drink. Cabin lights dimmed but the seatbelt sign was still illuminated. Nose to the sky, they continued their ascent.

Mark pulled the blind open. A red light flashed on the tip of the wing. Below them, Sydney's lights had condensed into a neon dot; the wide harbour was now just a puddle. But the city looked different somehow, full of sparkle and life.

The voice of the captain crackled through the cabin. 'Ladies and gentlemen, we're about to fly into an area of unexpected turbulence. Please remain in your seats and keep your seatbelt fastened.'

Through the bumps and drops of turbulence, Mark pictured the mechanics of the plane failing. Something inside him craved emergency, deserved disaster. He imagined shrieks of terror from other passengers ringing in his ears. Beeps and pings, lights on the floor, oxygen masks tumbling down. Flight attendants stumbling through the swaying ribbons of decompressing air, staggering backwards towards the safety of their seats. Mark braced for impact.

Who would miss him if he died? What regrets would he list, looking death in the face? Mark immediately thought of Ethan, of the irreverent helix of DNA. Stomachs plunged, propellers halted, engines powered down – now they were dropping out of the atmosphere. Gravity was winning. Bathed in darkness, Mark would disappear into the infinite roar of the sky, where the unforgiving altitude swallowed him alive.

A bell chimed. 'The captain has now turned off the seatbelt sign. You're free to move around the cabin.'

Hundreds of belts unclicked. Mark opened his eyes. The aircraft stabilised, its engine hummed, holding it in the air. Turbulence had passed. He switched his mobile phone back on.

There were three photographs of Ethan on his phone. In the first picture, the boy stood inside the rotunda at Observatory Hill Park; in another, he leaned against the trunk of an old fig tree. The Moreton Bay fig reminded Mark of his mother; she was obsessed with their majestic buttress roots. She loved their darkness, how strangler figs planted their seeds in the canopy of another tree. Once their roots were deep in the ground, they asphyxiated their host. It saddened him to think she'd never met Ethan. Like a Moreton Bay fig, her cancer strangled its host too.

Ethan took the last photo himself. A selfie, whatever the kids these days called it. He'd quickly grabbed Mark's phone and taken a candid shot of the two of them. Mark looked surprised, caught off guard. Ethan's grin was so wide he squinted. The sides of their faces were touching.

Looking at that photograph, nobody would know how much damage had unfolded between them. But Mark knew. He couldn't undo it. He'd shaken that baby – his son, his flesh and blood. No matter how much he suppressed the memory, altered his version of events, buried the truth, the damage would always be there. He didn't deserve Ethan's wide smile.

Trolleys blocked the aisles. A flight attendant handed Mark some whiskey and a green can of ginger ale. Clicking open the aluminium can – its hiss of carbonation – suddenly reminded Mark of Kate Levy sitting in the prison visitors room, sipping vending-machine soft drinks through a straw. It confused him at first, but if he was honest with himself, Mark knew exactly why that investigative reporter never came back to see him. Why she never finished writing the story. It was the evidence: somehow she'd got her hands on it. Even the most opinionated shaken-baby syndrome critics, champions of wrongful incarcerations and diagnostic flaws, couldn't deny his case's evidence. His baby's injuries were too atrocious to be accidental. No vitamin deficiency or congenital disease caused that sort of harm.

He carefully studied the three pictures of Ethan on his phone. Such a good kid, smart. Mark already missed his voice, his face, his curiosity. He took a deep swig of liquor from the plastic cup. His son's smile made his heart leap from his chest but it also made Mark feel like he couldn't breathe. If he erased Ethan's face, that smile would never haunt him. For a few seconds, his finger hovered over the rubbish bin icon. But Mark couldn't delete the pictures. Those pixels were more precious than anything he'd ever owned. He returned the phone to his pocket.

Mark rested his face against the window. Above the blanket of clouds, tinted blue by a scattering of moonlight, thousands of crisp stars decorated the night. Pinpricks of light fell through the sky. East to west, the horizon was dotted with hundreds of stories: the cooking fires of two celestial brothers, Achernar and Canopus; the male crow Wah, bringing flames to the indigenous people; the flying horse Pegasus; Aphrodite and Eros in the constellation Pisces. Irregular galaxies, blue dust clouds. Somewhere in that sky was another ancient myth: the star he'd given Claire.

Mark knew he'd had – and lost – some inconceivable thing. Like grasping for a scientific breakthrough just out of his reach, he'd touched it. Grazed it with his fingertip. But it didn't belong to him. He re-centred himself in the chair. Perhaps circumstances had thwarted him; he'd never discovered an original idea, made his mark. Mark just decided he'd failed and had shrunk his ambitions accordingly. But he'd never held himself accountable either; he'd just stopped trying. He chose to fail. Ethan reminded him of the importance of curiosity, of ideas, of exploration, of the allure of unfinished problems. To step back and wonder. To ask questions and make mistakes, fearlessly, like a child.

He took his phone out again and stared at Ethan's face. To look at something was to change it, and be changed by it. As the plane tilted in the sky, his universe realigned. Mark wasn't actually at its centre, his hardwired orientation was wrong. Something had shifted. Everywhere around him, protons, neutrons and electrons were spinning and fusing, but most of the universe was made of dark energy and dark matter – stuff he couldn't see. He'd forgotten why he fell in love with physics in the first place: its certainty didn't make it interesting; it was the discovery. The beauty of the unknown.

In scientific law, variables were always relative. Mark pulled up his sleeve and rubbed the faded tattoo on his arm, looking at each element in the formula.

E for Ethan. M for Mark. C for Claire.

Mark and Ethan were bound together by a constant; they were elegantly linked by the speed of light. Mass–energy equivalence. Affect one, change the other. Even if they lived on opposite sides of the country, didn't see each other again for another twelve years, father and son would be connected forever. Mark remembered that he wasn't absolute: he was still part of a single entity. Ethan would always be the product of his parents – $E=mc^2$ – and Mark could never stop being one piece of that equation.

His son had taught him that science was revision. Recognising errors and setting them straight. That physics was full of paradoxes and duality, always at odds with our intuition. Because in a cosmic accident, Mark had done one great thing, made his mark. He'd released some positive energy into the universe – Ethan. And now they were quantum entangled. Like a spaceship spinning out of control, Mark had spiralled out of orbit, but Ethan would be his ground control, carefully guiding him home.

The lights in the cabin dimmed. I forgive you, his son had said. Mark had often wondered if on hearing those words, he'd feel some kind of release. Finally stop punishing himself. Taste the sweetness of reprieve. But he still felt none of those things; he was just as weighed down as ever.

For the last twelve years, Mark's guilt had strangled him silently; he was like a helpless tree choking in the tight grip of a Moreton Bay fig. However, admitting to hurting his son – saying it out loud – felt like taking his first gasp for air. It gave Mark oxygen. Before now, he believed he'd always be moored by anchors of regret.

But maybe Ethan was right about time travel: we can't change what's already happened, but we can still change the future. His son's forgiveness had loosened something; it allowed Mark to uncover some dormant strength. That eventually he might untangle the knots that kept him tethered to the past. That one day Mark would be strong enough to lift those heavy anchors, cast out into the future, and finally forgive himself for his mistake.

∞

Ethan met Alison by the rotunda at Observatory Hill Park. He walked quickly up the hill, feeling the muscles in his shins stretch with the sloping incline, and stopped to turn around. Below him was a field of colour: green and yellow and orange. Summer was almost over and the season's palette was changing. A scattering of golden leaves peppered the ground.

From up there, Ethan saw all of Sydney: the sandstone city, the turquoise harbour, the pointed gleam of skyscrapers, The Rocks, the Harbour Bridge. A path intersected the huge lawn, cutting it into four sections. It made Ethan think of the cerebral cortex, the different grassy areas of each green lobe. Frontal, parietal, occipital and temporal lawns.

'Ethan!' Alison shouted, waving. Her hair had grown back around her ear, covering her surgery scar. Ethan's head was still a little patchy. She wore a purple dress with a frilly hem, which bounced as she walked up the hill, and carried a bunch of multicoloured helium balloons in her hand.

'What's with the balloons?'

Alison looked up at them, strings taut as they blew in the wind. 'Duh,' she said. 'They're for you.'

Ethan took the bunch in his hand. There were seven balloons – red, orange, yellow, green, blue, indigo and violet – just like wavelengths of the electromagnetic spectrum. A rainbow. He tied them to the bench.

Alison pointed to Ethan's plastic bag. 'What's in there?'

'Quark.'

'Your dead rabbit?'

Ethan nodded.

'Yuck,' she said. 'Why'd you bring him with you?'

'He's been in the freezer. But I wanted to bury him here, in this park. Do you think we could dig a hole?'

'What? Here?' Alison looked down at the grass beneath her feet. 'I'm pretty sure we're not allowed to do that.'

Ethan frowned. 'Why not?'

'Because I think the park belongs to the Queen.'

'She's in England. She won't know.'

Alison shrugged. 'I guess not.'

They started to dig a hole together, in the shadow of the colossal Moreton Bay fig tree and its tangled roots, using white plastic teaspoons. Digging with spoons was more difficult than Ethan expected. Maybe he should have brought a shovel.

'I have dirt under my fingernails.' Alison frowned.

When the hole was deep enough for the shoebox coffin, Ethan gently lowered Quark into the soil.

'What do we do next?'

Alison waved goodbye to the shoebox. 'You need to give a eulogy. That's a speech.'

'Goodbye, Quark.' Ethan scratched his head. 'You were named after an elementary particle and a fundamental constituent of matter, postulated as building blocks of hadrons. But you were so much more than that. You were a rabbit who liked to eat biscuits, and my very best pet. I'm sorry you didn't survive my botched attempt at time travel. But thank you for saving my life.'

Alison coughed.

'And thanks to Alison for saving my life too.'

'You know what?' she said brightly. 'Maybe Quark did survive. Maybe he's the one who successfully went backwards in time. He could be the leader of bunnies in Ancient Rome or something.'

Ethan kicked the pile of dirt back over the hole, covering the shoebox. 'I hope so. That would be a much happier ending to the story than spending the rest of eternity being dead in a box. Like what happened to Schrödinger's cat.'

Alison gave him a confused look. She placed a bunch of handpicked flowers on top of Quark's grave. 'When do you go back to school? I start next Wednesday.'

'Me too. But guess what? I'm going to uni as well.'

'You're too young to go to uni.'

'I know, but the physics department invited me to go to some cosmology lectures. Only if I can pass the mathematics requirements but it looks pretty easy. I'm a genius, remember?'

'Yeah, whatever. Your shoelaces are undone.'

Ethan untied the balloons from the bench. He'd sat here once with his father, on that exact seat, and eaten a cheeseburger. Fed the ibises. Talked about physics. He looked at his watch and then at the sky. High above the horizon, in the east, Ethan could see the moon. He pointed. 'Look!'

Alison shielded her face with her hand. 'It's a funny shape. And it's daytime. I thought the moon only came out at night.'

'Right now, it's a waxing gibbous moon so it rises earlier. But the shape of the moon is always the same, what changes is the reflected light. Even when we can't see it, the moon's still always there. Sometimes it's full and bright and sometimes it's covered in shadows. And because the moon is tidally locked to Earth, we never see its dark side.'

A strong gust of wind stole the strings from Ethan's grip and suddenly the helium balloons were carried away by the breeze.

'Oh no,' he said. 'I let them go.'

As they watched the balloons drift over the park and up into the sky, Ethan felt heavy. He thought about his mum and his dad, how his universe had expanded. Then he thought back to his father's words. There's too much gravity. It was everywhere. Even though the balloons floated high above them now, eventually they'd burst or deflate. Helium might leak until the balloons fell out of the sky; the heat of the sun might pop them. Gravity would get them in the end. Falling was inevitable.

Now Ethan understood. Phrases like the gravity of the situation made sense, and he realised why – when things were difficult – they were called heavy or weighty.

Gravity.

Ethan couldn't see it with his brain any more, but he felt it everywhere.

∞

Gravity makes tears run down our faces, and our chests heave and sink. It's the reason we drop to the ground and yell out our hurt. It can be paralytic, leaving us heavy in our beds, unable to rise and face the day. Gravity plays tricks on us: distorts space and time, bends the light. But gravity keeps our feet on the floor and stops us from floating far away into the atmosphere, disappearing into outer space. Because gravity doesn't just pull us down – it also pushes us up.

Gravitation shapes the universe. Forms tides, heats planetary cores. It's why fragments of matter clump together into planets and moons, why stars cluster into vast, rippling galaxies. Earth isn't going to crash into the sun, the moon won't collide with Earth – gravity keeps them safely in orbit. It always attracts and never repels; it brings the planets back.

Gravity is insistent. It firmly stands its ground. We never stop accelerating towards the centre of the Earth at 9.8 m/s². That curvature in the fabric of space-time is a phenomenon we experience every day, an invisible experience we all have in common.

None of us are weightless. Gravity extends to infinity.

And when stronger forces threaten to pull us apart, it's the weakest force that unites us. Gravity binds us together.

Acknowledgements

Thank you to my exceptional agent, Karolina Sutton, for championing *Relativity* from its first draft and offering the best advice at every juncture. I'm also grateful to my amazing international agents: Melissa Pimentel and everyone at Curtis Brown UK, Pippa Masson and all at Curtis Brown Australia, and Alexandra Machinist and all at ICM.

Enormous thanks to my phenomenal editors, Cate Blake and Karen Kosztolnyik: this book is infinitely stronger because of your magical brains. Thanks also to Ben Ball, Lou Ryan, Laura Thomas and Josh Durham for the spectacular cover, Rhian Davies, Heidi McCourt, Alysha Farry, and everyone at Penguin Australia, as well as Nikki Lusk and Emma Schwarcz for your sharp eyes. Further thanks to Jennifer Bergstrom, Becky Prager and all at Gallery Books.

To everyone who read *Relativity* in its various shapes over the years – Marcus Forsythe, Mark Scano, Adrienne Xu, Karen Riley, Jack Boag, Eliza Sarlos, Tim Willox, Eva Husson, Margot Watts, James Goodman-Stephens, Liv Hambrett, Geoff Orton, Josephine Rowe, Sofija Stefanovic, Elmo Keep, Dan Ducrou, Eva Schonstein, Luke Gerzina and anyone else I've missed – thank you for your generosity and encouragement. Adrian Fernand, your drive and intelligent feedback always pushed me to work harder and dig deeper – thank you for being my partner in crime. A million thanks to Sam Thorp, who had confidence in my writing before I ever did and helped me find Schrödinger's cat. I'm especially grateful to Brendan Gallagher, Angela Bennetts and Amy Gray for your insightful help. Most of all, my heartfelt thanks to Alison Fairley.

For your physics expertise, thank you, Paul Gregory and Joseph Roche. I'm indebted to Stewart Saunders and Jeanne North for guidance with all things neuroscience and medical, and to Rhoderic Chung. Thanks Benjamin Law, Renee Senogles, Kelly Fagan, Romy Ash, Emily Maguire, Nam Le, Christos Tsiolkas and Dominic Knight for your sage advice.

Writing this book would have been impossible without help from my Faber Academy crew: Amy Hoskin, Damien Gibson, Simon Murphy, Richard Reeves, Richard Skinner and Steve Watson. Special thanks to each of you for all the years of priceless editorial advice, friendship, solidarity and support.

Thank you to my parents – to my mother, Josephine Barcelon, for always encouraging me to read, and to my father, Michael Hayes, for always encouraging me to write. Extra thanks to Dad for pointing out constellations at our star-watching stone and showing me the moon. Thank you to Nerida and Robert for your continued support, and to my grandparents Marie Thérèse, Amparo, Francis Daniel and José. And Claudia, Hose, Peter, Froukje and Harry – you guys are the best.

Finally, a googolplexian of thanks to my son and husband for their boundless love and patience. Julian, you inspire me every moment of every day – thank you for teaching me how to tell stories and showing me how to write this one. You are my light and my constant; *Relativity* is my ode to you. And David, your unwavering belief and infinite kindness have sustained me through the brightest and darkest moments. I'll never be able to thank you enough for giving me time and space, and the universe.

Every year, thousands of infants across the world are injured or killed by abusive head trauma caused by violent shaking. These injuries and deaths are 100 per cent preventable. This book is dedicated to all the families affected by shaken baby syndrome and in memory of those babies who didn't survive.